Devoid of moonlight to guide them, coming in low westward from the East China Sea, lost to enemy radar because of the sea clutter, the two MH-53J Pave Low helos skirted the wide confluence of the Huangpu and the Yangtze deltas ten miles to their south. As sea clutter gave way to the low stratus and cumulonimbus clouds massed along the coast, the two choppers were still below the ChiCom coast radar net. The Pave Lows' look-down radar guided them up and over the contours of the earth in NOE—nap of the earth—flying, at times no more than fifty feet above the ground. The men aboard each chopper—four SEALs and the chopper crew—were hoping and praying the low flying would keep them undetected until they reached their target.

On all the aircraft specifications charts provided to avid journalists in the Iraqi War, the squat, fat MH-53J Pave Low hadn't been featured—it didn't look "sexy" enough in some editors' opinions. But it was the unmentioned Pave Lows, four of them—despite the Apaches' reaping all the glory in the press—that had struck the decisive blow against Saddam Insane. The Americans hoped they would do the same against the Chinese, but they knew the ChiComs would have a few tricks of their own. . . .

WW III: WARSHOT

Ian Slater

FAWCETT GOLD MEDAL • NEW YORK

A Fawcett Gold Medal Book
Published by Ballantine Books
Copyright © 1992 by Bunyip Enterprises, Inc.

Library of Congress Catalog Card Number: 92-90609

ISBN 0-449-14757-6

Manufactured in the United States of America

First Edition: October 1992
Fourth Printing: August 1993

For Marian, Serena, and Blair

ACKNOWLEDGMENTS

I would like to thank Professors Peter Petro and Charles Slonecker, who are colleagues and friends of mine at the University of British Columbia. Most of all I am indebted to my wife, Marian, whose patience, typing, and editorial skills continue to give me invaluable support in my work.

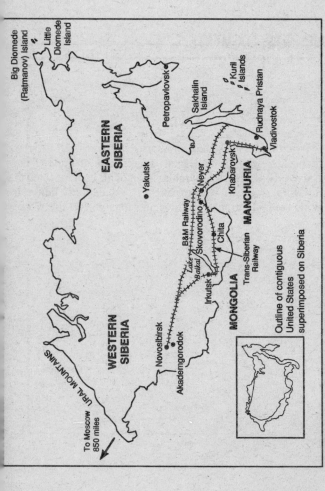

Big Diomede (Ratmanov) Island
Little Diomede Island

EASTERN SIBERIA

Petropavlovsk

Yakutsk

Sakhalin Island

Kuril Islands

Rudnaya Pristan

Vladivostok

Khabarovsk

Never

B&M Railway

MANCHURIA

Skovorodino

Lake Baikal

Chita

Irkutsk

Trans-Siberian Railway

MONGOLIA

WESTERN SIBERIA

Novosibirsk

Akademgorodok

URAL MOUNTAINS

To Moscow 850 miles

Outline of contiguous United States superimposed on Siberia

SIBERIA Scale: 1 inch = approx. 575 miles

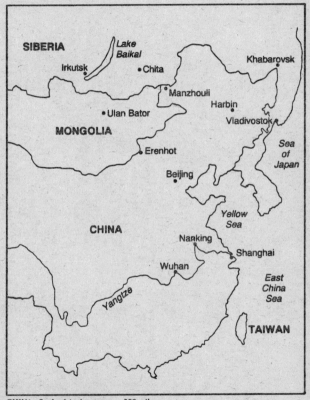

CHINA   Scale: 1 inch ≈ approx. 350 miles

CHAPTER ONE

THE THREE FIGURES dropped softly, catlike, from the chopper roaring above them, its rotors a blur against the winter moon. Their progress in the deep snow was unhurried, displaying an economy of movement, yet singular purpose. Their sixty-pound packs and two-meter skis lowered, the women pulled down their night vision goggles, clicked on the long skis, and, using herringbone steps, began to climb the ridge from the depression the chopper had used for cover. The baskets at the end of their poles disappeared six inches into fresh powder before biting into the last snowfall that had crusted under the impact of wind and sun across the vast taiga. At the ridge's summit a black, moonlit wilderness of pine, beech, and fir stretched in every direction, the air no longer polluted by the oily stench of the chopper's exhaust, but pure and smelling of that hard, cold purity that all skiers love.

The three women, in their thirties, were Olympic standard biathletes. In top shape they were as adept at firing the high-velocity .22 rifles dead on target as they were skiing the women's nine-mile or the men's twelve-mile cross-country course, each of them having practiced endlessly on the Les Saisles course at Albertville and on others before the war. Each woman's body was so well-conditioned that she could drop her rapid biathlon heartbeat to 145 per minute while firing on the range in the prone position, and to no more than 190 on the cross-country trails. They skied down

1

from the ridge in single file, and it wasn't until a minute later that the leader found it necessary to start double poling, her body in the white, skintight, four-way-stretch Lycra-nylon suit moving as if one with the white skis and poles.

As well as having to be beautiful, in top physical condition, and willing to volunteer for the three-day, seventy-mile crossing of the cease-fire's no-man's land, all three had been required to submit to a medical examination to ascertain whether any of them were having, or would have, their period during the crossing. Menstruation would almost certainly be a lure to any tracking dogs that might be accompanying patrols sent out along the enemy's edge of the four-hundred-mile-long, seventy-mile-wide DMZ. The merest whiff of blood, they knew, could be picked up for miles by the animals and would pose a risk to the entire mission. Normally this wouldn't be a problem—you could simply kill a dog with a single shot from the .22 with noise suppressor so as not to attract any further attention. But on this mission, they carried no weapons—at least none like a rifle or pistol, which would be a sure giveaway—only the two-apiece, razor-sharp "ice pick" daggers whose grips were the normal plastic rubberized and finger-contoured handles of the ski poles. These could be extracted quickly with one pull from the pole, screw threads being decided against because even a drop of moisture on a thread could freeze and make extraction harder. Anyway, it would take longer to unscrew rather than pull them. The rubber/nylex pole handles simply slipped out and back into the pole in a firm friction grip, the hairline of the join obscured by the pole's rubberized handle, which extended an inch farther down the pole than the join. Three skiers meant six daggers in all, each tipped with ricin pellets. The castor oil derivative took only seconds to work, as the needle-sharp point, upon being thrust forward, would break the ricin capsule—teardropped at its end like a solidified saffron drop of Canada balsam—

coating the tip with the poison even as it punctured the ricin and the victim's skin simultaneously, the poison causing a total collapse of the victim's central nervous system.

On flat terrain now, the three were moving in unison in leg-kick, pole-push strokes. Then, with an incline up the other side of a frozen stream approaching them, the leader moved from classic stroking to the freer skating slide, poles starting together, then one leg pushing the ski sideways, using the other to glide, then alternating.

Someone back at HQ had argued that while it was obvious they couldn't use a helicopter to cross the DMZ in such clear weather without it being detected and shot down, they should have at least used male commandos—until it was pointed out by the duty officer that even the tradition-bound British had conceded that now half their MI-5 counterespionage agents were women. Better at observation. Saw things men didn't. Besides, with three women there was a greater element of surprise. The enemy wouldn't expect it. Once the three had crossed the DMZ, using darkness as cover, they'd surely fit in much more quickly than three men. After all, what could be more natural than three good-looking foreign correspondents, all equipped with the necessary ID, vying craftily with one another to get a one-on-one interview with the famous American general whose daring if unconventional exploits from Iraq to Siberia had surpassed even those of the legendary Rommel and Schwarzkopf?

And then all it needed was a second, the needle-thin steel out, stab, and back in the pole. Or, if carried in separately— should they have to leave the poles outside—just as easily discarded behind a cabinet, in a wastebasket, anything nearby; the wound so thin, it would in effect be no more than a hat-pin-diameter stab. To make sure of this, having practiced with the optimum size needed to ensure depth without severe hemorrhaging, they had followed the lead of the British, who in the Iraqi War had consulted an eminent

Edinburgh pathologist on the best shape and size of the bayonet required to kill with minimum effort. There would be little if any blood, and the symptoms such that the victim's responses would more likely than not be interpreted as either heart attack or stroke. And giving him mouth-to-mouth would make it look even better if aides rushed in to help.

The cease-fire might last, but if it didn't—get Freeman, and the battle'd be half won. Freeman was like Patton—unpredictable and brilliant. Indeed, it had been someone at Marshal Yesov's HQ at Irkutsk who, remembering that Patton had represented the United States in the decathlon in the 1928 Olympics, thought of the idea of using the biathletes to get Freeman if the cease-fire between Siberia's sixty divisions and America's twelve broke.

One of the best friends the Americans had had before the cease-fire was a Siberian, Alexsandra Malof, from the JAO—Jewish Autonomous Oblast, or region—around Khabarovsk—whose underground movement had unearthed the secret of Baikal. In this four-hundred-mile-long, twenty-mile-wide lake—the deepest in the world, and holding a fifth of all the freshwater on earth—the Siberians had hidden a flotilla of small diesel subs beneath the winter ice. Nosing up through the thinner patches of ice, the toroidal, "Goodyear Man"-shaped minisubs had been able to launch a deadly missile offensive hundreds of miles eastward against the U.N.-sanctioned and outnumbered American force of ten divisions. The American force, under the command of General Douglas Freeman, was charged with preventing any further annexation of territory in what had been the Soviet Far East.

Now, after escaping from the Siberian jail in Port Baikal during the Allied commando raid that had destroyed the sub base, Alexsandra Malof was still on the run. Having headed south across the Siberian-Chinese border, then east to Harbin, the largest city in Manchuria, she was intent on getting back to the autonomous region in American-held Khabarovsk.

CHAPTER TWO

Harbin, Manchuria

"NOW!" SAID LATOV, sitting on the edge of the bed. It was half command, half plea. As head of the new Siberian Republic's consulate in Harbin, he was used to getting his own way, particularly with refugees like this one, desperately wanting the necessary travel documents so she could return to her home near Khabarovsk.

"No!" Alexsandra told him, taking his hand, moving it sulkily away from the thigh-revealing slit of her *qi pao*, the green dress clinging sensuously to her. "You kept me waiting," she said, sensing that if she gave in too easily, she'd have nothing left to bargain with.

For a moment Ilya Latov didn't answer her. He couldn't. He was too excited—she was still new to him. Three weeks ago he had seen her walking through Zhaolin Park by the river. Dressed in rags, she was shivering, her clothes lice-ridden, her Siberian fur boots tattered. Now the musky smell of her perfume which he'd brought her enveloped him, her lithe, silk-sheathed body exciting him in a reverie of expectation. Despite the darkness of the room here in the consulate annex, he could still see the outline of her breasts silhouetted clearly against the rime-covered window. Beneath all her outward sophistication, the finery he had provided for her, Latov couldn't think of her as any more than a Siberian peasant, a Jewish peasant at that, and he was determined to get every kopek's worth out of her. He tried again to slide his hand beneath the *qi pao*, feeling the warmth of her thigh. It made him feel young again. "I've been . . . busy," he said lamely, his arousal making his voice dry and cracked.

She pushed his hand away again. It was the only power she had. But soon she knew she would have to yield if she was to get the papers she so desperately needed to get out of Harbin, to head north, back to the JAO near Khabarovsk. It was now, thank God, in control of the Americans, following their push of the Siberians back as far as Baikal before the cease-fire following the first U.N.-declared war since Iraq in 1991.

Latov moved closer to her. He wanted her on top of him, sitting on him, rocking slowly back and forth side to side—to watch her breasts sway above him until he couldn't stand it anymore. He thought her by far the most beautiful woman he'd seen in months, or had he been away from Siberia too long—among the *kosoglazy*—the slant-eyed Chinese who, as far as he could remember, had been Siberia's most hated enemy?

"*Who* were you busy with?" Alexsandra asked moodily, sitting up stiffly against the wall, pulling her wrap tightly about her, drawing her feet up like a petulant school-girl. Her black hair caught the glow of colored lights outside. The Siberian consulate overlooked Zhaolin Park, where the Chinese were having the annual ice lantern festival. The consulate had been asked to douse its lights to heighten the effect, the kaleidoscopic hues they could see through the frosted windows produced by the battery-fed light bulbs frozen inside the ice sculptures and from swinging lanterns at the edges of the park. "I saw you with her," Alexsandra challenged Latov. "Walking in the park this afternoon."

"*Gospodi!*" he said exasperatedly. "She's my wife. What do you expect? That I should—"

Alexsandra swung her legs over the edge of the bed, reaching down for the heavy peasant fur boots she'd worn all the way on her escape from Lake Baikal, south then east, across the Mongolian-Chinese frontier and here to Harbin.

Latov reached out, took her shoulders, steadying her. "Look, if I refuse to go out with her, it would look suspicious. What do you expect?"

"Will *little* Ilya have to be home by eleven again?"

He ignored her baiting tone. In a way he liked it—he would enjoy hurting her even more. "The Chinese are giving one of their lunar new year parties," he explained lamely, his hands slipping about her, pulling her around so that her back was to him. He kissed her neck, her hair. "She's gone out with friends."

Alexsandra could smell his breath: wine and stale cigar smoke. "Won't you be missed?"

He felt his erection getting harder. "What do you want? First you're mad that I'm with her—then, if it wasn't for me, you'd still be wandering around in the park."

"I want you to tell me the truth, Ilya. I don't want anyone coming back—catching us here. You're a bigwig—the new Siberian consul. Who am I?" She turned suddenly to him. "A Jewess, a refugee forced south by the war. What would happen to me?"

She remembered all too vividly what had happened to her in the Port Baikal jail after she had been arrested in Khabarovsk as being a member of the *yevreyskie podpolie*—the Jewish underground—and shipped west on the Trans-Siberian. Had it not been for the Allied commando attack on Lake Baikal's southern township, during which a shell had blown open a wall of the jail, she and the other prisoners would never have escaped. She would still be there, having to endure more of the torture of the kind meted out by the OMONs—the Siberian Ministry of Interior's Black Berets—some of them women who, in true OMON style, had gleefully crippled several American POWs by driving needle-thin wire through their genitals. It hadn't taken her long to realize that the OMON thugs were no different from the KGB thugs who had raped her in the Baikal jail, that the *new* Siberian secret police were no better than the *old* Siberian KGB. Only the names had changed.

"She won't come back early," said Latov reassuringly, taking off his greatcoat, the sag of his belly revealed as the white bulge of his tuxedo. "They'll all be too busy stuffing themselves with grilled bear paws and stewed moose nose. The Chinese are barbarians. They'll eat anything—cow tendons, intestines—"

She laughed. "They think you're the ones that are barbarians."

He'd had enough of her teasing and suddenly released her, walked away from the bed and sat in a chair he dragged over from the corner of the room.

"Come here!" he ordered. Pulling her close to him, he felt her breasts pushing against him in the dark, her nipples hard in the cold of this caretaker's annex that he used for what he grandly called their "rendezvous." It was near freezing in the room. The Chinese didn't believe in heat, and had it not been for the small Japanese kerosene radiator in the room, they would have frozen. He knew that outside, enjoying the lantern festival, the Chinese would be wandering contentedly up and down the park in the subzero temperatures, licking ice cream; the big revolution in dreary Harbin, one of the worst-polluted cities in Manchuria, being the advent of a new flavor—strawberry—an ideological victory over the traditional and trusted vanilla.

"Are you telling me the truth?" she asked softly, yielding a little more to him. "There's no one—besides your wife?" She almost said, Another man perhaps? but that would be pushing him too far.

Even so, he uttered an oath under his breath, none of which she heard clearly, but nevertheless understood. It meant, what more do you want from me?

"I told you," he said sharply. "I've been busy. The Chinks are calling up more troops from the southern provinces, sending them up over the Nanking Bridge—to our border. You must have seen them passing through. I tell you, it's a logjam down there in Nanking. We've been trying to help them sort it out. All their other crossings over the Yangtze are flooded. Chinese have no idea of building approach roads or—''

"I don't care about Chinese roads,'' she said. "Just so long as you're telling me the truth—that there's no one else.'' She pushed her thigh between his legs. "You promise!''

"I swear,'' he said, at once impatient and gratified that she was so jealous. "I've been busy with Chink officials all day. Novosibirsk and Beijing don't want any misunderstanding.''

She knew what he meant—the Chinese and Russians had fought sporadic but bitter battles for a hundred years over the Amur River, which the Chinese called the "Black Dragon.'' The prize was the fertile river border areas around the northeasternmost corner of Manchuria, within the big hump formed by the river as it flowed eastward into the Sea of Okhotsk. Things had gotten so out of hand in the sixties that at one point soldiers of the Chinese People's Liberation Army had dropped their trousers and mooned the Russians watching them across the river. Many on both sides had been killed during the resulting border clashes. But why the sudden rapprochement between ancient enemies?

"I just want you to spend more time with me,'' she said, conciliatory, dropping now any suggestion that he might be fooling around with some other woman. She took his hand and placed it beneath her *qi pao*, telling him flippantly that it was nice Novosibirsk had "kissed and made up'' with the Chinese.

"We've not made up,'' Ilya retorted angrily. "It's convenient for Novosibirsk and Beijing to get on with one another just now.''

"Why?'' she asked, giggling, putting his hand inside her panties.

"Because—'' he said, gasping like a fish out of water, "if the cease-fire . . . if it doesn't hold . . . Novosibirsk would want . . . Beijing . . . an ally.'' He was babbling now.

"Here—let me do it," she said, unzipping the *qi pao* herself. He was so clumsy. "You mean you've spent all night discussing that?" she said, laughing openly at him. "The Americans won't break the cease-fire."

He was angered by her laughter, but too excited to chastise her.

She reached out in the darkness, her hand unzipping him, squeezing it, tugging it toward her, smelling it. "Enough war talk," she said softly. "I believe you. So long as you weren't with some slut."

He saw her shoulders visibly relax, her whole body, demeanor, softer, warmer now. Reaching frantically for his greatcoat, draped behind him over the chair, he got up, tipping over the chair in his urgency, flinging the coat onto the bed to take away the chill of the sheets. Then he lowered her to it.

"I'm sorry, Ilya," she said plaintively. "I'm so jealous. Sometimes—"

"*Ladno, golubchik,*" he said. It's all right, my sweet. "It's all—" She turned full on to him, squeezing him harder, moving its swollen tip in a fast, gentle whipping motion up and down against the damp tightness of her panties. He groaned with pleasure. "Go on—go on," he pleaded. "No—stop, stop. Tease me!"

She kissed the lobe of his ear, bit it. She hated him, his sour breath now reeking with nicotine and sweat.

He smelled like the OMON thugs, and she felt a rush of panic. She knew they wouldn't give up looking for her. Of all the prisoners who had escaped Baikal, she knew she had earned the OMON's special hatred. As well as being instrumental in helping the Americans to uncover the secret of the vast, frozen lake—the midget ship-to-surface-armed missile submarines that had almost turned the tide against the Americans, until the spectacular joint British SAS/American Delta commando raid on Baikal—she and other Jewish saboteurs from the JAO had wrecked part of the Trans-Siberian, in trying to stop the military support trains heading east from Novosibirsk.

The commandos had completely wrecked the sub base at Baikal. If Ilya even suspected who she really was, she knew she'd be shot—and most likely he, too, for having given her shelter from the OMON bloodhounds, albeit unknowingly. She heard him grunting, his body heavy, suffocating, his belly sliding in perspiration on hers, his arms, barely able to support his weight, shaking. She was still a prisoner. In order to get the necessary travel papers she so desperately needed, the very sex she was giving him as the price might well induce him to take his own good time issuing the papers. Why should he hurry? He might even refuse, just to keep her on tap.

He was covering her in wet kisses, the cloying mixture of vodka and stale breath flooding over her, his rutting rough and hard, confident he was exciting her. She sighed and gasped to maintain his illusion, and to take her mind off the sheer horror of it, wondered how she could possibly end the liaison she'd started when she had determined to "accidentally" bump into him in Zhaolin Park. And now she had more reason to get out of Harbin—to get north with the vital information of the massive Chinese buildup that was streaming over the Yangtze across the Nanking Bridge. The American satellites wouldn't pick it up through Harbin's souplike pollution, even if there was a satellite passing over Harbin.

Suddenly she had the answer. "Alexsandra—Alex—" cried Ilya. "I love you—I—"

Seized by inspiration, she pulled harder, slipped her shawl between them to stop the sucking noise of his sweat-slicked paunch slithering reptile-like against her, and pulled him harder into her, kissing him, her nails digging hard into his back, his mouth now moving quickly away from hers, kissing, slobbering over her breasts. "Harder!" she told him, and she could see them raping her in the jail at Baikal, her hatred of them so intense she feared she might never again be capable of genuine sexual love. She was crying, he mistaking it for passion, his thrusting becoming more violent. Through the maelstrom, she turned her head to the rime-covered window that looked out on the blurry pink glow of Zhaolin Park.

His rutting took on a manic quality, and, snorting frantically now like a pig, he drove her back against the headboard of the bed with such force that she heard a bone click in her neck, the pain shooting down her spine—then suddenly she felt lighter as the blubber rolled off her. It was panting, trying to talk, but unable—grunting incomprehensibly. Finally, gathering his spittle, he asked, "Was it good?"

"Prekrasno," wonderful, she said in the darkness, the room permeated now and then by the crimson light of swinging lanterns outside. The east was red. So was Ilya's back. When Mrs. Latov got through eating her grilled bear paw or stewed moose nose—the Chinese believed that eating animal parts imparted the animal's strength—and she returned to the consulate to find her darling Ilya's back so badly scratched, it would all be over for him. What would he tell her—that the Chinese comrades he'd been working late with had suddenly turned passionate? Then, Alexsandra knew, he'd have to issue her travel papers—as quickly as possible. She'd have her papers within hours. Why, he'd probably have the consulate limousine drive her to the outskirts, he'd be in such a hurry to bundle her off. Even so, it'd take him months to make it up with Madame Latov. Despite her soreness, feeling as if a red-hot poker had been shoved up inside her, Alexsandra smiled deliciously at Latov's predicament. And how could he possibly blame her? He'd probably boast for years about the woman who was driven so uncontrollable by his passion that she'd near skinned him alive.

The fat pig!

As he lit his cigarette, he saw her smiling. "It was that good, eh?"

"Yes," she said, without betraying her contempt, genuinely relaxing now. "It shouldn't be better!" she added, invoking an old Russian proverb that meant when things were going so well, one had no right to ask for anything more.

"Alexsandra . . ." he began as he started to dress.

"Yes?" It was becoming windy outside, fine snow striking the window like sand, the room pierced by flashes of red light from the wildly swinging lanterns. "What?" she said.

"It was nice," and with that he walked over and opened the door. The two Black Berets, their faces covered by the usual black balaclavas, walked in unhurriedly but moved purposefully, one standing to the side of the open door, the other coming over, handing Alexsandra her coat and shawl.

"And this time," said Ilya, as he was zipping up outside the door, looking back at them, "don't let her escape. Find out who her contacts are in the city—what other Jewish bastards are in the area—before you get rid of her. Understand?"

This angered the Black Beret closest to her. "Hell," he told his comrade when Latov was gone. "We weren't the bastards who blew the jail apart!"

The other Black Beret, still looking down at her, wasn't listening. Alexsandra stared at the balaclavas, the mark of their obsession with anonymity. Then, as if reading her thoughts, the one nearest—she could smell him—pulled up his mask and grinned. They knew it didn't matter whether she could identify them or not—it would do her no good now. She was finished. An interrogation session, maybe with help from their Chinese hosts—after all, she would be in a Chinese jail—and then execution as a spy. In China that meant a bullet into the neck, or would they insist on the OMON way and garrote her?

"Too bad the Americans won't know," one of them said to her. She was speechless with fright, shivering so violently she could hear her teeth chattering. ". . . about the Nanking Bridge," he continued. He glanced back at the other OMON by the door. "You think the Americans are in for a surprise, comrade?"

"I think so, comrade," the other answered. "I think so," and they both laughed. "I'll have a bit of that," the unmasked one said, watching her breasts rising and falling quickly in her panic.

"Left tit for me," said the other man.

"Picky bastard," joked his companion with mock severity. "You'll take what's left, comrade."

The unmasked one walked toward her. He had the crude, gold-capped teeth that had given Soviet dentistry a bad name, and when he smiled, it made him look even more malevolent.

"Marshal Yesov," he told her, bending down on his haunches so close she could smell a strong, cheesy odor pervading the dark room. "Marshal Yesov, my lovely, wants some information from you. All right?" He was unbuttoning his fly. "We want to know all about your yid underground. Its contacts with the Americans, understand?" She wasn't looking at him, but could smell him. Slowly he wound her hair about his wrists, forcing her to look up at him, her lips parted in pain. "You have contacts with Freeman's HQ, eh?" He now pushed her head down between his legs. "Tell Niki what you know."

CHAPTER THREE

Khabarovsk

ALREADY A LEGEND in his time, for his part in America's sweeping, outflanking armored movements of the Iraqi War and in the battles since, General Douglas

Freeman, a tall, silver-gray-haired officer whose clear blue eyes belied the weather-beaten exterior of middle age, was, for all his toughness, an optimistic man—a smile more his armor in Second Army than a frown. But when he scowled, as he was this late afternoon, striding as briskly as deep snow would allow and pulling his gloves on tightly against the bitter Siberian cold, his troops said he was a dead ringer for George C. Scott as Patton.

There was a swish of snow nearby.

" 'Scuse me, General?"

Freeman and his aide, Colonel Dick Norton, saw it was a reporter. Some of the press corps, particularly the Europeans, imitating Second Army's first-battalion alpine troops out of the winter training center high in the Sierra Nevadas, were finding it easier to get about on skis. The newsman's ID clip signified he was from one of the general's least liked papers, the *National Investigator*, one of the American La Roche tabloid chain. "Only thing they investigate," Freeman had once told Norton, "is tit and ass. That's it and that's all of it!"

" 'Scuse me, General?"

"Yes?" He knew the reporter was probably sniffing around for info about one of the men near the Baikal DMZ hundreds of miles to the east, who the night before had come in after four hours of guard duty and shot himself.

"You think Private Bronowski would have committed suicide, General, if he'd been back in the States when he got the news from his wife?"

Freeman kept walking, the squeak of his boots against the dry packed powder not letting up.

"No one likes being over here," said Freeman, not bothering to break his stride for the reporter or to look at him. "But we were sent here by the U.N. to do a job—to maintain the peace and to ensure that Siberia's annexation of Outer Mongolia doesn't spread any farther."

"Farther where?"

"*Inner* Mongolia," said Freeman, almost adding, *you fool*, his breath stabbing the air in short bursts of warmth. "Men are bound to get homesick. 'Course, I don't expect your story of his wife being screwed by a Pentagon pen pusher while he's stuck over here keeping the cease-fire helped any."

"We just report the news, General."

At that Freeman stopped and wheeled on the reporter, Dick Norton alarmed, the general looking as if he was within a couple of seconds of punching out the muckraker. The *National Investigator* reporter stood his ground. "General, you said no one likes being over here. Are you saying the president should recall—"

Freeman turned away and kept walking, Dick Norton informing the reporter, "We're here to keep the cease-fire. Period. If you'd like to ask any more questions, you should put them at the scheduled press conference—Khabarovsk HQ. Sixteen hundred hours."

The reporter moved off on his skis, still scribbling.

"By God!" muttered Freeman, pulling one glove so tight that the Gore-Tex looked grafted to his hand. "Can't stand that vermin."

"The blonde's a bit better-looking, I must admit," said Norton, trying to laugh it off.

"Rats!" said Freeman. "All of those La Roche reporters are rats." He looked across at Norton. "You see that boy's body? God damn, I've seen some horrible wounds in my time, but sticking a barrel in your mouth like that. Still, I haven't got much time for anyone who shoots himself over beaver. But you can understand, I suppose." His right fist hit the palm of his left. "Damn! Washington should have let me press Yesov's army when we had 'em on the run, Dick. Now they're safe as church mice west of Baikal. All those damned politicians back home. That's what it is." They were approaching the general's Quonset hut, the pillowed snow following the roof's half-moon bluish contour in the late afternoon light, the general pausing, watching the long trails of steam from the Quonset's vents

snaking high up into the pristine air. "But, no," added
Freeman bitterly. "Washington in its wisdom stopped
us—just as they did Schwarzkopf. 'Course," Freeman
conceded, "if Norman had gone farther west to run the
Republican Guard to ground, our armor over there
would've bogged down in the wet plains round Basra. But
here, Dick, *here* we could've finished Yesov's bastards off
before they got halfway across that—that damned ice
rink." The rink Freeman was referring to was the four-
hundred-mile-long Lake Baikal, now frozen solid. Norton
spotted a covey of reporters approaching them, hungry
on the scent of the suicide and bent, he warned Freeman,
on making an issue of poor morale throughout Second
Army.

They'd given Freeman good headlines for fighting Yesov's Siberians to a standstill then pushing them back across
Baikal, but now, with the suicide of one soldier, there was
blood in the air, and the less scrupulous among the press
corps had left their hosannas back in the bars of Khabarovsk. It was hooting time.

Freeman was smiling at the oncoming pack, most of them
on skis, telling Norton, "Not that blond bitch from the
Investigator. Leave her till last. First question for the brunette
from CBS. By God, I'd like to reconnoiter her, Dick."

"Cool it, General."

Freeman nodded as pleasantly as he could in minus forty.
"Ladies, gentlemen." Norton gave CBS the nod.

"General," began the brunette, flicking away strands of
nut-brown hair that just for a moment turned gold in the
dying rays of the sun. "Is it true that morale in Second
Army is at its lowest ebb since the signing of the cease-
fire?"

"Not at all. We're talking here—I presume you are
talking about the self-inflicted—"

"The suicide!"

"One soldier's tragedy hardly extends to a whole army,"
said Freeman.

"General?" interjected a French reporter from *Paris*

Match in a loud tone. "We've had rumors that the Siberian Interior Ministry is out to punish—is actively searching for collaborators who helped the British and American forces before the cease-fire."

Freeman was struck by the man's use of the phrase "actively searching for." He wondered what "passively searching for" would be. "We've had no such reports," Freeman told him truthfully. "What they do in the zone west of Baikal I can't say, but there'll be no tracking down of collaborators in our zone—that is, east of Baikal. We're not here to exact vengeance. We're here to keep the peace."

"You don't think any OMONs are after you personally, do you, General?"

"Hell, no!" Freeman laughed, looking down at the crowd which he always thought of as an audience. "Any of those black-bonneted bastards come to get me, I'll give them a Second Army welcome." He patted his waistband, beneath which he carried the Sig Sauer P-220, always loaded with a fifteen-round magazine of nine-millimeter Parabellum. "And if that isn't enough for 'em, I'll introduce them to my friend Charles *Winchester*." There were a few laughs from those who had been on the Second Army beat longest, who knew he was referring to the twelve-gauge riot gun, loaded with 00, that he kept by his bed. "Hell," continued the general, "the Winchester twelve hundred'll stop . . ." He paused, searching for an apt analogy.

"Amtrak!" suggested one of the reporters.

"Hell," the general joked, "anything'll stop Amtrak."

That was the headline in the next morning's *National Investigator*, Stateside: GENERAL SLAMS AMTRAK!

Marshal Yesov's aides delivered the headline and story to the Siberian commander. They had been instructed by him to monitor everything said by and about the general. They'd had a special file on him ever since he had fought so brilliantly in the Iraqi War.

CHAPTER FOUR

Irkutsk

MARSHAL YESOV AND the other Siberian generals had been delighted by the Iraqi War. It had been the *real'noe vremya*—"real-time"—testing range that told them which of the old Russian, now CIS, weapons needed to be junked. A case in point was the Scud. Moscow had said they'd updated it after the Iraqi War, but in Siberia, in Novosibirsk's satellite city, Akademgorodok, home of the republic's most eminent scientists, the joke amid the Siberians—who hated Moscow as much as they did the Americans—was that firing a Scud was like drinking a glass of cheap Moscow vodka: you never knew where you'd land!

Through front companies in Brussels, the world's arms capital, Yesov ordered shipments of the new Israeli Arrow antimissile missile in lieu of the American Patriot. It wasn't only that the American Patriot was unobtainable, even through third-party arms dealers, but that the Siberians had long suspected, even before *The New York Times* reporters, that the Patriot, highly lauded as it had been through media hype, was a missile with more of a reputation than it deserved. The Siberians' concern was that while the Patriot had brought down so many Scuds over Israel, it had not always destroyed the warhead, sometimes merely exploding the Scud's fuel tanks. Such hits were spectacular, especially to the millions of TV viewers—but they still left the warhead intact to fall and explode somewhere else. If you were aiming your missile at a large target—a city—this didn't matter so much. But Marshal Yesov had expressed concern that if Novosibirsk decided on a preemptive strike against the Americans, then a very specific targeting capability would be needed, together with an integrated in-depth, antiaircraft and antimissile-missile defense ring around Lake Baikal's western shore—which would be provided by the Mach-breaking Israeli Arrow. For Yesov, the new long-range 203mm howitzers operating within the deep AA defensive ring about west Baikal were the answer.

One of Yesov's younger generals, Minsky, commander of the Siberians' Far Eastern Military District's elite *udarnaya*—shock troops of the Tenth Guards Cavalry Division—was pressing for just such a strike, pontificating aloud about the vulnerability of the Americans. Minsky was an Afghanistan veteran, recently appointed CO of the Tenth Guards Division—its honorific of "Slutsk" earned by his forebears in the Battle in Byelorussia in the Great Patriotic War of 1942–45. As its commander, Minsky was keen to prove his worth against the Americans.

"To hell with the cease-fire!" he proclaimed defiantly in the Siberians' Irkutsk HQ. No general would have dared spoken in the marshal's presence like this in the old days. But since Gorbachev, Yeltsin, and now Chernko, the up-and-coming young "Turks," as Minsky's ilk were called, could get away with it—if they showed results, as Minsky had in suppressing breakaway minorities farther north in the Yakutsk region. "I say push the bastards back to the sea!" he enjoined his colleagues. "We outnumber them five to one at least."

Attending to his maps, Yesov said nothing. He was an old Soviet strategist of the Frunze Military Academy, a believer in the big battalions school of warfare dominated by artillery, the *Bog voyny*—"God of War"—and *zarnitsa*, or lightning war, behind the enemy's lines; not only behind the battlefield, but wherever possible within the enemy's supply base—in this case the United States itself. Having been a young soldier once himself, he well understood the impatience of Minsky's generation, but he had risen to be a marshal because he had never lost, and as much as the young men now scoffed at Lenin, one Leninist dictum had guided and would continue to guide all Yesov's actions: "It is a crime to undertake war with a better prepared opponent."

Minsky, however, highly decorated in the Afghanistan War, was undeterred by Yesov's Frunze Academy caution. He thought Yesov an old fogy. In turn, Yesov thought that dealing with Minsky was like staring down the laser sights of one of the new T-80's 135mm, the biggest MBT—main battle tank gun—in the world. One frontal shot against the tank's glacis armor plate wouldn't be enough to stop it. Sometimes, Yesov knew, it was more prudent to withdraw to defilade position—to sit and wait.

"The Americans are dug in," Minsky pressed. "Freezing their asses off. Snow—why, it's mother's milk to us. But not to the Americans. I say hit them before the ice starts to crack and close our roads." There being precious few roads at all in Siberia, the frozen rivers were the only trustworthy supply lines along which the logistics "tail" could keep up with the head. "Besides," added Minsky, indicating the map of eastern Siberia around Lake Baikal and south into Outer Mongolia, "we have the Trans-Siberian. In 'forty-five it only took us two months to move four armies across from the west. And during the cease-fire, we've been moving supplies across the taiga constantly. Why doesn't Novosibirsk attack?"

None of his colleagues answered. They were loyal to Minsky, but they knew his reference to Novosibirsk was really a dig at Yesov, who would have the final military say on whether to hold the cease-fire or not after Novosibirsk's political decision.

"Well, what are we going to do?" said Minsky.

"I don't know what you're going to do, General," said Yesov, putting on his greatcoat, his peaked, crimson-banded gray cap, and his gloves against the bitter winter cold. "But I'm going to dinner."

But Minsky was not easily put off. Inside the officers' mess he wondered aloud about the special vulnerability of Americans when they were so far from home. "I tell you, the Americans are crybabies. Three months away and they start to blubber for Mama."

"General Minsky," said Yesov quietly, his massive jaws demolishing thick, black bread, "perhaps the Americans will move against us."

The other officers, nonplussed, glanced at one another, but for Minsky there was no doubt.

"They won't," he said confidently. "Washington wouldn't permit Freeman to violate the cease-fire."

The marshal took out his cigarette case and lit a Sobraine, holding it meditatively between thumb and forefinger, both of which were stained a dark yellow with nicotine. "Perhaps, comrades. We'll see. But this Freeman—he has a flair for the unorthodox."

Just how unorthodox, Yesov could have had no idea.

CHAPTER FIVE

Khabarovsk

FREEMAN'S INSISTENCE THAT a team of navy SEAL—sea, air, and land—commandos be trained by deaf mutes, and that "Wolf dung! Lots of it!" be collected and brought to his HQ at Khabarovsk were two of the strangest orders issued by the commander of all American and Allied forces in eastern Siberia.

The victor of his daring nighttime commando raid on Pyongyang, North Korea's capital, early in the war, and of his equally audacious airborne attack on Ratmanov Island, in the Bering Strait, only twenty-five miles from Alaska, Freeman had never approved of the cease-fire agreed to by the White House. "If we don't finish it now," Freeman warned Washington, "we'll have to do it later at a higher cost." But, as Schwarzkopf was told not to pursue the Republican Guard in Iraq any farther, so Washington had similarly ordered Freeman not to press his rout of the Siberian Fifth Army, spearheaded by the once-famed but now badly mauled Thirty-first Stalingrad Division.

The general's order for wolf dung during the cease-fire Washington and Novosibirsk had pressed upon him, perplexed his aide, Dick Norton. But Freeman, as if his words were explanation enough, merely pointed out that "Intelligence reports all wolves have been taken from the Beijing Zoo and sent to the northern boundaries of the Beijing Military Region."

In his Khabarovsk Quonset hut HQ, Freeman was studying the huge twelve-by-six-foot map of eastern Siberia, its green, mountainous terrain to the south contrasting with the treeless humps and plains of Mongolia to the south and west. His eyes followed the outline of a huge rectangle, the western edge formed by Lake Baikal, the annexed Mongolian People's Republic to his south, the Yakutsk region of Siberia to his north, and behind him the Sea of Japan. There were many fancy military euphemisms for it, but every private in Freeman's Second Army knew what it meant if the cease-fire didn't hold. They'd be boxed in.

"Why can't the damn fools see it?" demanded Freeman. "Novosibirsk is playing Washington for a sucker—again. I don't trust those vodka-swilling sons of bitches as far as I can kick 'em." He turned from the map to face Norton and the other officers of his Khabarovsk HQ, some of them new boys flown in from Dutch Harbor, Alaska, on rotation. "You know what the new republics' military were doing when Bush and Gorby were shaking hands, gentlemen?"

Norton knew—it was a rite of passage for any newcomer to his staff as far as Freeman was concerned.

"Well," said Freeman, "there was a little mystery NATO couldn't figure out. You all remember NATO?"

"North American Trust Organization?" proffered a cocky if ill-advised young captain—obviously not a career soldier.

Freeman ignored the smartass remark, but he'd already noted the man's name: Tyler, M., a junior officer, liaison between Freeman's G-2, intelligence section, and his first armored division. Cheeky bastard like Tyler would be a good man to put in the lead tank, Freeman thought. With that kind of chutzpa, he'd keep going where others would stop. Secret of an armored thrust was that you must never stop; your mobility was the best chance of securing victory and survival.

"Well," continued Freeman, "our Russian friends in July, 1990—Soviet high command, to be exact—reported they had forty-one thousand tanks in Europe. Forty-one thousand, five hundred and eighty to be precise, gentlemen. Under the COFIE—conventional forces in Europe—treaty, a significant number of those tanks were to be destroyed, and so four months later the Soviets told us there were now only twenty thousand Soviet tanks in Europe. The question, however, gentlemen, was—I should say *is*—where did the other twenty thousand go? Scrap heap?" Freeman shook his head. "No, sir—*none* of them were junked. *Not a one!* We found out that many of the remainder were moved east of the Urals—out of Europe—just before the treaty document about 'tanks in *Europe*' was signed, and some were sent to the new central Asian republics. Now there were still eight thousand tanks missing, gentlemen, and if you're puzzled about them, I can tell you that it was revealed in *Sovetskaya Rossiya*—a *Russian* paper—that the missing eight thousand tanks had been put in 'storage bases' in western Siberia and central Asia. Tanks, gentlemen—T-72s with laser sighting, thermal imaging, and appliqué armor—all of which could be used against us at any time. So my standing order is to keep your powder dry and make damn sure none of your forward OPS doze off—'specially during blizzards when our air cover from here west to Baikal will effectively be reduced to zero, even with our infrared capability. Any observer falls asleep at his post, I'll have him flayed alive plus a hundred dollar fine for each man in the squad. Understand?''

''Yes, sir.''

''And the officer in charge busted to private.''

No one answered. Freeman was as frustrated as Norton had seen him. He had tried to warn the American people and the Congress of the danger a few days before, during his press conference in Khabarovsk, but for this he'd been attacked. Now, holding up one of the La Roche papers, he let the new members of his staff see the screaming four-inch headline: WARMONGER!

''What do you think?'' he asked his staff. ''Am I a warmonger? Anybody here think these jokers'll rest with American troops on Siberian soil? When they've got us surrounded north to Yakutsk, west beyond Lake Baikal, south to Mongolia?''

No one cared to answer him.

''Warmonger!'' he said, throwing the La Roche paper down. ''Well, they're right—*when* I see war coming. Like Churchill. My God, this is Saddam Insane all over again. Should have gone after that son of a bitch right into Baghdad. I'd have personally shot the mad bastard. Know how many Kurds we would have saved? Men, women, and children? Never mind Iraqis.'' Freeman snatched up his cap and the thick beech stick he'd honed to a pointer, his tone changing—as if suddenly, uncharacteristically, resigned to the foibles of Washington and the State Department doyennes of Foggy Bottom. ''Meanwhile,'' he continued in a world-weary voice, ''all those armchair fairies in State and the Pentagon are pumping the president full of—*restraint*.'' He said it as if it were a dirty word, the beech stick smacking hard against the massed divisions west of Baikal. ''Only *restraint* this crowd'll understand will come from the barrel of an M-1 tank. Which is why, gentlemen, if I'm any judge, I expect to be 'recalled for consultation' any day.''

If some of the officers were surprised, Dick Norton wasn't. He'd got the first fax copy of the *New York Times* that morning, and if, unlike the La Roche tabloids, the mainstream papers weren't exactly calling Freeman a warmonger—their more genteel prose amounted to the same thing. The *Times* had written:

> General Douglas Freeman has proved to have been not only a loyal implementor of U.S. national policy, but a prescient and brilliant soldier. The raid he led on Pyong-yang, the brilliant strategy that allowed the Allies to break out of the infamous Soviet-ringed Dortmund/ Bielefeld pocket on the north German plain earlier in this conflict, and his dashing seizure of the initiative once the Siberian military threat in Lake Baikal had been realized, have made his name synonymous in the history of American arms with "daring" and "brilliant," if at times "eccentric," leadership.
>
> This having been said, however, we believe that the time has come for Douglas Freeman to be recalled, as he was once the European threat was quashed. He is a fighting general, and not, as is increasingly being pointed out in the Congress, a peace general. He has done his job extraordinarily well, and the nation, as it did upon his return from Europe, should shower its honors upon him for his outstanding leadership of operation "Arctic Front," which made it possible for the present cease-fire to be instigated. But now it is time for someone else to take his place in Siberia. He is, as he was in Europe—and there is no easy way to say this—too "volatile" for the peace. He is a soldier's soldier, and one who has much to teach in the staff colleges of the nation. With the battlefield now thankfully silent, and with spring imminent, it is fitting that with a change in season there be a change in command, a transition from the time of war to a season of hope.

"By God!" Freeman had commented upon seeing the editorial, whipping off his reading glasses, conveying the impression he didn't really need "visual assist," when he plainly did. He was certain *The New York Times* and other papers were merely parroting administration policy, which he believed had been deliberately leaked to signal his end. "Where do those Pentagon fairies get that horse manure from, Dick? 'Season of hope'! Good God, don't they understand the Siberians outnumber us more than five to one?"

Dick Norton thought it inadvisable to remind the general that before the cease-fire, one of the Pentagon fairies he'd referred to had won the Silver Star in the vicious fighting on the road east of Skovordino, and that in his view Washington might be right. Norton looked down at the editorial. "Sounds like James Knutson to me—Yale, not the Pentagon."

"Well," grumped Freeman, his hands cupping a mug of coffee as he overlooked the frozen Amur River from his Khabarovsk HQ, the tall, war-scarred smokestacks reaching into the ice-cold blue, "it's an Ivy League fairy, then. Worst kind. Don't realize their freedom to pontificate upon national policy has been paid for in blood from Iwo Jima to this . . ." He paused, searching for the right word to describe the confluence of vast mountain ranges and endless taiga of fir, beech, larch, silver pine, and the steppe beyond Baikal. It was so vast, whole armies had been swallowed by and could hide in it without a trace. "Soon be spring," he said. But there was none of the optimism with which most others on his staff had been anticipating the coming of the season. "Ice'll start to melt. There'll be floods. Our tanks could be in a quagmire. Immobile." He took a sip of coffee, its steam condensing.

The HQ door banged open, a G-2 lieutenant stamping his feet, shucking off the snow. " 'Cept for the permafrost," Freeman went on. "That's rock-hard. But that won't help us when the rivers start to crack.." Norton could see that even as the general was speaking, his conversation about the cold was evidence of a much deeper concern about whether the cease-fire would hold. He wanted it to, but to be caught napping at any of the hundreds of weak points along the vast "box" was a heavier load than anyone else was carrying, here or back in the Pentagon. "What do you think, Dick?" Freeman asked. "Don't dress it up. You think they'll attack in winter?"

"No, sir—I think the cease-fire'll hold. Summer's the time for war in this country. They sure as hell won't try to move while Lake Baikal is frozen. We could reinforce our M-1 battalions on the western shore in a matter of hours— just scoot across that lake with close air support A-10 Thunderbolts riding shotgun. They'd soon sort out the T-72s. Look what they did on the road to Basra." Norton was talking about the massacre the Thunderbolts had wrought in the Iraqi desert with their Volkswagen-sized gun mount forward of the plane's titanium "bath" seat—the Thunderbolts' thirty-millimeter cannon chopping up Hussein's fleeing armored columns, sending them careening in panic. "Besides, General, Baikal won't even begin to melt till late spring—four, six weeks away at least."

"Maybe, Dick, but I don't trust 'em. I want to know the moment that son of a bitch starts to crack."

"Yes, sir."

"Under the *rules*," Freeman said contemptuously, putting down his cap, the beech stick's knobby end smacking the four-hundred-mile-long lake, "we can move anything but food supply trucks across the lake. Washington says anything else would give the wrong signal to Novosibirsk."

"Yes, sir. I know."

Freeman pulled his gloves on, deciding to leave after all, stretching the fur-lined leather into a fist. Dick Norton opened the door for him and immediately turned his face from the icy blast. "You tell me, Dick, the moment that ice starts to melt—first goddamn crack. You hear?"

"Yes, sir, but I honestly don't think you've anything to worry about."

As Freeman stepped out into swirling fresh snow, someone cried, "Look out, General!" Almost too late, the general stepped back, barely missed by two hooded skiers.

"God damn it!" exploded Freeman as they swooshed by.

"You okay, General?" asked Norton.

"Yes, yes," said Freeman brusquely, pulling up his collar. "Women drivers—what d'you expect? Man's not safe in his own camp."

Norton laughed with him. It was a comment that'd get him killed in the media, but Norton knew he held no prejudice against women—had used them as his lead pilots in the attack on Pyongyang. On the other hand, he'd vehemently opposed the idea of women in tanks—had said, quite rightly, there was no place "to piss in private."

CHAPTER SIX

IN THE HEADQUARTERS of Beijing MR, the most important of the seven military regions in China, the imperturbable General Cheng was perturbed. In one fell swoop, with Siberia's annexation of Outer Mongolia—to which Cheng had no doubt Ulan Bator had willingly agreed, given the Mongolians' ancient hatred of the Chinese—the traditional buffer zone between north China, Inner Mongolia, and Siberia had been removed. It wasn't just the stationing there of the Siberian Thirty-ninth Army with its "category one"—top readiness, armored and motor-rifle divisions—that concerned Cheng. They had always been posted on the Mongolian-Chinese border and had always been a thorn in China's side. But now several more divisions were stationed closer along the Mongolian-

Chinese border around Saynshand in the Gobi Desert. The annexation meant that not even the formalities of Siberian-Mongolian discussions were necessary before the Siberians could move their troops at will in and about Outer Mongolia, threatening China's enormous province of Inner Mongolia.

Cheng's concerns ranged from the grand strategic implications of Siberia's annexation of Mongolia to the myriad details that had to be attended to in running the world's largest army, which, though not as modernized as the Siberians' or the Americans', was nevertheless four million strong. Many of the reservist cadres were battle hardened and wise after unofficially fighting to help defeat the Americans in the Vietnam War, older cadres having fought the Americans to a standstill in Korea in the 1950s.

. But always it had been difficult for the PLA to keep within budget. In 1989, the time of Tiananmen, it had cost only thirteen U.S. cents a bullet to shoot Goddess of Democracy protesters; but now, with rampant inflation, the cost of ammunition had skyrocketed to twenty-five cents. Cheng knew this might not be a serious consideration for smaller armies, but for an army of four million, it was a headache. But Cheng was as resourceful as he was known to be cautious, and his connection with the American industrialist and newspaper magnate Jay La Roche was used to good effect, enabling him to buy U.S. supplies in the illegal arms trade through Brussels.

Cheng knew from his intelligence sources that La Roche was what even the Americans would call a degenerate—his bizarre sexual behavior had driven away his wife, who was now serving as a Wave, an American naval nurse, at Dutch Harbor in the American Aleutian island chain. But registered on the Shanghai, as well as the Tokyo, London, and Wall Street, exchange, La Roche, who Cheng plainly admitted to his colleagues would "sell his mother for a *fen*," was valuable to Beijing. La Roche had assured Cheng, and thus the People's Liberation Army, of access to anything they required, from bullets to nerve gas, which could be used against either Siberians or Americans—whoever violated Chinese territorial integrity.

Though La Roche always insisted on hard currency, Cheng had conserved brilliantly. While the Americans and Siberians were spending more and more on self-propelled artillery, for example, the PLA relied largely on the older-fashioned towing system. It meant that the crews weren't as well-protected as they would be in armor-plated, self-propelled howitzers, but Cheng knew that once a self-propelled vehicle broke down—an overheated bearing, a wiring malfunction, whatever—it stayed where it was and became the delight of enemy artillery gunners: a stationary target. With towed weapons, on the other hand, if something happened to the lead vehicle, the gun could be quickly uncoupled, broken down into its component parts, and if necessary moved by sheer muscle power—as had been done over the mountains and through the swamps of the thousand-mile Ho Chi Minh Trail. Cheng much preferred fighting to penny-pinching, the constant battle of refusing requests for more money making him increasingly unpopular among military commanders, and he yearned to show his mettle in combat.

As he signed a memo denying yet another exorbitant request for extra uniforms, General Cheng's foreign affairs phone began its insistent ring. It was the Foreign Ministry, informing him that the Siberian chargé d'affaires in Harbin, Ilya Latov, had conveyed the wish of General Yesov, commander in chief of the new Siberian forces, to meet tomorrow with his "esteemed" Chinese colleague in the border town of Erhlien. Cheng recognized instantly that there was significance in the Siberians having selected the Chinese town on the border and not Dzamïn Üüd, the town on Siberia's Mongolian side, where the Trans-Siberian spurline coming down through Ulan Bator reached the Chinese frontier. It was a gesture of respect, that Yesov would be coming to him, not vice versa. Still, Cheng was as suspicious of Yesov as Yesov and Freeman were of each other. What was the Siberian bear up to?

So as to maintain face and not show any sign of haste that might evidence the anxiety he felt, Cheng replied he would be pleased to meet the comrade from Siberia but not till the following evening. This, he knew, would necessitate Yesov taking the Trans-Mongolian express, unless the Siberian commander wanted to come by air and risk the Americans interpreting an overborder flight as a back door violation of the cease-fire. It would be a long journey for Yesov through the mountains south of Lake Baikal, down through the Selenga River valley into Mongolia, all the time enjoying the ceaseless loudspeaker rattle from the train's PA system.

Unable to stop or even control the PA system, Yesov would be subjected to the relentless, mind-numbing blare all the way down over the endless, brown, icy, treeless expanse. The great marshal of the United Siberian Republic would have to feast on the finest Mongolian cuisine of rancid blood sausage and slimy bowls of floating goats' ears and yellow mutton. Cheng calculated that by the time Yesov reached Erhlien on the Chinese side, a neat town compared to the Mongolian slum of Dzamïn Üüd, and was given proper food, he would be in a much more conducive mood to listen to the Chinese point of view to whatever proposal he might have. Cheng certainly wasn't going to cross the border to meet him. Apart from the filth of the Mongolian side, the mobile missile sites around Dzamïn Üüd, as part of the Gobi Desert defense, were all pointed at China. To meet there rather than in Erhlien would be an implicit acceptance of Siberia's annexation of the Mongolian frontier. It would be noon by the time the Trans-Mongolian reached the border, and over the vast, endless snow that covered the dormant grassland of the southern Gobi, vultures would be high in the hard, cloudless, blue sky, circling, waiting for the slightest mistake of any wayward traveler. Already many refugees from the north were said to have perished.

Before leaving for Erhlien, General Cheng, unsettled by the new Siberian republic flexing its muscle in Mongolia, decided it would be prudent to have the frontier units in

Beijing, Lanzhou, and Shenyang military regions in the far north of China, bordering on Siberia and Mongolia, on first-stage alert. The haunting fear of a sudden Mongol invasion sweeping down from the north across the plains of Inner Mongolia to Beijing was always a constant in the psyche of the Chinese, and foremost in the mind of whoever was head of the PLA. Indeed, the fear had been the reason for the construction of the Great Wall, the only man-made construct visible from outer space. Cheng, ever vigilant, would sometimes walk through the vast underground network of tunnels beneath Beijing, which had been constructed in the 1960s when the ferocity of the Chinese-Soviet battles over the disputed northern border areas around the Amur River had convinced the Chinese that a Soviet invasion was imminent.

As a final precaution prior to leaving the Beijing railway station for Erhlien, Cheng suddenly ordered carriages in his train to be switched. You could never be too careful. It would take only one Democracy Movement fanatic to kill you. He also ordered a fax be readied for one of La Roche's Shanghai companies, requesting replacement parts for civilian air transport. Indeed, Cheng, though he could never admit it officially, avoided air travel in China if at all possible. He had lost more people on the People's airline in the last year than he had on military maneuvers. In fact, the fax, which might or might not be sent, depending on his meeting with Yesov, had nothing to do with aircraft parts. But its invoice number code would tell La Roche's company that what the PLA needed was a delivery of ten thousand 203mm, 102-kilogram HE—high explosive—heavy artillery rounds with variable bag charges. The 203mm had a range of plus or minus eighteen miles and could do tremendous damage in either a creeping barrage or direct target fire. Cheng also ordered that, pending the meeting with Yesov, a requisition be made and held for four thousand AIF, or anti-infrared smoke rounds. These latter were normal smoke rounds infused with denser particles which prevented enemy infrared scopes from picking up body and engine heat signature, which they could do through normal smoke. These AIF rounds, Cheng knew, might be a little more difficult for La Roche to procure. He knew that La Roche might not be able to get them directly from Belgian or French factories because of the ridiculous U.S. human-rights-prompted embargo on such sales to China. But then, La Roche would do what he had done so often in the past—have the AIF shells stolen from his own country's army, either from the convoys resupplying Freeman's Vladivostok base out of Japan, or from the stockpiles in Vladivostok itself. He would then send them down on junks through the Tsushima Strait between South Korea and Japan into the Yellow Sea, where the junks, ostensibly bound for Taiwan, could be officially intercepted by the PLA navy's fast-attack coastal defense boats and unloaded on the China coast.

CHAPTER SEVEN

New York

IN THE OPULENT, dimly lit cocktail bar of the Il Trovatore on the fiftieth floor of La Roche Tower, Jay La Roche, who owned the tower and everything in it, looked out at the gilded blackness that was Manhattan—and part his. La Roche's empire, begun in perfume and pharmaceuticals, had expanded in a dozen different directions; and before the cease-fire, the war had catapulted him to the top ten of *Fortune*'s 500.

The waitress, who delivered his third Manhattan in the fifteen-karat-gold-lipped glass with gold-filigree leaf design, bent lower as she placed the silk coaster before him, lingering to wipe the table. The table was as clean "as a choirboy," as La Roche was fond of saying, but Francine, a long, lithe blonde with a starlet's body to match, knew that if she was to keep her job and the big tips that came with working at the Il Trovatore, she'd better linger as long and as frequently as possible. And as Jimmy, working bar, told her, low-cut dresses with "no visible panty line" were "de rigueur." Jimmy also informed Francine there was a "bonus" for "noninventoried services." She asked him what he meant. Jimmy told her she'd find out.

Jay was alone this evening, but Jimmy could read the signs and knew it wouldn't be long before La Roche wanted company. Dressed smartly in a tuxedo, La Roche had what Jimmy called "the look"—enigmatic, cold—like one of those long, deep-feeding fish Jimmy had heard about. Creatures who lived their entire lives in the dark, covered in poisonous antennae, who would lie in wait for hours, then suddenly dart, stun their prey, swallow their victim and move on, their only satisfaction the kill.

Jimmy knew the ritual by heart. After the third Manhattan, which La Roche was now sipping, he'd ring room service for a fourth drink to be taken up to his penthouse.

Soon La Roche was down to the cherry. Jimmy pulled over the next order chit and scooped ice into the daiquiri shaker. "Think you're about to be drafted, Francine. You been a good girl?" The question wasn't idle chatter—if she hadn't been, they'd all get it in the neck.

" 'Course," she said.

"Don't shit me, Francine. You been having it off with the fleet or what?"

"Screw you," she said. "When are those daiquiris going to be ready?"

He gave the flask a few extra shakes, the condensation catching the rosy glow of the bar, his voice using the chipped ice as cover. "Nothing personal, Francine, but Mr. La Roche wants the best. Have to understand that. You had a blood test?"

"You had yours?"

"Yeah," said Jimmy, unabashed. "But I'm careful, Francine. I don't go screwing about with anyone—after hours—know what I mean?"

"I haven't—"

"Hey—don't dance with me, honey. One of the juice-heads said she saw you down at Melville's with a fly-boy. If you two tore one off, sweetie, I hope you used a letter."

"I'm clean," she said. He topped up the daiquiris. "Listen, Francine, you've got it all wrong. It's for *your* own good, too, babe." He lowered his voice, careful that a group of American and Japanese businessmen two tables closer in than La Roche couldn't overhear—the Japanese being told through the booze and haze of blue smoke that with the Mideast wells aflame again, this time by Muslim fundamentalists in support of Siberia against America, North Slope oil was going to cost them a lot more than yen. "If you're dirty," Jimmy explained to Francine, "he'll get mad. He likes S and M, anyway. And that'd just give him an excuse—if you're dirty." Jimmy lifted his eyes. "Know what I mean?" He could tell she wasn't quite sure, though she was getting the drift—sort of. "You hear about his wife?"

Francine shrugged. "I heard a lot of yap."

"In Shanghai," said the barman. "Beat the crap out of her. She's lucky she got out in one piece. Just warnin' you, babe."

"I can handle it, Jack," she said, picking up the tray. "I think you're jealous. Maybe you didn't perform well enough for him."

"I'm still here, bitch. And don't call me Jack."

"My my, I think he *is* jealous," said Francine, balancing the tray. "Just a teensy-weensy bit."

La Roche snapped his fingers. She went over and came back without having delivered the daiquiris. "Mr. La Roche would like another drink, Jack," she said. "In his room."

"You're on, babe. You clean?"

She snatched up several coaster. "I suppose all *your* boyfriends are virgins, Jack?"

"Yes," he said, unequivocally. "How about yours?"

Francine didn't give a damn about Jimmy. Did he think that because she was just seventeen she hadn't been round the block or something, that she didn't know La Roche had you followed, that if you had made it with anyone else and hadn't passed the company medical, you were out on your ass?

She knew she was clean. The only thing she couldn't figure out was that if La Roche was so fussy—he probably knew she'd been to Melville's—if he was so damned uptight about prick poisons, why didn't he just keep a stable of girls on tap? How come he had to come down to the bar—*his* bar, for Chrissakes—and pretend that he'd somehow managed to pick you up? As if somehow he'd seduced you. Well, she didn't care—had a guy once who had to do it with a parrot in the room. He was rich, too, and anyway, Jay La Roche was one helluva lot richer than him. Made it kind of exciting, though, she thought, like in the movies.

When she entered the penthouse, the first thing Francine was aware of was its smell: strangely antiseptic, creating an ambience of cold detachment—an empty feeling. So much so that she half expected to see cover sheets on the furniture.

The apartment was spacious, yet not as big as she'd supposed. Everything in it seemed extraordinarily organized—nothing spontaneous about it. Even the paintings—mod art—seemed chosen to match the angular Scandinavian chaise longue. For all the art deco colors, and a stunning view of Central Park and beyond, it had an inhospitable air, and she felt a chill, despite the fact that the gold-braced thermostat was registering over seventy degrees. When he came out from the kitchenette to meet her, he was in a rich oxblood robe with yellow dragons, rampant, front and back, embroidered in gold thread. It clashed violently with the decor.

He pressed a button somewhere and the air began pulsating with a heavy rock bet.

"You like the Razors?" he asked.

"Yes, Mr. La Roche, but how did you know—"

"I know what music you like—if you call that shit music." He paused, but she knew it wasn't for want of anything to say, his eyes sweeping over her, taking in every detail, as if he could see right through her, knew all about her past and her future.

"I know what you eat," he said. "Come here." As she walked toward him, he reached over to the window wall and, without taking his eyes off her, pressed another button, and she saw the drapes moving toward one another, wiping out the view.

"My wife's boyfriend is back with her," he said. "Up in Alaska."

She was nonplussed, but quickly something told her, perhaps the obsessive neatness of the apartment, that if she showed any puzzlement, it would be dangerous. She said nothing.

"You know why?" La Roche went on, one hand extracting a small gold snuff box from the robe's right-hand pocket, his other hand holding the gold leaf which gave the cocaine a light saffron color. "You know why?" he repeated.

"No."

"Because," said La Roche, his lips in a thin smile, "he had to bail out over Ratmanov."

Francine was racing to keep up. All Ratmanov meant to her was that it was some hunk of rock off Alaska the Americans and Siberians had been fighting over before the cease-fire. A lot of men were killed.

"Yeah," said La Roche, "some Siberian nearly took Romeo's eye out." La Roche was still smiling, swirling the ice cubes in the glass.

" 'Course, he'll want to get back to flying soon as he can. Right?"

"Sure," agreed Francine. "I mean—it's only natural isn't it?"

"Yeah—well, I want him out of there—away from her." He took a gulp of the Manhattan. "That natural?"

"Yeah—sure, Mr. La Roche—"

"You know all it'll take to get him out of there?"

Francine shook her head. He handed her a thousand-dollar bill rolled tightly into a tube. Holding her hair back with one hand, she leaned forward.

"One phone call, sweetie. One fucking phone call. That's all." He held his hand out for the snuff box after she'd finished, and she watched his fingers covering it like an octopus. He laughed. "And a little campaign contribution."

She smiled, figuring it was the right thing to do. It was, but then, suddenly, his mood changed. He sat down in the plush leather swivel chair and turned away from her. For a moment Francine thought he was staring at the drapes, but then noticed he was holding a Christmas-card-sized photograph he must have taken from his robe pocket.

"She wants me back," he said. "I know it. Deep down I know it." He swung around to face Francine again. "But I was bad to her, Francine. You know what I mean?"

"I—I think so, Mr. La Roche." He was looking away from her again, back at the photo of his wife. "I have to pay for it, Francine." He was speaking softly, his head back hard against the rest, but Francine didn't hear him and didn't care—already feeling the rush. He got up, walked over toward her, and, taking her hand, led her into the kitchenette, opened a drawer and took out a small, glistening paring knife.

She froze.

"Don't worry," he said contemptuously. "I'm not going to hurt you. Come here." She hesitated. "Come here, you bitch."

Her heart thumping, she glanced at the door.

"Go—if you want," he said. "Think I'm going to cut you?"

"No . . ." she began uncertainly. He put down the knife, walked toward her, took her arms, pulled her hard up against him, staring at her, then released his grip. Her relief was audible as she stumbled back, rubbing her wrist. He held out his hand to her, and this time she came to him willingly, albeit hesitantly.

"Now watch," he said. "I told you I'm not going to hurt you." Deftly, quickly, he took the knife and, pulling the bodice of her dress toward him, sliced it open, then, hooking his left forefinger in the middle of her bra, cut the strap and dropped the knife into the sink, gazing at her breasts. Then, wordlessly, he led her into the bedroom and shut the door. He turned on a small bedside lamp, sat on the bedspread of pale blue silk and told her to take off his robe. He was getting big, she saw, but not fully aroused. He flung back the bed sheets and, from under the pillow, pulled out a strap—its buckle missing. He doubled it up and gave it to her. "Until I tell you to stop, Francine. You understand?"

"Are you sure you—" she began.

He screamed at her, "Until I tell you to stop! Understand?"

Before she could answer, he lay facedown, spread-eagled on the bed, his body much thinner than she had imagined— the robe probably had padded shoulders.

Only then in the dim peach glow of the lamp did she notice another photo of his wife Lana. He'd placed it so that he could see it as Francine began giving him the strap. He told her to do it harder and harder, and soon he was calling out his wife's name and Francine thought that that's all there'd be to it.

If Jay La Roche was thinking of his wife, she wasn't thinking of him. Still busy looking after the wounded that had come in prior to the cease-fire—the worst cases from ferocious tank battles along the Never-Skovorodino road north of the hump formed by the Amur River—Lieutenant Lana La Roche—née Brentwood—was far too occupied to think of anyone but her patients. And even if she'd had the time, she would have tried to avoid thinking of Jay—his kinky sex so vulgarly aggressive, to the minutest detail, that even the memory of their short and, for her, terrible marriage made her stomach churn. In her work she'd found a way of at least temporarily escaping the awful humiliations he had subjected her to in the bedroom while appearing to the outside world as a meticulously groomed and successful businessman, owner as well as chief executive officer of one of the world's largest industrial conglomerates.

Work also helped Lana forget his petty vindictiveness— his refusal to grant her a divorce on any grounds, unless she wanted to see her family—in particular, her father, a retired U.S. admiral, and her three brothers—smeared in his tabloids. At first she thought he was bluffing. Besides, with her youngest brother, David, who had served with distinction in the Allied Special Air Service/Delta Force commando raid against the submarine pens on Lake Baikal; her brother Ray's equally distinguished service as captain of a fast guided-missile frigate; and her eldest brother, Robert, serving as the captain of a Sea Wolf II Hunter/Killer; she quite frankly didn't see how La Roche could do anything against her family.

"You want to bet, baby?" Jay had sneered at her through coke-bright eyes. "I don't need your whole fucking family. Daddy'll do fine."

"What do you mean?" she'd asked him, flabbergasted.

La Roche had poured himself a half glass of scotch, downed it, then used a napkin to pat his sneering lips dry, staring into the distance, affecting the pose of someone in deep thought. "How about this for a headline? 'Admiral Brentwood Denies He Is Homosexual.' "

"But—But—" she'd said, flustered, angry, yet feeling utterly helpless before him. "He's not! Even if he was, so what—"

"You naive little bitch," retorted La Roche. "Don't you know anything? You sure as hell don't know how to fuck. Doesn't matter whether it's true or not. Hollywood wouldn't care—or would say they didn't care. Liz Taylor would

probably donate another of her pearl chokers to the Fight
AIDS Committee. But believe me, babe, in the rest of the
country—in the *navy*, for Chrissakes—'Admiral Denies
He's Gay.' Put that in a headline,'' he shrugged, ''and not
even Clarence Darrow could sue me. We—and by *we*,
sweetheart, I mean every goddamn paper I own, a hundred
and twenty-three to be exact—would only be reporting the
admiral's denial.'' His smile was pure evil. ''Freedom of
the press, right?'' It was the first time she'd ever hit him, or
at least tried to. The blow he delivered in return sent her
reeling across the plush-carpeted bedroom of their Shanghai
penthouse.

''That makes two black eyes you've got. You'd better
quit while you still have your teeth.''

That night, looking down on the Bund, watching Shanghai's waterfront lights smeared by the drizzling rain that
was falling over the Huangpu and farther north at the mouth
of the Yangtze, Lana felt as lonely and as homesick as she
thought anyone could be. All she had wanted to do then was
to go down and get aboard a ship, a junk, anything that
would float and take her away from Shanghai and Jay. But
realizing now the threat against her family was real, she had
no option but to stay. The war and her volunteering as a
Wave had allowed her the only possible escape. But even
her volunteering made La Roche look even better—the
successful businessman *and* patriot, unselfishly allowing his
wife to go and help the ''boys and gals,'' as he was fond of
putting it, at the front. Now and then he even sent La
Roche–sponsored concerts to entertain the troops. But Lana
knew that if she ever sued for divorce, his tabloids would
unleash a muckraking, albeit invented, offensive that would
totally bewilder as well as destroy her parents—if not her
brothers' careers.

But for Lana this night thousands of miles away from Jay
was one of the better ones in ''America's Siberia,'' the
name given to the remote naval hospital at Dutch Harbor,
which for many servicemen on rotation from duty in Siberia
was the first piece of America they had seen for months.

The weather was bad, as usual, wind, fog, and then eighty-mile-per-hour arctic winds—all within the space of an hour. But she didn't mind—she was on her way to see the man who had helped her mend. Frank Shirer was an American air ace she'd met briefly years before in Washington and who was now the man she wanted to marry—if that were ever possible. Shirer had been shot down during Freeman's attack on Ratmanov Island in the Bering Strait when the U.S. carrier *Salt Lake City*, from which Frank had led the second wave of Tomcats, launched its fighter bomber attack on the rock.

Both he and his radar intercept officer had baled out but were captured by the Siberian SPETSNAZ—the equivalent of allied Special Forces—and, with a cruelty that Lana could still not fathom, one of the SPETS commandos, trying to get Frank to reveal the exact location of the American carrier, had driven a ballpoint into Frank's left eye, leaving it hanging by the optic nerve. After the fall of Ratmanov, surgeons at Dutch Harbor had put back the eye, but the 20/20 vision demanded of a fighter pilot was gone. Yet as traumatic as it was for Frank Shirer—the man who had once shot down his coequal in the Siberian air force, Sergei Marchenko, after having been downed once by Marchenko himself—to contemplate the end of a brilliant career, it was made worse by the knowledge that Marchenko, whom he had thought he had downed for good over North Korea, had apparently survived. Marchenko's Fulcrum MiG-29 with its telltale *Ubiytsa yanki*—"Yankee Killer"—motif, had been sighted by Americans flying patrol over the Lake Baikal cease-fire line.

For Lana, however, the prospect of Frank being out of the war was something for which she was grateful.

For a moment, when she walked into Ward 5 and saw he was gone, all her professional cool left her and she panicked. Sometimes, for no known cause, an infection could develop in a patient overnight and—

She heard a whistle. " 'E's over 'ere!" It was a cockney voice that always reminded her and Frank of Eliza Doolittle's father in *My Fair Lady*. The voice belonged to an irreverent but well-meaning cockney whom they'd appropriately nicknamed "Doolittle" and who was convalescing from burns suffered when General Freeman, in one of the most controversial decisions of the war, had ordered in FAEs—fuel air explosive bombs—over the seven-square-mile Ratmanov Island in the Bering Strait. Freeman had used the overpressure of the air-detonated FAEs—a chemical mist of jellied ammonium nitrate, aluminum powder, and polystyrene soap—to detonate mines that the SPETS had laid in anticipation of Freeman's airborne invasion. Unfortunately, on the small, rocky island the explosion of the FAEs had also caused some "collateral damage," as the Pentagon had put it, amongst the joint British SAS/U.S. Delta Force commando detachment that had spearheaded the attack on Ratmanov.

"Fought 'e'd done a midnight flit on yer, did yer, Lieutenant?" asked Doolittle, his bandaged head nodding toward Frank's empty bed.

Lana smiled with relief, the cockney quickly dousing a cigarette in his tea mug before the ward sister—"Mother Attila," he called her—spotted him. "Me and Frank nipped out to the lounge for a bit of TV. 'Masterpiece Theatre.' Shakespeare." He nodded cheekily toward Frank, who was returning from the washroom. "Fought it about time 'e got a bit of bloody culture." The cockney winked at Lana. "But all 'e wants to do is ogle the nurses, 'e does—and read dirty mags. Glad you turned up. Gettin' right out of control 'e was. Right, mate?" he asked Shirer, who had shoved the reading glasses prescribed for him into the pocket of his hospital-issue robe.

"Yeah," continued Doolittle. " 'Ere I was tryin' to educate 'im, an' he's pervin' at centerfolds. Just as well 'e got his transfer."

"Transfer?" said Lana, completely taken aback.

"Washington," said Shirer, adding disgustedly, "Some damn desk job. Have to be there in a week."

"I'll see you two later," said the cockney. "Tat-ta."

*   *   *

Neither of them speaking, Frank and Lana walked out together to the TV lounge. They could hear the "Masterpiece Theatre" theme trumpeting, and saw the blue flickering of the screen. "Lousy reception," Frank said. "Atmospherics up here are really weird. Met guys say that if it wasn't for all the cold fronts socking us in, we'd see the aurora borealis. Least that'd be something."

They walked hand in hand through the lounge and got a disapproving look for it from one of the head nurses coming from the coffee room where they were headed.

"I don't want you to," Lana began, "but if you really had your heart set on it, why couldn't you go back to the carrier in some, you know, administrative—"

"God damn it—" he began, then checked himself. "Sorry. But lookit—if I can't fly, I don't want to be on the carrier. Seeing other guys suiting up—couldn't stand it."

"I know. Sorry—it was stupid of me—"

"No, no. You're right. I'll just—hell, I'll just have to settle into whatever they give me." He paused, both hands in his robe. "Unless . . ."

"Unless what?"

"Nothing." There was an awkward moment's silence, and without him saying a word, she knew what it was. Doolittle—the cockney—had been pumping him up again with stories about Adolf Galland, Germany's top air ace, commander of the Luftwaffe in World War Two, having flown and fought with only one eye, the other one glass. Every fighter pilot who had ever had an eye injury had heard about Galland. It was even said that Siberian ace Marchenko, who had reputedly suffered from a slight astigmatism, had trotted out the Galland story to get into flying school, before he'd submitted to a simple laser recontour of the cornea to correct the problem.

"That was in World War Two," said Lana sharply. "They never flew jets."

"Yes they did," replied Frank hastily. "Galland flew the Messerschmidt 263. If they'd produced enough of—"

"I don't want to hear about Galland," Lana said impatiently. "All I hear about is Galland and his damned glass eye."

"How about Bader?" Frank shot back. "British ace. Didn't have any legs. Can you imagine? Flew without legs. Everyone said it was impossible—thought it was going to be a big handicap. Guess what? It helped him out in a dive. Blood flow—didn't have so far to go. Could come out of a blackout quicker than anyone else. How about that?"

"That's great. I'm very happy for him. But I wish Doolittle would clam up for a while. He means well, I know, Frank, but look, hon, the sooner you face it—I mean *really* face it—the better. No one's going to let you take up multimillion-dollar aircraft with one eye. Not these days. Don't you think I've asked around?"

It took Shirer by surprise.

"Well, I have. If I had my druthers, I wouldn't see you near another plane, but I know how much it means—well anyway, the answer's the same. No deal. Besides, it—" She stopped herself.

"Go on."

"No, it doesn't matter."

"Go on."

They were no longer holding hands. "All right, I'll say it. Frank, you've got to think of other people as well as yourself. I know how much flying means to you. It's been your whole life—all you've ever cared about. But it's not just you. It's—"

"You're saying I'd be a danger to others?"

She looked straight at him. "Yes."

"Standard answer," he said dismissively, plugging in the kettle again for coffee, although it had just been on a raging boil.

"Because it's the *standard* truth," she said. "Anyway, you'd never pass the eye examination without your glasses."

"Thanks a million."

"Oh, don't be so childish. All I'm trying to do is help you. Frank—"

"All right, let's not talk about it anymore," he said. "You want sugar?"

"I love you," she said.

"You, too," he said, kissing her quickly on the cheek.

It bothered her—oh, not that they'd had another row about his inability to accept the end of his flying career. They'd had any number of "discussions" on that subject. It was him asking her if she wanted any sugar. He knew she never took it—her determination to keep on her diet had been reinforced by the sweet things he told her about her body during their most intimate moments—his "Venus de Milo," he had called her. Frank Shirer knew darn well that she *never* took sugar. He slipped his arm about her, pulling her closely to him, kissing her again on the cheek. Their fights had never ended like that—at least not so quickly. There'd always been a mini cold war before the thaw. He was up to something.

"Whatcha, mate?" asked Doolittle. It was the cockney's way of inquiring how you were doing.

"Fine," said Frank as they passed him on the way back to the ward. "Just fine."

Lana felt increasingly anxious. Something wasn't right. Suddenly she felt herself plunging into outright depression, brought on in part by the shock of realizing they'd be separated within the week. She'd never seen a transfer come through that fast. A week. The thought of being without him filled her with an ache of such longing she felt as empty as she had that night looking down on the Bund in Shanghai without any hope of escaping the pain. Her only consolation was that at least the war was over—the cease-fire intact.

CHAPTER EIGHT

MARSHAL YESOV HAD tired of the endless Mongolian vista of snow-covered pasturelands, unbroken except for the odd camel he could see from the train, and clumps of *yurts*—the circular, willow-framework-covered homes of the Mongols. An occasional curl of cow-dung smoke spiraled lazily up from the yurts' *toonos*, or chimneys, whose flaps opened a little more as the sun rose higher over the cloudless Gobi, where night temperatures were still often minus twenty-five and below.

Yesov also had had enough of the bowls of yellowish, glutinous goats' ears swimming in fat, delivered to him proudly by the Mongolians. As the train approached the Chinese border, Yesov noticed that patches of snow had already melted, revealing the yellow, caked earth which, blown up by the hot winds of summer, would form the great dust storms of the Gobi, which would sweep south over the Great Wall and on to Beijing, less than four hundred miles to the south. He would be glad to get his business done, and, though he wouldn't admit it to the Chinese who met him at Erhlien, glad to be on Chinese soil, away from the inedible muck the Mongolians served up, and glad, too, to get away from smiling in fraternal friendship with the Mongolian comrades while having to drink their vile traditional cup of sour camel milk mixed with salt tea.

"Na zdorovye"—To your health!—said Marshal Yesov, gratefully raising his cup of Chinese tea. Unlike the *Troe durokov*—"Three Stooges," the drunks who had bungled

the attempted putsch against Gorbachev back in '91—
Yesov preferred tea to alcohol, which he rarely consumed,
though he had a great reputation for doing so. What he
never told anyone was that whoever was attending bar at
official functions in Novosibirsk was always warned by one
of his aides, on pain of losing their job, that after the first
vodka toast, his glass was to be filled with water. This
enabled a sober Yesov to hear many things he would not
have otherwise, and to be one step ahead of his competitors.

In response to his *"Na zdorovye,"* Yesov expected to
hear, *"Gan bei!"*—Bottoms up!—the Chinese equivalent
of the toast he'd just made to the fraternal friendship
between Siberia and China. Instead General Cheng, still
standing, not yet having removed either cap or coat,
responded with a long-winded toast to the health and
fraternal friendship of *Marxist-Leninist principles.*

Yesov grunted and drank the tea. The Chinese were
paranoid about what had happened in the Soviet Union,
particularly with the breakaway Siberian union, and were
determined to prevent any such dissolution in China.
Accordingly, Marshal Yesov couched his introductory re-
marks in terms of "consolidation," as in the case of the
Siberian union having annexed—"with Ulan Bator's
invitation"—Outer Mongolia. This could hardly be seen,
Yesov pointed out with the first smile that had crossed his
face in two weeks, as aggression on the part of the Siberian
union. Far from a splitting up of constituent parts, it was, as
he said, a consolidation of two historical cousins into
"one."

Cheng sat expressionless. Beijing had already protested
the annexation of Outer Mongolia. He waited. There was a
long, pained silence, Yesov finally offering cigars, "Cu-
ban," giving Cheng the chance to comment either way on
his view of the annexation.

Cheng declined the cigar.

Seeing his opposite number clearly had no intention of
exchanging pleasantries, Yesov now came directly to the
point. "The Americans are up to no good. This cease-fire is

in reality a time of frantic resupply for their imperialist forces.'' Yesov leaned forward across the bare wooden table. ''It is the American-Japanese alliance. We both know Japan covets your Manchuria. The Japanese have always done so. And now with the oil wells set aflame in the Middle East by the Muslim fundamentalists, Japan is frantic, comrade. Frantic! She imports ninety percent of her oil from the Middle East. Without that oil she is nothing. But your vast coal reserves in Manchuria—''

''And in Siberia,'' put in Cheng suddenly.

''Yes—and those. Japan would like those, too, comrade. And the Americans are going to help her get them—and all the other raw materials you have in Manchuria. If you let them.''

Yesov pushed forward his cup for a refill, his gesture devoid of any sign that it was a request—more like a demand. A bluff, perhaps, thought Cheng.

''The only way for Freeman to defeat us, General—with his back to the sea—is for him to launch a *preemptive* flanking attack against us—a left hook, south, across the Amur, west through northeastern China and Mongolia, to come around behind us at Irkutsk, west of Lake Baikal. And soon—while the ground is still firm enough for their armor. Our intelligence confirms it.''

Still Cheng said nothing. He didn't believe all Yesov said for a minute, but there was a half-truth in the Russian's presentation that alone could quickly develop into a full-blown, ugly reality for China. No matter who started it, if fighting broke out again between the Siberians and Americans, the Siberians, in order to split the American forces between Lake Baikal and Khabarovsk, would need to launch a *right* hook from their eastern Mongolia, through China's Inner Mongolia and up across the Black Dragon—which Cheng noticed the marshal had still called the Amur. Such a counterattack would mean Freeman's forces would be split in two by the Siberian wedge coming out of Chinese territory. If Beijing permitted it. This was obviously what Yesov was here for: to come to an "understanding" so that the Chinese would permit, or rather turn a blind eye to, Siberian troops in transit on Chinese soil.

"Well then," proffered Yesov, his attention moving from the water-swollen leaves of the aromatic green tea to the general's impassive face. "If the Americans violated Chinese territory in attacking us, would you—would Beijing—have any objection to us sending forces up from Mongolia across the Amu—the river—to root them out?"

"If the Americans violate Chinese territory, they will be attacked immediately by the People's Liberation Army, Marshal, but as to your request of transit for Siberian troops, I would have to ask Beijing."

"Of course. When might we expect an answer?"

"In due course."

"The matter is urgent, as I'm sure you realize, Comrade Cheng. Intelligence reports tell us American armor is already massing along the hump."

"We will decide when we are ready, comrade."

It was one of the Chinese characteristics that most infuriated Yesov—the refusal to give you a definite yes or no on the spot. Of course, it had been the same in the old days with Moscow. Everything had to go to ten different committees, no one taking responsibility until it was too late. It reminded him of the story about Mao being asked whether he thought the invention of the wheel had been a forward or backward step for China. Mao considered the question and replied, "Too early to tell."

General Cheng rose, followed by Yesov. The meeting was over.

Cheng decided immediately to reinforce the Chinese presence on his side of the border, ordering two of the five armored divisions in Shenyang, the most northeastern province, north from Harbin to the banks of the Black Dragon River, together with five of Shenyang's fifteen infantry divisions and two artillery brigades. Even allowing for the fact that a Chinese division had five thousand less than a western division, it still meant a reinforcement of over 65,000 men.

But with Siberians, Americans, and the Chinese now caught in a tripartite of suspicion, Cheng was not content to rest. In addition to his having unilaterally ordered more troops north across the Yangtze to bolster the border defenses—which would take days to implement—other precautions must be taken. Accordingly, Cheng called an extraordinary meeting of both the Central Committee and the Military Commission, all the members having their offices in the luxurious Zhongnanhai compound on Beijing's Avenue of Eternal Peace. He explained the position succinctly, pointing out that it was imperative that neither the Siberians nor Americans violate Chinese territory. "It is clear, comrades, that if the Americans move south across the Black Dragon, Novosibirsk will have no objection to us moving troops through Siberian-held Mongolia to repulse them."

"But what if the Americans imposed sanctions upon us, General?" asked Chairman Nie. "As they did with Hussein?"

"It would have no effect, comrade," Cheng assured him. "One of their own has supplied and can go on supplying the PLA with whatever it requires." He meant La Roche. Cheng leaned forward on the table, his Medal of Merit ribbon for stopping "U.S. aggression in Korea" catching the fading, snow-reflected light that had penetrated the serenity of the Zhongnanhai, and for a moment he could hear the birds twittering outside above the two lakes. "While the Americans' high-tech victory over the incompetent Hussein might have been impressive to the western world, comrades, *here* the Americans are back in Asia. Here, comrades, they will not find demoralized, disloyal, badly supplied Republican Guards, but the People's Liberation Army, who, from the time of the Long March, know more about surviving and fighting on the land than anyone on earth."

There were knowing nods about the table, but Cheng was warming to his subject. The PLA had been, was, his life. "The Chinese infantryman travels light, comrades. His mobility in the mountains is legendary." Cheng stood up like a schoolmaster, knowing that all eyes were upon him. "This is precisely how General Sung, in 1950, under the very noses of the Americans, could move twelve divisions of the PLA, a hundred and sixty thousand men, comrades, from Manchuria across the Korean border to the Chosin Reservoir, and the Americans detected nothing until it was too late. The PLA's Ninth Field Army slaughtered the American marines. General Sung ordered his troops to kill these marines as you would snakes. And we did. Even by the U.S. imperialists' own admission, some marines went insane in the minus-thirty-four-degree battle. They cannot take it. And now they are far from home, comrades—their supply lines stretch across the Pacific. We would chop them to pieces."

"And they have *long* noses!" added Chairman Nie, which produced the only general laughter of the afternoon. It signified the Central Committee's confidence that Cheng clearly understood the situation and was prepared to meet any contingency in the far northeast. The Central Committee was also reassured by the knowledge that Cheng had an important American who could provide whatever matériel was needed—probably from South Korea, via Vietnam—should it become necessary.

After the meeting, Cheng was informed by his secretary that his request for artillery shells and AIF smoke rounds had been received in Shanghai and that Mr. Li, the cover name they used for La Roche himself, would be personally informed of the request in the interests of expediting delivery.

"*Hao.*" Good. Cheng nodded, and immediately placed another order by fax for three airport luggage-train, type-B axles. The "three" meant three thousand, and "type-B axles" stood for ERFB-BB shells.

These were extended-range, full-bore shells with a base bleed, so that immediately after firing, the gas was forced back into the shells' air wake instead of around the shells, where it would create drag. When the round hit, with little or no drag, it had twice the explosive power. "Two for the price of one," La Roche had told Cheng, but the "one" was very expensive, even more so than usual, because of the shady South African connection with the Canadian, Gerald Bull, who had invented the super-long gun.

It was Bull's research that made it possible for the ERFB-BB's rounds to be made, the long-range "bull" gun that maximized their efficiency already on order by Cheng. But Cheng wasn't a fool in the capitalist pool filled with sharks like La Roche: payment for the shells was contractually contingent upon the delivery of the guns first. Cheng already had a brigade of A1 Far 210mm howitzers, another offshoot of the Canadian's phenomenally effective six-wheel-mounted, thirty-five-mile-range gun, the longest-ranged mobile gun in the world. To get those, at three million dollars apiece, La Roche had to go personally to Austria to talk with Voest-Alpine SA and sell them a line that he was buying them on the quiet for the U.S. Army, for though Bull was dead, killed by the Israeli Mossad in Brussels shortly before the Iraqi War, the Americans were still touchy about Bull's South African connection. The ship the guns would be loaded on would suddenly "disappear" in a "local storm" somewhere in the East China Sea, en route to South Korea, its stated destination. On top of that, La Roche would skim off the insurance—and it would be substantial—from Lloyd's. During wartime there would be no chance of getting insurance, but this was a cease-fire and he could get Lloyd's to underwrite it. Cheng knew that the vision of the Lutine Bell sounding at Lloyd's in London, signaling another vessel lost at sea, would make La Roche smile. It would mean millions more for him, no matter that the base bleeds might well be being purchased for use against fellow Americans—along the Chinese-Siberian border—and how, if this was the case, because of the gun's ferocious accuracy, twice as many Americans would be killed and injured as under a normal artillery barrage.

*   *   *

While Cheng finalized troop dispositions for the battle defense of the borders, and the Siberian OMON Black Berets were taking Alexsandra Malof to the cells in Harbin, over five thousand miles away Jay La Roche was high, drunk, and aroused in his eightieth floor New York penthouse above the Il Trovatore bar, asking Francine what the hell she thought she was doing.

"What you told me, Mr. La Roche."

"Don't 'Mr. La Roche' me, you slut. You love it, don't you? You—" He lurched up from the bed, pulling the strap from her, flinging it across the room. "Don't have to be invited, do you? Like it, right? Bitch—" He lunged at her, both hands grabbing her breasts, losing his balance, falling back on the waterbed, the heavy slush sound mixing with Francine crying in pain on top of him.

"Shut up, you bitch!" They rolled off the bed onto the thick shag carpet, he still hanging on to her, letting go only when her rain of blows became too difficult to fend off. She was screaming at him. She ran to the bedroom door but couldn't open it. He laughed. There was a tearing noise like crushed cellophane, and she saw him pulling on a condom. For a moment or two he had his back to her and she saw him searching for something, then he swung around, holding his hand up victoriously, showing her the snuff box, flicking the lid open, snapping it shut, tossing it at her. "Take a snort!"

She did, and in a few moments felt another rush. "I don't want to hit you again, Mister—"

"Jay!"

"I don't want to hit you again, Jay."

"Turn around!"

"No—please, Mister—please, Jay," she gasped.

He jerked her hard toward him, then unsteadily swung her about, slamming her face first up against the wall, and she felt the searing pain as he entered her, and tepid liquid running down her legs onto the carpet as he poured the bourbon over her buttocks, the liquor spreading in a pool about her feet. "You've been to Melville's," he charged.

"Yes, but I—"

"You clean?"

"Yes, I—"

"The fuck you are. Thought you could pull a fast one on the boss eh? Eh?"

"No—no."

He smacked her hard on the buttocks with his left hand. "I'm not getting your shitty germs." She gasped again at the hot, raw pain inside her rectum. Her arms spread-eagled against the wall, nails hard into the wallpaper, she felt she was going to black out. He was breathing hard, panting, "Oh—oh—oh," calling out, "I love you, baby. I love you—" But she knew he was talking about his Lana. Now he was making blubbering, crying noises as he pumped her harder and harder, until he fell full against her, lathered in sweat, his breathing irregular, and then he was sobbing, clutching her waist, and off to her side she could see he was still clutching a picture of his wife. A moment later he staggered back from her, collapsing on the bed. "Get . . . get . . . out, you slut!" His voice was hoarse, and the next time he spoke, barely audible. "I'll get her back—you'll see. I'll get her back—"

Francine ran toward the bedroom door, expecting it to be locked, but this time it sprang open. She didn't know how he'd done it—the place was full of buttons and traps—and she didn't care, moving quickly out into the living room, lifting the phone, punching the bar button. "Jimmy—you gotta help me, I—"

"You in the penthouse?"

"Yes. For God's sake, Jimmy, he's—"

"He use the knife on the bra?"

"What—yes, why?"

"Get out, I'm on my way up. Meet you at the elevator—Francine?"

"Yeah?"

"You get out real quick. He's not finished, babe. Next cut won't be your clothes."

Francine dropped the phone, slipped off the chain, and a moment later was standing out in the hallway next to the elevator.

In the Il Trovatore, Jimmy had called over a waiter to fill in, walked quickly into the elevator and pushed the button for the penthouse floor. The moment the doors slid open, in she came, stark naked. Jimmy gave her his bar jacket, his other hand holding down the bypass lever, his thumb pushing the button for the thirteenth floor. She was shivering. "This is the only building in New York with a thirteenth floor," Jimmy said suddenly. "Wanta know why?"

"He's crazy." Her eyes were closed, her breathing rapid.

"He has it to show he's not superstitious," said Jimmy. "Says he doesn't believe in voodoo—destiny's in your own hands. Always quoting some guy called Neatcha."

"He's crazy."

"No doubt about it. But the money's good."

"Not if you're dead."

"You mean you won't keep it?"

"I mean I'm never going back."

"Sure," said Jimmy, watching the floor lights flit by. "And I'm Father Christmas." The elevator came to a halt. "A grand's good money."

"I mean it," she said.

"I know you do. Listen, if you want a good proctologist—a few stitches—five hundred bucks. No questions. That leaves you with five, sweetass."

"That supposed to be funny, Jimmy?"

"Don't get shitty, Francine. Just a joke. You're in one piece. Look on the bright side—you could be his wife."

"Huh—wonder why she divorced him?"

"Not divorced," said Jimmy, walking her to her apartment door. "Separated, honey. He isn't finished with her yet—or her boyfriend, the crackerjack ace." Jimmy seemed to like the idea. They heard someone coming up the exit stairs. They walked faster. Whoever it was stopped, then kept going up to the next floor.

"One of the boys," said Jimmy. "Probably wants to make sure you're still on the premises."

"Oh my God," she said.

"What?"

"My damn keys—I forgot my keys!"

"No sweat," said Jimmy, taking a credit card from his wallet and working open the door.

Once inside, she handed him back the jacket. "Thanks, Jimmy."

"Don't try to leave him, babe, like that Lana Brentwood dame. If I know anything, he ain't finished with her yet. And remember Hailey." Jimmy could see she didn't recognize the name. "Congressman," he explained. "Didn't do what La Roche wanted him to. Something about having his wife transferred. Congressman Hailey had an accident. La Roche's tabloids said it was suicide. Months later La Roche's wife was transferred to the Aleutians— another congressman in his pocket, I guess. So you be careful, hear?"

"Yeah."

"Francine?"

"Yeah?"

"You enjoy it?"

CHAPTER NINE

FOR MARSHAL YESOV, Beijing had given the answer, his forward observers reporting that from the ruins of Kublai Khan's Xanadu, 190 miles north of Beijing, on the Great North Plain, as far north as Manzhouli, just south of Siberia's Argunskiy Mountains, and in the northeast as far up as the Black Dragon River that formed the northernmost Siberian-Chinese frontier, Chinese garrisons were being reinforced to repulse any incursion by the Americans through northern China's river valleys into Siberia.

Yesov was so pleased with the Chinese action that he ordered all his forward observers and consulate liaison officers, like Ilya Latov in Harbin, to simply refer to the Amur as the "jiang"—the river—in deference to Chinese sensitivities. And if so much as one American footprint or one shell or one American helicopter was sighted straying, even for an instant, across the border, both Siberian and Chinese headquarters were to be notified immediately. Given their common watchdog duty, some of the Chinese and Siberian junior ranks formed congenial relations during their daily radio reports to each other on the status of the wide ribbon of frozen river, where temperatures had dropped to minus thirty in the passes. The cold was no special travail for the northern troops from Shenyang Military Region in China, or for the Siberians, but it was a torture for the Chinese regiments who came from south of the Yangtze. These southern Chinese regiments, some from as far away as Canton, hated the cold and were grateful that patrols were kept to a minimum so that the American helicopters buzzing up and down the border during the cease-fire would see nothing else but normal Chinese patrol activity along the western part of the Amur hump where the northern part of China's Inner Mongolia jutted like a blunt spearhead around Hulun Lake into the northeasternmost sector of Siberian Mongolia.

Finding that his eyes got tired after only a small time at the computer screens, Freeman had the reports run out on hard copy and was now going over them for any signs of an earlier than normal thaw, at the same time trying to put himself in Yesov's shoes should the Siberian commander decide to attack across the westernmost defensive line of the cease-fire, namely Lake Baikal. Freeman marked off possible Siberian jump-off points on the west bank of the four-hundred-mile lake, especially those down around the small port of Baikal at the southern end, which now lay in American hands under the terms of the cease-fire. If Yesov attacked, Freeman decided he would send in Stealth bombers to try to take out the line along the cliffs that formed the southern arm of the Trans-Siberian as it curved about the lake before dipping south into Mongolia. Even with Smart bombs, however, a rail line was notoriously difficult to take out, as ties and rails could by replaced in a matter of hours.

He poured another black coffee and looked at his watch. It was 0400, with only the cease-fire skeleton staff on duty. Even Dick Norton, who tried to keep pace with the general, had gone to bed. At times Freeman felt guilty for not having the time to think more about the welfare of his staff. He hadn't even thought much about Doreen, his wife, who had died only a short time before and for whose funeral he couldn't return—the battle for Ratmanov Island raging at the time. But he knew his first responsibility was to Second Army as a whole, knowing that a surprise attack, which neither Washington nor London nor any of the other Allies expected, could presage a disaster. Doreen, he was sure, would have been the first to understand. She had been the ideal serviceman's wife—uncomplaining, ready to follow at a moment's notice, and, if the truth be known, the source of much of his earlier strength when, as a young officer, he was trying to make his mark in a field crowded with other veterans of the Iraqi war. He had experienced both hosannas and hoots, the former when he'd led the raid on Pyongyang and reached Baikal, the latter when he'd used fuel air explosives over Ratmanov. La Roche's tabloids in particular had alternated between making him a saint and a "warmonger." Presently they were saying that he was a man "obsessed" by war, unable to see that "there could be an end to it."

They were right, he *was* a warrior—saw the world with a warrior's eye—but there was nothing he could do about that. It was the way he was made. When they walked on the spring grass, people marveled at the beauty of swallows sweeping low, so close to yet never quite touching the grass, their darting blue-metal sheen a thing of joy to watch. Freeman enjoyed watching them, too, but he knew that it was the feet of the people visiting the park that scared up insects which the swallows then swooped low to kill, and that this was every bit as much a part of the scene as was the beauty. Even the most tranquil scene he could remember— the tidal pools he and Doreen had seen around Monterey— were in fact miniature seas populated by creatures for whom battle was never ending. You fought or you died.

Dutch Harbor was in darkness. If the aurora borealis was "kicking up its 'eels," Doolittle said, "some ruddy great clouds are in the way, mate." But his fellow patient, Frank Shirer, wasn't listening. The flier, his convalescence rapidly coming to an end, was engrossed in the *Wall Street Journal* that Doolittle had given him. It wasn't a paper Frank normally perused. Neither did Doolittle, investment to the cockney constituting an eternal mystery. "Stocks" in his family were things Robin Hood was put in if the Sheriff of Nottingham ever caught him. Doolittle dragged heavily on his cigarette, glancing down at the Xeroxed page he'd inserted into the newspaper so that no passersby, including the MD he called "Joe Friday"—"Just the facts, soldier"—could see Frank studying it. "Bit of a fudge," Doolittle conceded.

"Fudge?" replied Frank. "It's downright cheating!"

"Well, mate, this is the first time I've ever 'eard that a man who wants to get 'imself killed is cheatin.' That's a new one, that is. Personally, I wouldn't do it—I've already done my bit, squire. For me it's out on the old compo— disabled soldiers' pension to you—and a deck chair on Brighton Beach, lookin' at the birds strolling' up an' down. An' I don't mean bloody sea gulls. Yep—that'll do me nicely, that will. Me, the deck chair, wiv a jar o' Flower's bitter." He exhaled, cigarette smoke appearing to come from every orifice in his head behind the bandages that covered the horrible burns he'd suffered during the taking of

Ratmanov Island. "And that's what I'd do if I were you, mate," he advised Frank Shirer. "Crikey, you've already done your bit for king and country. Besides, you got a good-lookin' bird. That Lana's a real corker, she is. All you need, mate, is the ruddy beach. Instead, what you want to do? Go up in one of them bloody death traps again."

Doolittle took another heavy drag on the Player's, leaned back and shook his head, hands together, head smoking again like a double boiler about to blow. He leaned over and, tapping the Xerox of the Snellen eye chart, told Frank conspiratorially, "Best day's Monday, see? When old Joe Friday 'sn't around. The new doc's a bit unsure of 'imself, so 'e's followin' the same bloody routine day after day. Same chart, same sequence. All you have to know is which letter's where. Right? He puts 'is black patch stick over your good eye and asks you what you see. You can make out the blur wiv your bad eye can't you?"

"Yes—just."

"There you are, then. 'E points to the third blur in the fourth row and you've got it. 'Cause you memorized the chart. Right? Piece o' cake!"

The smoke came pouring down from the cockney's nostrils like a dragon, and Frank drew back out of range.

"They're so many guys 'e's got to do, see?" explained Doolittle. "Even if he changes the routine from one blur to another, you memorize the chart, you've got it. Besides, you got one big thing going for you, old cock."

"Yeah," said Frank wryly. "I could be court-martialed."

The cockney laughed; which was appropriate, Frank thought. Doolittle wouldn't be the one on a charge.

"Nah, mate. Listen—what you forget is, none of these guys *wants* to pass the test. What they want—what *you'd* want, if you weren't so bloody daft—is to get home fast as they can, start usin' the old joystick in bed, not up in the blue fucking yonder."

For Doolittle, his "plan to put one over" on the authorities—in this case, a greenhorn MD fresh from medical school and not yet wise to the ways of the army—was a bit of a lark. But to Frank it meant a restless night of old dreams, of Adolf Galland, the one-eyed German Luftwaffe ace, of the British ace Douglas Bader and the Canadian Rosin, who, after a seven-year court battle with the army, had won the right to be a paratrooper, despite having only one eye. Visions of Lana invaded the dreams as she fought her way through the crowd of pilots, not saying a word; and through it all there was the crackle of fighter pilots mixing it up in a furball, a Soviet MiG-29 going into the radar-defying stall slide, Sergei Marchenko, the Mikoyan Works emblem on the Fulcrum's fuselage, coming at the Tomcat at Mach 1.2 in a steep dive, the MiG's thirty-millimeter cannon winking, followed by two white puffs as two Aphid air-to-air missiles streaked toward Shirer, his copilot yelling, "I've been hit"—and all because of information overload on the one good eye, misreading the Heads-Up display. He pulled the Tomcat hard out of the "Finger Four" formation, going into the scissors so as to get Marchenko to overfly him, get the Tomcat into the MiG's cone. But then it was the Tomcat, his radar intercept officer screaming, Marhenko's Fulcrum now in the Tomcat's cone of vulnerability. There was a bang, the Cat shuddering violently and Frank screaming at his RIO to get out. The next second he pulled the strip, heard the explosive bolts go, felt the wind tearing at his face, like rushing through some vast refrigerator, and heard the snap of his chute opening, the RIO's on fire, going down like a Roman candle.

"Shush!" said a calming voice. "You'll wake the whole ward." And then the voice was gone. It was dark, only the dim pinpoints of light on the IV drip monitors telling him he was still in hospital.

They had been the same nightmares that had plagued him for weeks, nightmares that he hadn't told Lana about and which had been responsible for his sudden mood shifts— unlike him, but which, he knew, Lana had noticed with increasing anxiety. And so finally, now, with the arctic wind howling mournfully about the hospital at Dutch Harbor, he made the decision. To hell with the nightmares. There was no way he wanted to live the rest of his life, like so many, haunted by regret. He'd have to find out in the only way he knew how. He'd do a bit of a "fudge," as Doolittle had put it. Besides, before they put him in a cockpit, he'd have to pass on ground simulators. There he wouldn't kill anyone if his single-eye vision couldn't cope. The worst he'd do would be to flunk the course. He'd risk a court-martial in the event that the green doctor wasn't as green as Doolittle figured.

He got up, put the hospital robe around him, and made his way quietly through the ward and to the right, toward the TV room. He could hear that someone else was watching—an old Johnny Carson rerun—Buddy Hackett telling a joke about a guy yowling, "Wah—wah—wah," with awful genital pain. ". . . So the guy goes to see doctor after doctor. Finally the only thing they could do, they said, was to remove his testicles. They didn't have any other answer. After his operation, the guy goes to a men's clothing store, buys a new suit, asks for a couple of ties, and asks for size thirty-four waist underpants. The clerk says he should get a size thirty-six. The guy tells the clerk he knows what he wants and it's a size thirty-four. Clerk runs a tape measure around the guy's waist and says, 'No, sir. If you wore a thirty-four you'd have terrible pain in the testicles.' Wah—wah—wah!"

Shirer roared laughing; he was feeling so good now that he'd made the decision. The man watching the show, another pilot who'd also been wounded over Ratmanov, was just sitting there, hands tremulous. "You okay?" asked Frank.

The pilot shook his head but kept looking up at Frank. For help. Shirer saw a packet of cigarettes in the man's robe pocket, and though he didn't smoke, he took one and lit it up for the guy and sat with him, watching the Carson show. The longer he sat there, the more he wondered if somehow he should take the guy's condition as a warning—

remembering one time how a top gun on *Salt Lake City* who graduated top of the class got shot down after fifteen missions. Everyone thought he was fine after, and he was, for seven more missions. Then bam! Everything came apart. Now, just hearing the sound of going on afterburner made him a head case.

When you were young you never thought you'd crack up.

It was the first time in months that General Freeman had seen his aide, Dick Norton, unshaven and in pajamas, the flannelet bottoms sticking out from underneath the greatcoat like red-and-white-striped barber poles. As he came through the door and pulled the blackout curtain aside, a flurry of snow blew in after him like an angry ghost. Despite the fact that his quarters were only ten yards from the HQ Quonset, Norton already looked half frozen. Freeman knew it must be urgent.

"Minus forty," said Norton, handing the general the SITREP, the buff-colored situation report folder with a crimson stripe across the right-hand corner and marked "Top Secret." It told Freeman there was marked activity all along the Siberian-Chinese border. The Chinese had been moving up the Shenyang army at night, but here and there in gaps through the cloud cover infrared satellite photos had detected them.

"Only thing we can do, Dick, is to keep a close eye on it. I want to see all SITREP reports over China, Secret and above. Hopefully, of course, everyone else is right and I'm wrong and the cease-fire'll hold. Maybe the Chinese are just being prudent—taking precautions. As I would. But if it doesn't hold, I don't want to be caught with my pants down."

"No, sir."

"Meanwhile—long as the Chinese keep out of it, we won't bother them."

The door flew open. A sergeant, his voice muffled by the khaki scarf that hid his face up to his eyes, staggered in, dusted with snow. Not bothering to look up, and certainly not expecting the general to be up and about at this hour, he stamped the snow off his boots, proclaiming to the skeleton headquarters staff, "I don't think this fuckin' berg'll ever thaw out!"

"Good!" answered Freeman to the startled soldier. "If we have to engage, son, I want hard ground under our tracks!"

CHAPTER TEN

"I MUST BE sure," insisted Yesov.

"I promise you, Marshal." It was Kirov, head of the KGB's "new and improved"—as Novosibirsk sarcastically put it—First Directorate, covering Canada and the U.S. "Once the signal arrives in—"

"Yes, yes, I know all that. But this is not enough, that your people are ready. The point is, your operation must precede my operation. That is vital. For me to begin 'Concert,' the American convoys must lose their ability to reinforce Freeman's Siberian garrison."

"Marshal, I can assure you—everything's in order. You can start Operation Concert as you have planned. My people will already be doing their part. This I guarantee."

"What is the code name you're using?" inquired Yesov. He wanted no mistakes, no matter how remote the possibility of two operations being accorded the same name.

" 'Ballet,' sir," said Kirov, smiling.

The marshal was not known for his sense of humor, and in any case looked blankly then sternly at Kirov, who seemed very pleased with himself with the joining of his, Kirov's, Operation Ballet with Yesov's Concert. "This is no joking matter, Kirov. My intention is to kill every American in my sight. Gorbachev—the fool—might have liked them. I do not.''

"Nor I, comrade.''

With that, the marshal of all the armies in the United Siberian Republic abruptly left. He was ready. Despite the sudden drop to minus forty degrees reported in the American sector, the long-range forecast was for a dramatic warming within the week, and only then another plunge in temperature.

CHAPTER ELEVEN

THE TWO BLACK Berets were having a little fun with the Jewess on the way, one holding her tightly in the back of the police van, the other feeling her beneath the long Mongolian peasant skirt she'd worn on the escape route from Baikal through Mongolia to Harbin. Only now did Alexsandra realize why Latov, without as much urging as she had thought would be necessary, had told her about the troop buildup on the Siberian-Chinese border and the movement of troops from the southern military regions across the Yangtze at Nanking, the approach roads to other bridges over the great Yellow River effectively useless because of the early spring floods in the warmer south.

Cold, she was shivering as much from fear as from the musty, bone-eating dampness of the cell in the Gong An Ju's—Public Security Bureau's—so-called new jail on Zhongyang Street. The Songhua River that ran past the jail was still frozen, but water beneath the ice seeped into the cells from around the embankment and from Stalin Park.

For some reason she didn't understand, instead of immediately dwelling on her situation—indeed, as she later realized, as a way of denying the terror her capture now held for her—she found herself thinking about how ironic it was that the Chinese, who took such pride in their self-reliance, insisted on retaining and paying homage to two foreigners: parks and streets were still being named after Marx and Stalin when the rest of the world, including the new CIS and the other Soviet republics, had torn down the demagogues of Marxi-Leninism.

A Mr. Lo, a PLA guard behind him, turned up promptly, officiously flashing his ID from Harbin's Public Security Bureau. He asked her, *"Ni hui shuo Zhongwen ma?"* Do you speak Chinese?

"Hui, yidian." I can, a little. Her accent was not good.

"Ni hui shuo Yingwen ma?" Do you speak English? Mr. Lo asked.

"Shide," she replied, and completely disarmed him by asking, "Why can't China think for herself? Why do you import foreigners to revere?" Not once, she pointed out, had she seen even a small park named after Mao. Mr. Lo, scrambling for an answer, explained that unlike the "running dog revisionists" of eastern Europe who had "betrayed" Marxism, China had remained loyal. As for her insult that China could not think for itself, he said China had always thought for herself. Mr. Lo explained that the Great Helmsman had expressly forbidden personality cults and the deification of any particular leader. This is why she had seen no Mao parks or statues.

"Did the Great Helmsman tell the Central Committee," Alexsandra asked, remaining seated calmly on the wooden stool, looking up at him, "to let Novosibirsk push you around? To send troops at their bidding?"

Mr. Lo struck her once, knocking her off the stool. His voice, if anything, was quieter than before. "You are a stupid woman. We do this as a protection against the American imperialists."

"The Americans won't invade China," Alexsandra shot

back contemptuously. She had learned enough from her previous interrogations to know that weakness only made them recognize their bullying for what it was, and in their guilt they lashed out—often more viciously than if you stood up to them. The guard hauled her roughly to her feet, putting her back on the stool.

"Ha!" said Lo. "Insolent! You *are* a stupid woman. You should have babies and concern yourself with wifely duties."

"One child per family, comrade!" retorted Alexsandra, but Mr. Lo was long experienced, too, in interrogation, and he suspected that her initial defiance was only *gongfen*—a centimeter—thin. The file he had been sent from her Lake Baikal interrogation had revealed the same pattern: a brazen attempt to tough out the questioning right from the start.

Very well, Mr. Lo thought. He did not have time to mess around with stupid foreigners. The Public Security Bureau had instructed him to find out who were her "cohorts" in Harbin.

She told him there were none. She had come all this way on her own.

Mr. Lo spoke to the guard, who answered respectfully and immediately left the cell, only to return a minute later with another guard, the second man carrying a wooden chair, to which they tied her and proceeded to beat her legs about the shins with split bamboo cane. She did all she could to withstand the pain but soon was biting her lip, tears running, whimpering like a whipped puppy.

"Who are your cohorts?" asked Mr. Lo quietly.

Alexsandra didn't answer.

"You are a bad woman!"

She said nothing.

"If you do not tell me in five minutes, I will turn you over to Black Berets. You understand?"

She understood it would be much longer than five minutes—any earlier and he'd lose face.

"You are a spy," said Mr. Lo. "Who are your cohorts?"

She could hear the slow drip of water from the wall

nearest the river, the cell so dark she could only make out a bead of sweat on Mr. Lo's face and the dull sheen of the guard's bayonet. Mr. Lo shook his finger at her. "We will put snakes in you. Do you wish this? Yes?"

She told herself there were no snakes in Harbin—the idiot man. It was too cold, but unconsciously she pressed her thighs together. It was a mistake. Lo now knew the long nose was more afraid than she made out. He whispered to the guard, who nodded, quickly tied her hands behind her, and left the room.

CHAPTER TWELVE

New York

APART FROM THE few guests from the Plaza who had dared brave the cold, briskly crossing from the luxurious comfort of the hotel to the chestnut barrow by the southeast entrance to the park, a jogger was the vendor's only customer.

"What can I tell ya!" complained the vendor. "I had 'em poifect, then bam, bam, bam. Everyone comes for lunch— all in a bunch—so now ya gotta wait."

"They look done enough," said the jogger, a tall, gangly man clad head to toe in a gray tracksuit, his goatee beard crusted with snow, his hood laced tightly. In front and back of the gray jacket, in Day-Glo tape, there was a sign announcing to the world: I DON'T CARRY CASH, CREDIT CARDS, OR WRISTWATCHES!

He kept jogging in place.

"You want them?" said the vendor, stirring the chestnuts

perfunctorily with his scoop. "You can have 'em. But they ain't cooked. Please yourself. 'S only five minutes they'll be done. What's your hurry?"

The gray man slid a hand inside the tracksuit's midriff pocket, peeking at a stopwatch attached to the pocket with a safety pin. "Got an appointment in five minutes."

The vendor pointed the scoop at the man's midriff. "Thought you had no valuables?"

The gray man shrugged. "Worth a try."

"Hey! Hey! Hey!" yelled the vendor, a limo passing fast by the curb, throwing up an icy wave of slush. "You sonofabitch!" Sticking his head under the barrow's meager awning, he turned to the gray man. "Big shot! Jay La Roche. Thinks he owns this fuckin' town."

"Probably does," said the tall man, still jogging on the spot.

"How you gonna pay me if you don't have no cash?"

The jogger bent down and extracted a five from his right sneaker. "Emergency funds." He winked.

"Yeah. Right," said the vendor, his grin thin with cynicism. "Some of those boys cut you up good, you hold out on 'em." He scooped up the chestnuts into one of the white bags and handed it to the man. "Four bucks."

The runner kept jogging in place while the vendor's hands did a number in his apron, frowning and mumbling something about not having change.

The jogger kept marking time until the vendor grunted and gave him four quarters before throwing on another fistful of chestnuts.

It was a dead drop—a note in the bottom of the paper bag with instructions for the next meet. Daytime meets were normally eschewed, but with the First Directorate under pressure from Yesov, Kirov had decreed that Operation Ballet should go ahead as fast as possible. The splash by Jay La Roche, or whoever it was in the limo, had nothing to do with it, but the vendor's reaction made it more convincing if the FBI or CIA had been watching, which the jogger doubted. The Americans hadn't yet broken a single three-man cell in the poisoned water crisis—PCBs dumped in New York's water supply earlier in the war. True, a member of one cell in Queens who had kicked off the sabotage at the Con Ed's Indian Point Nuclear Plant had reported to the jogger, his control, that he suspected he was being followed, but Control told him to relax—everybody in the plant who'd been on the shift and had clocked off twenty minutes before the bomb had exploded in the monitor room was being followed. Routine. Hell, since the water crisis, thousands of people were being followed.

Besides, Con Ed was turning out to be the cells' best friend, their PR busy talking down the sabotage as a "nut case," scared shitless that any sign of vulnerability at the Indian Point plant would start off fears of a meltdown, not only at Con Ed, but every friggin' nuclear plant in the country. The FBI, CIA, and White House were going along with the "nut case" story, too. The water supply poisoning had been cleaned up—many of the toxins leached out, water quality measurements taken constantly instead of once a day—and so now everyone was reassured on that score. But if radiation got loose, that'd be another story. The Americans were on the verge of panic—security was now so tight at nuclear plants, hell, they wouldn't let the president in without thumbprint ID for fear it might be a double.

The jogger kept moving, cracking the chestnuts on the run as he made his way along Central Park South, turning left on the Fifth Avenue dogleg, entering the park proper on the east side.

Down by the fountain a small man in a dark navy tracksuit doing stretching exercises started running a few seconds after the man in the gray had passed him, catching up to him by the dairy. They were both on the circuit pathway and headed down the mall before cutting across the Sheep Meadow to the snow-covered Strawberry Fields, where they slowed and drew level, blue and gray. "See you got your chestnuts okay," said the man in the blue.

"Yes," said the other man, temporarily out of breath.

They hadn't stopped but were walking fast in a strong, long-distance gait. "I thought the price was quite reasonable."

"Four dollars?"

"Yes."

"Well-cooked?"

"Best I've ever had."

"All right," said the smaller man, "I've got everyone set. Where's the main event going down?"

"No idea. All I was told was to get everyone in place."

"We've had everyone in place for ten fucking years," said the shorter man.

"You're impatient. Doesn't do to get in a hurry."

"We can't luck out much longer."

The gray man cracked one of the nuts, dropping the shells on the pathway as they passed under a copse of snow-drooping sugar maples. "If something's gone wrong," he told the shorter man, "you'd better tell me right now."

"Nothing's gone wrong. Everybody's a bit edgy, that's all."

"Why? What's the rush—after ten years? A day here or there doesn't matter."

"I dunno. Guess I'm stressed myself. I mean I don't really know how it works. Yeah—okay, so I organize the team, match the talent for the job. But I don't know how it's actually going to be done."

"You've no need to know," responded the man in gray, his breath visible in short puffs of mist. "Organizers aren't supposed to know. We can't all do one another's job."

"Huh," said the shorter man, grabbing several chestnuts from the packet. "That's what the CIA says is worst about our methods. We don't have cross expertise. So someone else can step in."

"That right?" said the man in gray. "So who did in their water supply? And knocked Con Ed out? We're doing all right. They're in a panic. All we have to remember is everybody does one thing and does it properly. It's worked so far—that's the only thing that matters."

"I'd still like to understand the guts of it."

"It's not classified," said the man in gray. "You can figure it out from any public library." He knew it was a barren response. One of the things you didn't do as a sleeper was to take out a lot of technical manuals from American libraries. It was a sure invitation to surveillance.

"What if something goes wrong?" said the shorter man. "Then I'd have to do it. Shit, this job's the most important thing any of us'll ever do. Right?"

"You could do it."

"That's like telling me I could be a—I dunno, Mario Andretti, 'cause I can drive. I mean, if something fizzes out—halfway through? If one of our guys is made and's taken out?"

"All right," said the taller man, "but let's keep up the pace. Joggers don't stroll." They increased the speed and he explained it—not only how they would simply sow further panic, but how they'd bring the country to its knees. "The old system of phones—still used in most places back home . . ." He meant the CIS. "They use analog-wave signals. Sound waves goes out through the telephone exchange, where you hear the clicks, electromechanical switches, then the signals go down cable pairs—or to conductors, if you like—to the next switch, and so on. At the receiving end the telephone converts the electrical wave back to sound. Now with digital—used all over America now—you use the binary scale—a series of zeros and ones representing any number you dial. Information's broken down the same way—into zeros and ones. Like fax. It's sent via the bipolar pulsing system. Follow me?"

"No."

"Okay, look. Christ, you've eaten all the nuts!"

"You can buy some more. What about this digital crap?"

"What I'm saying, it's a computer-based system that transmits all information—voice, data, you name it—in a binary code, so, for example, the number sixteen is one-zero-zero-zero-zero, ten is zero-one-zero-one-zero. Got that?"

"Sort of—not much good at math."

"Doesn't matter. Don't worry about it. The point is, what we get is a coded stream of pulses at 1.544 megacycles a second. That's over a million and a half pulses a second. Computer uses a wave form code. Anyway, just think of it as a whole bunch of pulses containing zeros and ones. Right?"

"Go on."

The taller man stopped for a moment to tie a lace, his gray tracksuit patched with sweat despite the cold, looking around to see if anyone was following, then started off again.

"Now, because you're dealing with all info in binary combinations of zeros and ones, you can process signals much faster and more cheaply than with the old mechanical switches that have to clunk through one, two, three, four, five . . . Follow that?"

"Yeah."

"Fine. Now digital networks all have to be synchronized, otherwise in a sequence of zeros and ones you wouldn't know where the start of a message or the end of it was. Only problem is, in order to have all the computers synchronized so they know where the start, middle, and end of a message is, you have to have 'em all keyed into a cesium atomic clock—it's got the most accurate beat in the world."

"That's why our guys are gonna hit the clock?"

"You win the car. Now, when you lose synchronization with the clock, you can 'free run' awhile without synchronization, but the ones and zeros start to pile up in no time, run into one another like rush hour on the turnpike. You have one big god-awful traffic jam. You with me?"

"Yeah."

"Okay. When that happens—a pileup—you're out of sync. Computer networks become a horizontal Tower of Babel. Most important thing—data circuits, like radar, are much more sensitive than voice circuits, so the data circuits pile up much faster, or, as the boys in the trade say, the 'byte error'—the slippage—becomes unmanageable. And it's garbage out. So a page of printout that should normally take half a second, runs two seconds. Loss factor four. And alarms aren't set off in the digital system the same way as they are in analog circuits. You can alter the alarms through interfering with the software, but—'' Another jogger was coming their way. When he passed, the man in gray turned about to double check, then continued. ''The weak link is that with the cesium-atomic-clock-synchronization system, everybody, and I mean *everybody*—that is, every computer—has to be on the same mark.''

''The same clock?''

''Right—including the military. No matter how many different codes there are, military has to use the same synchronization. So you hit the clock, military computers go out—AT and T's stations board in New Jersey lights up like the Fourth of July. Massive computer network breakdown. You remember the big screwups in the early 1990s?''

''No.''

''Biggest one was 'ninety—January twenty-ninth. Two twenty-five P.M. Hit every one of a hundred and fourteen big computers. Cost 'em over forty million. Year before in Paris, the big police computer went on the fritz—misread over thirty-nine thousand magnetized labels of drivers' licenses. Started charging auto drivers all over France with everything from rape to homicide. It was beautiful.''

''Doesn't the military have a backup?''

''Sure. Don't have to use land lines—can use satellite pulses—but if the cesium clock's out, it's all over except for the crystals.''

''What are they?''

''Crystals? Closest things to the cesium clock in their beat accuracy. Only trouble is, they have to keep them in 'double oven'—constant temperature. If you lose the clock, the idea is you go to 'holdover,' using the crystals as your drum.'' The tall man paused, then smiled. '' 'Course, if you cut off the electric power—no oven. That's what your third man in the cell is going to do.''

"So then all the defense computers are down?"

"You've got it. Military gets the old 'all circuits are busy' crap just like everybody else. The entire continental-based missile defense system of the United States shuts down because over ninety percent of all military phones in this country are slaved to AT and T and the other companies. Private enterprise at its best, my friend."

"What about the other carriers—Ma Bell and —"

"All in the same boat. The clock goes—they go. I love complex microchip technology. It's so easy to fuck up."

"When do we move?"

"When you see the ad."

They walked down toward the Swedish Cottage, where they said good-bye. They would not meet again. Everything was in place. The man in blue turned left and exited on West Eighty-first Street; the other walked into the American Museum of Natural History. There was a new acquisition of pre-Cambrian fossils. It put everything in perspective. The fossils were all that remained of an entire epoch. The Christians were right about that—in the end, it was all dust to dust, ashes to ashes.

The exhibit's attendant, who looked a little pre-Cambrian himself, gave the jogger a glance that said he wished visitors to the museum would be better dressed. Then again, he was mollified by the fact that, unlike the ruffians on the streets, here at least was a man of breeding, a man of cultural refinement.

The jogger looked up at the museum clock. It was 1300 hours. Kirov's "Ballet" was about to begin. What the man in gray hadn't told his cohort was that the really big payoff of such a massive computer screwup would be the havoc it would play with the navy's "burst" coded communications for its submarines at sea. They wouldn't know what the hell was going on, and if they came up near the surface to get emergency TACAMO—take charge and move out—aircraft messages, Novosibirsk would pick up the displacement bulge—the radiant heat difference between the sub and sea temperature—and BAM!—they'd be targeted by the Siberian fleet's Hunter/Killer subs before the Americans knew it.

"It's wonderful, isn't it?" commented the attendant for the pre-Cambrian exhibit.

"Certainly is."

CHAPTER THIRTEEN

Khabarovsk

FREEMAN WAS KNEELING, saying his prayers. There was a crack—like pine board splitting. He spun about, grabbed the riot gun—its five rounds filled with razor-sharp fléchettes—and aimed it at the door. He'd dismissed the reporter's rumor about a possible SPETSNAZ attack, but all the same . . .

There was no one at the door. He lifted the phone connecting him to the duty officer. "What in hell was that?"

"River, sir. Ice splitting."

"Call our Baikal command on the cease-fire line. Ask if the lake's breaking up."

"Yes, sir."

"And lieutenant . . ."

"Sir?"

"You wake me the moment you hear."

"Yes, General."

The duty officer rang back moments later, reporting, "Everything's fine at Baikal, sir. Nothing's moving."

"The world's moving, Lieutenant—we just aren't aware of it most of the time."

"Yes, sir."

Relieved, Freeman knelt to finish his prayer. "Almighty God, arm us. Amen."

Before putting out the light, he scribbled a memo to the padre who had given a sermon for twenty minutes—ten longer than necessary, in Freeman's view—a homily in which the padre had told the Second Army congregation that prayer may not indeed be heard by a supreme being but was a way of personally reminding ourselves of our individual responsibility to the collective spirit.

Freeman had been appalled. It wasn't enough, he told Norton, that he had to put up with weak-kneed strategists back in Washington—now he had to contend with God-damn revisionist priests who, rather than delivering the word of God straight and undiluted, had to stoop to secular interpretation of prayer so as not to offend the liberal fairies. The general, in an unprecedented move, had risen in the Quonset during the service and, looking about at the congregation of servicemen, helmet under his arm, declared, "With all due respect to the padre here, I feel it is my duty as your commanding officer to inform you that as far as I am concerned, God directly hears your prayers and will not fail us—*if* we prove worthy." As the padre's face grew redder by the second, Freeman had continued, "It is our bounden duty to thrash these neo-Communist sons of bitches in their new garb so soundly that they will never again doubt America's will."

On the memo pad by his bed he also scribbled an order to Colonel Dick Norton for immediate attention to Supply: "No fairy Bibles will be permitted in Second Army. King James version only. I don't want my men fighting and dying—should it come to that—with some namby-pamby 'God is my pal' version of some liberal New York hippy diocese. I expect your cooperation. Signed, General Douglas Freeman."

On the south bank, the Chinese side, of the Argun River, which formed the western side of the Amur, or Black

Dragon, hump, the first round to rupture the cease-fire was audible to the Chinese seconds before it hit them. Its staccato shuffling sounded like some giant steam locomotive moving rapidly in the blackness above them, the heat envelope of the 155mm HE head having concertinaed the frigid air. It landed a hundred yards behind them, its explosion lighting up what looked like glass-covered brambles as the hoarfrost melted from uprooted bushes that a moment before had been under a mantle of virgin snow and were now flying through the air in an eruption of black dirt and snow, shrapnel singing like bees, slashing into the advance battery of the Shenyang Military Region's Sixteenth Army, its 130mm field guns dug in under snow-camouflage netting high above the river.

Their forward observation posts, using the Soviet-made combination infrared laser range-finder, caught the flash of the second round two to three miles across the river, and the officer commanding the battery was on the radio to group army headquarters at Manzhouli, reporting that the direct fire was coming from high ground in the direction of Srednearaunsk in the hills on the American-held side. Within two minutes four other HE rounds had bracketed the Chinese position, killing one loader and exploding a Long March ammunition truck, and the Chinese battery had returned fire with six rounds of HE from their 130mm, thirteen-mile-range guns. Soon, in this, the southwestern sector of the Amur-Argun hump, firing erupted all along the line, especially along the west to east dip formed by the still extant wall of Genghis Khan forty-three miles east of Manzhouli. Quickly other American and Chinese batteries opened up on one another. American MLRSs—multiple launch rocket systems—lit up the night sky with what the MLRS troops called "white lasers," streaking salvos of thirteen-foot-long, nine-inch-diameter, 667-pound rockets —each rocket with a range of eighteen miles—twelve rockets fired at once from each of a dozen MLRS units spread along the length of the Khan wall. At times there were salvos of 120 rockets in one minute, 120 white parallel lines in the night sky, the rockets not designed to take out pinpoint targets, but to saturate a wide area and to sow chaos among the enemy troops. This they did, especially among the forward units of the Shenyang Sixteenth Army as the "coffee cups," or polyurethane foam containers, from 667-pound MLRS rockets, each carrying over six hundred antipersonnel/antimatériel submunitions, rained down. After each warhead's time had set off its "blowout" black powder charge, thousands of tiny submunition chutes were scattered over an oval-shaped area of several miles in which the M-77 submunitions exploded on contact, ripping through flesh and/or light armor. In the Chinese battery that had been first hit, there were twenty-six dead and over two hundred wounded in the first ten minutes of combat.

Within two hours three group armies—the Shenyang Military Region's Sixteenth, Sixty-fourth, and Thirty-ninth—were on the move, the spearhead of an attack on a seventy-five-mile front formed by the Twenty-seventh Army group, whose reputation had been made when they had swarmed down Changan Avenue and shot children as well as the young protesters of the Democracy Movement on the night of June 3–4, 1989, when above Tiananmen the voice of Big Brother in the loudspeakers had declared, "Your movement is bound to fail. It is foreign. This is China, not America."

"The Twenty-seventh," promised General Cheng, who had particularly ordered that the imperialist battery that had fired the first shot of the war be taken alive for all the world to see, "will know what to do with them after."

In General Freeman's Khabarovsk headquarters hundreds of miles to the north, the noise level of radio traffic was near deafening, the situation board, a computer screen blowup, showing fighting had broken out all along the border in the southwest sector of the hump. ChiCom divisions were already moving north en masse, fanning out toward Kulusutay to the east and Dauriya seventy miles to the west, and in the foothills of the four-thousand-foot-high Argunskiy mountain range the infamous Twenty-seventh had already crossed the border, men and equipment making good time across the frozen marshes just south of Genghis Khan's wall.

Freeman, for all his warnings about a breakdown of the cease-fire, was in shock, stunned now that it had actually happened. Staring at himself in the mirror, he slipped the nine-millimeter Parabellum into his waistband and was buttoning up his tunic as if in a state of hypnosis as Dick Norton knocked, waited, knocked again, then, alarmed at not receiving an answer, opened the door to the general's room. He took the general's silence for extreme calm under pressure, not realizing what a devastating blow it had been to Freeman.

Now that it had actually happened, it made no sense to Freeman. The American Second Army—*his* army—was suddenly in a war with *China*, a country of over a billion people. He didn't have to imagine what effect it would have on the American public—on the White House—the almost certain attempt of his enemies in and outside the Pentagon, if not on the president's staff itself, to hold him personally responsible for having broken the cease-fire. He was stunned by the supreme irony—that of all his warnings about the cease-fire being broken, the possibility that it would be broken by China had never, deep down, been seriously entertained by him. He had taken their border movements to be merely precautionary. But he knew that those against him back home, looking for a scapegoat, would recall his warnings about a possible cease-fire rupture, together with his wanting to pursue the Siberians before the cease-fire, and in it they would see him guilty of having made a preemptive strike.

The shock was wearing off now. He had always been contemptuous of Stalin's state of mind upon being informed that the Wehrmacht legions were upon him after he had signed the Hitler-Stalin Pact. Now, as much as he'd detested the Communist leader, Freeman knew what it must have felt like, but for Freeman the very recognition he was in shock was the signal he was on his way out of it.

"General!" It was Norton following him out into a river of khaki, some officers, still with white snow overlays on, passing about Freeman and Norton like rapids in a stream.

"What is it, Dick?"

"Sir—the Chinese are claiming we started it."

"Bullshit!"

Norton handed him a SATRECON photograph. It had been taken with an infrared sensor, a white spot like a pinpoint of overexposed film circled on the photo. Freeman felt his heart pounding.

"You can't see it with the naked eye," commented Norton, "but on computer enhancement they say you can actually see the black side blasts coming out of the muzzle brake. It's definitely a U.S. 155mm howitzer—towed, not self-propelled."

"So?"

Normally Norton would have lowered his voice for what he was about to tell the general, but in the near-frantic hubbub of the HQ it was unnecessary. "This was fired at oh five hundred hours, General. Ten minutes *before* the first report from our side of Chinese fire."

Freeman grunted, not wanting to acknowledge the frightening implication of Norton's words. "Probably took ten minutes for our reports to get passed down the line. You know how it is. Fog of war, Dick. The fog of—"

"We had the report within a minute, sir. It looks like we fired first." Norton continued, anticipating the general's next question, "We're trying to pinpoint the unit. Seems to be one of Five Corps' batteries near Kulusutay. They shouldn't be where they are, but maybe they saw ChiCom infantry on the move and changed positions for a better traverse. Anyway, we can't raise them—either their radio's out or—"

"Doesn't make any difference," said Freeman, and Norton knew the general was right. Whatever the cause, battle was joined.

The White House, however, demanded that responsibility for the first shot be "ascertained immediately. Repeat—immediately." The decoded Most Secret message from the White House added that "all hell" had broken out in the U.N.—the suspicion that Freeman had precipitated a war trumpeted to near certainty by the media, especially the La Roche chain of newspapers in the U.S. and abroad. Already *The New York Times* had obtained from an "anonymous" source another print of the photograph from the Pentagon showing the "first shot" SATRECON snap, which the *Times* said was "confirmed by independent analysis" to be genuine, the time on the photograph being automatically registered on such satellite overflights on the bottom right-hand corner of the photograph.

With three Chinese group armies, in excess of 121,000 men, coming at Second Army's left, or southern, flank—64,000 men—Freeman was in no mood to bother with the White House request, but knew if he didn't, he might be out of a job. He might be out of one anyway.

"Dick!"

"Sir?" It wasn't Norton answering but the communications duty officer cutting in.

"What is it, Major?"

"Sir, Five Corps HQ say they've tried to reach the battery that supposedly fired first, but there's no radio communication and the ChiComs are closing. Five Corps' G-2 estimates that unless we haul them out within the next ten to twelve hours, the ChiComs will overrun the position."

"Well, what in hell is Five Corps Air Cavalry doing?" demanded Freeman. "Sitting on their butts? Get the goddamn helos in there!"

"That's part of the problem, sir. It's still pretty cold, but the temperature's rising—so now we have a lot of fog and we've run into Qing Fives."

"Qing Fives!" retorted Freeman angrily, contemptuous of the Chinese fighter. "God damn it, Major, a Qing Five's just a bucket of crap with a jet engine strapped to it."

"Yes, sir. Our fighters'll make mincemeat of the Qings all right when they get there, but the best they can do is keep the ChiComs away from the Five Corps battery. Getting helos in there to get our boys out is another question. ChiComs are reportedly using surface-to-air missiles even against our light reconnaissance aircraft."

"God damn it!" said Freeman, glaring at the situation board. "Soviet munitions. What'd I tell you, Dick? Birds of a feather."

"Well, sir, the Siberians haven't moved."

"And thank God for that," replied Freeman. "Dick, send in a commando team to help get those Five Corps artillery battery guys out before the damn ChiComs overrun it." Freeman glanced up at the Special Forces availability board. "We have any SAS/Delta Force men around?"

"David Brentwood. Guy you used on Ratmanov's here somewhere in Khabarovsk."

"Where in Khabarovsk?"

"I don't know exact—"

"Well, find him, Dick. Tell him to get a team together—men he's worked with before—I don't want any screwups. Use Army Lynx helos to fly NOE. I want that SAS/D team in and out—fast. Tell them to rescue as many of our guys as possible and bring them straight to me. Try to get me the battery commander if possible so I can shoot the son of a bitch myself."

Norton was already making notes and issuing orders for the best NOE—nap of the earth—Lynx chopper pilots in the division even as the "tote" board above Freeman's HQ's radio row was going crazy with blipping red lights, each the size of a glowing cigarette tip and representing a ChiCom regimental advance of over two thousand men, the "reds" outnumbering the stationary "blues," the U.S. regiments, ten to one.

"What a screwup!" opined a radio operator, giving up his seat to his replacement, indicating the unofficial but widespread assessment of the situation.

"Shut up!" It was the duty officer reprimanding him.

Freeman held up his hand to intervene. "You got a complaint, soldier?"

The radio operator, who hadn't realized the general was nearby, visibly gulped. "Complaint . . . no, sir."

"Yes you have. We've got most of our divisions on Baikal's west shore to stave off a Siberian violation of the cease-fire, and instead I get hit on the southern flank by the Chinese. Well, son, you've got every right to be mad. So am I."

"Yes, sir."

Freeman, putting his arm around the operator, steered him toward the coffee urn. "Tell you fellas something else . . ." Everyone was listening. "I'm gonna change that. Right about now."

"Yes, General."

With that, Freeman ordered alternate divisions—every second division on the Baikal line—pulled out to head southeast to block the Chinese advance on his southern flank, and ordered AIRTAC strikes against the ChiCom divisions to hold them off long enough "until the alternate divisions from Baikal can reach the Chinese and attack! We're going to turn that goddamn 'yellow peril' into chop suey!"

The surge in morale that the general's words produced was palpable in the HQ hut, and Norton shook his head at the duty officer, smiling in admiration of Freeman's ability to so quickly raise the spirits of his troops. Freeman called Norton over. The general was still grinning, but his words told a different story. "Tell Washington I want every reserve, every ounce of gas, every bullet they've got, and I want it over here pronto. I know we can't do it all by airlift, but get those big C-7s started, Dick. And get 'em moving those convoys out from Pearl and the West Coast. I smell a big fucking rat—and his name's Yesov. If that son of a bitch violates the cease-fire at Baikal, we'll have a *two*-front war on our hands." He paused, Norton noting that he was short of breath. "Any sign of him moving, Dick?"

"No, sir." Norton indicated the met board. "There're blizzard conditions around Baikal, anyway."

"He could still move, Dick. Visibility or not. Besides, the temperature's rising. Doesn't feel like it, I know—but it is. Ice is starting to break up. Besides, blizzard's only thing that can stop our air force, laser bombs and all. Not even the Stealths can laser designate targets in that lot."

"I don't think he'll attack, General."

"By God, I hope you're right, Dick. Two-front war east and south. Our backs to the sea. Be a goddamn nightmare."

CHAPTER FOURTEEN

BETWEEN IRKUTSK, FORTY miles west of Lake Baikal, and the lake, in the village of Bol'shaya Rechka, a babushka wrapped her black scarf tightly around her head before she stepped out on her porch. As she stooped to grasp the two splintery pine sticks that stood up from the frozen paper cups of milk, she heard a squeaking noise that reminded her of her youth on the communes: tractors starting the harvest. Then, the giant, Popsicle-like milks at her side, she stood transfixed, staring through the thick white curtain of falling snow, the enormous shapes becoming more distinct by the second—armor—tanks and enormous field guns, their weight on bipods atop the biggest tractor tracks she'd ever seen. They were all around her, albino leviathans, crawling inexorably eastward toward Lake Baikal. After a while the old peasant woman stopped counting.

Each of the more than three hundred three-man-crewed Siberian T-72M main battle tanks—an APSDS, armor-piercing-fin-stabilized discarding sabot round, in its big

125mm gun—stopped seven miles from the western shore on the southern end of the four-hundred-mile-long, banana-shaped lake. The tank regiment's overall *komandir*, General Minsky of the Tenth Guards "Slutsk" Division, had at last been given the task he craved: his orders to spearhead the attack and defeat the Americans. He was eager but tense, his head tank regiment, with ninety-three of the "Slutsk" guards' division's 328 main battle tanks, assigned to undertake *zadacha dnia*—a total rout in the American sector in the southwestern Baikal. And the *zadacha dnia* had to be completed in no less than twenty-four hours, before the Americans could recover and regroup.

Minsky's initial artillery/tank attack in his sector would be followed by what Yesov had declared would be a merciless *presledovatelnyi boi*—a pursuit of lightning savagery—designed to finish off the retreating Americans on the ice before they reached the relative safety of the taiga twenty miles across the lake from the small town of Port Baikal. And following Minsky, ready to spread out north and south of him after his blitzkrieg, were the remainder of the four thousand tanks, advancing on a forty-eight-mile, or eighty-kilometer, front, the maximum that anyone like Yesov, trained at the Frunze Academy, felt comfortable with.

Immediately behind Minsky's ninety-three-tank spearhead came the regiment's forty-six BMPs—armored personnel carriers—with higher velocity and harder-hitting thirty-millimeter guns replacing the old seventy-three millimeters, and behind them the regiment's eighteen self-propelled 120mm, thirteen-mile-range guns, and the BM-21 multiple rocket launchers, forty tubes to each launcher.

The Slutsk division's artillery regiment of nine self-propelled S-3 152mm guns was kept as far back as possible, while up front Yesov had his self-propelled howitzers, their crews so razor-sharp that it would take them only seven minutes—under half the time required for the towed guns—to have the guns fully emplaced and ready for firing. These self-propelled howitzers were the new M-1974s, amphibious versions of the old M-1973, 152mm, 360-degree-rotation howitzer. Their drive sprockets, while well-protected—being located forward and beneath the sloping glacis plate—nevertheless squeaked like the unoiled rail cars of the Trans-Siberian, which, a few miles back on Minsky's right, or southern, flank, were even now hauling the supplies toward the lake, including a full range of main battle-tank 125mm HE, APDS, and HESH—heat, squash head—ammunition.

The babushka, now back inside her small bungalow, the wood-carved fretwork beneath the snow-filled window boxes shuddering like something alive, watched fearfully as the entire advance came to a halt. For a moment she could hear only the noise of mournful howling of the blizzard driving itself against the already snow-laden birch forest, but then she saw something that completely mystified her as the armored personnel carriers, with their blunt, bargelike snouts, advanced in line through the columns of main battle tanks and self-propelled artillery and, obeying flag signals—Yesov having banned any radio transmits—slowly turned left, northward, in unison, like a long line of prehistoric monoliths issuing forth enormous billowing clouds of thick, flour-white smoke into the white purity of the blizzard.

"Stranno!" Crazy! the babushka told her husband, an old reservist who had lost a leg in the final days before the cease-fire, during the American commando attack on the missile-launching midget subs' base at Baikal.

"They're making camouflage," he answered grumpily, cutting one of the rationed, brick-hard sugar cubes in half, clenching it between his teeth before sucking through the strong, hot, samovar-brewed tea, the samovar's brassy shine in stark contrast to the dank darkness of the cabin.

"What do you mean, camouflage?" she asked him. "It's crazy—the snow is already white—camouflage enough."

"You don't know anything," he grumped, the sugar only now starting to dissolve. "It's small-particle smoke," he explained. "Thicker than usual. It will stop the Americans' infrared scopes from seeing the heat exhaust of our tanks and big mobile guns when they begin the attack. Infrared can see through normal smoke.''

"It's crazy," she repeated.

"I'll tell you what's crazy," he told her, reaching for his crutch, a rough triangle of birch wood, its shoulder pad a small arc of rubber from an American Humvee, part of the American equipment captured in one of the last firefights around the southern end of the lake before the cease-fire. "It's crazy for us to stay up here. We'd best get down to the cellar before—"

There was a tremendous crash, the door flung open, the blizzard howling in—a half-dozen white-hooded, white-clothed figures barging in like angry ghosts.

"Idite!" You must go! ordered the lieutenant. "We are commandeering your house." The other men were already pushing past the babushka, two of them moving toward the basement, unraveling a coil of wire held between them.

"Idi!" Go! said the babushka. "Where to, pray?"

"Back," answered the lieutenant, using the AK-47 to motion westward over his shoulder in the general direction of Irkutsk.

"But that's over forty kilometers," she protested. The husband caught a glimpse of a blue-and-white-striped T-shirt as the lieutenant took off his white camouflage overlays to better handle the land lines that they were in the process of laying. The land lines would be much more secure for being sheathed, and so much less likely than wireless radio traffic to be jammed by American electronic countermeasures once the fighting started. The old man, however, was more interested in the blue-and-white T-shirt. It told him they were SPETS.

"Be quiet, Natasha," he cautioned his wife.

"They'll have a truck to take you back to Podkamennaya," said the lieutenant, sticking the AK-47 through the line spool.

"That's no good," protested the babushka defiantly. "That's still over twenty kilometers from Ir—"

"It's warming!" the lieutenant said. "On the lake the ice is starting to break up. It won't be such a cold walk."

"Come on!" said the husband. He knew the SPETS would have another kind of answer if they protested too much. Didn't she realize that a major attack was about to start? *"Radi Boga, tishe!"* For God's sake, be quiet! he told her, pushing at her with the crutch, anxious to get as far away as possible. Once the land lines were connected, hell would erupt.

CHAPTER FIFTEEN

Khabarovsk

"I TELL YOU," declared Freeman, "I don't trust the sons of bitches. They're going to hit us, Dick." He paused, looking at the map. "God damn this snow!" His hand swept up, covering the entire north-south axis of the lake. "No way we can protect it all, so we have to narrow the field. If he penetrates our defenses and gets on that ice—four hundred miles." He shook his head at the thought. "He could move a division anywhere across there in less than—"

"Well, I know aerial reconnaissance doesn't show anything because of the blizzard, General. But there's no IR report either. Not a sign they're advancing."

"Could be using IR suppressor smoke. If only I could launch a preemptive strike on Irkutsk or—"

"We'd be condemned by every country in the U.N.," cut in Norton. "As well as our allies. Fighting to push back the Chinese is one thing, sir, but us breaking the cease-fire with the Siberians would—''

"You're right, dammit!" conceded Freeman, turning away from the map to the tote-board display, trying to put himself in Yesov's shoes. "Great weakness of a democracy, Dick. We can only finish a war—can't start it."

"Would you want it any other way?" proffered Norton, anticipating the question might be asked in the news conference about to start in the briefing room.

Freeman didn't answer, but his grimace was reply enough. "Hell, I'm in trouble enough with Washington, trying to convince them Beijing started this crap on our southern sector." Peering down over his reading glasses, he swept his hand over the midsection of the map. " 'Course, Yesov couldn't spread himself too thin, either. Even if he had every division of his—he wouldn't risk a four-hundred-mile-long front. Soon as the bad weather lifted, our TACAIR'd rip him to pieces." The general took off his glasses and pinched the bridge of his nose in his fatigue. "Then again, we can't hold very much of it, either, having to move most of our forces south to help push the Chinks back."

Norton experienced a surge of panic, instinctively look-ing around for any media types who might have somehow wandered through security from the briefing room, where even now chairs were scraping the Quonset hut floor as a "gaggle" of over 120 media "vultures," as Freeman called them, from around the world were assembling. They were hungry for General Douglas Freeman's latest assessment of, and explanation for, what the Chinese and others in the U.N. were calling "an unprovoked imperialist attack upon the People's Republic of China," and one that would be "severely punished by the People's Liberation Army."

"General," urged Norton, "you'd better be careful what you say. If the La Roche papers got hold of something like that . . .''

Freeman was looking at him, amused. "What the hell're you talking about?"

" 'Chinks,' " said Norton. "They get hold of something like that, General, and you'll have every civil rights group from here to—"

"Ah, to hell with them. You know I don't mean any disrespect toward the little yellow bastards. Damn good soldiers. Only color I care about is anyone who's yellow inside."

"*I* know that, General, but—well, you know what newspapers are like. I think we'd better stick to 'Chi-Coms,' " Norton advised, pointing out that ironically it was the gutter press of the La Roche papers, who were the *real* racists, who would make such a big deal of such a slip.

La Roche's tabloids were already talking about "swarms" of Chinese Communists attacking the American positions in the southwest corner of the Amur hump—"swarms" creating the none-too-subtle implication that the Americans were being attacked by subhumans. On the front, with American casualties mounting not because of the Chinese numbers, but because of their tenacity and skill, U.S. soldiers were already making their ironic comments on the La Roche reporters, telling sergeants they'd just shot "another swarm" when only one ChiCom fell.

"They're all out there, sir!" It was the general's briefing room aide, in charge of setting up the appropriate charts and maps.

Freeman turned away from Baikal, ran a comb through his gray shock of hair, put his forage cap on, square and center, and hitched his trousers a notch, careful to make sure his tunic waistband was over the nine-millimeter Parabellum with which he'd replaced the old Hi-Vel .22 automatic that he used to carry and sleep with beneath his pillow. He'd debated about replacing that Hi-Vel—he'd had it all through Europe and Korea, and it had become a kind of talisman—but he liked the Sig Sauer better, and anyway, he hated staying with anything because of superstition. Said it bred "lack of self-confidence." Didn't go with ball players not changing their underwear because they believed it brought them luck. "Hell, only reason they make another home run is because one whiff of 'em'd knock any baseman off the bag.''

As the general and Norton stepped into the press room, Norton was momentarily blinded by the multiple explosions of flashbulbs amid the mass of mike-clutching reporters, already in a feeding frenzy over what the Chinese incursion meant and what wording the general was going to use and what Washington thought about the general and was it true that they were keeping him on a tight leash?

The general looked serious yet not grim, concerned but not stressed, the furrows in his brow as much a signal to those members of the press who already knew him that *he*, not the press corps, was going to set the agenda, and that the television klieg lights were too bright. He held his hands up for silence. ''Ladies and gentlemen, before I take any questions, I wish to clarify an unfortunate error reported by some of you.''

''Who?'' shouted one young reporter, a woman—mid-twenties, good-looking, her red hair conspicuous in the glare, the strap of the Pentax camera slung about her neck bisecting her breastline, making her figure even more prominent as she lunged forward with a fishing-rod-like boom mike, her emerald-green eyes keen with the determination not to let her inexperience stand in her way. ''Unfortunate error by whom, General?'' she shouted.

Freeman wanted to say, ''By the toilet newspapers of the La Roche chain,'' but Norton's cough by his side cautioned him from being specific, to remember what he himself had told Norton—that ''vexatious reporters are the most venomous, vengeful bastards in the world.''

''It's been reported,'' Freeman began, ''that our positions in the southwestern sector of the Amur hump have been attacked by 'swarms' of Chinese infantry. Now I'm here to tell you the Chinese have never attacked in swarms here, in Korea, or anywhere else. That was a myth concocted by overeager reporters trying to win brownie points with fat, unfit editors back home.'' There were ripples of laughter, and Norton starting a coughing fit. "Chinese infantry," Freeman proceeded, hands akimbo, "seldom attack above regimental level. And they attack well-defined targets—they don't *swarm* over anything. Like any other army, the Chinese army—"

Norton coughed, whispering, "Don't offend Taiwan."

". . . The Chinese *Communists*," continued Freeman, "have never launched 'hordes' or 'swarms,' as one of your colleagues put it. That's a bunch of coon—dirt." There was more laughter. "And those stories about one in ten Chinese infantry being properly armed, the other nine yahooing and beating bamboo until they get a chance to pick up a dead man's weapon, are a figment of some reporter's imagination. Now, admittedly that might have occurred here and there in Korea, but not here. The People's Liberation Army's weapons are simple, highly reliable, and they've got plenty of 'em. I can assure you we are not beating swarms—we are *fighting* highly trained ground troops on their own ground."

"You mean you don't think we can win? Another Vietnam?" Even some of the older reporters turned around, surprised by the redhead's chutzpa, though most of them, Norton suspected, were drawn as much by her cleavage as she once again thrust the mike above her colleagues' heads toward the general.

"Not at all," replied Freeman icily. "What I'm saying is that the enemy is formidable but that I believe the American soldier can and will regain lost ground and—"

"But can we win, General?" The redhead's mike was barely a foot from Freeman's face, other reporters ducking out of the boom's way. The general didn't notice; he was reading a scribbled note, hastily passed from the duty officer to Norton and thence to the general.

"That's all. Thank you," he announced crisply, and was gone. The uproar from the media reminded Norton of rock and roll aficionados just informed of a no-show.

"Where?" demanded Freeman, whipping off his forage

cap in the Ops room, throwing it down on the table before the map of Lake Baikal, the hum of computers and bursts of radio traffic stabbing in the background.

"Here," said Norton, indicating a point just north of the southernmost end of the lake. His fingers slid farther along. "And here." Then he tapped a third position farther north of the other two, and like them, on the western side of the lake.

"Estimated strength?" asked Freeman.

"Four, possibly six, divisions. Least a hundred thousand men," the duty officer cut in. "G-2 suspects SPETS troops are the spearheads. Whatever the troop concentration, General—we're looking at three breakthrough points."

"Satellite-confirmed?" pressed Freeman. He wasn't about to commit any reserves to possible feints by Yesov until, in the absence of aerial reconnaissance reports, he had confirmed visual sightings.

"Infrared-confirmed in each case, General. They're moving east, all right. Straight toward our Three Corps at Port Baikal. No doubt about it."

"Radio intercepts?"

"Nothing there, sir. Apparently Yesov's got them moving by flag signal and sheathed land line. So we have no intercepts."

"Now lookit, Jimmy," Freeman replied, his eyes fixing his duty officer. "I don't want another Skovorodino road trap here." The duty officer was aware that there were no roads along most of the lake, but knew immediately what Freeman meant. Were they fake tanks—as they'd been at Skovorodino before the cease-fire—giving off infrared signatures in hopes of dummying Freeman into committing his revetted armor at Port Baikal to precisely the *wrong* places, leaving Port Baikal largely defenseless?

"I've already thought of that one, sir. No, sir, it's the real thing, all right. Infrared images were *moving*."

"Flashlights can move. How about our ground sensors?"

"Got that one covered, too, General. Snow muffles the sensors all right, so nothing registered for a while. But then

Port Baikal started registering definite shakes—horizontal movement—mile-and-a-half-advance rumble. They're main battle tanks, sir—they're not driving fake tanks around on truck chassis, if that's what you're concerned about.'' The duty officer turned and snatched up a SITREP sheet, saving the best evidence for last. ''Besides, one of our patrols out of Port Baikal, halfway down to Kultuk at the southern end of the lake, got an LAW round off. He was up a tree, General—literally. Put his shot right through the tank's cupola. Said the thing went up like the Fourth of July. Kept rolling—couple of Siberians tried to get out. On fire when they hit the snow.''

''And our patrol?'' inquired Freeman.

''Not so good, General. Three confirmed dead—two missing—but the other four got back to Port Baikal.''

Freeman was nodding, looking worriedly at the map, the three points, fifty miles apart, now marked with red circles—a large S inside of each. A 150-mile-long front. ''How did our patrol get back so fast? Ahead of the Siberian tanks?''

''They used four Arrows.''

Freeman nodded. The Arrows weren't the Israeli antimissile missiles, but the small snow vehicles that young David Brentwood and his SAS/Delta commando team had used to go across the lake before the cease-fire to take out the midget sub pens at Port Baikal.

''We, gentlemen,'' said Freeman, looking from the duty officer to Norton and back, ''are in a fix. If we recall any of our troops we've ordered south against the ChiComs, the ChiComs'll punch an even bigger hole through our southern flank. But if I don't stop this Siberian triple play''—his knuckle rapped the middle of the three red circles marking the 150-mile-wide Siberian offensive—''our boys'll have to hightail it across that ice—leave all our heavy equipment behind if they're to make it in time.'' He dismissed the idea of such a retreat as quickly as it had occurred to him. It was the worst-case scenario. ''Any sign of the weather clearing?''

" 'Fraid not, General," answered the duty officer, showing him the isobar printout from Harvey Simmet, the senior met officer. "It's warming, but that's only going to mean more fog, and they're only miles from our boys on the lake. Even if we call in TACAIR now that we more or less know their positions, our A-10s are gonna have one hell of a time with IFF." He meant identifying friend or foe.

Freeman knew the duty officer was right and recalled that even in the relatively unlimited visibility of Operation Desert Storm, Schwarzkopf had lost over twenty percent of those killed in action to "friendly fire," these so-called "fratricidal" casualties ten times higher than in any military action in the twentieth century, including World War Two and Vietnam. "That cunning bastard Yesov," said Freeman, facing the map, "knows damn well we can't use TACAIR when he's so close. And you know why he's so close?" Freeman turned around, eyes bright with anger. "Because those fairies back in Washington insisted on a *cease-fire*! All right—Dick, now listen up. I want all our units north of the Siberian midpoint here on the west side of the lake to pull south fast as they can, to reinforce the units between the midpoint—designation S-Two—and the Siberians' southernmost point at the end of the lake, designation S-Three. That'll buy us some time. Now when that northernmost part of Yesov's assault line, S-One, reaches the lake, it'll start to pivot south . . ."

Already Norton was seeing the general's plan, and not for the first time was filled with admiration at the sheer speed of Freeman's analysis. This wasn't grace under pressure—it was brilliance. "Right," said Norton, "and when they pivot, their armor will have to come out onto the ice—"

"And so will their southern arm," said Freeman. "S-Three. They'll try to pincer us, box us in, with their triple play—their armor coming at us through the taiga west of the lake, down from the north on the ice, and up from the south on the ice." Freeman was smiling at Norton. "The *marshal* is going to get a big surprise, Dick. Son of a bitch waited until the warming started, figuring I couldn't move armor east fast enough through the thaw—least not as far as Lake Baikal's west shore—to stop him. Well—he's right. But that cocky bastard is in for an earlier springtime than he anticipated, gentlemen.''

Freeman was positively beaming. Striding to the huge wall map, he took the Day-Glo marker pen and drew a crimson slash line from the Siberian mid, or S-Two, position, east across the lake, drawing another line parallel to it east across the lake from the S-Three position farther south. ''Those tramtracks are our corridor, gentlemen. Fifty miles wide south to north on our front, twenty miles deep west to east from Port Baikal to the lake's eastern shore. Now Dick, I want volunteers to lay the flare lines for the corridor a mile or so out from the western edge of the lake. Then once that's done, tell the TACAIR boys to hit anything outside the corridor.''

Now the duty officer was starting to see it. The flares would mark the outer limits of the American defense—any Siberian tanks north or south that ventured out onto the ice, attempting to encircle and cut off the Americans from the far eastern shore in a pincer movement, would have to forego the formidable protection of the dense taiga. Even in heavy fog their infrared signatures would be more easily picked up on the completely uncluttered background of the ice. It would be a killing ground for the A-10 Thunderbolts' thirty-millimeter guns, a killing ground that would be as devastating for the Siberians as the Basra road had been for the fleeing Iraqi armor. Just as the Republican Guards' tanks had broken out from their underground shelters to do battle, only to be slaughtered in the open, the Siberian tanks would be doomed the moment they emerged from the thick cover of shoreline taiga.

Convinced he was approaching the crowning moment of his career, Freeman tried but simply could not contain his excitement, knowing that snatching victory from such an apparently massive defeat would astonish the world and forever place him in the annals of warfare.

Meanwhile, as the babushka and her husband were driven

west of the lake toward Podkamennaya township, General Minsky's regiment sat still, including the BMPs which, though stationary, were still churning out thick, white smoke into the already thick whiteness of the blizzard. Waiting.

CHAPTER SIXTEEN

Aleutian Islands, Alaska

AS IF THE lineup outside the doctor's office at the Dutch Harbor hospital wasn't creating enough pressure on the new young ophthalmologist, no one could find the pointer he'd brought with him to use for the Snellen eye chart. It was a small detail, but it flustered him, as more and more it seemed he was losing control of the situation just when he wanted to be most impressive in the wounded veterans' sight. And to top it off, an obstreperous patient—a limey by his accent—was loudly complaining outside the doctor's office. " 'Ere, what's the bloody 'oldup, then? 'Aven't got all bloody week 'ave we?"

"You know the army," commented another patient. "Hurry up and wait!"

"Well," said Doolittle, "we ain't in the bloody army, are we? This is the senior bloody service."

"Would you behave yourself!" It was "Mother Attila," the head nurse, Doolittle's fellow Britisher assigned to the Allied naval hospital. She was big and heavy, her trajectory so unpredictable they had begun to call her "Scud." "I'll put you on report," she threatened the cockney.

"Oh dear!" retorted Doolittle insolently. "Terrified I am, that's wot. Bloody terrified!"

She was taking out her pen when the ophthalmologist, red-faced and harassed, appeared at the door. "Nurse, you haven't seen my pointer, have you?"

"In your trousers, mate!" said the cockney.

There was a roar of laughter from the queue, the doctor's head withdrawing quickly to his examination room, and Doolittle now definitely on the Scud's report.

Even more flustered now, the young ophthalmologist smiled apologetically at Shirer, who, during Doolittle's diversionary play, had been sitting patiently in the hard-seated examination chair. "Can't seem to find my occluder—sight blocker. Well, just place your hand over one eye."

"Fine," said Frank. "Which line?"

"Wha—uh, any line."

"Read it all?" said Frank, feigning surprise, and was reciting it by heart when he had a moment of inspiration, hesitated, then said, "Last letter, fourth line—bit blurry—an E or an F."

The doctor glanced up at him, convinced that this pilot—he looked back at the file—Shirer knew very well it was an F and, like so many others, was probably trying to fudge it in an attempt to eke out a little more rest and recreation if at all possible. It was known he was keen on a young nurse, Lana La Roche. Well, the young ophthalmologist thought, I might be green, but not that green. He wasn't about to underwrite malingerers, and he told Shirer straight, "I guess you don't want to hear it, Major, but you're fit for flying duty again."

Frank mumbled an obscenity, taking the RTD—return to duty—slip with feigned reluctance. The head nurse and Doolittle were still arguing outside. It was getting on the doctor's nerves. He knew he shouldn't have wasted so much time looking for the damn pointer, but he'd had it since medical school and it had become like a charm to him. He rose, opened the door and called out briskly, "Next!" It was Doolittle, only his eyes and nose visible, the remainder of his head still bandaged.

"Right!" said the doctor, sitting on the stool in front of

the examination chair. "What letters can you make out?"
    "Where?"
    "On the chart."
    "What fucking chart?"

That afternoon, Frank Shirer was officially posted back on the active duty list, but the day was to end in disappointment. It hadn't occurred to him that once he got back on the active list he would be assigned anything else but fighters. However, with not enough fighters to go around, and his earlier experience of flying 727s coming up on the Pentagon's screen, he was assigned to Far East Bomber Command, Nayoro, Japan. B-52s. For Shirer it was like being told you'd been assigned to driving a Mack truck after having been at the wheel of Alfa-Romeos.

Lana was delighted. With Japan so close to Siberia, only F-111s and one or two of the precious few Stealth B-2 bombers were being used, as far as she knew—the long-distance B-52s merely on reserve standby.
    "Too bad," she lied. "But it'll help you to have a new challenge."
    "*Challenge!* I can fly a B-52 blindfolded."
    "Is it that easy?"
    "Well, no, but hell, after flying Tomcats. They don't call B-52s 'BUFFs'—big ugly fat fellows—for nothing. Anyway, they're not using B-52s over there—least not where it counts."
    "Oh?" Lana said, sounding disappointed. "Too bad, hon."
    He turned to her. "You serious?"
    "Of course."
    "Really?"
    "Yes."
    "I'll grow old in B-52s," he said morosely.
    "When will you be shipping out?"
    He handed her the fax. "Tomorrow. They don't waste any time once you're fit, do they?"

"Well, it's what you wanted. I mean at least you'll be flying and—"

"Yeah, sure."

It was a bright clear day over Roosevelt Island, with Manhattan towering against a background of a hard blue winter sky. Johnny Ferrago bent down to hoist his six-year-old daughter Linda onto his shoulders so she could see over the crowd gathering for the opening of the third water tunnel. Johnny was what was known in the excavating business as a "sandhog," one of the "unsung thousands," as *The New York Times* editorial put it, who, risking deafness, silicosis, and a range of other subterranean maladies, not to mention cave-ins, had labored for the past ten years to keep not only Manhattan, but the whole of New York alive. Blasting and drilling over seven hundred feet below ground, the sandhogs had carved out a sixty-mile-long, twenty-foot diameter *third* tunnel. This would boost the 1.5-billion-ton capacity of New York's water supply to 2.25 billion—the third tunnel taking the strain off one and two, which, fed by the underground aqueducts coming down from the Hillsview Reservoir, passed under the Bronx, exiting on West Thirty-fourth.

"Daddy?"

"Yes, hon?"

"Won't all the water be dirty?"

Ferrago's wife, Lenore, smiled as he pulled young Linda forward over his head and, looking up, ostrichlike, said, "Hey, what you think your daddy's been doin' all this time? That water's clean as you can get."

Ferrago's twelve-year-old son, Danny, his face all but covered by the collar of his parka and earmuffs, grumbled, "Can't be clean as snow water."

"What the hell you talking about?" said Johnny.

"You shouldn't say that, Daddy," came Linda's voice from above.

"Sorry, little girl. But that water's passed the sniffer test, Danny. Better than half the bottled water you can buy."

"What's a sniffer test?" asked Danny sullenly, wanting to know, but his pride at odds with his curiosity.

They could hear a murmur in the crowd of several thousand strong, someone saying the governor, with police escort, was approaching. He wasn't—it was traffic control cops on bikes keeping everyone behind the tape. "Sniffer test," Johnny Ferrago explained to Danny, "is done by a lady who sniffs the water. Right? Like a wine tester."

"They don't drink it, Daddy."

"Sure they do, Lindy—"

"No, Daddy. I saw it on 'Mister Rogers.' They spit it out."

"She means wine tasting," put in Lenore, his wife.

"Oh," said Johnny, looking up at his daughter. "That's right, honey. They don't drink the wine. Maybe the lady doesn't drink the water, but it's the best test they have." He looked down again at Danny, to include him in the conversation. "Some people can smell bacteria better than a machine. How about that, eh, Danny?"

"Yeah," said Danny. "I can't see anything."

"Well, you 'scuse yourself," Johnny told him, "and move up front. Your mom can't hold you up. You're too big."

"Don't want to go up front."

"All right then, stop squawkin'."

"I'm not squawkin'."

"All right, you two," said Lenore. "Cool it. We're supposed to be having fun. Remember?"

"How do they clean the water, Daddy?" asked his daughter, her head bending down over his.

"Don't have to, honey. Sunshine kills a lot of the bugs, and all the other bad stuff settles down in a big dam."

"What's a dam?"

"Well, place where you collect water. Lots of it. Keep it still so all the bad stuff can settle out. Then they put a seki disk—sort of like a black and white lid—down into the water. They have to be able to see it for at least two meters—that's just higher than Daddy. If they can still see the disk, then the water's safe.''

"How come we drink bottled water, then?" pressed Danny.

"Don't be a smartass, Danny," said Ferrago sharply. "Because I don't like all that chlorine they put in tap water, that's why.''

"Miss Lawson at school says they put fluoride in it. It's good for your teeth.''

"Yeah, well," said Johnny, "far as I'm concerned, the jury's still out on that one.''

"What's a jury, Daddy?" asked Linda.

"Never mind," said Johnny crabbily. "You keep your eyes on all the people going up there on the dais—the stand. You see the mayor's limo yet?''

"No.''

"Can *you* see 'em?" Ferrago asked his wife irritably.

"No. Just a few motorcycle cops." She nudged Johnny, lowering her voice. "Don't let Danny get on your nerves. He's just pushing your buttons.''

"Yeah, well, he's doin' a damn good job.''

Linda started jumping up and down on his shoulders as the band began to warm up.

"What's the big deal anyway?" said Danny. "It's boring.''

Lenore Ferrago reached in front of Johnny, grabbed the shoulder of Danny's jacket and gave it a good shake. "The big deal, Danny, is that your father has spent the last ten years digging that tunnel, and without it all those flashy Manhattan offices up there would be empty. A lot of men got killed in that tunnel, and a lot of others got silicosis, and—''

"What's sili—" began Danny, unrepentant.

"Lungs fill up with dust," said Johnny matter-of-factly.

The dignitaries were collecting now on the flag-draped dais decorated in front of the "head frame" that had taken Johnny and hundreds of others down countless times beneath the East River, where they'd had to continue blasting through bedrock. Apart from increasing the city's water supply, a third tunnel would allow the old aqueducts, many of whose huge valves had all but rusted away, to be maintained. Without the new tunnel, what now were maintenance crises for New York would soon become a colossal disaster.

For Johnny and the hundreds of other sandhogs who had spent so much of their lives in the subterranean tunnel and complex of risers, or overflow shafts, and who knew every inch of it, there was a shared feeling that it wasn't so much New York's tunnel as *theirs*. Despite all the problems, its on-and-off-again financial history, the biggest job of its kind in the history of the world had not only provided the sandhogs with work at some of the highest blue collar wages around, but had given them a deep sense of purpose, the kind that for a tradesman sometimes comes only once in a lifetime. They knew that without water, *everything* in New York—from flushing a toilet and mixing martinis to life-saving hospitals—would come to an abrupt halt. And a disease-ridden halt at that.

While Lenore was trying to convey something of what it had meant to their son, Johnny recalled the time he had been pinned for hours by a fall in one of the riser tunnels that led up to the street and the manhole covers that millions of New Yorkers walked over daily without a thought of the unseen world that kept their seeing world going. He wondered, too, about his future. The question of how many of the workers would be kept on hadn't been settled—or rather, that's what the union had been told. Ferrago and his friends, however, believed that the city officials already knew who'd be kept on, but not wanting to precipitate any "job action" that might mar the opening celebration, hadn't yet released the information. What they did know was that because of the war there'd been a lot of talk about cutting the completion ceremonies to a bare minimum: the mayor, a few local politicians, the police band, and that'd be it. But the mayor had overridden any such cutbacks, arguing, with unexpected support from the *Post* and the *Times*, that it was precisely *because* of the war that a very public celebration of America's industrial know-how and determination, evidenced in the world's largest tunnel, should be held. It would demonstrate once again, especially to the Siberians, that this was a "can-do" nation whose role as the "arsenal and foundry" of democracy could surmount industrial and logistical problems that would have confounded most others.

"There must be fifty people up there," commented Lenore, indicating the dais through the thicket of heads in front of her. "There's even an admiral. What's he in charge of—they sail boats in the tunnel?"

"Matter of fact, they do," Johnny answered. "Little prop-driven TV robot jobs. Push through all the crap and take pictures of any fractures 'fore they get a chance to get any bigger and blow. Those gases build up and that baby explodes, those brokers in Wall Street are gonna get more than their ankles wet, I can tell you. Stock exchange'd be goddamned swamped."

"Daddy, you shouldn't say that—"

"Yeah, sorry, Lindy."

"So what's the admiral—" began Lenore, her voice drowned out by the throaty roar of a V formation of Harley-Davidsons, the mayor's limo drawing to a halt in front of the dais, the serious men with the shades, despite the pale winter light, on either side of him looking hard beyond the line of uniformed policemen at the tape.

"How come you're not up there, Daddy?" Linda called out.

"They're VDs, stupid," said Danny. A Sousa march crashed into the air.

"*What?*" said Johnny, straining down to hear Danny, and seeing Lenore laughing so hard she looked like she'd fall down.

"He means VIPs!" she explained.

"Jesus," said Johnny. "I hope so."

"Don't call me stupid!" said Linda, bending toward Danny so that Johnny had to take a quick, jerking step forward to keep his balance.

Johnny saw Lenore standing on her toes, waving, calling out to someone. "Johnny—it's Mike Ricardo. Thought they weren't going to come . . . Over here, Mike!" Ricardo, a small, wiry man, made his way through the crowd, his New York Yankees cap lost from view now and then as the crowd moved forward, someone saying something about a movie star. Johnny and Lenore had got to know Mike and Betty Ricardo when both men had been working on the Bronx section of number three.

"Hiya, Johnny!" called Ricardo.

"Hey, Mike. What's the story—thought you and the missus were gonna watch Notre Dame?"

"Nah. Betty says I got square eyes already. So what the hell? Figured I'd give her a day out."

"Big deal," said Lenore.

Ricardo grinned. "She's havin' a ball. Stuffing herself with candy floss." He jerked his thumb in the direction of the dais. "I think she's got a thing for the mayor."

Lenore shook her head. Mike always had an answer.

"Listen, Johnny—" Ricardo started, but had to repeat himself; the band was killing Sousa with the base drum. "You want to come over to Pete's place after, for a few beers?"

Johnny nodded toward Lenore. "Have to check with the boss here."

"Pete's looking at a Camaro," cut in Ricardo, indicating a copy of the *Post* classifieds. "Wants us to give it the once-over."

"Before or after the beers?" Lenore sighed.

"Well, you know . . ." said Ricardo, grinning.

"Yeah," she said resignedly, "I do. Well," she turned to Johnny, her elbow pressing his, "be home by midnight."

"Yeah," he replied, but it was said as if he hadn't really heard. The truth was, he was in shock. The ad for the Camaro was the tip-off for another ad in the Personals:

Man in early thirties desires live-in companion. Sexual preference not important. Must like cats and be prepared to share household chores. No Republicans.

He'd been waiting so long that now it was here, he suddenly felt he was no longer ready. "Yeah," he answered. "No problem."

"Ladies and gentlemen," began one of the politicians, a Democratic representative for New York. "It's my pleasure and privilege to introduce you to—"

"I can't see," grumbled Danny.

After all the waiting—all the years—it took only three hours to answer the ad, to drive up to the Hillsview Reservoir.

When Johnny returned that evening, he was in a hell of a mood, and they were saying there'd been more power "outs" at Con Ed. So he knew everyone had been working, that the ad had been the signal for all of them.

"Danny!" yelled Johnny Ferrago, his shadow enormous in the candlelit kitchen. "Get away from there!"

Young Danny jumped back from the kitchen sink and, despite a brave effort, began crying. "I forgot."

"Well don't. What'd I tell you in the car?"

"I forgot," repeated Danny, now clinging to his mother, who drew him close.

"Lay off, Johnny," she told him. "He just forgot. What's the big panic anyway? You said you'd turned off all the water."

Johnny rose, picked up the cup Danny had been about to use and put it in the dishwasher. "There's still water in the pipes."

"I thought you said you ran it out?"

"You can't run it all out. Besides, from what they say on the radio, one drop'd be enough to kill you."

"How come they don't know how to fix it quicker?" complained Lenore. "Last time some idiot poisoned the water, they—"

"Because, last time was just peanuts," snapped Johnny, his metaphors going to hell with his temper. "Car radio says this time it's much bigger. Poured it over the spillways, apparently. So I don't want any of you going anywhere near taps. And Danny—stop your goddamn blubbering!"

"Why can't we use the toilet, Daddy?" asked Linda.

"Because you can't flush it, that's why," Johnny told her gruffly, pouring himself another scotch—putting in a dash of the bottled mineral water.

"I don't like using that poopy seat," said Linda, referring to the portable camper toilet in the basement. "It's scary down there."

"And how come Con Ed's on the fritz again?" said Lenore.

Johnny ignored her, turning to Linda. "Tell Mummy when you want to go down," he said. "You can use the big flashlight—that's what it's there for." His tone continued to be gruff, angry at his own bad temper but unable to rein it in. "It won't be for long," he said. "You all right, Danny?"

"No. I'm thirsty."

"Come over here," Johnny told him, and gave him a glass of the bottled water. "There y'are." Danny gulped the water. "Taste good?" inquired Johnny in a conciliatory tone.

Danny shook his head vigorously from side to side.

"For Chrissakes, Danny! You're spilling it. Can't you—"

Lenore interceded, quickly yet gently ushering the children into their bedroom off the hallway. Danny was still grumping. "It's not time for bed."

"You don't have to go to bed," Lenore assured them. "Just sit and play or do—"

"Why can't we watch TV, Mommy?" asked Linda.

" 'Cause," answered Danny, "there isn't any power, stupid."

"Don't you call me stupid—"

"Knock it off!" yelled Johnny from the dark recesses of the kitchen. "Or I'll tan both of you."

There was silence, Lenore aware for the first time she could remember that she could no longer hear even the faint hum of their refrigerator as she hustled and cajoled the children to get into their pajamas. If they were quick, she'd read them a story—"by candlelight!"

"Haven't cleaned my teeth," said Danny.

"All right," said Lenore, "Then go—no, wait a minute. I'll bring the brush in here with some bottled water."

"Yuk!"

Out in the kitchen, the shadow of her arm stretching like a huge derrick in the candlelight, Lenore poured the mineral water sparingly into a Big Bird cup. "This is getting to be a real pain," she said. "How long do you think we'll be without power and water?"

Johnny shrugged. "Probably won't get full power back for weeks, from what the radio says. It'll be staggered, I guess. Brownouts—a bit here, a bit there. As for water?" He turned his scotch and Canada Dry club soda nearer the candle. "No idea."

"What kind of people could do that?" she asked, screwing the cap back on. "Blowing up power stations is one thing, but poisoning the water—that's—that's sick."

"So was Agent Orange," said Johnny, sipping his scotch.

"That's different," Lenore said, reaching to put the bottle into the refrigerator from habit.

"Sure," said Johnny. "You weren't in Vietnam."

"Neither were you," she said, an edge to her voice. She really didn't know how long she could put up with the inconvenience. They'd most likely close the schools, and then, God help her, the kids would be home all day. "Anyway, that was war."

"Christ! What do you think this is?" he shot back. "No worse than what we did to the Vietnamese."

She peered in the flickering candlelight at an unrecognizable shape deep in the refrigerator's vegetable bin. "My God—what's this?"

"What?"

"This—" She made a noise as if she was picking up a snake, the lump in the plastic bag half solid, half liquid, squishy. She held it out toward him, outstretched fingers like laboratory tongs, face grimacing with repulsion. "It's a cucumber—I think. Or was." She was heading toward the bathroom, holding it at arm's length.

"You can't flush it," Johnny reminded her.

She stood motionless in the hallway. "Well, where can I put it?"

"Put it in the goddamn garbage." They heard the wailings of more sirens—gunshots.

"Looters," Johnny said. "Now we'll see how our fellow Americans behave when the lights go out."

"Well, they're not all like that," she said. "Would you go looting?"

" 'Course not. What a dumb question."

"See?" she said good-naturedly. "*You* wouldn't." She couldn't tell whether he was smiling or not in the shadow of the candle's glow.

"Johnny—no! No!" she yelled.

"What the hell—"

"Look, the Jameses'—oh my God, she's got her kitchen tap running. I'm sure of it—look, she's leaning over with the kettle to—she mustn't have heard that radio announcement you—oh my God, Johnny—"

She dropped the bag in the kitchen garbage pail, then grabbed the phone. It was dead. Slamming it down, she ran out the kitchen door, clattering down the darkened steps onto the crazy-stone backyard, yelling as she called out to her neighbor across the lane, an elderly woman—from where Lenore was, a small figure bending in a soft square of a camp light. "No—no, Mrs. James—"

"Daddy? Daddy? What's the matter?" called out Linda.

"Nothing," Ferrago replied. "Go to sleep." It was 8:04 P.M.

At 8:05 P.M., when Lenore Ferrago had pounded on her neighbor's back door she so terrified the elderly Mrs. James that the woman dropped the cat's filled water dish, the plastic bowl creating an enormous shadow in the candlelight as it bounced high against the dishwasher before banging to the floor and rolling, toplike, already empty of water and reverberating as it spun to a stop on the pale green linoleum floor.

"Martha!" bellowed Mrs. James's husband. "You okay?"

When he came in from the living room, the cat meowing safely behind him, his wife had one hand on her heart, the other on the doorknob, using it as a rest as she opened the back door. "It's—It's all right," she assured her husband, weakly waving for Lenore to come in. "It's Lenore Ferrago."

"Sorry," began Lenore, "but you mustn't use the water!" She paused for breath. ". . . Radio's warning everyone in the Bronx, Westchester, not to—" She had to stop.

Mr. James picked up the newspaper he'd been reading, peered through his bifocals then quickly pulled one of the kitchen chairs out from the table toward Lenore. "Here, sit down. You'll have a heart attack."

Lenore took the chair but hurried on. "Someone's apparently put poison in the water supply."

"Good gracious!" said Mrs. James. "Not again." She turned to her husband. "Les, put the radio on—"

"Can't put it on, Martha. No power."

"No, no, Betty's—the battery radio. I think it's in her third drawer down. You know, the Walkman."

Les James doubled up the paper and, taking a flashlight from the top of the fridge, moved off to get the radio.

"Les!"

His wife's shout struck James with the force of a physical blow. By the time he had returned to the kitchen, she was crumpled on the floor, the cat, having licked up some of the spilled water, already in convulsions, writhing in an agony the likes of which he had never seen, nor wanted to ever again.

In that tiny kitchen the threat to the eleven million people in New York had become real, and meanwhile, all over the state and indeed the nation, the threat was becoming a palpable nightmare of sudden yet agonized death, its full extent withheld from the American public not by any government decision, but by increasing power failures resulting in communication brownouts.

When the news of the explosion in Hillsboro first hit the streets, there was confusion over the name. Some reporters confused it with the Hillsview Reservoir. Others thought it was the Hillsboro of movie fame, the stand-in for Dayton, Tennessee, made famous or infamous, depending on the point of view, by its "Monkey Trial" in 1925, wherein newspaper luminary H. L. Mencken, writing for the *Boston Globe*, reported the clash of the Titans, when presidential hopeful William Jennings Bryan and the great defense attorney Clarence Darrow battled it out over the Tennessee school law forbidding the teaching of evolution.

But the Hillsboro in question was in Wisconsin, and there was no confusion on the part of the "sleeper" SPETS team, suspected by FBI investigators later to have consisted of two cells of three men each, which, using heavy eighty-one-millimeter mortars, blew the cesium clock building to hell, also knocking out the electric "feed-in" for the backup atomic clock.

Kirov's "Ballet" had begun. AT&T's big "tote board" in New Jersey went crazy, the byte—eight bits to a byte—slippage in every mainframe computer irreversible. This meant not only that Lana La Roche, née Brentwood, couldn't phone from Dutch Harbor to California to find out whether Frank Shirer was as yet in overseas B-52 training or had been caught in the helter-skelter sabotage that was apparently breaking out all over the U.S., but also that all defense computers and most phone lines were down.

In fact, Shirer was already en route to Nayoro, for

Freeman had sent out an urgent request for BUFFs. No one knew why, because while the "big ugly fat fellows" could bomb from thirty thousand feet outside most AA missile envelopes, all the pilots, including Frank, knew that you simply wouldn't have the accuracy from that height, and certainly not in the blizzard conditions.

In any event, even if the U.S. phone networks hadn't been shut down, Lana wouldn't have been told where Shirer was. But if the shutdown of all personal calls was a trial for the ordinary citizen, the Defense Department had a much more serious problem. *All* ICBM silo computers were down, including those inside NORAD's Cheyenne Mountain and those responsible for the prearranged coded "burst" messages to American submarines, like Robert Brentwood's USS *Reagan*, a dual purpose SSBN/SSN, ICBM/Hunter-Killer Sea Wolf II.

In the Pacific Northwest, in Washington State, another sub, the USS *Corpus Christi*, a 16,000-ton Trident II, her gold crew aboard, slid effortlessly through the long, moonlit race of water stretching out from the Bangor Base into Hood Canal. The pine-scented banks slipped by like spiked velvet, and the "boomer"—as they called the intercontinental ballistic missile Trident—headed out to join the First Pacific Fleet several thousand miles west nor'west of Bangor. She was to become part of the hectic American buildup and resupply of Second Army, or rather, one of the hidden protectors of the convoys racing to satisfy the enormous appetite for matériel created by the logistics of fighting a two-front war across the other side of the world.

The OOD—officer of the deck—Ben Cashell, reported, "Degaussing station coming up," informing the captain and the crew in the redded-out control room beneath the sail that the sub was entering the huge "magnetic wiping" shed which would temporarily erase the *Corpus Christi*'s telltale magnetic signature. At the very least, her signature would be sufficiently altered so that it couldn't be easily identified by any of the Siberian nuclear subs. Some of the Sibirs, as they were known by the U.S. submarines, had passive sonar arrays—big spools of transparent, oil-filled cable that housed listening mikes, which they trolled hundreds of yards behind them in the oceanic sound channels off the American west coast.

Cashell, a native of the drier regions of Texas before he graduated from Annapolis as the first black to be so rapidly promoted to executive officer aboard Tridents IIs, reveled in the sheer natural beauty of the deep-water sound, the fresh ocean smell mingling with that of the pine forests that swept right down to the sea, the moon a silver disk above the heavy, dark foliage of the timbered hillsides—all of it elemental in its mystery. He heard the depth readout from control and looked farther down at the bow, watching the thin line of phosphorescence, caused as much by the incoming tide as by the sub's egress speed, and he knew that soon, a moment he always savored—once they were beyond the sound and approaching patrol speed—the *Corpus Christi*'s thin line of foam would become a creamy bow wave before the ''cut-out'' speed. Then there would be no visible bow wave at all, just a continuous, oily-looking hump of water sliding over the forward section as the sub, carrying ten MIRV nuclear warheads on each of its twenty-four missiles—more than all the explosive power used in World War II—headed quietly out to deep water.

For some, the subs represented a monstrous intrusion into nature's realm, but for Cashell the ship immersed in the sea represented not a conflict, but a harmony between man and nature. Far from violating the integrity of the natural realm, the sub became part of it, its very shape—a giant forty-two-foot-wide, 560-foot-long cylinder with a bulbous bow like that of a great whale, and streamlined sail, diving planes, and pressure hull—moving in concert like the fins of a great fish in a perfect marriage of function and form. And because of this, unlike the older submarines of World War II, which had to make most of their torpedo attacks on the surface, the Tridents and their smaller cousins, the Sea Wolfs, attacked from below. Here even the enormous bulk of the 16,000-ton Trident, a whale compared to the smaller Sea Wolf, was as responsive as any marine mammal to the slightest change in the ocean's environment.

Corpus Christi was all but through the "chicken wire" of the degaussing station and when Cashell saw the light he thought it was a hunter's flashlight blink from shore. Then the starboard lookout yelled, "Incoming!" That's all Cashell remembered.

The first blink was followed by two others—three ninety-four-pound Hellfire antitank missiles.

No one in the sub's control was hit, but fourteen seamen on the forward starboard side were killed instantly when one of the sub's Mark-48 torpedoes exploded beneath them following the Hellfire's impact, the antitank missile ripping open the hull forward of the sail at the waterline, wiping out all bow-inset sonar sensors as well as gutting the torpedo room. Three more men were found dead, trapped in the tangled wreckage of the forward section's fourth level, another five having survived by being sucked out after the initial inrush of water which had doused fires immediately. As the sub had been on the surface, these five managed to swim ashore. But the sub, barely kept afloat by a chief of the boat who had quickly ordered all affected compartments sealed off from the rest of the ship, was effectively out of commission for what the Bremerton yard boss later estimated would be at least six months.

In San Diego the Aegis-equipped guided missile cruiser, the *Santa Fe*, had been sunk, the torpedoes used in the attack thought by both the CIA and FBI to have been two of three stolen from the San Diego Naval Yards during the Super Bowl game, the attention of perimeter guards diverted. Subsequent spectroscopic analysis, however, proved that the torpedoes, though definitely U.S. Mk-48s, had come from the Canadian west coast naval base of Esquimalt. Presumably they had been smuggled across at some point along the three-thousand-mile U.S.–Canada border by "illegals" who, like their cohorts in the U.S., had entered North America during the Gorbachev-Bush honeymoon, possibly having slipped in from a Russian trawler in for "repairs" at one of Canada's ports. The CIA in particular drew the president's attention to the "peculiar reluctance" of CSIS—Canadian Security Intelligence Service—to follow suspected illegals across their border into the U.S. "They're very good in Signals Intelligence, sir," reported presidential press secretary Trainor. "But when it comes to HUMINT . . ." He shook his head.

"Quite so, I'm afraid," agreed British liaison officer Brigadier General Soames, representing Her Majesty's government in the crisis. "Canadians are rather reserved in this area, I'm afraid. Not their line of country at all, really. They wait to be invited. RSVP, if you get my drift."

"I do," said President Mayne glumly. "Novosibirsk must love it."

"Oh yes. Novosibirsk, St. Petersburg—they're very fond of Ottawa. Home away from home. Cold as well."

The only thing seriously challenging the CIA's theory of the origins of the torpedoes was that the dredged remains of the two that had sunk *Santa Fe* and killed over 140 U.S. sailors indicated that several critical gearing sprockets had been constructed of nylex, a steel-hard plastic sheathed in fiberglass. The only reason for this would have been to make them undetectable at airports where, contrary to somber international agreement, metal detection scans of diplomatic bags were routinely carried out by CIA "ground crews." All of which would suggest that the two torpedoes could had been smuggled in by air, piece by piece. Whatever the reason, in a concomitant sabotage attack in San Diego, eight F-4 Phantoms were total write-offs, the forty-million-dollar-apiece aircraft destroyed not by the explosion of the airfield's ammunition dump, as was first reported, but by surface-to-surface handheld "shoot and forget" missiles of undetermined type, most likely twenty-one-pound, night-firing, U.S. Dragon antitank guided missiles with a one-thousand-yard effective range.

Out on the harbor another handheld missile struck only one of the densely packed planes in the forward starboard parking area of the carrier *John F. Kennedy*, but five

McDonnell Douglas F-18 Hornet fighters disintegrated as the fire from the first spewed out, engulfing the other four. Five men were killed on the carrier's deck, two in PRIFLY control, eleven injured forward of the island, and three were still unaccounted for. In all, a court-martial was a certainty for the senior officer on duty at the time, unless he could explain to the board of inquiry why, contrary to general practice, the five planes were parked on the flight deck instead of being distributed around various shore bases until the carrier had cleared port. The fact that one of the shore bases had been hit at about the same time would be no defense.

A motor pool's cyclone-wire fence at Fort Hood, Texas, was penetrated and twenty-five "Hummers," or "Humvees"—the army replacements for the old Jeep—were destroyed by fire. It was later discovered that this act of sabotage, however, was sheer vandalism by local teenagers, completely unconnected with the more highly organized and selective attacks launched in other parts of the country by now reactivated "sleepers."

Five thousand miles away, under cover of the blizzard, Minsky's six batteries of Siberian BM-21 multiple rocket launchers broke the cease-fire, unleashing their salvos at 1100 hours, delivering 2,160 122mm rockets on a quarter square mile within two and a half minutes—the most intense bombardment by MLRs, or tube artillery, since the Iraqi War.

For the American III Corps stationed at Port Baikal on the forward line of the cease-fire, along the southwestern edge of the lake, it was nothing less than a catastrophic eruption, high V's of jagged ice blocks, snow, and black frozen earth exploding in their midst. Over 230 were killed outright, hundreds more wounded by the hot, metallic rain of the shrapnel, scores of others concussed by the simultaneous pummeling of air that accompanied the massive rocket offensive. Within the next three minutes, by 1105 hours, the Americans' 155mm howitzers were returning fire, at least those whose crews had not been taken out by the Siberian MRL attack.

Ground sensors at III Corps HQ indicated Siberian armor moving east rapidly toward them, already deep into the DMZ. Over a hundred American Abrams M1A1 fifty-five-ton main battle tanks moved forward to meet them, another hundred opening fire from their revetment areas behind the frozen lake's treeline, their 120mm guns in defilade position, though the Siberian tanks' exact positions could not be ascertained because of the anti-infrared smoke screen created by Minsky's armored personnel carriers. Forward Siberian observers, however, *could* see the U.S. infrared blurs that were the III Corps echelons' exhausts, the Siberian observation point then directing the Siberian self-propelled 122mms as the latter opened fire in a sustained thunder whose shock waves denuded trees of snow in the taiga.

The U.S. M1A1s immediately returned fire, but their maximum four-thousand-meter range was of no avail, falling into dead air, the Siberians' self-propelled 122mms' thirteen-mile overreach putting Minsky's batteries well outside harm's way from the American tanks' fire.

Apache squadrons now rose en masse from behind the protective barrier of the 3,200-foot Primorskiy mountain range north of Port Baikal, heading low across the Angara River, intent on redressing the imbalance, and on the "hi-pole" Siberian radars the Apache gunships appeared like so many gnats.

"At least sixty," Minsky's aide informed him, all heading for the Siberian armor, obviously leaving the less agile and, for the helicopters at least, less dangerous, less mobile, self-propelled Siberian artillery until later, their first priority undoubtedly Minsky's scores of front-line T-80s.

The fate of the Apaches, however, only confirmed Freeman's countless warnings to Washington about how the cease-fire would prove to be nothing more than a time for the Siberians to dig in. Minsky's phalanx of AA guns and missile batteries, dug in and waiting beneath their snow "lizard" pattern camouflage nets, were about to create a bowel-chilling sense of déjà vu at American HQ in Khabarovsk, the frantic atmosphere of unrelenting radio traffic filling Freeman's control center with the nightmarish visions of the Siberians' deadly feint on the Never-Skovorodino road. There, fake inflatable Siberian tanks, lamps for infrared inside, had suckered Freeman's gunships into the Siberian-held territory where the Apaches were destroyed in a deadly crossfire of AA guns, missile batteries, and vertical area mines, bloodying Freeman's Second Army in what was the lowest point in the American pre-cease-fire campaign.

Freeman had been awakened as soon as the attack on Baikal was radioed through, and entering the din of the HQ Quonset at Khabarovsk, he was advised by Dick Norton that in addition to the attack on III Corps at Port Baikal, large formations of Siberian motorized infantry were moving north against III Corps from fifty miles south of Baikal, around Kultuk; and north of Baikal, a second Siberian-armor-led spearhead was materializing, heading south from Maloye Goloustnoye.

A schoolboy could have seen it was a pincer movement, as Freeman had predicted, designed to hit III Corps frontally and from both sides, to encircle the 36,000 men of American III Corps.

What to do about it, however, given the worsening blizzard conditions, was an entirely different matter. The problems were legion. Despite state-of-the-art Doppler radar, CAS—close air support—Freeman's immediate and obvious first step, wasn't possible now in the whiteout conditions. Unless he wanted to risk dozens of collisions between the fighters and the swarms of Apache gunships and other helicopters below, already rushing ammo resupply westward from Kabansk, eighty-five miles northeast of Baikal across the lake.

To add to his worries, Freeman was informed that patrols out of Kultuk near the cliff-top tunnels high above the lake, a small but important railhead held by a company under a Major Truet, were completely cut off from Port Baikal fifty miles to the north.

Freeman would have been even more worried had he known that many of the Siberians' three thousand attacking tanks were towing *Siamsky bliznets*—"Siamese twin"— T-72 mock-ups, infrared signatures from the hauled mock-ups being emitted through the use of cheap twelve-volt battery-powered heaters. This doubled the potential targets for the Apache gunships, at least for those that could manage to get below the whiteout or fly closer to the ground than could the fighters. A Hellfire optically tracked antitank round for each of these targets, even if the helos got through Baikal's AA ring defense, guaranteed the depletion of the Americans' already strained supply of the expensive ninety-five-pound missiles. The logistics involved in a battle area more than twice the size of Iraq were rapidly limiting Freeman's options.

CHAPTER SEVENTEEN

WHEN THE PLA guard came into the cell, he was smiling, telling Alexsandra Malof he had brought her some refreshment: *bai chi*—"white tea," he explained in perhaps the only English he knew, tipping up the thermos and handing her the hot water—without a speck of tea in it. "Ha! Ha!"

He knew she wouldn't think it funny, but he'd underes-

timated her energy despite having gone thirty-six hours
without food or water. Most prisoners were so cowed, they
had no strength left for a retort. He certainly wasn't used to
a mere woman prisoner causing trouble, but that's what he
got. With a flick of her wrist, she threw the boiling water
into his face, the completely unrelated thought racing across
her mind that the Chinese made the best thermoses in the
world. The moment he yelled, hands to his face, she kicked
him hard in the groin and he collapsed, the submachine gun
rattling on the damp flagstone floor. The last time she'd
seen a soldier prone was the Siberian who'd raped her in
Baikal. She lifted the wooden stool high above her and
brought it down on the man's head, the green cloth of his
PLA cap turning dark with blood in the dirty yellow light of
the passageway as she frantically pulled the slung AK-47
from his arm. She could hear footsteps—two, perhaps
three, guards—coming down the hall toward her cell. She
stood back from the door.

There were two of them. The cell exploded in cordite
smoke and the ripping tar-paper sound of the AK-47's
burst, both men hit, one already dead on the floor, the other
flung back against the corridor wall as if bodily lifted and
thrown by some giant hand.

She was running down the grimy corridor, her left hand
swishing the hair away from her eyes, right hand gripping the
submachine gun, her breath steam as she ran into the colder
air bleeding in from the entrance of the jail. As she reached
the door, she swung the AK-47 in the direction of the duty
guard's desk, and seeing he wasn't there, realized he must
have been one of the two she'd shot. When she pushed hard,
opening the door, the frigid air outside stung her.

Someone shouted, but she was already beyond the
penumbra of the lone arc light outside the jail—into the
dark, where she dropped the heavy gun in the snow and kept
running, glimpsing fog rising from the Songhua River by
Stalin Park on her left as it spread smokelike, coursing
eerily about the multicolored ice sculptures of Zhaolin Park.

One of the city's old Soviet onion-domed spires pierced a bluish blur of moon. Fog was everywhere, spilling out from the boat dock to Sankeshu Station. She could hear police whistles behind her. Glancing back, she glimpsed a dim shape—one of the ice sculptures, a dragon, headless in the fog.

Not knowing where to go—the foreign consulates friendly to America and its allies bound to be the first to be cordoned off—she paused in the pitch-black dampness, seeing the fog clearing, cloud swallowing the moon, and she leaned against a high wall, suddenly feeling dizzy from her exertion and weak from having gone so long without food or water.

She made the decision to go to the Guoji Fandian Hotel on Dazhi Street. Latov had taken her there a couple of times. The manager would no doubt recognize her—two barbarians for dinner—but wouldn't be surprised to see her, the hotel catering to many international tourists. If only she could get to a friendly foreigner who would get the message out about the massive Chinese buildup taking place via the Nanking Bridge. It was a long shot, but there would still be foreigners caught in China by the war, waiting for exit visas from the Public Security Bureau. It was risky, but if she did it with brio, she might succeed. If she did, she knew she would save thousands of American lives and hit back at Latov and his Chinese comrades. Their one big mistake—a typically Chinese delay, she thought—was not to have issued her immediately with the bright orange prison clothes which would have doomed any effort to simply walk into the lobby of the Fandian.

The first foreigner she saw as she entered was a small, blue-striped-suited man with moustache, bald head, and wrinkled brow—obviously a European. He wouldn't do. Even sitting he looked harried, a worrier, his gaze fixed on the lobby's slime-rimmed, dried-up fish pond, its fountain encrusted with a coppery greenish detritus, the man looking at it forlornly, as if his future was as bleak as that of the nonexistent fish.

A second man, an Indonesian, wearing a Muslim *songkok*

cap, his bags by the reception desk, looked more promising. Medium height, potbellied, smiling, talking with the Chinese clerk, he seemed at ease as he filled in the card, then pulled the English edition of *China Daily* from the pile on the counter and moved off toward the restaurant. Unhurried, he was skimming the front page with only a modicum of interest, turning the paper over, revealing a gold wristwatch as he did so. An affluent man, and Indonesia a neutral in the war. If she could get to him, maybe . . .

She decided it was too risky. His business connections with China would be too precious for him to risk doing anything for her. She might offer herself as the price—ask him to send the fax and wait for a confirmation of receipt before keeping her end of the bargain. But he could turn her in just as easily after. She could hear a siren in the distance.

A porter—early twenties by the look of him, Eurasian—was being bawled out by the manager, who was calling him a *lan xuesheng*—"a lazy student"—and "a turtle," the worst kind of insult, telling him to hurry up and take the Indonesian's suitcases up to a second-floor room. The incident convinced Alexsandra that the Indonesian would be a bad choice, for only someone who traveled a lot in China would choose the second floor over the higher, more scenic suites above the ground-level smog. Room service was quicker on the second floor, and when the elevators broke down, with or without an accompanying fire, you had a chance to get out from the second floor, the fire escapes any farther up sure to be too decrepit and ill-maintained to work. She watched the student sullenly pick up the suitcase, heard him murmur, *"Cao nide xing!"*—Fuck your name!—to the empty fish pond, and followed him up the first flight of stairs to the second floor, eager to get to him before he reached the two women floor minders who, in stained white smocks, would be smiling, asking her room number so as to jot it down for future reference—fornication with unregistered guests being strictly forbidden in the people's hotels.

"*Wo shi Meiguo ren,*" I am an American, she whispered to the porter, the energy she'd expended catching up with him on the stairs exhausting her. "*Ni keyi bangmang ma?*" Can you help me?

He took her to be an American. She was a big nose and white—her Chinese fractured. He glanced at her but did not pause, and kept walking down the stained red paisley carpet that clashed incongruously with a Guilin mountain design of turquoise silk tapestry that covered most of the waterstained wall. The air was heavy with stale cigarette smoke, and this, combined with the kerosene-fired heat, made it difficult for her to breathe. The two white-jacketed minders folding linen were putting it desultorily on a trolley. One of them asked her the room number.

"*Er ling si,*" 204, said the porter grumpily as he strode on impatiently with the heavy suitcases.

Once he opened the door, she stepped inside and closed it behind him. She began to speak. Quickly he held up his finger, shaking his head vigorously. It was her fatigue that had made her so momentarily careless. Of course, not all foreign-designated rooms would be bugged, but you could never be certain which ones the Public Security Bureau had decided to listen to on any given night. He indicated the bathroom and tried to flush the toilet. It didn't work and it took him a minute to reconnect the chain to the pull lever.

When finally it gurgled loudly and coughed, she moved closer to him. "I want you to take this to the Baltic legations," she told him, keeping her voice as low as possible despite the noise of the toilet. The Estonians, Lithuanians, and Latvians, she knew, shared the same trade legation in Harbin, and if a message could be got to them, they would love nothing better than to pass it on to the Americans. Only now she realized her mistake, the sudden alarm in his face telling her he'd completely misunderstood, having thought she, like most foreigners, had wanted to change money, getting more yuan on the black market than from the official exchange rate. Perhaps he didn't even know there was a war going on yet. Beijing's iron-fist control over the media made it more likely than not.

"I cannot give you money," she told him truthfully. "I have none. They took it all away at—" He stared at her. Did he understand or not? She felt unable to go on, her legs trembling from fatigue and tension. Seeing a thermos on the table by the frost-covered window, she poured a cup and, her fingers shaking now, tore open a bag of green tea, spilling half of it, stirring the leaves frantically, watching them swell, and blowing on the hot liquid. The student porter looked at his watch, as if that would somehow enlighten him about what had happened. Alexsandra sipped the tea. It was glorious. It seemed to give her instant strength. Sitting on the edge of the bed, seeing her disheveled appearance in the wall mirror, she put down the tea, turned to him and slowly, without taking her eyes off his, opened her blouse.

He looked away, then looked back, walked toward her, and buried his head between her breasts like a child.

"Will you help me?" she intoned, stroking his head gently. He stood back abruptly, looking down at the floor, ashamed, then nodded. Quickly she scribbled a note and gave it to him. "The Baltic legation. You must throw it over the wall. You understand? Be careful—it will be surrounded."

"And you?" Now he dared to look up at her. "You cannot stay here."

"No."

"You must take a taxi."

"Where?"

"The place I will give you. They will help hide you from the police."

She smiled, doing up her blouse. "You are not a turtle."

It was the only time he smiled. "You must wait here. I will go for a taxi."

"I have no money for a taxi—"

"No matter. We must help each other."

At that moment Alexsandra could have cried, taken him in her arms, made love—done anything that would make this young man happy.

"Wait here," he instructed her. "I will send up a friend and he will take you to the taxi stand down from the hotel." He walked toward the door, hesitated, glancing back—the noise of the toilet subsiding. He walked closer to her. "You must not walk out too quickly. It will raise suspicion. You must be—"

"Natural," she said. "Unafraid."

"Just so."

Ten minutes passed, her fear more intense with every second, every footfall she heard. Soon there was the sound of a trolley—more footsteps, fading; then knocking on the door. Her heart jolted. What a fool she'd been—but where else could she have gone? The door opened. Another porter, a smaller, stockier man, a little older than the other, beckoned to her quickly while looking down the corridor.

Once in the lobby, he led her to a taxi, and though she tried to walk more slowly than usual, the intense cold quickened her pace and in a moment she was inside the taxi and whisked out into the night. How the Chinese loved secrecy—it came with their mother's milk, from having to contend all their lives with the paranoia of the regime. "I will let you out next street," said the driver, whom she could not see beyond his dim outline behind the wheel. "You go out next street—to your left. There will be another taxi waiting. Ask to go to Stalin Park for the festivities."

Before she could answer, the cab had stopped. She knew nothing of festivities in Stalin Park—it must be thirty below, the only people out those watching the ice sculptures and—

The driver reached over and quickly pushed open the door. "Out!"

The cab was gone. Alexsandra found herself alone again in the darkness as she started hesitantly to walk down the two blocks, crusted snow crunching beneath her feet so loudly that she felt everyone in the street must hear her. She saw the dark shape of another cab. Sensing a trap, she stopped. The air was pungent with coal smoke that made the fog seem heavy and gritty, even more suffocating than it had been in the hotel. She glimpsed a small flame illuminate the darkness, the waiting cab driver lighting a cigarette. She breathed in deeply, felt giddy, almost slipping on an icy patch as she steered herself resolutely but nervously toward the cab. Her whole body felt in the grip of a deep, damp cold, and she thought of the tea she'd had at the hotel— Long Jin. She would remember the tea forever, even if—

"Ganjin!" Hurry up! came the driver's rough command, and the back door flew open. She stood there, hesitating, trying to think.

"Stalin Park—yes?" said the driver.

"Yes."

"Then hop in. We must hurry!"

As they drove off, the taxi quickly gaining speed, she thought it impossible that he could find his way through the dimly lit, fog-swirling world, but at one point she could see the speedometer needle quivering on a hundred kilometers an hour. They hit a dip and for a second she was suspended, her head tapping the car's roof before she crashed back down on the seat. She smelled and felt dust all about her, as granular as that from the Gobi Desert. The car braked. A Mao-suited figure—a woman, how old it was impossible to tell—opened the door.

"Come," and the next moment she found herself following the bent black figure down a narrow hutong to a small mud brick house pungent with the smell of something overripe, on the verge of rotting, and vegetables frying. She was shown to a single-cell-sized room, a lone tallow candle burning on a small wall table, flickering in a draft.

"You must stay here," the woman told her. "The busybodies are everywhere. Worse now there is war."

The busybodies, she found out, as the old woman brought her tea, were the neighborhood grannies—nosey parkers with red armbands. Fanatically loyal to the party and much more feared than their male counterparts, these were the bullies of the one-child-a-family rule and other party edicts, spies who, despite their age or because of it, were much more dangerous than the police—for their job, and one they followed with zeal, was to know everything that was going on with everyone in the street.

"Sooner or later they would find out," the old woman told her. "So we will try to get you north as quickly as we can."

"Who are you?" asked Alexsandra, cupping the tea as much for warmth as for nourishment. "I mean—not your name—but why do you do this? You are so kind to a stranger."

"Tiananmen," said the woman simply. "There are many like us," and suddenly a burden was upon her and she shuffled away.

Young Xiao Ping, a kitchen helper at the Fandian Hotel who had been sent to the Baltic legation by the porter to deliver the note, had no difficulty whatsoever. Despite snow now falling heavily, and the poor street lighting as in all Chinese cities—the recent order of the Harbin people's council to dim streetlamps still further adding fuel to the rumors of war—Xiao Ping simply wrapped the message about the Nanking Bridge in a clean linen pillowcase from the Fandian Hotel, the hotel's monogram carefully removed, and tossed it over the legation wall, well away from the main gate, which might be under surveillance. The rock-weighted pillowcase landed softly in the compound on the other side of the wall. It hadn't occurred to Xiao Ping to wrap it in any other color than white, and in any case by morning it was completely covered with snow.

"Where is she now?" asked Latov, seated at the Siberian consulate table at the banquet celebrating the Chinese lunar new year, the Public Security Bureau man standing behind him, in a waiter's uniform, informing Latov that the PSB car had had difficulty following her from the hotel in the fog. To have followed the cab too closely would have given the PSB car away.

"You idiots!" said Latov, though still smiling, raising his glass as his Chinese host began an interminable speech about the new and glorious socialist brotherhood between the new United Siberian Republic and the People's Republic of China.

"Don't worry, comrade," the PSB man assured him. "We know the general area. All we have to do is carry out a house-to-house search. And we have already identified at least two contacts she made at the hotel. Two porters."

"Have you picked them up?"

"No, we were waiting until we told—"

"Do so. Immediately."

"Must I remind you, comrade," replied the PSB man, offended by the Siberian's tone, "that you are our guest in Harbin?"

Latov did not even deign to turn about, bored though he was with his Chinese host's babbling about socialist brotherhood. "And *you* forget, comrade," he told the PSB man, "that we've purposely let her escape so that we might break this entire northern ring of spies and saboteurs. If you fail, it'll be your head in Beijing, comrade."

"And yours, comrade, in Novosibirsk."

"Where are my men?" snapped Latov. He meant the Black Berets.

"At your legation."

"Tell them I want them to be in on the search for her. They know what she looks like."

It was a stupid thing to say, and Latov regretted it the moment he had uttered it, feeling the PSB man's contempt almost immediately.

"We have no difficulty recognizing foreigners, comrade."

"You mean barbarians?" said Latov.

"As you wish."

"I want my men involved in the search," insisted Latov. "You find out who's hiding her. But when that's done, she's to be brought back to me. That was the agreement. She's a Siberian national."

"She's a Siberian whore."

"As you wish, but she is *my* whore and I will punish her."

"We will see."

"You'll do as you're told, comrade, or else you'll find yourself on the Amur front."

"You mean the Black Dragon front, comrade?"

"It's forty below up there, comrade."

"We Chinese are used to the cold."

Latov gave a contemptuous snort and reached for his wine. "It's forty below and the Americans are shooting at you, comrade."

"Not for long," said the PSB man. "We know how to deal with Americans. We defeated them in Korea. They ran away."

"Well . . ." Latov conceded, finally seeing the sniping was getting them nowhere. "That's one thing we can agree on, comrade. We both want to defeat the Americans. So you find the girl and let my men return her to me. Agreed?" Latov waited. "I apologize for any untoward remark."

The PSB man nodded curtly. He knew the barbarian didn't mean it, but nevertheless it allowed the PSB to save face. Nodding abruptly, he left.

"What was all that about?" Latov's wife asked him.

"Ah—" said Latov dismissively, reaching for black fungus, a Manchurian delicacy, "a prisoner giving us trouble."

"Since when are you concerned with Chinese prisoners?"

"I'm not. She's Siberian."

"One of our people?" said Latov's wife, surprised.

"No. A Jew."

"Oh—Stalin knew what to do with *them*."

CHAPTER EIGHTEEN

IN LESS THAN two hours American III Corps had suffered twenty percent casualties, seven thousand killed or wounded, against Yesov's first echelons. Anything over thirty percent casualty level and the U.S. commanders knew that III Corps would no longer have enough fire power to withstand an onslaught by a second echelon Siberian attack. The printout on the analysis computers in Freeman's Khabarovsk headquarters was unequivocal. The LER—loss exchange ratio—of 22.6:1 would mean that the troops manning the 155mm howitzers and the M-1 tanks on Lake Baikal's southwestern shore would have to destroy twenty-three Russian guns for every American gun lost merely to stay even. To make matters worse, 155mm batteries had to be diverted left and right of III Corps' defense line—that is, south and north of III Corps' front at Baikal—in order to meet Yesov's flanking attacks. This meant in the next hour that as the tracks of the M-1 tanks fought to grip the watery mirror finish of the lake—translucent in places down to thirty and sixty feet—the cold statistics of the loss exchange ratio jumped to 50:1.

The Apaches were swarming now over the vast, snow-covered taiga from the Primorskiy range, their 4,400-yard fire-and-forget Hellfire air-to-ground missiles streaking down in crimson balls, taking out thirty-two targets, Siberian T-80s, in spectacular explosions, of which fourteen were actual tanks going up. The remaining eighteen were *poddelki*—fakes—Yesov's vertical aerial mines and mobile mounted ZSU twenty-three-millimeter Shilko AA gun quads and Kuadrat surface-to-air missiles taking out eleven of the sixty Apaches.

It was such a loss rate that Freeman knew he couldn't sustain III Corps' present position, the situation aggravated by the blizzard, which prevented any effective close fighter air support. And so, his counterattack effort in tatters almost as quickly as he had launched it, Freeman, in an order that all but choked him, instructed the remaining 29,000 men of III Corps to effect forthwith a fighting withdrawal across the seventeen-mile-wide lake and to set up a second line of defense in the taiga along the lake's eastern shore. Hopefully it would give him time to rush in support, both men and matériel, from Khabarovsk, and Skovorodino, the latter atop the Amur River hump.

It was the only thing Freeman could do. And Yesov knew it. Refusing to yield to Minsky's impatience, the marshal had held his massive, taiga-hidden formations in place, waiting for the temperature to fall while the lake, remaining frozen, would result in a less hard ice/air interface. This widened the V's, or the cone-shaped eruptions, of the Siberians' howitzers exploding on the lake, sending more shards of splinter ice and white-hot metal fragments even lower to the ground over an even wider area.

The perimeter of the American III Corps was now a bloody mess of body parts, interspersed with the junk of shattered matériel and gutted tanks burning fiercely, the explosions of their fifty rounds of high explosive, squash head, and discarding sabot ammo killing and maiming more Americans than Yesov's howitzers.

In the U.S., the latest and, to date, most devastating attack of Operation Ballet was that experienced by the U.S. Navy during a five-minute heavy mortar barrage of Miramar Naval Air Station. This attack totally destroyed or put out of action an entire squadron of twenty-six F-15E Strike Eagles—a confidence-shattering display for the American "top guns" of just how vulnerable high-tech aircraft were to the determined and highly trained infiltration units. All ten men in the two SPETS mortar crews were killed by perimeter guards at Miramar, but not before shrapnel from their last 200mm, fifty-five-pound rounds sliced open the fuel tanks of two Lockheed "Fat Alberts." The cavernous transports, replete with the new snow/taiga pattern, replacing their old NATO green/gray/khaki splotch camouflage, were in the process of loading 650 marines to relieve British Commonwealth cease-fire troops guarding the Allies' R&R barracks along the Amur River outside Khabarovsk. In the explosion, so enormous local residents thought it was a nuclear bomb, 570 marines died, some killed by their own ammunition set off by the fire, all of them charred beyond recognition, most, teeth showing through the black leathery grins, still strapped to their seats.

Apart from the terrible loss of life, it wasn't the millions of dollars wasted in destroyed equipment that shook Americans, who well understood their industrial capacity was still the best in the world. But all over the country the ghosts of Vietnam arose in the American psyche, invaded by memories of the infamous Tet Offensive, when the North Vietnamese Army, through infiltrators, had brought the war to the Americans' doorsteps in Saigon, a turning point in the only war America had lost. Worse, the attacks on the sub at Bangor in Washington State and on the carrier *John F. Kennedy* in San Diego were the first on the West Coast since the Second World War, when one of the big Japanese I-class subs had shelled the oil installations near Santa Barbara, and Point Estevan on Canada's Vancouver Island. That enemy was again bringing the war to the forty-eight contiguous U.S. states, and the repercussions of this shook Washington to its foundations.

Trainor couldn't remember the president being so angry. As Mayne subconsciously massaged his forehead, reading the reports streaming in from Hillsboro, San Diego, Bangor, and Miramar, his aide knew, if no one else did, that the

President of the United States was on the verge of a migraine attack, so that the next file Trainor brought him contained two sumatriptan pills taped to a report of the marines who had been killed in the attack on Miramar. The sumatriptan were perfectly legal and, Trainor knew, were prescribed for more than one senator, but in the rough-and-tumble world of politics, Trainor was as discreet as possible with the medication, fearing that some boozy congressman, doing three times as much damage to his body with his afterwork martinis, might make political capital of it.

It was a grim morning all around, the simultaneous successes of the attacks on Hillsboro, Bangor, Miramar, and the rest proof positive that Novosibirsk's network of "sleepers" were wreaking havoc on American morale, quite apart from the human and matériel carnage they'd already inflicted on America's ability to wage war.

"How long till I go on?" Mayne asked Trainor.

"Two minutes, Mr. President."

Mayne closed the latest damage reports and went over his speech once more. As the red light went on and Mayne cleared his throat and shuffled his papers, readying for his extraordinary address to the nation, David Brentwood, Lana Brentwood's younger brother, attached to Britain's SAS and now on a long-awaited honeymoon in the Canadian Rockies, was being urgently summoned, like so many other Americans, for immediate return to active service.

Across the Pacific it was dusk along the Black Dragon River on China's northern border, and Colonel Soong, commanding the Fourth Battalion of the People's Liberation Army's Shenyang XVI Corps, was readying his nine hundred men to overrun the position just north of Manzhouli, from where the Chinese army had first been shelled and which had precipitated their entry into the war. Soong had designated five attack points so as to break up the enemy's fire, which he estimated was battalion size with three batteries of eight guns each, together with a headquarters battery containing communication and fire control.

With about ten men per gun crew plus ammunition and support troops, the U.S. battalion on the hill, Soong estimated, would number around five hundred men.

It had been a fierce fight, with the enemy's 155mms having the advantage of the high ground even as they had pulled back to the horseshoe-shaped summit of the mountain designated A-7 in the Argunskiy range, and Soong knew it would become even fiercer, the dead lying everywhere as he ordered his three companies to regroup for yet another assault. Nearby, off to his left, he saw what he guessed must have been one of the most forward American fire-control spotters, the man's torso missing an arm, his other sliced neatly through. The American's shoulder patch, stuck to his shoulder's shattered bone and showing the screaming eagle of the Eighty-first Airborne, had been cut neatly in half by shrapnel, as if sliced through with a band saw, blood congealing purple against the snow in the fading light.

Soong took it as a good omen, and, crouching, made his way through the dead clumps of uprooted aspen and pine, their earth-clogged roots dark against the now freezing snow, the acrid stench of cordite and the singed-meat smell of burning bodies heavy in the air. Soong was so occupied making sure the slope leading down to the river, still a half mile ahead, wasn't mined, that he didn't notice a mottled-green-camouflaged enemy helo—American—a Blackhawk UH-60A, hung up in tall pine a hundred yards to his right.

Normally Soong would have been back with his battalion HQ staff and not so far forward with his troops, but the capture of A-7 Mountain had become a top priority of General Cheng's, and indeed PLA photographers had been sent to record the event. The battle of the Black Dragon River, which Beijing was now calling it—"Black Dragon" having much stronger patriotic connotations than "Mount A-7"—was a misnomer, as southwest of the Amur hump near A-7 there was no Amur. But for Beijing the battle for A-7 came to symbolize the war for the Amur hump as a whole, and a victory on the mountain would be a showcase victory early in the war against the Americans.

Colonel Soong, now ordering up heavy mortars, was determined to lead the final attack. He was disappointed that there seemed to be so few dead about, no more than a dozen or so, suggesting that despite the distances involved from Chita to the northwest and from Khabarovsk to the east, the Americans might already have managed to withdraw most of the battery crews and spiked the guns. If so, the fierce battle so far might now suddenly give way to a hollow victory, one that, if the enemy had managed to be snatched from the surrounding Chinese battalions, would deny Cheng the crushing total victory he and Beijing so urgently desired. As if in answer, he heard a shout from a company commander off to his left, a long burst of AK-47 fire, and then the steady *chump, chump, chump* of a U.S. Marine Mk-19 throwing out high-velocity forty-millimeter anti-personnel/armor-piercing grenades from its linked belts no more than a thousand meters away, from some unseen clearing deep within the taiga.

At a rate of fire of over 350 rounds per minute, the American grenade gun was a deadly weapon in any situation. In defense it was particularly formidable, capable of breaking up the most determined infantry assault, its persistent dull thumping filling in the vacuum created by the temporary lull in 155mm artillery fire, the latter having dropped off in intensity under the ox-horn-shaped advance of the Shenyang army's IX Corps.

Exhorting his men not to stop, Soong moved forward into an area of taiga that had the strange appearance of having suffered a forest fire without the trees being burned, as leaves and whole branches were shredded by the flaying shrapnel of the grenades. He heard a shuffle of air, felt the increasing pressure on his eardrums, and dove to ground, using the body of a dead comrade as protection. Only now could he properly see the American chopper wedged high in the branches of two trees, its shattered rotors no doubt responsible in part for the fallen foliage. When he saw a body in it move—the pilot's—and a fall of snow, he instinctively raised his Kalashnikov, but it was the whole chopper moving.

Whether from concussion of the incoming 155mms or from the wind groaning through the trees, or both, the American helo slid, tail first, another foot or two, then stopped, its scraping noise against the branches barely ceasing before he spotted the body moving again against the angle at which the aircraft was leaning. Firing a long burst, Soong saw the body jerking in violent spasm, and watched the chopper suddenly plunge another ten feet, tail first, upended in the pine, the now dead pilot still in harness, head and arms dangling from the twisted fuselage, blood pouring from his neck, splattering the snow and branches beneath.

It wasn't that Soong particularly hated Americans, that he hadn't even thought of taking the American captive, but there were no real provisions for POWs. In Beijing's opinion they cost too much.

As Soong's battalion moved forward, taking out the grenade gun at high cost—over seventeen dead—the Shenyang infantry came across more American choppers that had been brought down by the highly effective ChiCom antiaircraft fire. Equally as deadly, in Soong's view, was the fact that the enemy battery itself was so far from American air bases in Siberia, that even after succeeding with hazardous air-to-air refueling, the would-be rescue helicopters could have had only enough petrol for several—no more than five to ten—minutes or so over the besieged summit. The upturned chopper in the trees nearest him moved again, and instinctively he raised his Kalashnikov and swung toward it, but the only thing moving was the chopper itself, a local gust sending the craft crashing down.

Advancing once again, Soong concluded from the relatively few enemy dead he was now seeing, and the failed chopper rescue, that Shenyang's XVI Corps was on the tail of a panicked American withdrawal to A-7's summit. He could have no idea that five thousand miles away across the

Pacific, many in the continental United States itself were on the brink of such panic.

CHAPTER NINETEEN

". . . MY FELLOW AMERICANS, nothing is more repugnant to our sense of justice and fair play than the curtailing of individual rights. But the unprecedented and coordinated enemy attacks on our ports and other bases *within* the United States not only constitute a grave threat to the vital supply lines to our troops in Siberia, but also constitute a grave threat to all of us here at home.''

When Trainor reached the press room, another aide, a younger man, wide-eyed and pasty-faced from the cataclysm of bad news that was spewing through the White House fax machines, asked, "What the hell are they doing? I mean—the military attacks, yes, but now we've got news of forest fires in California, the southwest. Man-made. I mean what the hell do they hope to achieve by—''

"Chaos,'' answered Trainor simply. "On a scale we've never seen before.'' Trainor glanced up at the bank of press room TVs. It was probably the first presidential speech in years written entirely by the chief executive himself.

". . . This administration therefore has no alternative but to invoke the Emergency Powers Act. Under this act, stricter access and exit controls for all U.S. ports, civil and military facilities and bases will immediately be put into effect. These are already in operation in most of our bases around the world, but they will be extended to all bases in Hawaii and within the continental United States itself. This will mean that normal policing, arrest, and detention procedures will have to be shortened so as to best use our limited resources and manpower in combatting sabotage within.''

The president was looking straight at his audience. ''I realize this will involve inconveniences for many of us, and the implementation of restrictions on individual liberty, which is as repugnant to you as it is to me. But there are times, and this is one of them, when, if a free society is to remain free, it must be prepared to expect as much from those at home as those we send to do our battles abroad— for those at home to do as much as they can to support and protect those brave men and women who are at this very moment fighting and dying in Siberia and on the sea lanes leading to that embattled place.

''. . . And so, beginning at ten P.M. Eastern Standard Time tomorrow, the following federal agencies will be authorized to use extraordinary measures to meet the threat of extraordinary times. The Federal Bureau of Investigation . . .''

A sound man, earphones comically high on his head, cords trailing behind him, appeared from the dark fringe of the klieg lights and handed another sheaf of papers to Trainor, returning from the press room. The Wisconsin sub ''farm,'' a vast acreage of VLF—very low frequency— aerial array for contacting submarines at sea, had been attacked. Apparently, a pack of stray dogs and cats had been let loose at several points on the northern side, setting vibration and heat sensors off, diverting most of the security guards' attention from the real point of entry on the southern perimeter, which had been penetrated by saboteurs; someone later reported having seen a weather forecast news chopper in the area. In any event, the demolition on the farm for the second time in the war was such that already nine of the North Pacific sub fleet, including the USS *Reagan*, had not received their burst messages updating the positions of submarine friends and foes.

Hawkeye TACAMOS—take charge and move out aircraft—had been ordered aloft from the West Coast stations to take over the always tricky task of making radio contact with the subs at their next rendezvous points. But it was always more complicated than it seemed. The Hawkeyes' rotodomes' 360-degree sweeps had ranges of up to three hundred miles, with overlap patterns so they could cover all nine subs that had already missed their first call, together with the overlap patterns necessary to reach another six nuclear subs in the Pacific due for call-in within the next twelve hours. This meant the endurance of the half-dozen allocated planes and their crews would be stretched to the limit—that quite simply, some of the subs would not be reached. Meanwhile, a large Siberian fleet was now in the process of gathering in the fog-shrouded seas where the Kuro Siwo, or Japanese current, meets the ice-cold waters south of the Aleutians.

The New York Times argued that the president was "overreacting" to the sabotage, while the *Washington Post* editorial agreed with the adoption of the Emergency Powers Act, the *Post* tempering its approval, however, with the warning that "emergency contingency planning must not usurp reasoned restraint," that there was a danger of the restriction of individual liberties becoming a "habit all too easy for a majority to accept as the new norm." The *Washington Post* also joined the *Times*, the *Christian Science Monitor*, the *L.A. Times*, and other major newspapers in recommending that an "oversight body" representing all segments of society should be established as soon as possible to monitor the Emergency Powers Act.

While looking soberly concerned, "wholeheartedly" welcoming the idea of oversight committees, the country's police chiefs were ecstatic, but played it down in front of the press conferences.

For the first time since the Vietnam War, editorial offices raged with argument—calm debate no longer possible in the atmosphere of growing panic—about whether or not to release certain stories and sow further fear. One holdout was Peter Ovan, the editor of a small New Hampshire daily, the *Logan Examiner*. The short, balding editor argued that a tip he'd received, confirmed by a second source, about a small team of arsonists who had been able to start a fire that gutted the Lockheed Stealth fighter plant at Burbank, California, should be told to the American people. "If the government can't protect one of our most vital defense plants," argued Ovan, "then what hope've we got?"

"Hell," responded the Pentagon chief of PR, "anyone can start a fire, Mr. Ovan."

"That supposed to comfort me, Major?" responded Ovan, shifting the phone from one shoulder to another, tearing off a fax of a reported sniper attack on the approach road to the "secret" Savannah River atomic weapons production plant in South Carolina. It was a better story, in Ovan's opinion, for the truth was that if he wanted to nail the administration for incompetence, the Stealth fire story wasn't the best. Besides, he'd already run a column on the open secret among the pilots of the 450th Tactical Group at Nelles Air Force Base in Nevada that the twin-engined multimillion-dollar Stealth fighter, with swept wings and V tail, had been flown at night since 1983 and was responsible for many UFO sightings over the mountains and deserts of the western United States. More importantly, in the pilots' opinion, it was perhaps the most overrated plane in history. Inherently unstable and therefore remarkably maneuverable, kept on the edge by its computers, the Stealth fighter hadn't proved to be the ultimate "radar evader" after all. The Soviets had designed low frequency detection sets that could pick up the fighters almost as quickly as they could the Stealth B-2 bomber. It was one of the reasons the B-52 program had been drastically cut, ostensibly for "economic reasons."

As it turned out, Ovan didn't run either the Stealth or the Savannah River sniper stories in the *Logan Examiner*, for at 9:00 A.M., just before he was to go to press, his wife rang, saying there was an urgent Federal Express overnight courier envelope for him from Washington, D.C.

Cautious by nature, and made more so, given the rash of

reported crazies and sabotage, Ovan asked his wife the sender's address. He could hear the rustle of Ida handling the plastic envelope. "Ida! Don't open it!"

"I'm not. I'm looking for an—it's from a Mr. Carlisle. Internal Revenue Service, Washington."

"Since when do the IRS use courier?" Ovan asked.

"Since most of the phones aren't working," said Ida.

"All right, have Billy run it down here. I'll go over it with the rod." He meant the metal detector he kept in the office as a precaution against crank mail.

"You be careful," said Ida. "All this violence in New York." To Ida, all violence happened in New York— another country. "I think you should call the sheriff's office."

Ovan considered it for a moment, his pride battling the pressure of his deadline. Still, the IRS gave him a turn. Rumor was, everyone gets audited sometime. "All right. Have Billy take it to the sheriff's office first."

Seventeen minutes later the local police car pulled up outside the *Logan Examiner*. When the sheriff walked in, Ovan was busy tapping the computer keys, selecting type size for the leader.

"Pete, we opened your package."

"Then I guess it wasn't a bomb?" Ovan replied wryly.

"Sort of."

Ovan's fingers stopped on the keyboard. "What you mean, 'sort of'?"

The sheriff opened the plastic bag and showed him. It was a fish wrapped in an old copy of the *Logan Examiner*.

Ovan's hands came off the keys. "You tell Ida about this?"

"No one 'cept the deputy. I told your Billy to stay up at the station."

"You checked the sender?" asked Ovan. "Carlisle— IRS?"

"Yep. Put a radio call through all the way to Washington. Phones there aren't working too good."

"Well?" said Ovan impatiently.

"No such person. Besides, Pete, IRS don't send dead fish."

"How 'bout live ones?" reparteed Ovan, but he didn't think it was funny himself. He thanked the sheriff for calling personally, asking him not to tell Billy.

Ovan's assistant, a young, freckle-faced coed, Mary, had just finished trimming the ads as he walked over to the window and pulled out a cigarette. He always asked Mary if she minded whether he smoked, and she always said no, she didn't, when they both knew she did. But this time he didn't ask. He just lit up and inhaled deeply, looking out on the sunlit folds of virginal winter snow—deep and crisp and even, he thought. "Drop the leader," he said glumly.

Mary looked up, surprised. "The story about the Stealth—"

"Do as I say," he snapped. "We'll run that NBA payoff scam instead." He exhaled, bluish smoke filling the small room. "Everyone likes baseball."

"*Basket*ball," Mary quietly corrected him.

But he hadn't heard her. He was furious, and rang the CIA public relations major whose staff had been ringing the newspapers to hold back the Stealth sabotage story. The major was polite, given Ovan's tirade about receiving the dead fish.

"Mr. Ovan—if you'll let me speak for a moment, sir . . ."

"Go on, then!" grumped Ovan finally.

"We don't operate that way, sir. I'm not going to pretend that I'm not glad you're holding the story, but we don't work that way, Mr. Ovan."

"I shouldn't damn well think so," said Ovan, his voice now an asthmatic wheeze. "Christ, that's just the kind of thing we're fighting against over there, goddamn it! In Siberia!"

"Exactly," concurred the major. "Look, we'll have the FBI—this kind of thing is really their jurisdiction—look into it, if you like."

"Yes I would."

"Fine. I'll have them contact you as soon as possible."

"Appreciate it," said Ovan brusquely, but grateful nevertheless.

When the major hung up, he shook his hand as if it had been on fire. "Boy, was he steamed."

The petite second lieutenant nodded. "I could hear him from here. Did he buy it?"

"Yeah. Hook, line, and sinker. He won't print." The major paused. "You didn't leave anything did you?"

"Nothing," answered the lieutenant. "Dumped everything. Plastic gloves—everything."

"Good!" and they went into their little Federal Express routine, laughing. "When it *absolutely! positively!* has to be there overnight . . ."

Later that day the editor of the *Atlanta Journal* in Georgia received an anonymous tip that in addition to a sniper attack on the road to the Savannah River plant, there had been two explosions near its three nuclear reactors. None had been perforated, but a truck carrying thirty drums of nuclear waste was blown clear off the road. At least four of the drums had ruptured, spilling their deadly poison, which, in a heavy rainfall, was now believed to have entered the water table through the porous soil.

The editor of the *Journal*, upon being paid a visit by the CIA after running the story, said he wouldn't give the name of the tipster even if he knew it.

"Was it from New England?" the CIA asked. "From Logan?"

"Who's Logan?"

"Place in New England."

The editor shook his head. "We get all kinds of courier mail from all over the country. Especially now, the phone systems are so—"

"Yeah, yeah," said the CIA agent, and left.

In the maze of Brooklyn's back streets and in the vandalized cores of dozens of American inner cities that had decayed in the seventies, been rejuvenated in the eighties, only to die again the nineties, the dealers and users passed through America's night with impunity, the police out-numbered and often outgunned—if not by the accuracy, then by the sheer number of weapons on the street. Most of all the police were consistently outmaneuvered by the high-priced lawyers who had the gunmen back out on the streets often in less time than it had taken for the police to book them.

In a Brooklyn alley not far from the bridge, there was a tinny noise of underground ventilation, gray steam bleeding into the night, many of the users already shooting up in the galleries, freebasing, the real "badasses" on crack levitat-ing, not knowing where they were or what they were doing, TVs left on, screens flickering blue, as the president's speech containing the phrases "arrest on reasonable suspi-cion" and "suspension of habeas corpus" was being broadcast. So many stations were carrying the address that some of the "dudes" uptown, the suppliers like Bobby "Bad-Ass" Duguid, were cussing and instructing their boys to turn off "that prezeedential shit, man," Duguid demanding "video" instead—his favorite, "Wrestlin' Witches."

Duguid's preppy lawyer detested wresting, especially the degrading sight of women in mud. In fact he hated everything about Bobby Duguid except the vast amounts of money he had to launder for Bobby and "muh associates—'Smith, Smith and Wesson.' Ha! Ha! Ha!" The young lawyer liked something else, too—the raw power of a man like Duguid, who could daily "rip off the system," as Bobby so accurately put it, and not even "touch the money, man." Bobby made it a point of never carrying cash, and let it be known in the intricate, psychosis-webbed world of drugs that he never carried it. His lawyer handled that, a sight Bobby loved to see—fine striped shirts, his "whitey," with the Cartier watches and Rockport shoes, handling the lucre with tear-off surgical gloves, terrified of catching "dis-eeze from muh clientele!"

At ten-thirty, outside one of the dozens of Harlem

galleries owned and supplied by Duguid and his associates, the four men in the unmarked police car from the Sixth Precinct, the Alamo, knew that if they didn't move within the next five minutes, even the crackheads who didn't know what planet they were on would slip away into the garbage-tainted air. But they'd been ordered to wait. "No cart before the friggin' horse," as their chief had put it. "When we hit, it's all got to happen simultaneously. I don't want that roach in his flamingo-pink whorehouse uptown to get tipped off. Praise God for President Mayne. I'll vote for him till I die."

There had been a rough chorus of heartfelt amens.

The steam was still rising, going this way and that like some living thing fuming but in confusion, a red and blue neon slashing the vaporous cloud every four seconds, infusing it with a surrealistic look, hard on the eyes.

"No need for all this palaver," said one of the four-member squad, the short-barrel, pump-action shotgun in his right hand. "What's the difference? With this new Emergency Powers thing, we could pick him up in the morning, right? We could be home getting sleep by now."

"Johnny," said a detached, in-charge voice from the backseat, "once these friggin' lawyers hear Mayne's speech, they're gonna go ape and tip off every slimeball in the territory."

"So where can they go?" asked the policeman with the shotgun. "We shut all the fucking airports to Canada and Mexico."

"They don't have to leave the country," said the man from the back. "Just hide out till the emergency power's repealed. Then we'll be back to square—"

The radio crackled, its volume low. "Car forty-five. A code one-eight-seven on Jefferson one-four-eight-nine. Corner store—7-Eleven." A 187 was a homicide, Jefferson, the other side of town. It was the "get ready" code to foil the smartasses who might be listening in on police radios.

"All right, Phil," said the lieutenant in the backseat, patting the man in the front who had the shotgun. "You do the kick. I'll be on your left, Marty to your right. José stays with the car. Got it?"

"Got it."

The radio crackled again. "Ah, car forty-five, that one-eight-seven on Jefferson's bein' looked after." It meant the alley behind the shooting gallery was now covered.

"Right! Remember," said the lieutenant, "no one out to the back door or you'll get your balls blown off. Drabinsky's got a pump back there and he's so fucking short he can't aim any higher than your prick."

"How the hell he get on the force?" whispered Phil, opening the front passenger door.

"Aerobics," said the detective. "Stretches, Simmons tapes, ah-one and ah-two and ah—"

As they slipped through the steam, the detective felt his stomach muscles tightening. Sometimes the kick didn't work, then it was a shmoozle and you ended up having to either shoot the friggin' lock off or use the ram log. By the time you got in, they'd all rushed for the back, and then it got really dangerous. Finding their way blocked, they turned and headed back, spaced out and wild, knowing they were trapped and that if they rushed you, most of them would probably get away. "At Duguid's uptown," said Phil quietly, "I'll be they've got Jeeves answering the door." He was nervous but he loved it. Tonight especially, "reasonable suspicion" meant no announcement, no badge shit, no Miranda.

Entering the crumbling brownstone, they heard an odd scrabbling noise, and the gut-thumping beat of rock in the air. There was a candle halfway up the stairs—the power long disconnected.

Phil saw a soft light issuing from beneath the second floor door and heard the scrabbling noise again—a rat scurrying into the darkness over newspapers on the stairs. He could smell human excrement. They walked up slowly, the candle flickering, now only the slit of light beneath the door to see by, the stink becoming worse.

"Ready?" whispered Phil.

"Ready."

When Phil hit the door, it was so rotten it caved in. He was on the floor looking up through a cloud of dust and crud, the air reeking of dirty bodies, maybe fifteen or more junkies, some astonished, cigarettes, bottles held motionless in their hands, stilled for a second before they broke for the rear door. There was movement on the left side of the hallway. Phil's flashlight picked out a man, his pants down. The man's right hand flashed to his pocket. Phil fired twice, the blast lifting the man off the floor, slamming him against a doorjamb. A woman, breasts flying, came running through the dust-filled gloom, screaming her head off, tried to touch the man but couldn't—blood everywhere. Now they were all coming back from a rear door—a mad-eyed sprinter, dirty T-shirt and jeans, some red thing in his hair, a shooter in each hand. He got off two wild rounds before they took him out, too. The man behind dropped his gun and raised his hands but was knocked flat by a scrawny teenager, BORN TO RAISE HELL on his chest. Phil gave him the butt, full face, and he was down. Phil heard his left ear ringing like an express train as the lieutenant fired twice.

"Be cool! Be cool!" came a voice from the hysteria of candlelight and dust.

"Put her out!" yelled Phil. One of the crackheads—a Latin—was on fire, her blouse ablaze, but no one did anything. Phil stepped forward, knocked her down, covered her with his jacket and began stomping out flame, the dust rising like talc, the smell of singed hair joining the sickly sweet smell of "dude rube," the local wino rotgut.

"Hey, man!" It was a white male, transvestite, early thirties, cadaverous, unshaven, wild-eyed. "Where's your warrant?"

"Hey!" said another. "That's right, brother. You ain't got no right to bust in—"

"You know," said Phil, standing up, resting his .38 on the white one's nose, "I think this one's a saboteur, Lieutenant."

"Armed as well," said Marty, extracting a switchblade from the man's handbag.

"What the—"

"Shut your face, Greta!" Phil said. "Now all of you against the wall—move!" He and the lieutenant started kicking legs apart. The alley team came in looking disappointed. "You bastards have all the fun," said Drabinsky. "All we got was tiddly-dick—some crackhead trying to hide in a friggin' garbage can."

"Well," said Phil, clicking the cuffs on the last of the addicts, "I wouldn't sweat it, Drab. Downtown says we can put in for all the overtime we need." Drabinsky followed Phil out, helping to steer the last cracker down the spotlighted stairs past the other cops, the high, spitting crackle of walkie-talkies calling in the meat wagons through the hysteria of the crackers screaming, an arm shooter smiling, eyes glazed, not caring.

"Drabinsky," said Phil, "for the first time in this country we're gonna clean house."

Drabinsky shifted the weight of the shotgun to the other hand. "Is it true? We can bring 'em in, lock 'em up for three months without—"

"No," said Phil. "Six."

"Six weeks or six months?"

"Months!" said Phil. "Six fucking months! Everybody's gonna get well, Drab. Give us all the time we need. You think you've seen plea bargaining—it'll be a buyer's market for songbirds." Taking off the flak jacket, he put on his police jacket and zipped it up. "How do you like them apples?"

"Christ," said Drabinsky, the full implications washing over him. "What I wouldn't give to be in Miami."

"Greedy!" Phil said, smacking him on the shoulder. "That's your trouble."

"Damn right!"

When they got back to the precinct, they thought there was a party on. Bobby "Bad-Ass" Duguid, the tall black

man in flamingo-pink suit, hat, and white mink coat, was in
the cage with his lawyer and assorted entourage.

"His hair's all wet," said Phil. Duguid's eyes were afire
with rage, his lawyer, pale white, beside him.

"Yeah," agreed the sergeant. "I'm very worried about
that, Phil, because if Mr. Duguid gets a cold, we could be
sued."

"You motherfuckers aren't gonna get away with this.
You hear me, whitey?"

Another policeman, his Puerto Rican accent cutting
through the hubbub, handed Phil a wax-paper package.
"Guess what we found him doin'?"

"In his Jacuzzi," said Phil, "wanking himself off?"

"No," said another cop. "*She* was wanking him."

"Where's *she*?" asked Phil.

"Downstairs," said the Puerto Rican cop. "But lookee
here. Have a look at the package."

"My, my," said Phil. "Sarge, you see what we have
here? Plastique."

"You mother!" yelled Duguid, a hand coming out of his
mink through the bars. "That's a plant and you know it."

"Well then, Mr. Duguid," said the sergeant, "we'll
have to put this aside for evidence." It joined another two
plastic bags, large ones, heavy-duty, each bag containing
firearms, including two Uzis, four AK-47s, and a grenade
launcher.

Under the Emergency Powers Act, Mr. Duguid was
confined for six months, pending "further investigations,"
including intensive audit by the IRS and investigation into
the illegal importation of prohibited semiautomatic and
automatic weapons.

Asked about reports of widespread persecution on "Good
Morning America,' the FBI spokesperson, Jennifer Lean,
replied, "Sir, we've known for years that ever since the
lessening of tensions between Premier Gorbachev and
President Bush, a large number of 'illegals'—spies and

potential saboteurs—have been placed in strategic areas for just such a situation. We also know that these people did not come with large amounts of money. This would, of course, have immediately raised suspicion, or at least alerted the immigration officials. The question, then—''

''You mean,'' interjected the interviewer, ''that the money used to purchase such weapons was drug related— that 'illegals' are or were involved with using drug money to finance their clandestine war efforts?''

''The money had to come from somewhere,'' said the FBI spokesperson, ''incredibilized,'' as she later put it to her colleagues, that the TV host could be so dumb. It was pointed out to her, however, that a good interviewer isn't afraid to appear naive so they can get the guest to give them answers they want.

Privately, most of the FBI agents believed the ''illegals'' had brought in all the money they needed by diplomatic pouch years before, and that drug money wasn't involved.

While Duguid was being photographed, scowling, to update his file, twelve miles south of Port Baikal, Jason Thomis of Charlie Company—or the ''forgotten company,'' as they were calling themselves—from III Corps' Second Infantry Battalion, was digging in with the rest of his platoon along the rail line that ran parallel to the cliffs from between Baikal and Kultuk at the southernmost end of the lake. Thomis's company had high, precipitous ice-sheathed cliffs behind them, the surface of the frozen lake hundreds of feet below. It allowed them to look down on the blizzard-covered lake as far north as Baikal, the thick whiteness about Baikal trembling and flashing crimson with the thunder of war. Occasionally they could spot A-10 Thunderbolts coming from the far eastern side of the lake after protective F-15 Strike Eagles had penetrated the screen of MiG-29 Fulcrums that had come screaming eastward out of Irkutsk, led by the Siberian ace, Sergei Marchenko. But for the American Eagles, having won the furball with the MiGs and driving the Fulcrums off, it was all in vain. For though the A-10 Thunderbolts were now free to dive beneath the blizzard to engage the enemy ground targets, they reappeared only seconds later without having fired a shot, their pilots confounded by the zero visibility, Minsky's forward Siberian armored spearheads being so close to the fleeing Americans that it was near impossible to tell friend from foe.

The U.S. M-60 and M-1 tanks were so close in most cases to the Siberian armor that the A-10s were forced to rise and circle like frustrated birds of prey waiting for the weather to clear, which it didn't. And all the while the A-10s continued to burn up their precious Avgas as the battle raged beneath them. Now and then an A-10 would make another attempt, only to reemerge, frustrated from being unable to differentiate between the American and Siberian tanks. Many of the American and the pursuing Siberian units were so near one another that even accurate fire from the A-10s' thirty-millimeter nose cannons, while it would have no doubt set Siberian tanks ablaze, would, through the resultant explosions, have done as much or even more injury to the American ground troops.

Now and then Thomis could see a bulge of dull orange light in the cotton-wool-like cover of the blizzard, the backflash of Siberian-acquired Aerospatiale, MILAN 2,500-yard and HOT 5,000-yard-range antitank missiles. The few that didn't hit the American targets failed not because they had encountered the kind of thick, anti-infrared smoke that Minsky's troops were using as cover, but because the armored U.S. target had crashed through the splitting ice opened up by the pounding of Minsky's eighteen-gun batteries of amphibious M-1974 122mm howitzers.

In addition to hearing the howitzers' distant thumps, Thomis and his buddies could see contrails of the Siberians' Multiple Rocket launches arcing momentarily above the blizzard. Unleashed in ripple fire sequence, the fifteen-foot-long, three-hundred-kilogram, twenty-four-mile-range HE and fragmentation rockets were being fired from scores of twenty-ton ZIL-135 trucks which, with sixteen missiles apiece, created *plotnost*, or saturation density, completely devastating a square mile at a time. It was the equivalent of several battalions of field guns sustaining rapid fire for ten minutes, and four times as great as the mind-numbing pounding of Berlin in World War II by the Red Army's Katusha rockets.

In addition to this, Yesov's northern arm, each of his batallions equipped with eighteen mobile trailers of forty B-M21 rocket tube launchers, was unleashing 720-round salvos of the 122mm projectiles screaming down into the American positions. The scarlet trails of the rockets, momentarily visible in the swirling fog and snow, appeared to Thomis and the rest of Charlie Company like hundreds of ribbons before disappearing, the rockets crashing in thunderous unison, momentarily swelling the blizzard in huge blisters of flame.

"Where in the hell's *our* MLRs?" Thomis asked no one in particular as the rumble and crash of the artillery and rocket barrages rolled across the icy plain up through the fog, the broken ice-floe sea beneath. All was quiet for the moment, but the northward storm was rolling ever southward, coming closer, the deceptively lazy orange and green tracer arcing out of the swirling white candy-floss roof above the lake only making the danger more, not less ominous.

"Coming up from Khabarovsk," answered Valdez, manning the Squad Automatic Weapon next to him, traversing the SAW left to right so that its arc of fire, should there be an attack from the taiga, would be able to swing through 180 degrees without endangering any of the other men in the foxholes.

"Anyway," said another C Company infantryman, "no friggin' good firing our MLRs into that lot. Take out as many of our boys as they would the Siberians."

"Then how about the fucking Siberians?" said Thomis agitatedly. "Their rockets must be hitting their own guys."

"Sibirs don't mind taking out a few of their own."

"Neither does Freeman," said someone.

"Bullshit!" snapped a corporal. "He had to do that on Ratmanov, man. Without the air strike, he'd have lost more marines than he saved."

"Yeah, well, you weren't there, were you, Ricky boy?"

"Knock it off, you guys!" interjected the platoon's sergeant. "Cut the yap and watch your front."

"What the fuck for?" challenged Thomis. "What are we gonna do if armor comes out of those trees, Sarge? Throw fuckin' snowballs at it?"

"The Hueys'll be here by then," answered the sergeant.

"Oh yeah?" pressed Thomis. "When?"

"Soon."

But none came. Thomis and his buddies cared nothing about the logistical nightmare that had descended upon Freeman's headquarters—that was HQ's problem. All that second platoon, C Company, wanted was "out," and no amount of explanation by their CO, Major Truet, could make them see that Freeman, as CINCFE—Commander in Chief Far East—had to divide his already overextended chopper forces, especially his Apache gunships, to try to inflict what damage they could west of the lake on Minsky's airfields while ordering what Chinook and Huey transports he had south to the Chinese border. The simple fact was that Charlie Company, the farthest south of III Corps, was simply too far to reach, given that those choppers not assigned to attack the Siberians' thrust, now in progress on III Corps' main front around Port Baikal, were urgently needed to stem the ChiCom breakthrough farther south.

CHAPTER TWENTY

IN AND AROUND the battle of Port Baikal at the southern end of the lake, American III Corps, reeling from the forward elements of Yesov's right hook, spearheaded by Minsky's armored regiments, was rapidly approaching disaster. For the Americans it was a carnage unparalleled in American arms, for not since the marines' fighting retreat from Chosin Reservoir in the Korean War had there been such a savaging of Americans at close quarters. At one point an entire company, Bravo, from III Corps' motorized division, was lost within five minutes, disappearing into the lake in a massive sinkhole as the ice, already *treshchina-pauk*—"spider splintered," as the Siberians called it—by the pounding of their artillery, suddenly gave way beneath the 103-ton American HETS—heavy equipment transport rigs—and armor that tumbled into the five-thousand-foot deep.

Twenty-three men who had managed to escape the sinking trucks clambered frantically for a grip hold on jagged chunks of car-sized ice floating in the freshwater sea. Other clumps of water-sodden men, having been spilled from the trucks and trailer units as vehicles careened off the ice, were now slithering on the mirrored finish of the floes like so many stricken animals. Many of them died like animals, clubbed to death by OMON and SPETS commandos, who, preferring not to waste ammunition or give their positions away by shooting, moved like ghosts through the blizzard, their white overlays making them indistinguishable from the Americans whom they beat to death, referring

to it in their reports to Yesov's HQ as the *reznya tyuleney*—
"seal slaughter." To be sure that the American public,
especially U.S. students eligible for the draft, got the
message, SPETS video close-ups of American dead, though
not how they died, were quickly sold to French TV and
CBN by Novosibirsk's Ministry of Information. Within an
hour photographs of hideously bluish-black bodies of American dead were flashed around the world, the French TV
anchorman, André Focault, in Paris, talking "of the unnecessary and undeniable carnage, the direst result of General
Douglas Freeman's violation of the ceasefire . . . spawned
by American arrogance in Asia."

The La Roche networks and newspapers had a field day
with the stills of decapitated Americans littering the blood-
smeared floes, the La Roche tabloids calling for Freeman's
"immediate recall." Only the Jewish lobby, many of whom
knew what it meant to live under Siberian domination in the
Jewish Autonomous Oblast, spoke out against what they
called the blatant bias of the networks in showing "such
revolting pictures of our dead."

The networks said they were just reporting the news.

But whatever was said, or shown on the networks,
nothing could really convey the full horror of the reality, the
smell of disemboweled Americans, or rather what was left
of them after the Siberian 203mm howitzers rained down on
III Corps' retreating east flank, a retreat that area commanders were frankly reporting to Freeman was becoming a
"rout." Except for three rifle companies, over three hundred men cut off in the vicinity of S-Three, southernmost of
the Siberian breakthroughs, the American line had simply
collapsed as men, panicked by the world of shifting,
disintegrating ice beneath them, fought each other to get on
the few remaining trucks, which in turn were slowed by the
necessity of having to put on chains, the blizzard dumping
fresh snow on the lake, the ice around and in the corridor
marked out for III Corps disintegrating like splintered glass
as Minsky's 203mm kept up their relentless barrage, the

OMONs and SPETS on the periphery clubbing and drowning any III Corps stragglers.

North and south of III Corps, the rolling barrages of the Siberian artillery kept up, Yesov's pincers already beginning to close the trap. Minsky's guns midway between the north and south pincers "overshot" III Corps, creating a virtual moat between the main body of the retreating Americans and the western shore of the lake, still ten miles eastward. The fury of the Siberian bear, as Yesov was being called, and Minsky's Slutsk division, was being described by many as unstoppable—the Siberian pincers moving as inexorably as two lava flows of a volcano, "spewing death," as Iran Radio ecstatically proclaimed, on the Americans, who were "futilely" trying to outrun its fury. In fact more Siberians were wounded, though not as many killed, than Americans. But for Freeman's III Corps, given the overwhelming number of Siberian divisions—over forty-four in all, versus the Americans' eleven—it was an unmitigated disaster. The mood was quickly conveyed to everybody else in Second Army, including David Brentwood, who, like his former SAS/D colleagues-in-arms— Lou Salvini from Brooklyn, and the Welshman, "Choir" Williams—was now arriving in Khabarovsk in response to Freeman's order for the SAS/D team to reassemble. Another comrade of David, the profane Aussie Lewis, was already in Khabarovsk on what he thought was going to be some well-deserved R&R.

David Brentwood was in Khabarovsk less than half an hour before he realized how grim the situation was, how III Corps' retreat was a humiliation that eclipsed any prior victory by Second Army before the cease-fire. To make matters worse, while temperatures north of the lake around Yakutsk continued plummeting, those around the Amur hump in the areas between latitude forty-two and fifty, covering northeastern China, Mongolia, and southern Siberia, were continuing to rise in Yesov's favor, as his meterological offices had predicted. These warmer temperatures were turning the already inadequate sixteen-hundred-mile Siberian Khabarovsk and Baikal roadway into quagmires for the U.S. armor, artillery, and trucks trying to relieve Baikal. The sixty-three-ton M1A1s atop their heavy extractor/transporters, and the eleven-thousand-pound M978 road tankers needed to satisfy the voracious two-gallon-per-mile thirst of the M-1, along with the hundreds of ten-ton trucks hauling vitally needed spare parts, were all bogging down into the "slush stew," as Norton called it.

When the survivors of the decimated III Corps began arriving at the naval hospital at Dutch Harbor, Alaska, Lana Brentwood's fear for Frank Shirer grew proportionately. She thought she had seen it all earlier in the war—the terribly deformed burn victims of ships that had been hit by missiles, resulting superheated temperatures melting faces like wax or suffocating them in toxic smoke. Others, like her brother Ray, were considered the unluckiest of all, having lost part of their face because of either fire or deadly AG—aboveground—submunitions, needle-crammed bomb-lets detonated while in the air directly over a target. Ray's face had been partially reconstructed through surgery by laser, the very kind of technology that had ironically allowed enemy pilots like the Siberian ace Sergei March-enko to have so accurately delivered their laser glide bombs against the American ships.

As Lana saw more and more men being carried in on the stretchers, she felt a growing sense of helplessness, and knew that the lucky ones had been those who had died on the ice floes in hypothermia's final, perversely warm, sleep. The men being brought in here at Dutch Harbor would have to undergo months of pain-filled surgery during facial reconstruction and limb amputation—if they survived that long. Of course, a few, she knew, would come through it stronger than before—like Ray, who had the "stick-to-itiveness," as her father used to describe it, to fight the pain as well as the deep depression and, worst of all, the hatred of one's own image in the mirror. Ray had come back—not merely to survive, but to go on, after being decorated for surface attacks against enemy subs off California. Robert, too, also navy, captain of the USS *Reagan*, and young David, a Marine Corps graduate now with the joint British/American SAS/Delta commandos, were of the same stuff. Always pushing themselves. Lana was as dismayed by her brothers as she was proud of them. No matter what anyone said, she was convinced there was something very different about men's and women's psychological makeup. Even her father, who first wanted Robert to rest on his laurels after winning the Navy Cross for action above and beyond the call of duty in the terrible Arctic Hunter/Killer battles off Spitzbergen Trench, was now speaking admiringly of Robert's decision, after a near-miss escape from a ruptured SSN during the Arctic sub battles, to volunteer for SEAL duty—considered the toughest in the navy. Not only had Robert upgraded the "escape" drills, but he had submitted his name for the SAL, Special Assignment List.

Young David was no better, Lana thought proudly. Quieter than either Ray or Robert, who was oldest, he'd been bitten by the same warrior bug. All three were married, David just, Ray with two children, and Robert's wife Rosemary with one on the way. So what made them do it? Hadn't they done enough? Lana thought, too, of Frank—well, of course he was no better, just as anxious to go off into danger—to prove what? None were fools—all had admitted to her in their different ways, though certainly not among themselves, that their fear in action sometimes all but paralyzed them. So why did they do it? Was it no more than sibling rivalry? Still, that didn't explain Frank. Her anger at them was her love—for she admired them enormously at the same time, as she did Frank. Whatever the reason, they were brave, and unlike the sleazeballs of Jay La Roche et al., selfishness had no part of it.

When the young lieutenant from Freeman's headquarters found the Australian, Lewis, in full winter combat uniform

complete with white overlay, his face covered in white
camouflage lotion against the reflection of the weak spring
sun from the snow, Lewis was perfectly still, the stock of
his beloved Haskins M500 single-shot, bolt-action, sniper
rifle firm against his cheek as he took steady aim through the
rifle's ten-power scope. Only one of its .50-caliber bullets
would be needed to take out a man at a distance of 1.2
miles. An enemy would be hit before he ever heard the
sharp crack, the depleted uranium slug exploding his head
like a melon. A combination HE and incendiary bullet from
the same Haskins was capable of striking a much bigger
target, like a chopper, exploding its fuel tank, which Lewis
had amply demonstrated against a Hind A gunship when the
Siberian chopper had followed the SAS/Delta team during
their attack on the midget sub pens.

"Sergeant Lewis?" Freeman's young lieutenant inquired.

"Who are you, mate?" asked Lewis, not stirring a
muscle, the Haskins straight as a die, betraying no movement.

"Lieutenant Stimson, sir, General Freeman's—"

"All right, all right—shush now, and for Gawd's sake
get yer loaf down. Heard you a bloody mile away. Not
exactly Captain Thunderbolt, are ya?"

Young Stimson was nonplussed. "Captain Thunderbolt?" He thought of an A-10.

"Yeah—Thunderbolt," repeated Lewis, still not mov-
ing. "Bushranger—y'know—highwayman back 'ome.
Robbed the bloody government and kept it for himself.
That's the ticket, eh? What's on your mind?"

"General Freeman's HQ—"

"Uh-oh," said Aussie, still not moving. "Bloody trouble . . ."

Stimson didn't know whether the Australian was referring
to Freeman or his target—whatever it was.

"Ah, I don't under—" began Stimson.

" 'Ere," said Lewis as he rolled away from the Haskins,

slapping out the bipod legs, his impish grin made fierce-looking by the camouflage cream. "Go on, 'ave a Captain Cook. Polar bears!"

Stimson had heard Australians spoke another language, but he got the gist of it, lay down on the patch of snow and lifted the rifle.

"Fuzz button's on your right," instructed Lewis, and in a second the blobs, probably a quarter mile away, suddenly jumped into focus. It was a woman, or rather one part of her, that Lewis had zeroed in on.

"How'd you like to grab onto those, mate?" he asked young Stimson. "Biggest nungas I've ever seen. Whadda ya reckon?"

Stimson was stunned by the magnification—the woman's bust completely filling the scope. Then she turned and he caught a glimpse of her face. The contrast from what he'd expected was so striking, his eye started back from the scope and he looked up incredulously at the Australian. "She's . . ." He didn't know quite how to put it for a second. "Ugly!"

"You reckon?" said Aussie, who in a second was down by the rifle on the offside, using his left eye to sight. "Ah, she's not that bad, son. Call 'emselves Polar Bear Club. Skinny-dip through the fucking ice."

Stimson was standing up, brushing the snow off him. "She's—She's got a moustache!"

"Aw, don't be fussy, mate! Give her a Gillette for a present, I will. Fix her up in a flash. Anyway, it's not 'er bloody moustache I'm interested in." Lewis winked.

Stimson was still trying to regain his composure as an officer and a gentleman.

"Her tits, mate!" said Lewis. "Didn't you see 'em? *Magnificent*. I don't want one of those skinny birds—fucking model. I want big nungas." Lewis thrust his hands, bowl shaped, out in front of him. "To here—know what I mean?"

"I get the general idea."

Lewis bent over, snapped the cover on the sight, and

clipped the bipod legs beneath the barrel. "How long you been over here, Stimmo?"

"Two months."

"*Two*—no wonder you're particular," said Aussie. "Listen, mate—that's the first bird I've seen worth looking at. That Yesov—the bastard—he's hiding 'em all somewhere. Shipped all their younger women west. Conscription, you see. You remember that. If we're heading back into Baikal—you remember that." The Aussie paused. " 'Course, back there big tits probably mean a bra full of hand grenades comin' at you. Gotta be careful." He glanced back down the river. "I agree with you 'bout Olga's moustache." He made a face. "Hairy armpits, too—hairy armpits are the limit, Stimmo. Pong too much. Right? Still—all the same in the dark, eh?"

Stimson had never met an Australian before. He'd heard they could be rough, but—

"So what's Freeman want?"

"Don't know. I'm just the gofer."

"No hint?"

"No hint."

"Well, that's nice, isn't it? Here I am, R and R—well-deserved, I might add—and first time Yesov farts, I'm called up. I tell you, Stimmo," said Lewis, smacking the young American on the back, "it's diabolical. What's your first name, mate?"

As a mere lieutenant, Stimson didn't exactly stand on ceremony, but after all, he was HQ staff and he'd never been so casually addressed by an NCO before. Nevertheless, he found himself answering, "Raymond," before he knew it.

Grinning, the gregarious Australian put out his hand. "Goodo, Ray. Everyone calls me Aussie."

Stimson nodded.

"Well, Ray," said Aussie, "I just hope there are Sheilas wherever we're goin'."

"I doubt it."

"Thought you said you didn't know?"

"Well, no, I don't, but I don't think you'll be going back home."

"Yeah, well—you're probably right there." They walked over the crunching snow toward Stimson's Humvee. "Another Aussie mate and me were billeted on an English estate," began Lewis as they climbed in and buckled up. "Before the war—in training down at Hereford. Anyway, this Pommie sergeant—a Brit—tells my mate, 'You Aussies are too crude. Got no subtlety. Watch me,' he says. So we watch this Brit Lothario chatting up the lady of the manor, nattering on about nature, the farm, how nature's grand, hinting that the mating season wouldn't be far off. So my mate, a corporal from Mundubbera—says he gets the Brit's message, you see—like you have to sort of introduce the idea of sex more gradual, subtlelike. Talk about nature and stuff—like you just don't hit it, wham! Right?"

"Right," said Stimson, driving over the potholes back to Freeman's HQ.

"Yeah, right," continued Aussie. "Well, my corporal gets this idea, see—like how to approach the lady more indirectly, see if he could get a bit. So he goes into the barn that night and paints a gee-gee—a horse—green."

Stimson looked across at Lewis.

"Yeah," Lewis assured him. "*Green*. Anyway, in the morning everyone gets up for breakfast, wandering down past the manor house. The lady of the manor's up as usual, smiling and greeting us. My mate watches her go up to the paddock as usual and sidles up next to her, lights a cigarette as she's looking out at the animals. 'Good morning, my lady,' he says, real polite like—tips his hat.

" 'Morning,' she says, and my mate gives one of our blokes the office."

"The office?" asks Stimson.

"The office—the signal."

"Oh—"

"Yeah—so, bam! Barn door opens and out runs the gee-gee. My mate turns to the lady and says, real casual like, 'Look—a green horse! How about a fuck?' "

Stimson was appalled. Lewis doubled up, barely able to hold the rifle steady in the Humvee. Stimson was shaking his head. For a few seconds he actually felt sorry for the Siberians. "You're sick, man."

"Bullshit!" said Aussie, one hand gripping the roll bar. The Siberian roads were unbelievably bad. "I'm horny."

Stimson didn't know what to make of it all, but then he didn't know what had gone before, the SAS/Delta training quite simply the toughest in the world. In the SAS there were no drill instructors screaming at you; they talked softly—the training did it all. With over an eighty percent failure rate, only the toughest men managed to climb Wales' Brecon Beacons in gale conditions with ninety-pound packs of bricks, every brick numbered. Only the toughest could survive being forced to live off the land, having to eat rats raw—the slightest smoke, if you cooked them, being a dead giveaway—and learning to live for days in a shallow trench, not moving, defecating by pushing it down slowly to the slightly deeper depression dug in the trench.

The SAS had been unknown until May 6, 1980, when millions sat enthralled before their TV sets all over the world, watching as the SAS commandos stormed the Iranian embassy in London, freeing the hostages in a dazzling, blitzkrieglike display of rappeling, stun grenade and machine gun assault. And yet the SAS ability to immediately distinguish a hostage from a terrorist, the latter often changing places at the last minute in the hope of confusing would-be rescuers, was only one of their skills. In order to merely pass the course, an SAS trooper had to be able to enter a room, shoot, kill, and be capable of rolling, clearing a jammed gun, and come up shooting dead on target within seconds. They were men whose natural dispositions lay in self-reliance, but who paradoxically were required to get along as a team.

But young Stimson knew little or none of this, and had seen only the wild, slightly ridiculous side of a man whom death had stalked from Ratmanov Island to Baikal. And not all, he knew, were like Lewis. David Brentwood, about Stimson's own age, they said, was quiet, reserved, more like the SAS Welshman they called Choir Williams, and like Salvini, the American Delta commando, both of whom were now also on their way to Freeman's HQ.

Near Kultuk, Thomis, hunched in his foxhole, was complaining again, brushing fresh snow off his white overlay. "Let's get out of these friggin' foxholes while we still got the breath."

"Where you gonna go, Thomis?" asked Valdez, fingering the safety on the SAW. "Frappin' great cliff behind you, man."

"Yeah, well, let's pull back into those railway tunnels. Least we'd get some cover."

"Oh yeah?" posited Emory, who hailed from Georgia. "Those tunnels, man, they're just big coffins waiting for you."

"Hey listen, Georgia—I'd rather have a ton o' fucking concrete over my head than this friggin' snow hole. This ain't gonna stop shit!"

The sergeant let them bitch. It wasn't as if they'd give away their position to the Siberians, who must know it already. Besides, he'd sent patrols out.

Emory thought he heard a creaking noise—but he'd been hearing creaking noises, "like tanks," all night despite the fact that Charlie Company's forward patrols and those from the combat support company strung out farther north along the rail line had reported no enemy in sight.

"Holy Toledo!" said Valdez. "Will you look at that!" No one had to—the red tails of the Siberian MLRs north of them streaking out from Minsky's southernmost flank were arcing out of the fog higher above the lake, their fiery parabolas, seen only briefly above the fog before they disappeared, followed by more speckling in the blizzard, like explosions of firecrackers beneath some vast sheet, where Thomis knew Americans were dying.

Only three seconds later, which told Charlie Company the MLRs were hitting about forty miles away, would they hear the sound of the MLR explosions amid the steady rumble of the big self-propelled Siberian 203mms and the sounds, like wood splitting, of more fracture zones opening up in the lake's ice cover, trapping so many Americans in the retreat.

"The Siberians were in the rail tunnels," said Valdez, "near Port Baikal, where they had those midget subs on the rail tracks, ready to slide 'em into the lake. Tunnels didn't help them none when that SAS/Delta team hit 'em."

"So?" charged Thomis.

"So they got roasted, man. Southern-fried. That Brentwood guy and his outfit popped an AT round in that tunnel, and *boom!* Scratch one midget."

"Lucky shot!" said Thomis unconvincingly.

"I thought there were two Brentwood guys in that attack," said Emory. "One SAS, the other in the navy or—"

"Two Brentwoods? Three?" said Thomis, spitting into the snow. "What's the difference, man?"

"I heard there was three of 'em—in the family, I mean."

"So the three of them are fucking nuts!" growled Thomis, stamping his feet, the snow having melted beneath his boots, so that he had to bunch up snow in front of his foxhole to make his shoulder position against the M-16 more comfortable. "I'd still rather be in one of those tunnels—get some concrete covering my ass—than stuck out here like a fucking tree."

"Tunnels are fucking death traps," said Valdez. "Concussion'd pop your eyeballs."

"So you been told." Thomis looked away, knowing he'd been caught out on a fundamental point. He knew Valdez was technically right about concussion in a shelter, but knowing Valdez was right didn't matter. Psychologically, being stuck in a foxhole was a hell of a lot worse, as far as Thomis was concerned. "Huh! Way I heard it, it was a lucky shot that S/D team got in that tunnel. That mad fuckin' Aussie that fired it—"

"Jesus, man, who gives a shit who fired it?"

"Well, that Aussie said it was a lucky shot. Said so in the *Stars and Stripes.*"

"So now you believe the fuckin' papers?" countered Valdez. "I'm tellin' you once and for all—tunnels are bad news. Besides, if you want to go hide, man—"

"Hey, hey, Davy Crockett," countered Thomis, "don't give me your hero shit. You want to hide your ass just as much as I do." Thomis looked around. "Like everybody does. Ain't that right?" He looked at Emory on his left for support, but Emory wasn't going to get involved, so Thomis shot an angry glance back at Valdez over his right shoulder. "Point I'm makin', *Juan*, is that SAS/Delta team were the A-one cream of the crop. The best—and they knew just what they were looking for. The tunnel they blasted was no accident—it was their mission to get the sub pen, man. Sibirs'll just come at us willy-nilly. We're in a tunnel, we stand a better chance."

"Man," cut in the corporal from New York, "wish to fuck that S/D team was here now."

"Yeah," said Thomis. "Well, they ain't. Probably sunnin' 'emselves in Khabarovsk. They say it's gettin' nice and warm there."

"Yeah," said Valdez. "Minus ten instead of minus thirty. Great."

"Yeah. Well, put it this way—I'd rather be there than here."

"So what's new?"

"Relax," said the sergeant. "It's gonna warm up here pretty soon."

A machine gunner at the end of a three-man trench made grunting noises. "Very funny, Sarge. 'Gonna warm up'!"

"Yeah," said Thomis. "Regular fuckin' riot. Heeeere's Jay Leno! Still say we'd be better off in a fuckin' tunnel."

"We'd be better off if those SAS/Delta commandos were here," said the machine gunner.

"Dreamer!" said Thomis. "They're probably pissed in Khabarovsk and deep in poontang!"

"Shit!" It was their platoon sergeant putting down the field phone in disgust. "Our land line to HQ is cut."

"So we use the radio," said Valdez.

"Yeah, so they can jam it," said Thomis. "Nice goin', Valdez."

"Knock if off," said the sergeant.

"Maybe it was an accident," said Emory. "Tree fallin' or somethin'."

"Right!" said Thomis. "A tree—knocked over by a fucking T-80. You're as stupid as Valdez."

"Thomis!" warned the sergeant. "Knock it off!"

Thomis was shaking his head, his breath like puffs of smoke in the night air. "A tree falling—Jesus!"

He was terrified.

Aussie's immediate inquiry on seeing David Brentwood was to ask him about his honeymoon. "Has it fallen off yet?"

David ignored the Australian's vulgarity. The four of them—David, Aussie, Choir Williams, and Salvini—liked one another well enough when they'd been in action, but away from the fighting for a while, each had, albeit briefly, entered a world in which war was no longer the norm, and where fear of death was talked about, so that now their civilian-heightened sensibilities inhibited a camaraderie that for most of them only exhibited itself under fire.

"You look chipper!" Aussie informed David as they shook hands. "Been doin' the old in-out, have you? She teach you a few tricks?"

"How you been doing, Aussie?" asked David.

"Lousy. Since the cease-fire went down the tube, there's been no more beer."

"Oh, the poor fellow!" chimed in Choir Williams, winking at Salvini. "Deprived, are we, Lewis?"

"Nuts!" put in Salvini. "I saw cases of our stuff, piled up in Vladivostok."

"Japanese beer," said Aussie. "Horse piss. Nah, I mean the old Tsingtao. Chinese stuff. Beautiful big bottles, too. Drink that stuff all day and no hangover. Nothing."

"Oh yeah?" asked Salvini skeptically. "What's so special about it?"

"Don't ask," warned Brentwood, smiling across at Choir.

"Okay," said Aussie. "So you've heard it before, smartass. But Salvini's ignorant. He's from Brooklyn, and it's my duty to educate the poor sod."

"When the Germans had the beer concession in China," began Choir, imitating Aussie as best he could.

"Quiet, you Welsh bastard!" cut in Aussie, Stimson telling them that Freeman and his aide, Colonel Norton, were coming across the quad from the HQ communications hut. Aussie took no notice. "The Krauts bottled their beer under the old German Purity Law of 1516. No preservatives allowed. Now, when old Mao Cow Dung beat Cash My Check in 'forty-nine and booted out all the foreign devils, they still kept the Kraut beer factory in Tsingtao."

"If you say so, professor," jibed Choir.

"I do say so and—"

"Atten-hun!" called Stimson. The SAS/Delta team snapped to it, but despite Freeman's entrance, Stimson sensed an air of equality about the men. There was no disrespect toward the general—he was, even if under attack from the media, especially the La Roche newspaper empire, already a renowned figure to the men he commanded—the new American army's Patton. Besides, the more media scumbags attacked him, the more his men would defend him—at least those not under fire around Lake Baikal. There, his general strategy was neither divined nor, if understood, countenanced, Freeman's headquarters' bulletins quoting "tactical necessity" affording little comfort to those like Private Thomis in Charlie Company who knew that the possibility of being overrun was growing by the hour.

But here in the briefing hut, at least, Freeman's reputation was secure—so far, his knowledge of the minutiae of battle legendary, as was his fury against many Pentagon directives, such as the one that had distributed "Technicolor" condoms to the white-camouflaged troops in the Siberian midwinter.

"At ease, gentlemen," said Freeman, taking off his heavy winter coat, the outline of the nine-millimeter Sig Sauer barely visible beneath his tunic. "No time to waste. I've called you here because we're getting the ass kicked out of us on that lake and I have to find some way of taking the pressure off those boys. At the same time, I've got to stop this breakthrough down south around Manzhouli in Chinese Mongolia. With those ChiCom divisions swinging west, Yesov's moving east. They'll close the box on our boys—what's left of them—around Baikal and split our entire east-west Khabarovsk/Baikal supply line in two. As if that isn't enough, my G-2 tells me northern Siberian divisions are moving south toward the lake from up north around Yakutsk to get us in a three-way squeeze. Now the Pentagon has 'suggested' I withdraw all forces to Khabarovsk—buy time to consolidate for a summer counterattack. Colonel Norton here concurs."

There was a long silence, Stimson struck by the fact that none of the four SAS/Delta veterans made the slightest attempt to venture an opinion, though he sensed that none of them was afraid to speak up. It was as if they were telling Freeman, "It's your decision. That's why you get a general's pay."

Stimson was wrong. The truth was that all of them, including Norton, already knew what he was going to say. Their silence was their consent. They were with him. Now it was now merely a matter of details.

"Where you going to hit them, General?" asked David Brentwood.

Jesus! thought Stimson. He's being clobbered left, right, and center, and he's talking about going on the *attack?*

"Nizhneangarsk," Freeman said, then turned abruptly to the map, knuckle rapping the northern end of the four-hundred-mile lake. "The railhead on the BAM—Baikal to Amur mainline. We cut that—we cut the bulk of *their* supplies for their army of the north and for Yesov's left hook farther south across the lake. That is part one of three, gentlemen. Any one of the three fails and we are in the manure up to our neck.'' Freeman saw the frown on young Stimson's face. "You ill, Lieutenant?"

"Ah, no, sir. I'm fine."

"You look ill. Come on, spit it out, son."

"Well, sir, ah . . . '' Stimson was glancing nervously at the map, estimating that Nizhneangarsk was at least fourteen hundred miles northwest of Khabarovsk, and wondering why in heck no one else had seen the problem. "Sir," he began, "I know flying conditions aren't much good right now."

"Aren't much good?" said Norton. "They're appalling."

"Yes," agreed Stimson, "but I was wondering, sir— well, why don't we just bomb the railway? Wouldn't that be much—'' He stopped.

None of the others exchanged knowing glances or in any way tried to make him feel embarrassed. The lieutenant was young, and all young men, even the brightest from West Point, had to learn. Freeman took out his George C. Scott reading glasses and opened a red-diagonal-striped green file, showing the lieutenant the ARPs—area reconnaissance photos—taken by F-4G Phantoms and a few Stealth F-117As, the latter having gone in bravely despite the low impulse radar that had undone the defensive blocking action of their radar-resilient angular technology. Two of the Stealths and Phantoms had paid for it, though, and had gone down in the enfilade of heavy radar-guided AA fire.

"Son," began Freeman, "let me tell you something the public don't know, something our fliers learned in Vietnam, had to relearn in Iraq, and what their granddaddies knew when they were fighting the Luftwaffe. At any time—I stress at any time—rail lines, especially railway bridges, where the enemy can sink pontoons right next to the busted-up bridge a couple of inches under the water to fool reconnaissance and run the box cars across at night, are notoriously difficult to knock out."

"But with Smart bombs—'' began Stimson.

Freeman nodded impatiently, tapping the stills taken

from the black-and-white video shots through the thicket of AA fire around the Nizhneangarsk rail head. "Problem is, son—and here we're ignoring the flak and the fact they've got 'smart' AA defenses up there—problem is the damn snow." He showed the lieutenant the pertinent reconnaissance photos—the rail lines and black ties scattered about like broken sticks in the snow. The next photo, time-marked twenty-four hours later, showed the same photo view, the rails back together in working order, the next photo showing the rails scattered again. In the fourth and last photo the rails and ties were all in place once more.

"Same area," Freeman assured him. "The thing is, Lieutenant, ground sensors we air dropped outside the immediate area of the station registered movement at the rail head *within an hour* of our Stealths' air attack. *Heavy movement.*"

"Tanks moving up?" proffered Stimson.

Freeman slipped his glasses off. "No. Our analysts are sure of that—it'd be a different overpressure, weight of the vehicles, if it had been tanks. No, it was rolling stock, all right, moving through the area we'd just plastered—half an hour after we'd bombed it and lost four aircraft into the bargain. Those broken tracks and ties you see are fake. Extruded plastic, we thought. Point is, they were just shiftin' them around, son. Meanwhile the snow kept covering the real line two, three hundred yards away. Our bombs were just blowing up snow. So we sent in Smart bombs—to lock in on the real, snow-covered lines. Then we found we'd been wrong. They weren't plastic lines they were using to fool our recon cameras, they were genuine rail lines, spares just moved around after each attack to make it look as if we'd hit the main line. No, son, it's the same old story. Had to do it with Charlie in 'Nam—had to do it with that son of a bitch Insane in Iraq. You have to go in on the ground. We'll use the Airborne. It's the only way."

"Where do we fit in, General?" asked Aussie Lewis.

Freeman gave the four SAS/D men an enigmatic smile.

"Well, I thought after that sub base you knocked out, you boys'd be bored up there. Had enough of that lake, haven't you?"

Before they could answer, Freeman moved closer to the map and, using his glasses as a pointer, tapped the northern sector—not of the lake, but of the southwest corner of the Amur hump, on the Siberian-Chinese border. "We're in this war, gentlemen, because the Chinese said we broke the cease-fire. Right here." He was tapping A-7. "Well, whether we did or not, we've got to get our boys out of there. We've tried sending in choppers—they've been blown to bits." He turned to David Brentwood. "What we need is a small, well-equipped commando force, flying in NOE to go in, secure a chopper LZ on the top of that damn mountain before the ChiComs overrun it. Now, our boys weren't supposed to be in that area anyway—at least not that close to the border—and we've had no communication from them. But we can sort out blame later. Most of all, I want to get as many of them out as I can. You game for it. Lewis?"

NOE, nap of the earth—flying in which the choppers were often no more than twenty feet above the treeline, following the land's contours by radar alone—didn't particularly worry Lewis, but Choir Williams, he knew, hated it. "Well, General—Choir's your boy for NOE. Gives him a high, it does."

"Good," said Freeman, grabbing his coat. "I'll leave you with Norton to figure out the details." He paused. "As fast as you can, boys. Meanwhile, I promise you I'm gonna hit those bastards of Yesov's up at Nizhneangarsk. If I can stop the son of a bitch's offensive from getting east of the lake, then I can wheel what's left of Three Corps south to reinforce our boys ranged against the ChiComs. Bring Cheng to a standstill. And if your brother does his bit, Brentwood, we might just be able to launch a counterattack. Defeat into victory, eh?" With that, a question still on David Brentwood's lips, Freeman was gone.

"Over here, gentlemen," Norton informed them.

"We've already got the choppers' fuel and sundries allocated for you. Now—weapons." He looked at David Brentwood, who everyone instinctively knew would lead the raid on the mountain.

"Excuse me, sir, but what's all this about my brother? Robert or Ray? I don't—"

"Robert. The submariner. SEAL man, too, right?"

"Robert?"

"Yes." Norton's tone informed David that he would be told no more. "Sorry," said Norton, "but it's on a need-to-know basis. And you don't need to know. All I can tell you is that he's step number three."

"A Heck 7.6-millimeter barrel for me," said Lewis without further ado, referring to the Heckler and Koch machine gun. "Run short of ammo, we can strip the Siberians."

"You, Brentwood," said Norton. "The same?" And immediately David Brentwood was drawn into the urgent preparations.

A SEAL team for the third part of Freeman's plan had been needed so quickly that there was no time to bring them from their CONUS—continental United States—NAVSPECWARGRU—Navy Special Warfare Group—at either Coronado, California, or Little Creek, Virginia. Instead, Freeman had requested the nearest SEAL contingent, Team Nine from Pearl Harbor, and had personally requested submariner captain Robert Brentwood of the Sea Wolf–Hunter/Killer USS *Reagan* to join the team as leader.

CINCPAC—Commander in Chief Pacific—Admiral Leahy responded in Top Secret "immediate" cable that this wasn't possible. The admiral had nothing against brothers serving in the same theater—the services were replete with such cases—but Robert Brentwood, captain of the *Reagan*'s blue crew, was now back at sea on a seventy-day war patrol around the southern Kuril Islands north of Japan, guarding the vital entrances to the Sea of Okhotsk, and so would not be back in Pearl for the gold crew changeover for another fourteen days. Furthermore, because of the "strain on TACAMO aircraft" following the sabotage of the sub communication aerial in Wisconsin, Admiral Leahy said it might not be possible for the TACAMO aircraft assigned the USS *Reagan* to contact the sub for several days.

"All right, Dick," Freeman had told Norton. "Now we've *requested*, I'll pull rank. I'm *ordering* it as Commander in Chief Far East. I want Robert Brentwood because that submariner performed magnificently in Baikal before these jokers pulled a cease-fire on me. So did young David Brentwood. That's why I put them on my list. They're men I've worked with before, and when you're in a corner—"

"Pearl also points out that he's too old, General," interrupted Norton. "Robert Brentwood, I mean. At forty-four, he's pushing it even for a sub captain, let alone the SEALs. They usually limit entry to SEAL Special Ops to twenty-seven-year-olds."

"God damn it, Dick! You know the age of the oldest Tornado pilot in the Iraqi War?" Before Norton could give him an answer, Freeman charged on. "A *Tornado* pilot, Dick. Those boys went in on the deck. Needed goddamn windscreen wipers to keep the sand off their cockpits. Most dangerous air missions of all. *Fifty-nine*. That's how old he was, Dick. Fifty-nine. A fifty-nine-year-old Brit. A granddaddy, and some pen pusher in Pearl's telling me forty-four's over the hill?"

"Not exactly, sir but—well, you have to admit, for what you have in mind it's going to be pretty rigorous."

"Life's rigorous, Dick," said Freeman, turning to the wall map. "And I need someone I can personally trust and know on this one." Taking up the Day-Glo pen, he circled Nizhneangarsk terminus. "Now Nizhneangarsk's mine." Next he moved the marker south to the Siberian-Chinese border area around A-7. "The SAS/Delta boys'll have to take care of this one, number two. But," he turned back to Dick Norton, "no way we can break through south of

Baikal and stop Cheng unless Robert Brentwood does his
job. And it has to be done before the full moon. So you tell
CINCPAC I want Robert Brentwood out of that pig boat if
he has to put every goddamn TACAMO onto the *Reagan*,
and I want him in Pearl within forty-eight hours for a
week's refresher course. Send them the details—Most
Secret, need-to-know basis only.''

"Yes, General. But they will have to know the specific
target sooner or later."

"Later. Not over the air—coded or otherwise. When he
gets here."

"Yes, sir."

Robert Brentwood was passing through the USS *Reagan*'s "Blood Alley," the redded-out narrow corridor
between the banks of the Sea Wolf's missile fire-control
computers, into the ethereal blue of the sonar room, where
he had just been handed the millisecond "burst"
transmission received via the long, trailing, low-frequency
aerial. He preferred using the quick pop-up, high-
frequency mast to receive transmits—the time needed to
reel in the longer VLF could be the margin between life
and death in the tight turning war of the Hunter/Killers.
Besides, with sound passing through water at four times
the speed it moved through air, the "reel-in" now under
way could be heard miles away, despite the fact that the
hydrophones' spools were heavily insulated to prevent
noise shorts from alerting the enemy. But after the
catastrophic breakdown of the computer-phone networks in
the States, the VLF had been his only bet of picking up the
TACAMO aircraft.

Robert Brentwood was tense, but it was more the content
of the burst message than the reel-in that made him so, and
only Hale, his executive officer, could sense it. The
message had been brief and to the point—pickup for
transport to Pearl to be made by a carrier-borne chopper at
0400 the next morning.

"Don't they realize we'll be violating the first rule of a

war patrol?'' said Brentwood, handing back the decoded message to Hale.

"Must be important then," said the XO, by way of making his skipper feel better about having to surface. "Besides, we have air superiority."

"It's not enemy air that I'm concerned about. It's those Alfas. They can pick us up breaking surface a hundred miles away through the sound channel." Brentwood turned around to the officer of the deck, Merrick. "What's state of sea topside?"

"Beaufort scale—eight. Gale force," said the OOD. "Should be enough turbulence to cover our bust-through noise. Might have to be a wet pickup for you, though, Captain."

"Well, better me wet than you guys."

"Have to agree with you there, sir," responded Merrick easily.

"Any idea what they want you for?" asked Hale.

"No, but it's from CINC–Far East, so I figure Freeman's behind it."

"Maybe more subs in Lake Baikal?" proffered Merrick.

"Possibly. I hope not. Too darn cold."

The pickup by a navy Sea King helo, and the transfer to Pearl via one of *Salt Lake City*'s Mach 2.3 F-14 Tomcats, went much more smoothly than Robert Brentwood had anticipated. Apart from being told he was to be taken to the BUD school at Pearl Harbor, Brentwood was still in the dark about the operation, and on his arrival in Pearl he discovered that not even Chief Petty Officer Brady, the "Bullfrog," the chief and most senior instructor at the Navy Special Warfare Group, knew much more than he and the six enlisted men who, besides the Bullfrog, would make up the SEAL team requested by Freeman.

"Well," said the Bullfrog happily, "one thing we all know, gentlemen. BUD doesn't stand for Budweiser."

"Thought it did!" said one of the enlisted seven.

Basic underwater demolition training was essential for

the SEALs, and was one of the prerequisites for wearing the coveted badge, a trident grasped in the eagle's right talon, a flintlock pistol held in the other, the anchor between them.

"Beach clearance?" posited one of the men.

"Come on, chiefie!" pressed another of the SEALs, such informality allowed nowhere else in the navy except in the tightly knit band of elite UD teams.

"Honest to God, Reilly," replied the chief. "I haven't been told the specific area. None of us'll know till week's end. Freeman's orders. Till then we'll be doing a rerun of motivation week in Pearl." He had everyone's undivided attention. "Motivation week" was the sanitized naval version of what used to be called "hell" week. It meant a week of CDU—combat demolition unit—training, a week of deliberate sleep deprivation to slow your responses and wear you down, weed out the weak ones—if there were any. Drop-out rate was fifty-one percent.

Part of the treatment involved flying the men over to the outer island of Kauai, to the muddy taro fields around the Wailua River where the men would have to avoid detection by a squad of instructors, one of the methods being to stick a reed in their mouths while lying submerged in the mud, waiting for the searchers to pass by. Problem was, every now and then a leech draped itself over the straw and the air was cut off. In the past, some men came up purple-faced, gasping wildly for air, only to attract the attention of the instructors, thereby failing that part of the course.

The eight-man team—Robert Brentwood, the Bullfrog, and the other six enlisted men—knew, of course, that regardless of whatever the specific mission was, they'd be issued with special UBA—underwater breathing apparatus—specifically, the military version of the COBRA—closed-circuit oxygen breathing apparatus—a rebreather system which, apart from not issuing any telltale bubbles while you were going into a beach, for example, allowed the swimmer by means of the carbon dioxide filter canister to rebreathe the same gas, additional oxygen being bled as needed from a front waist tank into the inflatable bag. It was much better than the standard SCUBA, or *scaphandre-autonome*, system. There were still problems, however, and during the motivation week, one diver, Seaman Michael Rose—his last name reminding Robert Brentwood of his wife Rosemary back in England—ran into what the chief's report blandly designated as some "difficulty" at 120 feet in Pearl. Being in saltwater, the helium inject needed at that depth to prevent nitrogen narcosis, or "nitrogen drunkenness," was bleeding in too slowly, and Rose, despite his wrist fathometer, lost all sense of direction, going *down* to 240 feet, thinking he was going up, before being located by the Bullfrog and Robert Brentwood.

On the third day, the team, under Brentwood's direction, practiced egressing from a submerged sub's forward escape hatch with the sub under way at one and a half knots. For Brentwood it was the first real indication of what their mission might be. On the fourth day, the eight of them were split into four two-man UDT-IBS—underwater demolition teams; the IBS, or inflatable small boat issued each of the four pairs, a thirteen-and-a-half-foot-long F-470 fiberglass-hulled Zodiac. Each pair of SEALs was then assigned to a landing craft.

The first of the four two-man teams consisted of Brentwood and Dennison, a stocky man who, despite his shorter height, was probably the strongest swimmer of the group, and who possessed a wry sense of humor. As the landing craft started its run, he crouched low in the Zodiac on its outboard side and then, on the signal from Brentwood, rolled over the rubber boat's outer tube into the roiling water on the landing craft's port side, a quarter mile out from Pearl's sub net.

Brentwood followed and they began casting, Dennison unreeling a .065-gauge nylon fishingline marked "for feel" every one hundred feet, at which point Robert Brentwood let a knot-marked lead sinker line down to the bottom, quickly recording the depth by scratching it on his plastic knee slate and noting any other underwater obstructions, apart from the sub net, that an amphibious landing might encounter, including the positions of channel markers and angle of breakwater to the beach. Each number-two man in the four two-man teams had to keep radio contact with the other team via waterproof cigarette-pack-size walkie-talkies, it being vital for the teams to act in concert to effect a proper "extraction" or pickup. If the Zodiacs didn't cut out from the LCTs at the same time, on full throttle—the muffled thirty-five horsepower outboards streaking at right angles from the landing craft to pick up the swimmers, each man's left hand raised high to mark his position—there wouldn't be a second chance to be "snared" by the rubber loop held outboard from the fast-moving Zodiac. Once a swimmer's arm passed through the loop, he would immediately bend his arm to a V and kick toward the Zodiac as an LCT crewman, grabbing his webbed belt at midriff, hauled him quickly aboard, where he would ready himself in turn to "snare" the second man, until all eight swimmers had been accounted for. The four rubber boats would then turn and head out to sea, away from the enemy shore, to await their submarine pickup.

"You did good," Bullfrog told Dennison. "Remember, we lost more marines from drowning off Tarawa than we did from Jap shore fire. If we'd known just how deep some of them holes were in that coral, we could have saved a lot of guys." The chief hesitated for a moment, then added, "But we still got a problem."

For the moment the other seven men, including Robert Brentwood, said nothing, sitting back on the gunwales of the tender, exhausted from more than six hours in the water. Brentwood, though he didn't show it, was sure he was the most fatigued. He was old enough to be some of these men's father.

"What problem?" asked Dennison, reaching tiredly for a squeeze bottle of Gatorade. "None of us drowned!"

"Speak for yourself," put in Rose, the California tan of the twenty-five-year-old contrasting with the stubble of what had been a full head of straw-colored hair.

"No," conceded the chief. "Swimming was okay. But it was a screwup on the walkie-talkies."

"Hell," said Dennison, "ours worked fine. Didn't it, Captain? Waterproof one hundred percent."

"Oh, they all worked fine," said the chief. "That's the problem."

"Did Pearl pick it up?" put in Brentwood. "On the hydrophones?"

"Pearl!" said the chief. "Captain, they heard you up off Diamond Head. Frightened the fish in Hanauma Bay." He grinned. "So now you guys know why you were made to learn American Standard." He meant the sign language used by the deaf and mute.

"Hold on!" said Robert Brentwood. "I don't know anything about sign language."

"Oh—" said the Bullfrog, clearly caught off base for the first time since the refresher courses had begun. "Special orders from General Freeman, sir. Thought you knew."

"Hell, no!" answered Robert, who, despite the normal give-and-take of profanity in the service, wasn't in the habit of swearing, even mildly.

"Then, Captain," said the chief, "you're going to have to learn, sir. Rose—you're the best with a bunch of fives." The chief turned back to the commander of the USS *Reagan*. "You have twenty-four hours, Captain."

Brentwood gave an "Aye aye, chief"—the only situation in which the captain of one of the most powerful warships in history would have done so, at least so obligingly. Besides, Brentwood's momentary annoyance was mitigated by the growing conviction that he was now solving the puzzle of the mission's precise location. Well aware, as a commander himself, of the "need-to-know" rationale for keeping an operation secret until the last, he couldn't help taking pride in the certainty that he had divined Freeman's plan. He wondered whether any of the enlisted men had put it together—a sub approach offshore, casting for obstacles, sinker line depth measurements, width of approach . . . General Douglas Freeman was about to do another Mac-

Arthur, another Inchon, launch a daring seaborne invasion across the China Sea. And unless he, Brentwood, was all wet, the SSN USS *Reagan* would be used to insert a survey UDT—underwater demolition team. And, once the underwater terrain was known, the *Reagan* would most likely use its torpedoes to clear any major underwater obstruction just prior to the amphibious assault.

The giveaway from Brentwood was the concern over the walkie-talkies. If they were going to be that close to shore that they had to worry about the walkie-talkie sound being picked up by a beach garrison, then it had to be a pre-invasion mission. The final clue was the sign language. It meant they were going to be very close to the enemy, plus sign language wouldn't help you in the dark. A dawn invasion. He put this last conclusion to the Bullfrog without revealing any of his other deductions, and couldn't resist a quiet satisfaction in seeing the chief completely surprised.

The chief looked quizzically at him, and Brentwood got the distinct impression the chief was thinking that perhaps at forty-four the sub skipper *was* getting a bit old for it. "Dark's no problem," responded the chief, explaining, "We'd have PVs." It wasn't equipment that they used on a sub much—unless they surfaced at night—and the Bullfrog could see Brentwood had been caught off base. "Infrared," added the chief, unconsciously adding insult to Brentwood's injured pride. "Same kind they used in the Iraqi War. Pick up hand signals no problem. Warm arms in a cold sea—stick out like you got a hard-on."

For the Bullfrog it was a joke, but everyone else was too tired. Including swimming time, they'd been "refreshing" themselves with all the minutiae of SEAL underwater techniques for thirty hours without a break. Still, as fatigued as he was, Brentwood recalled the Bullfrog's earlier mention of Tarawa. It mightn't be that the SEALs would go in during the daylight, given the chief's mention of the PV goggles, but you'd have to be crazy to try a massive amphibious landing at night. Then again, a lot of people had thought Freeman was crazy for making a night attack on Pyongyang—until he'd pulled it off.

"Right, gentlemen," said the chief. "Six hours sleep and we start on some lovely abutments."

"Where?" asked Rose. "Down on Waikiki?"

"Doesn't matter," put in Smythe, a tall string bean of a man. "What matters is how big these mothers are, eh?" He turned to the Bullfrog. "How big are they, chiefie?"

"Mothers are big," answered the Bullfrog truthfully. "Quartermaster's got us down for primacord with demolition knots, with three-foot trailer cords to tie your charge to the master primacord."

"Be using bladders?" asked Smythe.

"Yup," confirmed the chief. "We'll all need tits." He was referring to Schantz bag/basket flotation packs that would take most of the weight of the explosive charges off the swimmers.

"Heavy fuckers, then?" said Reilly. "If we got Schantzes."

"What's the load?" added Rose. Everybody seemed to come to life with the prospect of having to suffer more than they had already. "Fifty pounds?"

"A tad more, Rosie," said the chief, smiling. "An even hundred."

"Jesus!" said Rose, and Smythe whistled. "We gonna refloat the *Arizona*?"

"We'll do a splash-run practice tomorrow," announced the chief. "Oh five hundred. I'll designate flank swimmers and fuse pullers. I'll have it ready by breakfast. Remember now, light meal, gents—don't want anybody sinking."

"Light meal," quipped Dennison. "If I'm still alive."

As they dismissed, young Rose told Robert Brentwood that the scuttlebutt around Pearl was that the Chinese had some kind of long-range rockets by some lake in far western China and that the SEALs were going to hit them.

"Well, if it's the scuttlebutt, you can be sure it's wrong."

"You got it figured out, then, skipper?"

"Well, Rose," Brentwood answered, still unused to uttering his wife's name so far away from her, "I'll tell you what I think, providing you keep it to yourself. No use violating need-to-know before we have to."

"Absolutely, Captain."

"Freeman's going to launch an attack from Korea—across the Yellow Sea—against China's right flank. Shantung peninsula's my guess. Just over two hundred miles due west of Inchon."

Rose paled. "Jesus! But . . . they'd chop us to pieces."

Robert Brentwood smiled. "To do that, the ChiComs'll have to withdraw troops from their northern borders."

Now Rose saw the light. "Take the pressure off our guys up there."

"Right. 'Course, we'll have to skedaddle on out of there once they start pouring down from the north toward the peninsula."

"What if they don't go for it?"

"Rose, what would you think Washington'd do if enemy troops landed on the Baja peninsula? Way I figure it, Freeman's going to do another MacArthur—the unexpected—and we're going in at night to take out the underwater obstacles."

Robert Brentwood would soon be glad he hadn't told the others of his hunch. After all, being half right doesn't get you the kewpie doll. He was a first-rate navy man, but was talking through his hat. He was no politician, and as things stood, Washington, virtually under siege at home, had no intentions of expanding the war further by invading China. Such a move would be implicitly taken by Taiwan as the green light for it to attack, and that flash point could ignite all of Asia.

CHAPTER TWENTY-ONE

Harbin

THE HUTONG STANK, the truck which normally collected the night carts' cargo delayed because of the snowfall. From the tiny window, Alexsandra could see two-wheel pushcarts sitting forlornly at the end of the hutongs, abandoned. The granny brigade seemed oblivious to the stench. Much more offensive to them was the odor of their Siberian allies, many of whom were now in Harbin, frequenting the unofficial brothels that lay in the clutter of dwellings along the riverbank. Like most whites, the Siberians smelled of old, wet dog, and this morning, as the granny brigade—its three members' red armbands vivid against the snow, their aged backs bent like vultures looking for carrion—made their way up the hutong, soldiers, both PLA and Siberians, descended to assist in the continuing search for the spy, Alexsandra Malof.

The underground had managed to hide her successfully from the granny brigade so far by keeping her in the claustrophobic room which she had since discovered lay in the rear of a small bicycle repair shop, one of those allowed under the party's "liberalization" program. The alleyways had remained choked with snow, and piles of it were accumulating at the end of the alley, as one of the wonders of China—complete snow removal by hand—took place each day as people emerged silently from the hutong's hovels to clear the narrow byways on command of the local committee. The grannies as usual were supervising, noting

who was where, who was absent, stopping every now and
then, assiduously sniffing the snow-cleansed air for the taint
of wet dog.

"There's a foreigner here!" announced the smallest of
the grannies, all three dressed in identical padded and faded
navy-blue Mao suits. It was an announcement clearly meant
for everyone to hear, the three of them turning crooked
necks, watching the two dozen or so people from their
hutong silently busy with wooden push shovels and bramble
brooms, the latter whisking against the bare flagstones, long
crystals of ice snaking along in crazy patterns.

"There's a foreigner here!" The brooms kept whisking,
as if no one could hear her, save for an old man who,
straightening up, looked about, confused, unsure of whether
he'd heard a command.

The few children who had been playing quickly disappeared, swallowed by the hovels as if struck by some silent,
felt message from their parents. The grannies also split up,
their heads moving now with an extraordinary agility for
their age as they shuffled along, noting the numbers of the
houses, the smallest granny blowing her whistle shrilly.

Within minutes the street security committee arrived:
three young zealots, their gender hidden under identical
Mao suits, red armbands at large. They had a right to
inspect each house indicated by the granny brigade. A
policeman would normally accompany them—at least, this
was the party regulation—but with a war going on against
the American imperialists, the security committees had
assumed greater authority, engendering more fear than
usual in every soul in every hutong in the city of 2.7
million.

Soon an army policeman, his thick, cotton-padded,
olive-green winter uniform flecked with snow, appeared,
walking in from the direction of the main road.

There were no histrionics for the Lings, who ran the
repair shop. Besides, there was nowhere to go. As Mr. Ling
looked out the window of his cramped kitchen, he spotted a
khaki truck, its tire treads choked with packed snow, PLA

troops spilling out of it, a dozen heading left down the main road, another dozen or so to the right, encircling the hutong. Directly behind Ling's repair shop lay more cluttered, snowcapped hovels leading down to the frozen river. Ling knew it was quite hopeless. He was surrounded. Besides, if there was the slightest opposition, they'd take his eight-year-old son, his only child, away as well. He went in and told Alexsandra they had discovered her. He was sorry. Their eyes met only for a moment in the grim morning light, and in that moment they both understood there was nothing they could do. To run was futile; she might as well save her strength.

The charges were that she and Ling, as "running dog jackals" of the "fascist pro-democracy movement," were guilty of treasonous "antirevolutionary" activity.

"I could smell her!" pronounced the diminutive granny victoriously. "I could smell her!"

Mr. Ling looked at the old woman with quiet contempt. "You smell nothing but your own fear."

Within minutes the Public Security man arrived and Alexsandra and Ling were shackled, hands behind their backs, the chain passing around the front of the waist between their legs and back up to a metal collar. She was taken out to the PSB car, a battered blue Fiat, Ling to a police motorcycle and sidecar nearby. "Someone has betrayed us!" he yelled back at the hutong.

The PSB rider slapped him across the ear with a rough suede driving glove. *"Zhu kou!"* Shut up!

The moment Alexsandra felt herself pushed into the small blue Fiat, its upholstery a dusty faded-gray velour, she experienced a strange sense of relief—the warmth of the car's heater was luxurious. It was the warmest she'd been for days, and in her relief came the sudden smothering fear that if she was so weak as to have already surrendered to this slight creature comfort, what would she tell the PSB interrogators once faced with another bone-aching cold cell? Even the Yakuts of her native Siberia, who lived in the region where the temperature often dropped below minus sixty, grudgingly admired the legendary ability of the northern Chinese to endure the cold. Her fear of dying cold was, she knew, as irrational as having hoped she would ever be free. Her rape by the Siberians at Baikal had never left her.

And what was it all worth—her silence? She didn't even know whether the message about the Nanking Bridge had gotten through. Yet all this now paled next to her simple but overwhelming desire to be warm again, her craving for even the smallest candle subduing all reason, all prior resolve. For now she knew it would almost certainly end with a bullet in the neck, the traditional party execution for counterrevolutionaries. Most likely it would be a public affair, as public and as exaggerated as her arrest, a warning to all those who might have sympathy with the pro-democracy movement. And if she was cold, she would shiver as she knelt and they would think it was fear. If only to deny them that, she longed to be warm.

CHAPTER TWENTY-TWO

AS FREEMAN FINALIZED preparations for his attack on Nizhneangarsk, Major Truet's Charlie Company, cut off from the main body of III Corps, waited anxiously at the southern end of the lake, still dug in, facing westward, the rail tracks and concrete tunnels atop the cliff overlooking the lake a hundred yards behind them. In the night the moonlit fringe of the boreal forest stood like an impenetrable curtain barely a hundred yards in front of them, the snowdrifts so high they'd climbed halfway up the trunks of the trees whose branches were now stiff to breaking point from the weight of snow.

Despite Thomis's incurable pessimism, the rest of second platoon remained confident that Freeman would eventually get evacuation choppers across the lake from the east. But for now all they could do was wait, all available choppers busy ferrying what men they could find in the hell that lay beneath the cloud covering the lake. The sound of Yesov's juggernaut was still rolling and thundering, the Siberians now getting behind as well as in front of III Corps to finish off what was left of the American retreat. Though knowing this, Thomis remained bitterly disappointed at the choppers' failure, so far, to rescue him, and he continued to argue forcefully that they should move back to the cover of the tunnels.

When it came, the weak, creaking sound of the Siberian reserve armor no more than half a mile away sounded like unoiled rail cars, the occasional clankiness of more tanks moving through the forest belying the awesome power of the main battle tanks. Each T-72 weighed 49,000 pounds and was outfitted with a 125mm smoothbore, one of the largest tank cannons in the world. They moved at no more than fifteen miles per hour, until General Minsky gave the order for a thirty-five-mile-per-hour burst of speed as they approached the edge of the treeline beyond which lay C Company. Cold was seeping down from the forest's edge, pouring into the foxholes and trenches around Thomis and his buddies like dry ice, at times obscuring the slit openings between the log-raft cover of some of Charlie Company's trenches.

What Thomis, Valdez, Emory—the Georgian—and others couldn't figure out was how, with the treeline so thick at the forest edge, the tanks could hope to exit directly in front of the trenches—unless the Siberians intended bringing bulldozers forward. But this would give Charlie Company time to triangulate mortar attacks which, while they mightn't harm the tanks, would give C Company's antitank crews more time and pin down the Siberian infantry. But then, Siberian tactics weren't known for showing particular concern for numbers of troops lost, so long as the objective was obtained. And anyway, Thomis hissed, it didn't matter "what the fuck their strategy is, man—where in hell we gonna go, with a sheer hundred-fifty-foot drop behind us?"

"Jump into the lake!" opined Valdez nervously.

Thomis was stamping his feet to keep warm. "Very fucking amusing, Valdez."

A reconnaissance patrol from C Company was almost shot as it scurried back from the treeline, their report succinct: "Fuckers are everywhere. Headin' straight for us."

"How far?" asked Major Truet.

"Half a mile—maybe less."

"We could try rappeling down the cliff," said Emory.

Thomis sneered. "Oh, terrific," he said, cupping his hands about the M-16's breech to stop it freezing up, "and while we're going down, what the fuck you think the Siberians'll be doing? Having tea? Anyway, where the hell would we go on the ice—taking a fucking stroll while they pick us off from the cliffs?"

No one answered. Thomis was a pain, but on this one his pessimism was justified. Valdez said the tanks were probably farther in the woods than anyone thought, that maybe they'd turn—run parallel *to* the tracks—and would go past Charlie Company, not *toward* them. Maybe they were going along some logging road, north toward Port Baikal to reinforce Yesov's attack on the retreating III Corps.

"Jesus!" said Thomis, looking behind him, down out over the moon-bathed white cloud that obscured the lake.

"What?" asked Valdez, but then he saw, as Thomis had, what looked like a canal, or rather, a long, jagged slit in the ice; in fact, it was through a narrow break in the cloud cover that he and the rest in the squad glimpsed the flashes of the guns. They'd been at it all day and now, through his Starlight binoculars, Valdez for one could see clearly, in the surreal-looking green world of the night vision glasses, the slaughter of the remnants of III Corps caught out on the ice. "They're being massa—" began Valdez.

"Shut up!" hissed Thomis. "Listen!"

The creak of the tanks had stopped. To the right of second platoon's heavy machine gun trench and scattered foxholes, a branch collapsed, the snow pouring down from the tree like sugar. Valdez slid his M-16 forward on the frozen ice rest he'd sculptured in front of him.

"Hold it!" cautioned Emory softly. "Maybe it just fell."

" 'Course it fucking fell!" hissed Thomis. "You idiot!"

Emory took no offense. He knew it was Thomis's fear talking, the same kind of fear that had suddenly made his own mouth dry as sandpaper.

"No firing!" said the lieutenant softly, yet urgently, his voice on the walkie-talkie distinct, without a trace of static, as he turned the volume as low as he possibly could. He was listening so intently that he seemed to feel everything at once, the wind moaning through the trees, snow plopping down here and there, a crack of a branch, the distant crackle of small arms fire on the lake below, and in the distance the scream of more Siberian rocket salvos, their fiery tails a fizzing white in the night goggles, his concentration and the weight of the goggles giving him a cluster headache that started to radiate down his right arm.

"Bastards!" said Thomis, by which he meant, What the hell were the Siberians up to?

"No such luck," Thomis heard the lieutenant reply in answer to Valdez's hope that C Company was being bypassed by the Siberians.

Another patrol sent out earlier following the rail tracks south of C Company's position had spotted an enemy troop concentration—at least five hundred, possibly brigade size—collecting around Kultuk. There was absolutely no doubt about it—Charlie Company was trapped between Kultuk twenty-five miles to the south and Port Baikal twenty miles to the north, and by cliffs above the artillery-ruptured ice behind them.

Suddenly someone said they could hear a chopper. "One of ours!" said Emory.

"One of theirs!" countered Thomis.

The truth was, it was impossible to tell amid the cacophony of echoes rebounding about the cliffs.

"I told you," said Valdez. "Old Doug said he'd try to get evac through to us."

"*Old Doug*'s in Khabarovsk!" said Thomis.

"Can it!" ordered Truet, who could hear them as he came down the line. But excitement was rising. Emory said it sounded like a Chinook. Throw all the crap out of it—seats, fire extinguishers, rescue winch—you could get forty or so men in a C-47, evac a whole platoon. More if you jettisoned your weapons. Truet said nothing; raising expectations was bad news if you couldn't follow through. "Men'll lose confidence in your leadership," they told him at West Point, and he knew they were right.

Thomis was in the worst state, and only Emory knew what was eating away at him. Thomis and his wife had had a real dustup the night before he'd shipped out from Frisco. All the way through the tunnel they'd argued because he'd smacked young Wendy—she was ten—that morning for giving lip to her mother. He tried to make up, telling her he'd buy her something really nice for her eleventh birthday, but she'd gone into the big sulk. He'd hit her pretty hard—on the backside—and now he was thinking about how he used to kneel down, say her prayers with her. "Jesus, tender shepherd, hear me . . ." "Honest to God," he'd told Emory in a quieter moment, "I'd've given my right hand not to have left her like that—hurting her. Her old man goes off, doesn't come back, all she'll remember—"

The "chunka-chunka" sound—a C-47?—grew louder, and a few of the guys started to get wound up.

"Easy now," the sergeant told them. "Watch your perimeter."

Thomis promised God right there and then that if he ever got out of it, he'd never hit Wendy again. Wouldn't take any crap, but he'd never hit her—never. He could smell her warm, baby-powder smell after her bath—and her hair golden, just like her mom's. There was another fall of snow from the trees, and he wondered whether other men in the line were making deals with the Almighty. Just get me out of this, God, and I promise . . .

In the dank cell, the Harbin Public Security Bureau guards had difficulty attaching the small alligator clamps to Ling's testicles. Ling was so terrified, despite his determination not to show it, that his sheer fright and the cold combined to shrink the skin around the scrotum into a small, tight, corrugated ball with the consistency of tough old elephant skin. One of the guards jerked hard on the single rope tie that passed through Ling's arms and around his neck. The guard had a lot of practice, having been very active in the Thirty-eighth Army's "police action" against "antisocial elements" following Tiananmen Square in the summer of '89. He had tied the arms of many of the hooligans of the pro-democracy movement before they'd been executed.

"What did the Jew woman tell you?" asked the PSB interrogator.

Ling was silent, his gaze downcast, fixed on a spot of rat droppings to better focus his resistance.

"The white woman you had hiding in your house," said the interrogator. "What did she tell you?"

Ling shook his head.

"She told you nothing?" proffered the interrogator. Ling's head moved, but it seemed more a stiffening of his own will than an answer. Personally, the interrogator had told his superior, he'd much rather talk to the comrade—to convince Ling in a calm, logical manner that helping the Siberian Jewess against his own people was treason, an act not only against the party, but against the people. And the party loved the people. The Siberian at the consulate, however—Latov—was in a hurry to break the underground movement in Harbin, the major distribution center of food and munitions not only for Cheng's armies fighting the Americans around Manzhouli, but for Chinese divisions spread along the Manchurian-Siberian border.

Ling didn't feel the electric shock he'd braced himself for. Instead, the interrogator suddenly leapt out of his wooden chair with a bull-like roar, the current having short-circuited along the table. "You idiot!" he shouted, slapping one of the guards so hard that the man's cap went flying. The other guard fumbled with the wires again while the interrogator strode angrily up and down the side of the cell farthest from the table. The shock had jolted his nerves so badly he had lit another cigarette while one was already on the go. He told the guard to turn up the amperage, and when the shock hit Ling, his scream could be heard in Stalin Park. Ling blacked out and had almost choked, the idiot guard having forgotten the tongue clamp and having turned the amperage too high.

The interrogator, his nerves rattled for the second time, reminded the guards that if they didn't get results quickly, then someone would be taking their rice bowl to the front, and they would be thrown into the battle for A-7. American gangsters had already inflicted seventeen percent casualties on the PLA, and though they would be undoubtedly overrun, they were putting up a fierce resistance.

"Disconnect the wires," ordered the interrogator. "You fools will kill him before he can talk." He turned on the man at the door. "Well, just don't stand there—go and get the boy from the hutong." It was a thing the interrogator didn't like to do, but now his job was much more than an internal matter of running a Democracy Movement cell to ground; it was war between the American imperialists and the People's Army. Whatever was necessary had to be done.

While they were waiting for the boy, Ling's wife was dragged screaming from her cell farther down the corridor. The interrogator put a cigarette into Ling's mouth. Ling spat it out, but it was as if the interrogator didn't see it. "I don't dislike you, comrade,'' he told Ling, his tone affecting sincerity. ''I admire your courage.'' Ling tried to spit at him, but it had no direction or force, merely dribbling down the faint stubble of his sallow chin.

''Now!'' said the interrogator, throwing down the cigarette he'd barely started, grinding it into the time-polished floor and shaking his finger like a schoolmaster. ''You have made me very angry.'' A half-running, half-shuffling noise came closer to the cell, and in the dirty saffron light of the corridor Ling saw his wife, crumpled between the sweating arms of her captors.

''Put her in the next cell!'' the interrogator commanded. Mrs. Ling had not looked at her husband, fearing it would weaken both their resolve, and both knowing he was a dead man.

''We'll let them think about it for a while,'' announced the interrogator, now lighting another cigarette. ''Let's see the Siberian whore.'' The two guards followed him eagerly from Ling's cell. Not only did they want to see her tortured, but if someone didn't talk soon, they'd be in Manzhouli.

The helicopter now was high above Charlie Company in the darkness, but whether it was in front or behind them, or coming down directly overhead, was difficult to tell, the heat wash of its rotor column and engines presenting no more than a white blurred image in Thomis's night vision goggles, icy gusts of snow stinging their faces like sand.

The next instant, the treeline a hundred yards in front of them was vibrant in light, the fuel air explosive detonated overhead, then came the sounds of men screaming, on fire, scrambling frantically from their foxholes, rolling desperately in the snow; other men leaving their positions, running to help, only to be machine-gunned as the Siberian Mi-28 Havoc, its silhouette often mistaken for the American Apache, pulled out of its 150-mile-per-hour dive. The Havoc turned in a deadly pirouette, its slaved fifty-millimeter still firing, the gun's flame suppressor hiding its position except from those directly in its thermal-image range finder, and they were now dead or wounded. The Havoc's stream of .50s was hitting them at point-blank range, bodies disintegrating as the depleted uranium armor-piercing, explosive-head bullets tore into the men of Charlie Company, including the two-man AA team forty feet from Thomis, their charred bodies still burning, flung back from their air-to-air Stinger, the shadow of its barrel flickering on the snow in response to the crackling, spitting fire now raging in the curtain of flame that was the forest's edge. Tall birch burned like oil-soaked torches, and beech trees exploded from the superheated gases. As the burned barbecue smell filled Thomis's nostrils, he was crying, the Havoc now only faintly visible before it disappeared into the blackness above the forest.

"Stay where you are!" the sergeant was yelling. "Emory, get the fuck back! Stay back!"

Emory was throwing his groundsheet over someone, stomping its edges to smother the fire, but the groundsheet billowed and rose in a soft burst of flame, Valdez seeming to have melted, what was left of his skin dripping like hot wax slipping away from his face, his eyes cooked white, glaring into the burning night. Some of the fuel air gel had splashed onto Emory, and he was slapping it, trying to get rid of it as he stumbled back to his foxhole. The supreme irony was that a radio signal had just come in from Freeman's HQ informing Major Truet that an evac of C Company—wounded having first priority—would be attempted within the next hour.

Ammunition on the American dead bodies was still cooking off—exploding from the heat—and the sergeant was shouting at everyone to keep their heads down, that an evac would soon be on its way. Thomis, upending his M-16, resting the barrel on his right foot, pulled the trigger, the sound of the shot lost in the general melee; his foxhole, like so many others, was filled with the reek of cordite and urine.

"Look to your front!" the sergeant was yelling, his voice on the edge of hysteria.

"Medic!" shouted Thomis.

The medic heard him, but there were so many others who had also been hit, it would be another ten minutes before he could reach Thomis. "Use your field dressing," he shouted, and Thomis, hands trembling, felt for his field dressing pack beneath his helmet band.

Inside his 1V13 heavy-armored artillery command vehicle, General Minsky moved from the folding seat immediately beneath the turret—the dull, thick vibration from the 8/600 generator pulsing through his body as he folded the traverse table—easing himself forward to use the PW-1 periscope sight through which, by determining polar coordinates, he could double-check the firing position of the 203mm battery and train the battery's master gun. But the blizzard was still in progress, and he moved back to the traverse table, having to rely on previously computed positions as he readied for the next phase of the shock attack, a two-inch broken red line indicating the positions of the isolated American company as reported by the Havoc.

Minsky missed the open vent days of the Afghan War. Here it was so cold you had no option but to have everyone shut up, relying on the NBC—nuclear, biological, chemical—air filter for fresh air. Even so, diesel fumes still got through, and at times made him feel nauseated. Still, the battle as recorded on the command vehicle's data terminal was going well, the Slutsk division living up to its reputation. Its radio operator—aboard this, Minsky's state-of-the-art command vehicle—was picking up some of the frantic radio traffic from the Americans just hit by the Havoc.

CHAPTER TWENTY-THREE

"BY GOD," SAID Freeman on being told that III Corps was effectively off the board, "they'll pay for this, Dick! I'll teach those sluts and Yesov's other Mongol hordes that butchering Americans comes at a high cost. Two for one."

Norton thought it unwise at that moment to point out that the Siberian divisions were not exactly Mongols. But the Pentagon, knowing of Freeman's affection for the "Good Book," had succinctly cautioned the general against too hasty a reaction by somewhat sanctimoniously reminding him that "vengeance is mine, saith the Lord."

"And I," Freeman had replied, "am his sword!" Gathering the last of his gear for phase one of his three-phase counterattack, the general was looking at the 241 section of the ONC E-7 chart showing the southern end of Lake Baikal, where the remnants of III Corps were being devoured by Yesov's armor. "Even the goddamn weather's against us."

"Should lift in about forty-eight hours, General," Norton tried to reassure him. "It's getting colder up north 'round Yakutsk, but the met boys predict quite a jump in temperatures round the Siberian-Mongolian border."

"Well," said Freeman, shaking his head at the enormity of what was happening on the lake, over five thousand casualties already reported, Medevac and MUST—Medical Unit Self-Contained—units overextended. "Jump in temperature might clear the weather, but it'll be too damn late, Dick. Only jump that'll count will be the Airborne's over Nizhneangarsk—and that won't be any good unless the

SEAL team does what it's supposed to. Each part of the plan depends on the other.''

"I know that, sir."

"Now listen—if we insert that SEAL team and have trouble extracting, I don't want them written off. Left on their lonesome. Understand?"

"Yes, sir."

"If they say they're in trouble, you get an SAS/Delta team in there with everything they've got to provide cover." Freeman held up his hand to stay Norton's objections. "Yes, yes, I know, it might put any rescue team in the hole, but it's a matter of policy—Americans have to do everything to get our boys out if they get in a jam. Hell, that's what we're all about."

"We could move a team in now," suggested Norton.

"I don't want to increase the traffic unless absolutely necessary. If anyone gets spotted prematurely, the SEALs' whole operation'd be shot. Besides, closest S/D team we've got is the one going in on A-7 to help out that goddamn battery that started this whole thing. You're right—they'd be the closest to the SEAL objective, but we can only use them *after* they secure a perimeter for a chopper withdrawal of the battery. *If* they manage that."

"That'd be one for the books," commented Norton. "Younger brother rescuing the older hand."

Freeman looked blankly at Norton, the general's mind having been so preoccupied with the minutiae of preparation for what would be his and history's biggest airborne invasion since Arnhem in '44, he had momentarily forgotten that two of the three Brentwoods would be in action at more or less the same time. The general paid it no mind. It was hardly unprecedented; brothers in Second Army were fighting a lot closer together than young David Brentwood would be at Manzhouli and Robert farther south. The general also paid it no mind because he knew that if Robert Brentwood's SEAL team met heavy resistance, his entire three-pronged counterattack plan against the Siberian-ChiCom alliance would fail, and it was a thought he didn't want to entertain. It was the first time Norton had seen Freeman willfully turning away from an unpleasant possibility, which was a measure not only of how badly the war was going for Second Army and how tired the general was, but above all, just how vital the SEAL mission would be along with Freeman's impending jump over Nizhneangarsk.

Freeman turned his attention to the map of the naval supply line, stretching all the way from America's west coast through the Kuril Island gaps, immediately north of Japan, through the Sea of Okhotsk to Siberia. It was another possible weak link, for if the Siberian Alfa Hunter/Killer subs could plug the narrow, shallow gaps between the Kurils—the gateway to the Sea of Okhotsk—then the enemy could quite literally turn off the oil supply to Freeman's entire Second Army, the general reminding Norton of George Patton's famous dictum: "My men can eat their boots, but my tanks gotta have gas!" Which for just one M1A1 meant two and a half gallons for every mile.

Even as Freeman spoke, the sonar operator aboard the Sea Wolf USS *Reagan* on war patrol just east of the Kuril Islands heard a faint pulse through the undersea "frying" of shrimps clicking and whales moaning, and alerted the executive officer, Hale, now captain in Robert Brentwood's absence; Merrick, in turn, had moved up to be the XO. When Hale heard the sonar *bong* by his bunk, he got up so fast, he knocked over the picture of his wife and two children, and within a minute—still stuffing his shirt inside his trousers—was standing inside the brass rail that skirted the scope island in *Reagan*'s redded-out combat control center. He wanted coffee, but Robert Brentwood had strictly enforced his no-liquid, no-food rule in the CCC.

"What've we got, Sonar?" Hale asked raspily, looking at the three-tiered green screen.

"Unidentified submarine, sir. Suspected hostile by nature of sound."

"Signature?"

"Negative." It meant there wasn't enough noise being emitted by the unidentified craft as yet to get a "prop-print" from the computer library, which could identify a specific vessel by matching its in-transit sound which, like the sound of every human being, had an individual "voice" print. But sometimes the enemy tried to add a baffle, a steel plate welded here or there, or extra acoustic, sound-absorbing tile on the superstructure to alter their noise signature. Even so, a good operator, like leading sonarman Rogers—whose higher-range hearing hadn't been damaged by too much "hard rock" music when he was younger—could often identify the class of ship from a sound which, to someone else's hearing, would have been the faintest pulsing of a prop.

"I'd say an Alfa," said Rogers, adding, "Might have flaked," indicating that the fast, forty-five-knot Hunter/ Killer Alfa might have lost part of its anechoic paint, designed to absorb rather than reflect the ping of a searching sub's "active" sonar. But Hale had the USS *Reagan*'s sonar on "passive"—listening mode only, the sub itself on silent running. While its nuclear reactor was unable to be shut down completely, it was heavily muffled, the reactor crew wearing their yellow booties, not only to prevent them from transferring any possible radioactive particles from the "coffeepot" or nuclear reactor throughout the sub, but to prevent even the sound of footsteps radiating through the hull.

"Sir—correction," said Rogers. "Louder now. It's a diesel—a quiet one, all right, but a diesel beat for sure. Ten thousand yards—closing!"

"Print out possible hostiles," ordered Hale, also informing the crew quickly, calmly, "Mr. Merrick retains the deck. I have the con." They were now well beyond the relatively shallow shelf of the Kuril Gap, into deeper water. Merrick, as XO in Brentwood's absence, immediately took up his position as officer of the deck behind the two planesmen, noting one whose face was beaded in perspiration. Wordlessly, he pulled out a damp tissue from the flip-up box and, so as not to alarm the planesman or divert his attention, he simply said, "Wiping," and drew the tissue across the man's forehead. A millisecond lost because of stinging perspiration in the eyes could put them all dead in the path of a torpedo or SUBROC. Sonar's auxiliary screen was now a column of brown X's, signifying the different classes of diesel to the right of each, listing speed—surfaced and dived—displacement, missiles, radar arrays, sonars, and officer/crew complement.

"Your best estimate?" Hale asked Rogers. They had worked together on the nuclear submarine *Roosevelt*, which, after sinking an enemy sub and sustaining considerable damage herself, had to be scuttled in the Arctic lest her vital coding machines be captured.

"Present speed, submerged," said Rogers, his tone controlled and assured. "Plus or minus twenty-five knots. Displacement . . . plus or minus two point five. I'd say Soviet Kilo class. Three thousand eight hundred yards and closing. Bearing zero-three-niner."

"Man battle stations!" ordered Hale, the chime alert bonging softly throughout the submarine. "Speed?"

"Twenty knots," answered Rogers.

"Hard left rudder to one-three-five degrees," ordered Hale.

"Left rudder to one-three-five degrees," confirmed Rogers, the diving officer watching rudder and trim control.

"Bearing?" asked Hale.

"Zero-three-niner," came the response.

"Mark! Range?"

"Four thousand."

"Angle on the bow," said Hale, beginning the litany of his attack. "Starboard one-four. Firing point procedures. Master one-zero. Tube one."

"Firing point procedures. Master one-zero. Tube one," came the confirmation. "Solution ready, sir. Weapons ready. Ship ready."

"Final bearing and shoot," announced Hale. "Master one-zero. Tube one."

Bearing and speed confirmed, the firing officer took over the procedure. "Stand by! Shoot! Fire! . . . One fired and running." The sine wave that was the other sub changed its vector on the screen, then fired.

"Shift to zero-eight-five," commanded Hale, gripping the periscope island rail, anticipating the turn.

"Zero-eight-five, sir."

"Very well. Fire two."

"Fire two. Two fired and running, sir."

"Take her to four hundred. Maximum angle two-zero degrees."

"Four hundred. Maximum two-zero degrees."

The second Mk-48 of *Reagan*'s two Mk-48s was homing in, the enemy unable to shake off its lock-on.

The visible sound blip of the other sub hastily, and now noisily, retreating, suddenly swelled from the size of a pinhead to that of a quarter then just as quickly shrank, becoming two microdots of light on the screen, fading, sliding slowly down the screen into nothingness. It was 0129 hours. It had all happened in just under seven minutes.

It was only ten minutes later, at 0139, that Hale and his crew received the information via an urgent TACAMO VHF "burst" message that they had sunk a Setoshio class diesel electric, not a Soviet Kilo; the Setoshio class's displacement 2.2 thousand tons, a diesel, similar to that of the Soviet Kilo, also with six torpedo tubes but a JDF— Japanese defense force attack submarine—the *Reagan*'s attack killing all seventy-five men aboard. No bodies had so far been found, or any other substantial wreckage, the identification having come instead from the contents of the pressurized garbage chute, packets of Shogun noodles floating to the surface and spotted by a JDF ASW patrol boat off the Kuril Islands.

Hale immediately knew that like Captain Will Rogers of the Aegis cruiser USS *Vincennes*, who had shot down an

Iraqi airliner by mistake in 1988—and unlike the captain of a USS guided missile frigate *Stark*, who in 1987 had allowed his ship to be fired on first—he would be completely exonerated by the navy.

He also knew that the Japanese defense force sub shouldn't have been in the grid, that it had strayed out of its predetermined patrol area—most likely lured by a Russian HUK probing the strait near the Japanese's sacrosanct islands—yet neither he, Rogers, nor the firing officer would ever be the same again. But in the massive conflict raging all about them, whatever stayed with them, no matter how deep it ran, would have to run silently aboard the *Reagan*.

Eleven minutes later, at 0150, the downed sub's big diesel imploded, the noise momentarily deafening Rogers, so that only his training made him hit the "squelch volume" button rather than tearing off his headset, the noise so loud it smothered all sea sound within a three-mile radius.

It was no surprise then that the *Reagan* didn't hear the Alfa that had been lying quietly on the bottom beyond the Kuril gap closest to Japan. By the time Rogers' sonar did pick it up and Hale ordered the sharp turn, it was too late, the Alfa having had ample time to hear the *Reagan* firing earlier, to have already vectored in the Americans. The Alfa captain had fired his three twenty-one-inch-diameter, surface-to-surface, torpedo-launched SUBROCS, each of the four-thousand-pound warheads when detonated above the surface capable of killing any submarine to a depth of three thousand feet, well beyond most subs' crush depth. With the *Reagan* level at fifteen hundred, the first SUBROC exploded above the *Reagan*'s hull, forward of its sail.

Hale heard the fire alarm go off for aft compartment three, above the torpedoes, the temperature gauge already registering 122 degrees Fahrenheit, the sub quickly filling with the pungent reek of an electrical fire.

"Inject Lock!" he ordered, hoping the freon gas would extinguish the fire. Within seconds, over the intercom and above cries of men in the sealed-off section, he could hear the freon hissing into compartment three and then a tremendous explosion as an oxygen tank ruptured, its noise bursting eardrums, its contents blowtorching the 122 degrees Fahrenheit to 628 degrees Fahrenheit, plastic fixtures spontaneously combusting, sending more choking toxic fumes throughout the boat.

In the next moment, two torpedos exploded, ripping the sub apart forward of the sail, the pressure, at three thousand feet over 130,000 pounds per square foot, driving the mortally wounded sub down toward the bottom in excess of a hundred miles an hour. First Officer Merrick and Sonarman Rogers barely made it from Control into the six-man forward "pop-out" escape capsule with three others, but the release mechanism wouldn't work, weighed down by what sounded like a pile of junk blown back from the disemboweled forward section. Then quite unexpectedly they heard the pile of metal above shifting like a collapsed barn in a hurricane, the debris that had been holding them down suddenly jettisoned.

"Release arm!" ordered Hale. There was a sound like a small grenade as the escape hatch burst free of the control section. But the Sea Wolf by then was already too deep—well over crush depth of four thousand feet—the sub plummeting at over 120 miles an hour, the release capsule shooting up from it through the water column like a cork released from a bottomless column.

"Jesus Christ!" It was the voice of a bosun aboard a U.S. Trident sub a hundred miles east of the Kuril gap, the Trident picking up the death throes of the *Reagan*, the agonizing warping of her bulkheads astonishing, like a dying whale, heard via the sound channel as clearly as if it had been only ten miles away. The sine wave that was the plummeting *Reagan* was drooping like a U of green pasta on the green screen, the dot of the escape capsule streaking up through the Trident's three trace sonar "windows" at terrific speed, its noise, like a rush of ice scatter, heard by everyone aboard the Trident. Then there was a tremendous wallop, like a space capsule smashing into the earth, the *Reagan*'s escape module hitting the air-water interface, its cone shape pancaked by pressures for which it wasn't designed. Its blip on the Trident's screen now resembled nothing so much as coffee grounds sliding down an opaque window—the slow rain of detritus all that remained of the *Reagan*'s capsule and crew, falling lifelessly and silently back into the very deep from which they had sought to escape.

"Poor bastards!" said the Trident's bosun. No one else spoke.

By the time the news was being conveyed to Robert Brentwood that he had just lost his second submarine, this time with all hands going down with her, he was about to learn that the target of his mission—"Operation Country Garden"—would constitute the third phase of Freeman's unexpected counterattack against Yesov.

The other seven members of the SEAL team were as eager as Brentwood had been, but just as taciturn in not showing their expectation—a nonchalant stance, typical of the swimmer commandoes, tempered by the knowledge that whatever the mission was, it was bound to be highly dangerous. It was at this moment of unspoken tension that Brentwood experienced an attack of free-floating anxiety. This time it was guilt, which he irrationally yet understandably felt for not having been in the combat control center when the *Reagan* had been caught out and destroyed. All her crew had been lost, all men he had made it his business to know, his extended family, many of whom had served aboard the *Roosevelt* before he'd had to scuttle her in the high Arctic. And now he had not been with them.

After all, he had detected the Alfa that had mortally wounded the *Roosevelt*, had made it pay for the blast from one of its twenty-one-foot-long torpedoes, which had resulted in a hairline fracture in the *Roosevelt*'s reactor. Brentwood knew that for him, as for some of the other men who had been farther away from the radiation-contaminated water before it had been pumped out, the "borderline" 250-rad dosage of radioactivity he'd received could kill him before his time.

He had been surprised to learn from the doctors in the Oxford radiation clinic that the same dosage could have widely different effects on its victims. Some went on living without apparent damage, as he had so far—then, quite suddenly, as the result of high stress, a man with the same dosage would rapidly decline in health. The psychological factor, in the words of the military MDs, was all but unmeasurable. You never knew. Brentwood now felt doubly at risk, enmeshed by depression upon hearing of the *Reagan*.

Had he been aboard, maybe he would have trailed the hydrophone array a little longer instead of relying solely on the inboard built-in hull sensors, and thus might have picked up the *whoosh!* of the Alfa's torpedoes or SUBROCS—whatever had hit her.

Ranged against his depression, there was his wife Rosemary in England to think about, and the impending birth of their first child. All his training told him he'd have to put the *Reagan* behind him. It wasn't his fault. Everybody made mistakes in their job. Yet he knew from his experience after he'd scuttled the *Roosevelt* that for the foreseeable future he would be plagued by a disturbing, dream-filled sleep—a parade of faces known and served with, now gone. Or was it all stress-induced premonition parading in the guise of memory—a foreshadowing of the SEALs' mission outcome? He had a look at the 3D mock-up of the China coast that had spawned the rumors of an amphibious invasion, rumors bolstered by the fact that their refresher courses here at Pearl had included depth sounding and obstacle clearance. Another rumor—this one correct—was that word of Freeman's target had arrived by "handcuffed-satchel" courier in Pearl.

By the time Robert Brentwood and the seven others were assembled in the "shed," the briefing officer from Freeman's HQ—drawing on what a U.S. president had once counseled—reminded the eight-man SEAL team that in crisis situations you *never* have all the information you want. You nevertheless have to make a decision based on whatever information you do have. What Freeman's G-2 intelligence section and the CIA knew before they received the vital information from the underground Democracy Movement was that the bridge over the Yangtze was considered one of the engineering wonders of the world—certainly more impressive to many Chinese than the Great Wall, its guard towers built along the 1,500-mile-long, dragon-backed barrier against Ghengis Khan.

One of the reasons for the Chinese reverence toward the great bridge was that during the bitter Sino-Soviet disputes of the sixties, Khrushchev had suddenly pulled out all Russian advisers, including the plans for the bridge—in effect saying to Beijing, "If you're so damn smart, build it yourselves." To the world's astonishment, especially the Siberians—for whom the bridge was now so vital—the Chinese did build it themselves, producing one of the greatest engineering feats of all time. Not only did the mighty bridge, nine piers in all, support a deck with 2.8 miles of road way, but it had a railroad on a lower second deck that spanned the great river for over four miles. When Mao and his Communists crossed the river on April 23, 1949, chasing out the Nationalists, they had also, for the first time, united the two Chinas: that "cold" China of the north, the country of the "noodle eaters," and the warmer country of "rice eaters" south of the Yangtze.

"The Nanking Bridge," began the SEAL briefing officer without ceremony—he might as well have been talking about the Ventura Freeway—"is the largest bridge over the Yangtze. Vital link between north and south China at any time but now—with early rains flooding out the approach roads to the other crossings—this Nanking baby is their only one, especially given its rail-hauling capacity." He switched on the projector, and Brentwood could hear the quiet whir of the air fan, which was strangely comforting,

given the monumental task that eight men now realized lay
before them. "Air force," continued the briefing officer,
"haven't been able to get anywhere near it. It's not only the
lousy weather, but the AA ring around this sucker is
something else. Five times denser than it ever was around
Hanoi. SAM sites, ZSU AA batteries—you name it, they've
got it—including a nifty little number they bought from
Israel—the Arrow Mach Two plus. Nasty. Besides . . ."
He dimmed the lights and focused the black-and-white
blowup of a blurred satellite picture of the bridge which
they used in Pearl for a scale mock-up. It always amazed
Brentwood that they claimed a camera on some of the
satellites in geosynchronous orbit, like the K-16, could read
a newspaper in Red Square. All he could see was a black
blur indicating the bridge, the latter circled in white on the
slide.

"Difficult to make out with the naked eye," conceded the
briefer, as if reading Brentwood's thoughts. "But under the
magnifier, you can see the nine piers all right. Set on
concrete blocks. Now, the big problem is that this was built
in the heyday of Red China's paranoia about America."

"Had a touch of that ourselves, didn't we?" asked Rose.

The briefing officer shrugged the comment off; his
grandpa had said something about it—a Senator Joe Mc-
Cartney . . . or something. "Yeah. Well, what you've got
to remember is that this bridge has, like I say, nine piers,
and it's a truss bridge—that is, there are V-shaped steel
supports arcing out either side from each of the nine
concrete piers. These steel arcs hold up eight individual
sections between the nine piers. I repeat, eight *individual*
sections. It's not all one span."

Brentwood was right on it. "So even if we blow a hole in
one section—if we don't take out the whole span, they just
build over the hole."

"Right. And even if you hit the top level, there's a
second, the rail deck, underneath. So you're going to have
to knock out a pier or bring down a whole section between

piers. ChiComs knew what the hell they were doing, not building it in one continuous span. They built eight of the bastards in the event of war. The problem is, in order to get enough high explosive to blow out a pier, you'd have to drill deep holes for the charges.''

"And the Commies don't like that!" said the Bullfrog, Brady.

"Nah," said the briefer, scrunching up his face, adopting Brady's tone. "Make too much noise, and concrete dust might hit a sampan, get in their chop suey. Probably get Melvin Belli to sue the shit out of you."

"That sounds fair," said Rose.

"That's all we need," said Dennison, who was just coming out of a messy divorce. "More fucking lawyers!"

"What we need, gentlemen," said the briefing officer, "is to insert you clandestinely and have you do what damage you can. Now, we can't drill into the pier, so you're going to have to get high enough above the pier's waterline to attach the HE to the trusses, place the explosives near the bottom of the V-shaped steel supports where they're embedded into the concrete. Remember, this isn't the movies. It's not the blast per se that'll bring the steel supports down, but the heat generated for a second or two—just long enough to soften the steel so it'll droop like taffy on a fork, and then the whole damn shebang'll come tumbling down. It's all in raising the temperature high enough to plasticize the steel for a split second or two. Failing that, go for an 'earmuff' HE charge on two piers supporting one of the spans. If you don't get a span, they'll just lay a few planks across the hole from a half-assed explosion, like they did on that Baghdad bridge we hit in the Iraqi War. Traffic'd be going across it within twenty-four hours. Freeman wants this sucker closed down for a week—two, if possible—and one span coming down'll accomplish that—sever the ChiCom supply line."

"While we're hitting them in the north?" put in Dennison. "That's a gamble, isn't it? We're in enough shit up north already—Three Corps is getting chopped to pieces. What's going to stop Yesov long enough for Freeman to wheel his muscle south against the Siberian-ChiCom border?''

"General Freeman's attending to that right now," answered the briefer. "Your job will be to knock out the bridge.''

"Well, sir," Rose said wryly, turning to Brentwood. "You were right—it's 'clearance' work all right." The others laughed, Brentwood responding in kind.

"Ah, what the hell?" he said. "Same country anyhow.''

"Okay," said the briefer. "We can't take you in by sub, as first hoped." He looked at Brentwood. "That's why you were seconded, Captain. But we've had to scrub that idea. ChiCom sub nets at the mouth of the Yangtze are too well placed—set just deep enough for their guided missile destroyers and gunboats to skittle over, but too shallow for any of our subs." He turned to Brentwood. "Sorry about that, sir. We thought originally we could have you take the team in via—''

"Then I'm excused," joked Brentwood, getting up as if to leave.

It got the biggest laugh of the day, which was just as well—the details of the task facing them were not encouraging.

Insertion would be by two Pave Low choppers, rather than one, in the event one was hit or experienced mechanical difficulties, flying low, nap of the earth, to avoid radar. They would take off from the carrier USS *Salt Lake City* on station 320 miles out in the South China Sea, outside the Nanking AA perimeter.

Extraction would be by the same method. If the SEALs got into difficulty, the SOS emergency code word or signature selected by Bullfrog Brady to initiate an SAS/ Delta interdiction would be "Mars." The Bullfrog had thought hard and long about the code word. While the Yangtze was a hell of a lot warmer than the Manzhouli front where the S/D team were now en route to, it was all relative. For though no ice would be on the Yangtze, it would be cold enough.

Even with the protection afforded by the trapped layer of body-heated water in the men's rubber suits, the temperatures would be below minus forty degrees Fahrenheit. While the suits would protect a man who would otherwise freeze up in twenty-three minutes in such water, even a suit-protected swimmer working a closed-circuit UBA, such as the COBRA rebreather, could be so exhausted, his lips so cold that it would be hard to form words properly. Anything beginning with an S was particularly difficult and had in the past sounded like an F on an emergency radio band. M words were the easiest to pronounce, no matter how cold you were. In any event, the Bullfrog hoped there would be no need to use it.

"And everyone go over your sign language," added the briefer. "With no radio, it'll be sign language on the surface, feel line when submerged, and penlights only in an emergency. Study the model all you like for the next couple of hours. We leave for the carrier at oh four hundred, and you'll go in tomorrow evening at eighteen hundred hours. Two squads, four men each. Designation Echo One— Captain Brentwood the boss; Echo Two—CPO Brady the boss. Flight to the Nanking drop-off seven miles south of the city and upstream will be three hundred twenty miles from *Salt Lake City*. One and a half to two hours, depending on head winds. Pickup four hours after drop-off. River currents estimated four to six knots. You'll take thirty-five horsepower outboards on the Zodiacs, but only use them if you have to in strong local cross-currents. Questions?"

"Choppers have the range without in-flight refueling?" asked Dennison.

"No sweat. Auxiliary fuel tanks, detachable."

"He makes it sound like a training run," said one of Echo Two's four-man squad.

"If you don't screw up—it will be," said young Rose,

his desire for reassurance dressed up as a question. "Right, Bullfrog?"

"Yeah," said Brady, turning to Brentwood. "Right, Captain?"

"What? Oh yes—absolutely. What is it the Brits say? 'Piece of cake'?"

"Yeah," Bullfrog told Rose, "that's it. Piece of cake. No sweat."

CHAPTER TWENTY-FOUR

COLONEL SOONG'S FOURTH Battalion traveled light, as did all PLA infantry. They had even discarded their NBC masks, confident that the Americans were too squeamish to use gas unless it was used on them first. Besides, the PLA had discovered a moderately effective method of dealing with gas: they ran away from it. Oh, part of their force would be lost in any such attack, but maneuvers involving tear gas had demonstrated how valuable time was lost donning cumbersome gear. And rapidly changing local wind and humidity conditions had taught Beijing what the Pentagon had discovered years before—that at best a commander could contemplate using gas only as a tactical, that is, local, weapon in a tight corner during a large battle, and not as a wider strategic weapon.

In any event, General Cheng had saved the PLA millions of yuan by not purchasing gas masks, protective clothing, and sophisticated robot sniffers through paying the money instead to La Roche Industries for better artillery shells. In doing so, Cheng had also enabled his divisions, unencumbered by the heavy NBC protective gear, to move faster on foot than any other army. It counted for Soong's battalions closing in so quickly on the southern side of the 3,770-foot-high Argunskiy 7. Even without his spotters, Soong could tell from the less intense yet more localized area of bombardment that the enemy battery, after losing most of their guns in their retreat to A-7, had regrouped atop the six acres of heavy timber that formed the horseshoe-shaped western part of the mountain's snow-covered summit. Not surprisingly, Soong's supporting artillery had been slower to move up than his infantry, but based on the PLA's *yuji paodui*—mobile guerrilla artillery units—all of his artillery was capable of being borne by hand, broken down like so many pieces of a Lego set, with even the wheels of each gun in four segments, so that the guns could be hauled piecemeal and assembled by manpower alone. It was an old PLA tactic, but one the PLA knew continued to astonish more mechanized foes whose trucks were more often than not stopped by the taiga.

CHAPTER TWENTY-FIVE

DAVID BRENTWOOD SAT on the thin, hard seat by the door of the AC-130H—a four-engine Lockheed C-130 transport converted to a Spectre gunship—and checked his wrist altimeter and watch. It was 0607. Thirty thousand feet and no moon—as dark "as a bloody coal mine in a blackout," as Aussie Lewis put it.

At 0611 David readied himself to lead the stick of the HALO-C—high altitude, low opening circle—jump from thirty thousand feet, after which the Spectre aircraft would rapidly descend in ever-widening circles, all the while pouring down fire into the mountain's collar of timber that surrounded and ran about the lip of A-7's horseshoe-shaped summit.

Hopefully his SAS/D team would be able to inject sufficient firepower on the ground to secure a perimeter around the horseshoe long enough for the battered survivors of the 155mm battery—no one knew how many there would be, due to the break in radio contact—to get to the northern edge of the horseshoe clearing. Providing a secure perimeter could be achieved, the area, no more than two acres, could be used as a landing zone for rescue helicopters which would follow on from the Kalga strip ninety miles to the northeast, lying in the valley between the Argunskiy and Nerchinskiy ranges. But it would work only if the SAS/D team could gather in the remaining defenders—probably by now no more than a score or so—fast enough, and lead them to the clearing before the whole mountain was overrun by the advancing ChiCom battalions.

"Check masks!" ordered Brentwood, standing up, one gloved hand gripping the canvas webbing, the other making sure his oxygen mask seal was secure. "Infrared goggles. Check!" Next he held up his left arm, tapping its wrist altimeter, looking down the line of fifteen SAS/Delta men who would accompany him, hearing himself breathing in the mask like some trapped animal lumbering forward as he carried the inverted Bergen pack that would dangle beneath him in the fall and which would carry everything from ammunition to a winter-issue 4,200-calorie MRE—meal ready to eat, otherwise known as Meals Refused by Everybody.

Everything changes and everything remains the same. It was the last phrase David Brentwood thought of as he dove from the Spectre into the void above A-7, the frigid air screaming about him in its banshee rage.

Aussie Lewis went out after him, then came Salvini, Choir Williams leading the S/D troop of one officer—David Brentwood—and fifteen men, each SAS man a veteran, and most graduates of either SAS's CQB—Close Quarter Battle—"house" in Hereford near the Welsh Black Mountains or of Fort Bragg's four-roomed "shooting house," where they had been trained relentlessly for rapid deployment surgical strikes.

During the two-minute free fall, his arms and legs out in "frog" steering position—simultaneously braking and guiding his fall, careful not to "grab air" too much in front of him lest he put himself into a spin, and shifting the weight of his pack away from his center line—David could hear the feral roar of the AC-130 still in its pylon turn far beneath them.

The air force brass called the AC-130 an "aircraft capable of substantial support firepower." To the crew of fourteen who manned the converted Lockheeds, however, the AC-130 was simply called "Spectre" or "Spooky Two." And until this morning the official designation given the plane by the Chinese High Command was "special operations enemy gunship." But from the moment it began unleashing its deadly thunder over the mountain, the AC-130 would be forever known as the "Flying Dragon." It was so named because of the long, thin, red tongues spewing down parabolas of fire from the left side of the aircraft where its two 7.62mm, seven-barreled, twenty-millimeter Vulcan Gatling guns, forty-millimeter Bofors pompoms, and 105mm howitzer filled the air with hot metal.

The worst part for the Chinese below was the fact that the dragon was not flying blind, merely shooting for effect, its IRR—imaging infrared—and LLTV—low light television—sensors mounted mid-belly between the "Black Crow" radio direction-finder pod and the twin Vulcans showing up the Chinese infantry as clear white dots on the flickering gray screen. In this way the gunship's target computers, in attaining their own vectors, were overcoming the failure, following the initial ChiCom attacks, to receive any radio beacon guide from the 155mm battery. The infrared sensors also obviated the necessity for using the two-kilowatt 1.5-million-candlepower searchlight mounted near the plane's tail, a fact which the five gunners aboard the Spectre appreciated, for while the beam would have better illuminated the moving targets below, it would also have pointed directly back to them.

Colonel Soong gave the order to cease firing at the dragon and to hit the ground, an order calculated by him to both conserve ammunition and as the only real way of combating the infrared sensors which could identify moving targets much more readily than stationary ones.

It was probably the only order of Soong's that had ever been disobeyed, for it was a natural human reaction to turn on whatever was shooting down at you, the Spectre's 105mm shells and the ChiCom enfilades of small arms fire rounds filling the air with multiple high-pitched whistles, the smallest piece of the white-hot metal penetrating skin and bone as if they were butter. The very air was vibrating with the sustained roar of the Spectre's weapons, the howitzer's gunners in particular priding themselves on having one of the thirty-two-pound rounds "en route" even as the preceding one was exploding, the noise drowning the steady pulsation of the aircraft's four turbo props, HE and shrapnel continuing to crash into the ChiCom positions. The ChiCom infantry return fire was ineffective, literally bouncing off the 6,900 pounds of armor plate that encased the Spectre, whose highly incendiary metal-alloy rounds from its four-clip forty-millimeter pompoms kept exploding among Soong's hapless infantry.

Then, as quickly as it had begun, it ended with the Spectre's fire-control officer's command to break off the attack, an order which, apart from the obvious, told all crew members that the S/D "skydivers" circle was now entering the DAW—designated air window—above the landing zone.

As he approached nearly 120 mph, the thunder-filled air that was streaming past his oxygen mask and over his tethered ammo pack below him seemed colder to Aussie Lewis than in any of the other jumps he'd made. He was nearing the chute-opening height of 2,500 feet, the ear-shattering noise caused by the Spectre's covering fire now ended, the irregular circle of snow that was the two-acre clearing on A-7's summit rushing up at him. He checked the wrist altimeter, saw it was 2,900 feet, pulled the rip cord and felt, then heard, the "snap": the jerk of the two-ply, banana-shaped chute opening. Immediately he began playing out his weapons/equipment pack twenty feet below on the tether to lessen his landing impact, and started working the riser cords, pouring air quickly from the left- to right-side panels, sliding into a spiraling corkscrew trajectory that would bring him away from the snow-covered timber around the clearing. Each of the fifteen SAS/D men knew he had to establish a perimeter fast.

There was another snap, but this time it was followed by the steady tattoo of a machine gun, and Aussie Lewis saw red tracer climbing lazily toward him, its deceptively graceful arcs curving past him. His feet hit the snowy ground and he tumbled, the tracer arcs lowering in his general direction. "Don't shoot, you stupid bastards!" he yelled ineffectually into his mask, furious, for all his training to be cool, and at heart deeply and truly afraid of only one thing—the ever present possibility in each rescue mission that you could end up as "collateral damage," killed by "friendly fire." Everyone on the SAS/D team was more aware than most in Freeman's Second Army of the acute danger of being hit by your own side—that even in America's most successful war, in Iraq, twenty-four percent, 35 of the 148 Americans killed, died because they were mistaken by their own side as the enemy. It was a percentage that Brentwood, Lewis, Salvini, Choir Williams, and the rest knew could double here in as many minutes, given the fact they'd been unable to make radio contact with those they were attempting to rescue.

Dragged a few feet by the chute, Lewis punched the release, and within a minute had hauled the Bergen pack across the waist-deep snow and had the Heckler & Koch 11 A1 out of its wrap. The butt stock of the forty-inch-long gun in place, its safety off, his thumb moved from the white S through E to full automatic as naturally as he breathed, the gun's barrel tooled to accept either the old NATO 5.6mm round or the heavier but harder-hitting Siberian 7.62mm—Soviet surplus. It had been an important consideration, given the unlikelihood of being resupplied by air should they find it necessary to counterattack into the timber, where, if their ammo ran out—some ammo boxes would inevitably be lost—they might have to use abandoned ChiCom-Soviet 7.62mm in their attempt to secure a perimeter.

Snapping out the bipod, Lewis planted the gun left of a shattered tree stump at the edge of the clearing and unwrapped the spare barrel, placing it by his side should he be forced to overheat the first barrel in what he already expected to be a massive counterattack by the ChiCom. The one thing on which the SAS/D team was depending was that most, if not all, of the artillery battery's gunners they were trying to extract would have Starlight infrared binoculars and/or goggles, so that although not being in radio contact, they would readily make out fellow American shapes in the clearing. Even so, it was risky, for it was possible that a PLA patrol had penetrated farther into the timber about the clearing than anticipated, the tracer coming at Lewis just before he touched down a case in point.

Through his own "bug eyes" Lewis could see the infrared blur of Brentwood, who had made a perfect walk-away landing, immediately taking up his position to the right of Lewis on the westernmost arc of the snowy, horseshoe-shaped clearing. Meanwhile, Salvini, Choir Williams, and others were spreading left of Lewis around the eastern curve of the horseshoe. Then, through the trees, he saw a shape moving through a clump of pine that had been stripped of their needles by what he guessed must have been artillery and mortar rounds, the stripped trees looking strangely naked, like so many huge, torn umbrellas upended in the snow. And through this wild, denuded wood, Lewis saw shapes moving; several others, their outline more indistinct because of a stand of unshelled timber, following the first; Lewis and the other SAS/D men who'd spotted them, holding their fire while peering anxiously through their nighttime goggles to make a clear friend-or-foe identification.

CHAPTER TWENTY-SIX

DEVOID OF STAR- or moonlight to guide them, coming in low westward from the East China Sea, lost to enemy radar because of the sea clutter, the two MH-53J Pave Low helos carrying four SEALs apiece skirted the wide confluence of the Huangpu and the Yangtze deltas ten miles to their south. Sea clutter gave way to the low stratus and cumulonimbus thunderheads massing along the coast, and the two SOS—special operations squadron—choppers were still below the ChiCom coast radar net, their look-down radar guiding them up and over the contours of the earth, no more than fifty feet above ground. The seven men aboard each chopper—four SEALs and the chopper's crew of three—were hoping and praying NOE flying would keep them undetected.

On all the aircraft specifications charts provided to avid journalists in the Iraqi War, the big, fat, squat Pave Low hadn't been featured—it didn't look ''sexy'' enough in some editors' opinions. But it was the unmentioned Pave Lows, four of them—despite the Apaches reaping all the glory in the press—that had struck the decisive blow against Saddam Hussein. Loaded with DEPNAV—the highly precise deep-penetration navigation computer—and nap of the earth early warning equipment, including their Doppler radar, the four Pave Lows had *led* the four Apaches in the predawn darkness of January 17, 1991. Flying low and deep

across the Iraqi border into the western desert, the Apaches'
Hellfire took out two critical "overlapping zone" radar
sites, thus assuring a "radar-black" hole. Then pouring
through the hole came the undetected Allied air forces,
delivering the first thunder of Desert Storm.

With insertion by air rather than by submarine having
been decided on by Freeman because of the unknown
configuration of sub nets at the mouth of the Yangtze and
Huangpu, Robert Brentwood felt even more that he was the
odd man out among the SEALs. Though with his rank he
was the "wheel"—the senior officer in charge of Operation
Country Garden—he was at least ten to fifteen years older
than most of the two four-man Echo One and Echo Two
teams.

And there were dozens of details he had to worry about,
any of which, if not attended to, could foul up the mission.
Even the relatively quiet purr of the muffled thirty-five
horsepower outboard engines, should they have to use
them, might be picked up by river traffic, though during the
bull-pen briefing board *Salt Lake City*, intelligence reports
had assured him that the noise wouldn't be heard amid the
distinctive and unvarying two-stroke putt-putting sound of
the Chinese barges. The Chinese apparently used the same
engines on all their waterways. It was as if, in his free-
floating anxiety before the mission, his mind, keyed for
action, needed to alight on some concrete detail as a
temporary way of escape, a way of filling in the time before
the inevitable unknown.

But the other SEALs were giving all their attention to
their weapons. In the first Pave Low, carrying Brentwood's
Echo One team, Rose was checking the number-four
buckshot cartridges for his AAI—Aircraft Armaments
Inc.—"double S," or silent shotgun. Using a plastic pusher
piston, the gun could send the buckshot out at over four
hundred feet a second, the shell's expanding metal preventing any gases escaping; meaning that if the weapon had to
be used, its only sound would be the soft click of the double

S's firing pin. Apart from the explosives, the remainder of the SEALs' small but lethal arsenal included Smith & Wesson .38 pistols, fragmentation and smoke grenades, emergency flares, and in Bullfrog Brady's Echo Two team, a Smith & Wesson Model 76 submachine gun carried by Echo Two's radio operator. In Echo One, Robert Brentwood was also armed with a Smith & Wesson Model 76, while Diver First Class Dennison packed a Stoner MK-23 with a 150-round belt-box feed.

In Echo One's last-minute check, Brentwood had Rose, Dennison, and Medical Corpsman Smythe—who was also Echo One's radio operator—make sure each of the three thirty-second-fuse Claymore mines was in the semi-inflated boat, trusting that Brady was making the same equipment check aboard the Echo Two Pave Low, a quarter mile aft of them. Unconsciously, Brentwood felt for the Griptite sheath of the high-carbon steel knife strapped to his calf and for the small, pen-sized signal light. Glancing at the C-4 plastique explosive packs, he detected an odor that shouldn't be aboard the helo. He'd ordered everyone to eat one of the regional Chinese meals before they'd taken off from the carrier. ChiComs could smell American food a hundred yards away. More than one U.S. soldier had died in Korea and 'Nam because of that, the Americans' red meat diet especially detectable by Asians.

"Everyone on rice and fish before we took off?"

Dennison, Rose, and Smythe all nodded affirmatively, the perfume-like smell of gum apparently coming from the chopper's electronic warfare officer. Brentwood told him to get rid of it.

"Well, gentlemen," Brentwood noted, to ease the tension a little, "according to my GPS here, we're right on the money." The handheld global positioning system, fed by satellite atomic clocks in orbit, was giving him a second-by-second readout of precisely where they were over the velvety blackness of rice fields south of Taizhou, just seventy miles east of Nanking. "We're exactly five hundred and eighty-eight miles east sou'east of Beijing. Error factor—no more than twenty yards—in case you were wondering where you are."

"Reminds me of a story," said Smythe, his voice made tremulous by the rotor's vibration. "This guy's at an outdoor Indian convention—"

"Is he Indian?" asked Rose.

"What? Yeah, 'course he's Indian," said Smythe. "Anyway, the head honcho asks him what tribe he's from—ticking 'em off on a clipboard, right? Indian guy says, 'I'm a member of the Farkarwee tribe.' Head honcho looks down, reads through the whole list from Apache to Sioux, says to the guy, 'You sure? I can't find the Farkarwee tribe on the list. How many are you?'

" 'Only me and my granddad,' says the guy. 'But I know we're definitely the Farkarwee tribe.' "

Smythe shook his head, like he was the guy with the clipboard. "Head honcho didn't know what to do. Didn't want to offend the guy, but he couldn't find the tribe. Maybe it was extinct, wiped out? So he asks the guy again. Says, 'You sure it's the Farkarwee tribe?'

" 'Sure I'm sure,' says the Indian.

" 'You positive?' says the head honcho. ' 'Cause it's not on my—'

" 'Look,' the Indian says, 'there're only two of us left, but I know we're the Farkarwee tribe.'

" 'How can you be so sure?' asked the head honcho.

" 'Because,' says the Indian, 'every mornin' when we were comin' across the country to this convention, my grandfather'd go out in front of the tepee, put up his hands and say, 'Where the fark are we?' "

Brentwood saw the cargo hold light go to red. They were five minutes from the landing zone. Once they reached it, they would rappel from the chopper down onto the muddy bank seven miles south on the river's western bank, where the Yangtze, straightening out upstream, was at least three miles wide. A seven-mile-long, spatula-shaped island lay three-quarters of the way across from their touchdown point on the western shore. Both four-man teams and Zodiacs would be out and the chopper gone within three minutes, the men having to take out the Zodiacs semi-inflated. "Like pallbearers!" as Rose had indelicately put it during the briefing. Full inflation of the rubber boats by carbon dioxide cartridge would take place once they were outside the chopper, moments before carrying them to the riverbank.

The Pave Lows banked left to the southwest in a wide, end sweep that would be longer than a direct run in, but would keep them low over the rice fields and levees and, most importantly, clear of the three 425-foot towers situated north of the bridge.

Two minutes from the insertion point, the Paves' pilots went from manual to hover coupler. The latter's computer-fed data from the gyroscope inertial guidance system and altimeter automatically altered trim and yaw through rotor control to keep the chopper coming in on a steady vector low over the levees, toward the preprogrammed drop-off point by the river, now four minutes away.

The pulsating red light turned to amber.

As leader of Echo One, Brentwood, like Brady leading Echo Two, would have preferred a drop-off point closer to the bridge, and to land on the eastern, down-channel traffic side, but most of Nanking's population lived on the eastern shore. Besides, the island would shield them from the more populated eastern bank.

Inside the cargo hold, Brentwood felt the tremulous vibration prior to the drop-off, saw the amber light switch to green.

"Go!" said the copilot, and the Pave Low's gaping door ramp opened. Within seconds Brentwood's Echo One and Brady's Echo Two teams were both out of the choppers. The second Robert Brentwood touched ground, the smell of riverbank mud and human excrement from the rice fields snatched his breath away. Then his infrared goggles revealed a broad shimmering expanse that was the river, and before it a gradually sloping gray that was the riverbank. From the first step in his rubber reef walkers, which doubled as fin slippers, he could feel an icy wind moaning about his rubber suit. Through the infrared, the shimmering negative-like image that was the expanse of river became crazy-quilted, dark patches caused by gusts that had ruffled the surface and suddenly lowered the temperature of the water-air interface.

Brentwood heard the gentle hiss of air as Brady pulled the carbon dioxide cartridge on the other team's boat. A moment later he heard another hiss, Dennison pulling the cord on Echo One, Brentwood feeling the gunwales of the rubber boat stiffening against his thigh as he caught a glimpse of Dennison steadying the WOX-5 underwater gun, its rocket projectiles against the belt-feed drums of ammunition for the minigun. The latter, a cut-down 7.62mm Gatling, had a hitherto unheard of firing rate of six thousand rounds a minute, another weapon Robert Brentwood fervently hoped they wouldn't have to use.

Echo Two's RTO—radio telephone operator—Petty Officer Jensen, had already slipped aboard Brady's boat, his AN/PRC-77 radio in its waterproof pack on the back of his inflatable black life-preserver vest.

Farther back in Echo One, in a last minute check, Brentwood, his left hand firmly gripping the forward starboard lug of the boat, slid his right hand over the waterproof holster of his stainless steel Smith & Wesson nine-millimeter Hush Puppy.

As Dennison, Rose, Brentwood, and Corpsman Smythe eased the boat into the ice-chilled water, Echo Two's four-man team and their 1,300 pounds of equipment were already pushing off, making a sucking sound on the sloping bank, which seemed to them as loud as a gunshot. But Brentwood knew it was probably no noisier than a rat plopping into the river mud, the last of the four SEALs in Brady's Echo Two ahead of them having stepped into a knee-deep silt hole. Brentwood pushed the thought of water rats out of his mind. It was one of the reasons he used to tell his younger brothers that he joined the pig boats—the submarines—and not the surface navy. In a sub there wasn't enough room for a rat to hide.

Waiting several seconds for Echo Two to make some distance before his Echo One pushed off, Brentwood could already hear a distant putt-putting: river boats. He was surprised, however, that there wasn't more sound, given the volume of water traffic Freeman's HQ had told them to expect. Glancing at his GPS through the infrared goggles, he saw it was 2250. The current was running around three to six knots, and so all being well, using paddle assist, they could expect to be in the vicinity of the bridge well within the hour, only using the engines in the event of unpredictable swirl holes. Pickup, unless something went wrong and they were forced to go SOS on the emergency band, would be at 0300 hours. "Ample time," as the briefer aboard *Salt Lake City* had put it, to recon the shore defenses near the bridge and slip in unseen, using the faint navigation lights on the sampans as pointers for the channel approach to the piers. If either boat thought they had been sighted, the decision to either start the outboard engine as cover or to engage would be left up to Brady, commanding Echo Two, and Brentwood in Echo One.

The two small boats caught the current, Echo Two already well offshore about a hundred yards ahead, Robert Brentwood back in Echo One, wishing dearly that the Chinese would never imagine, let alone suspect, such a daring raid.

The four men of Echo Two in Brady's boat had a bad fright within thirty seconds of shoving off when an enormous barge—its navigation lights air-raid blinkered, port and starboard lights mere pinpricks in the vast blackness of the Yangtze—all but capsized the twelve-foot-long, six-foot-wide rubber boat, heavily laden as it was with anchor, ropes, tackle, C-4 plastique, and weapons. Brady, in the bow of Echo Two, only managed to see the barge, loaded with four rail-car tankers heading for the tank farm downriver of the Nanking Bridge, at the last moment, giving Echo Two a bare two seconds to avoid it, the barge's wash alone threatening to swamp them as Brady managed to swing the Zodiac's tiller, putting her bow on to the barge's waves. The tank farm, faintly visible through the recon photos despite the smog over Nanking, had itself been a tempting target for the SEALs, but one that they'd rightly decided to forego in lieu of blowing up the bridge to sever the ChiCom supply line.

Another surprise for Echo Two, being the first boat out, was that though they had been told by Freeman's HQ that according to China's river traffic laws the right lane was the downriver route, in fact the rule, as evidenced by the sight of the enormous barge in the middle of the river, was made by the boats' captains. It was the oldest rule in the world, on the river or anywhere else: the biggest won. Normally it would have been of little moment to the SEALs, but it made for an added hazard in their clandestine mission, Brady making a mental note of it for their debriefing.

The two boats—Echo One a hundred yards farther back, due to its later push-off, Brady farther toward the right shore—were about fifty yards apart going downriver. The smell of China washed over them, the odors of Nanking, like the few lights the great metropolis showed in the darkness, less exotic than anticipated—difficult to isolate in fact, beneath the pervasive smell of the ordure from the fields on either side of the mighty river.

CHAPTER TWENTY-SEVEN

NOW AUSSIE LEWIS saw the shape of an American helmet coming out of the artillery-cropped copse of aspen, and gave a low whistle. "Hey, mate! Buddy! Over here!"

The man, about thirty feet away, silhouetted by a moon break in the clouds, stopped dead, then fell, his weapon spitting fire. As Lewis rolled, firing his HK in a tight, overbody arc, his face splattered by snow, he was aware of a searing sensation in his left foot. There was more firing off to his right from Choir Williams, and the man who'd fired at Lewis fell screaming, hands flailing in the snow for his dropped weapon. Lewis gave him a full burst and, in Lewis's infrared goggles, the man's body jumped, was still, then became a flapping gray. Lewis could smell a burning, rubbery odor where the man—who Lewis thought had obviously mistaken him for a Russian—had clipped Lewis's left boot, singeing part of the Vibram sole. Lewis's foot felt wet, but whether it was blood or snow, he couldn't tell; he felt for the elastic-band-held medipac on the side of his helmet. SAS and Delta were bred to be tough. They were also taught it was false heroics—stupid—not to take a shot of morphine if it could keep you fighting rather than being a burden on your buddies.

It was David Brentwood who, under cover of a long burst of 5.56mm from Choir Williams's HK 11 A1, made the dash across to Lewis to break the news. It had been discovered that the man they'd shot and a second one brought down by a Delta trooper on the northern side of the horseshoe of timber didn't have dog tags. Special Forces—SEALs, the SAS, and Delta Force—did the same thing if they were on clandestine ops—but not regular army artillery. They never, but *never*, took off their dog tags. Some widow might miss out on the $50,000 death benefit.

"Christ!" said Lewis as the import of Brentwood's "no ID" information hit him. "What you think, Davey? OMONS or SPETS?"

"Has to be Special Forces of some kind," David Brentwood conceded. As he spoke, he saw more shapes slipping through the artillery-denuded pine into the thicker timber encircling the mountaintop clearing.

"Freeman was right," said David Brentwood in a whisper. "We didn't start the war."

"Cunning bastards!" hissed Lewis, now grimacing, a sharp, hot pain piercing his ankle. "Siberian bastards started it—shelled the ChiComs themselves, made 'em think it was us to get the ChiComs in on their side."

"Freeman's not going to like this," said Brentwood, in what had to be the understatement of the war so far.

"Fuck Freeman!" hissed Lewis. "*I* don't fuckin' like it. We'd better get out of here, Davey. And fast. Fuckin' Sibirs aren't gonna want witnesses."

"Why the hell didn't *they* get out?" asked David. "I mean, why the hell—" Then he stopped, the answer frighteningly obvious. As he had told Lewis, the Siberians— Novosibirsk, to be correct—obviously hadn't wanted their SPETS, OMONS, whichever, to get out. Obviously, all they'd been told was to shell the ChiCom positions and hold.

"Purple-flare time, mate," said Lewis. "Get those friggin' Wokkas in here fast." He meant the CH-47 Chinook evac choppers from Kalga. There was nothing to rescue now but themselves, and they had to get out the word about who had really broken the cease-fire. It wouldn't be believed by the ChiComs, of course. In any case, Beijing was probably now only concerned with having the opportunity to gain more territory. But maybe the truth would make some difference to internal Chinese resistance.

Flickering high above them, the parachute flare turned night to day, transforming the two acres of snow into an undulating mauve blanket. It also unleashed a fierce Siberian counterattack. In seconds the air was flailed with the crack and whistle of small arms fire punctuated by the stomach-punching *crump-crump-crump* of heavy hundred-millimeter mortars.

"Least the ChiComs won't use their artillery this close to their own," said Aussie Lewis, clipping in another mag and immediately realizing the foolishness of his remark. Both he and David Brentwood knew that, unlike the Americans, the Chinese commander would have no compunction about sacrificing a hundred or so infantry—more—to gain a position. And every SAS/D man on the mountaintop now knew that the Siberians, caught out in their deception, would be more intent on killing Americans than worrying about being overrun by the Chinese.

"Jesus—what a mess!" uttered Aussie, his words lost to the feral roar of David Brentwood's Heckler & Koch submachine gun and the crash of mortars. "Where are those friggin' chop—" began a Delta trooper ten yards to Brentwood's left, but he never finished, decapitated by shrapnel, the stump of what had been his neck bubbling white with blood in David's infrared goggles.

CHAPTER TWENTY-EIGHT

HIS F-15 AND F-18 strikers already aloft from Yerofey Pavlovich, Second Army's forwardmost air base, flying ahead to provide an air umbrella, the pilots searching for breaks in the blizzard but not finding them, General Freeman looked at his watch. It was 0200 hours, cold, and still overcast. He tapped the pilot of the C-130 transport. "Let's go, son! Can't wait here all night."

With that, the big Hercules lumbered forward on the Marsden steel-web runway, followed by another whose 220 paratroopers, together with Freeman and his 219 paratroopers in the first aircraft, would be responsible for securing the Nizhneangarsk drop zone—a frozen salt marsh ten miles east of Lake Baikal's northern end. The remaining airborne troops would follow and be jumping from eight much longer, 245-foot C-5 Galaxies, each holding 345 men.

Freeman had few worries about the two-hour, 575-mile flight to the BAM—Baikal-Amur mainline—railhead at

Nizhneangarsk. Although there would be three thousand
men in all, the biggest airborne operation since the disas-
trous American and Allied drop over Arnhem in '44, he was
confident the Siberians wouldn't be expecting him. As
added insurance, a USAF squadron of Wild Weasels,
electronic jammers, was already airborne to scramble the
radars ringing Yesov's crack Sixty-fourth Division at Nizhneangarsk. The problem would be, once the Siberians made
visual contact, how quickly Yesov's Nizhneangarsk garrison could move up their heavy artillery and tanks to the
drop zone. Freeman regretted the operation had to be
carried out at dawn, but with any operation involving more
than a hundred men, he knew it would have been suicidal to
try it at night, when the zone on the frozen marsh was no
more than a quarter-mile square in the taiga.

The jamming around Nizhneangarsk was only partly
successful, the Wild Weasels, four hundred miles from
Yerofey Pavlovich, coming under attack by a squadron of
MiG Fulcrums, diving from fifteen thousand. Freeman's
assumption that the Siberians could be fought off by the
Eagles and F-18s proved correct—most of the furballs, or
dogfights, going in the Americans' favor—but one C-130
transport was taken out; whether by the Fulcrums or
friendly fire was not known. In the confusion of dogfights
and thick cloud, no one knew. What Freeman, aboard the
lead Hercules, did know, however, was that already over
three hundred of his paratroopers were dead, cutting his
force to two-thirds before he'd even reached the drop zone.

Inside the roar of the Hercules, the beefy-faced jumpmaster stood up, both gloved hands outstretched in front of
him, palms forward as if about to push against an invisible
wall, his voice raised against the thundering roar of the
engines. "Get ready!"

There was a long shuffling noise, the heavily laden
paratroopers still sitting, but moving closer now to the edge
of the long plank seats.

"Stand up!" yelled the jumpmaster.

"Stand up!" repeated Freeman, the first of the stick, but at this moment no longer the boss aboard the aircraft.

The jumpmaster's hands moved from the palms-out front position to his sides, as if he was describing the big one that got away, and as one the paratroopers rose awkwardly with their heavy gear, hooked up and checked that snap hooks were clipped on properly to the overhead cable without allowing too much slack on the long yellow static line. Each man checked the static line of the man in front of him.

The light still red, the jumpmaster's right hand shot out, down to the right like an umpire pointing at the bag. Obediently Freeman, as the first of the stick, crouched at the door, looking out into the enormity of a swirling gray world of cloud mixing furiously with snow, his tight chin strap giving his face an older yet even more determined look than usual. The red light turned green.

"Go!"

The stick fell out as smoothly as could be expected under the circumstances, only one paratrooper fouling—his fifteen-foot static line still holding the deployment bag, but his connector links breaking too early in a wind shear. He was jerked hard against the fuselage, the soft, crimson explosion of his head seen but not heard by the next two men in line.

Four "Saran-wrapped" Lynx helicopters going out on the skids of their C-130 transport also got into trouble. Despite the multiple braking chutes on the C-130's palette, the latter crashed through the ice cover of a pond at the edge of the salt marsh, disappearing in about fifteen feet of water. Another badly damaged Lynx was lost when its palette, having been blown off course into the timber, ended up in a mass of splintered treetops, dangling chute segments hanging forlornly, ripped by severed branches that had been broken off like matchsticks under the impact. Several of the branches had pierced the weather-protective wrap of the helo, impaling fuselage and tail rotors, warping the chopper's main blades and its chaff dispensers. The result was thousands of varying lengths of the silvered antiradar foil blown about aimlessly in the storm like silver streamers from some abandoned New Year's party.

One of the two remaining Lynxes' AH1's landing skis had been bent, but a paratrooper master sergeant had it fixed within five minutes—taking his assault knife, stripping a fir branch and lashing it with parachute cord to the ski, just as he would have splinted a broken leg. There was a tree-toppling crash that resounded throughout the entire drop area—one of the six eighteen-mile-range ultralightweight titanium 155mm field howitzers hitting and passing through the marsh ice. The other five guns, though two were almost buried in snowdrifts, were quickly assembled and their small but powerful-tracked vehicle haulers brought up, as well as Humvee-mounted PADS—positive azimuth determining gyro systems.

The PADS meant that within ten minutes the howitzers were laying direct Copperhead and RAP—right with boat tail—HE rounds fire against the BAM railhead just over three miles to the south. The accuracy of the four-round-a-minute fire was also due to one of the Lynx choppers serving as "fire control" after it and the only other serviceable Lynx had hauled their "baskets"—flip-bottomed mesh boxes of Heat-SFW, self-forging high-explosive, antitank warhead mines—scattering them in a rough circle around the quarter-mile-square drop zone. This left only one side, a southern exit toward the BAM, open for the attack on Nizhneangarsk Station itself—an attack that hopefully would not only sever the vital east-west supply line afforded Yesov by the BAM railway, but also cut off the Siberian Sixty-fourth and other divisions already moving east between Baikal and Yerofey Pavlovich.

For the moment, despite the loss of some of his bombers and helos, Freeman was as satisfied as a commander could expect to be—with only a two percent casualty rate of sprained ankles and jarred spines. Except for the man lost aboard the C-130, there had been no concussion-caused deaths, scores of men landing on the frozen, reed-tufted marsh, feet flying out from under them on the ice before they could roll properly and release their chutes.

Colonel General Litvinov, the military commander of all Siberian northern forces, including Kirensk garrison, 140 miles northwest of the north end of Lake Baikal, received a panicky call from Nizhneangarsk. It was from the recently appointed commander of the railhead's two infantry regiments—4,500 men, eighty tanks, thirty-six 122mm self-propelled howitzers, twenty-eight armored personnel carriers, and two antitank batteries of fifty-five men each. The commander's tone was rising by the second, for despite bad weather moving in—another arctic blizzard forecast— patrols were reporting that beneath the heavy overcast, American airborne troops in their hundreds, possibly thousands, were landing only four miles away in the taiga.

Litvinov, however, remained calm. He could afford to be; he was well away from Nizhneangarsk. Besides, he was under strict orders from Novosibirsk to keep his division of eighteen thousand—six thousand fighting men and twelve thousand in support—at Kirensk. Marshal Yesov had stressed that the Kirensk division must be so held for possible deployment to Yakutsk, eight hundred miles to the northeast, should the Americans decide to attack there. Along with Novosibirsk, Irkutsk, and Krasnoyarsk, Yakutsk was one of the most strategically and industrially important cities in Siberia.

"What can we do?" shouted the general from Nizhnean- garsk, whose two regiments had been assigned the specific responsibility of guarding the BAM railhead, his anxiety fueled by the memory of his one-time superior at Nizhnean- garsk. The latter had been arrested by the OMON before the cease-fire for what Novosibirsk was pleased to call "insuf- ficient initiative" in having failed to recapture those pris- oners who had escaped through the taiga following the Allied raid on Port Baikal. Whether or not this was the real reason for his execution or a cover for a power struggle in

Novosibirsk, the general had been court-martialed and shot by OMON enforcers.

"Uspokoysya, idiot!" Calm down, you idiot! Litvinov shouted into the phone. "You've nothing to worry about."

"You say that—you're not here. There must be . . ." The line was crackling, and he told Kirensk that one of the American *Dikie volki* was jamming.

"The *what?"*

"Dikie volki! Dikie volki!" Wild Wolves! Wild Wolves! repeated the Nizhneangarsk general.

"Diki lasochki!" Wild *Weasels*! corrected Litvinov.

"I don't care what you call them," said the Nizhneangarsk commander, "they're already cutting . . . communica—"

"Put your deputy on the extension," demanded Litvinov. "Immediately. And you stay on the line."

When the two Nizhneangarsk officers were on the line, Litvinov curtly announced, "General, you're dismissed. Colonel, you are now commanding general of Nizhneangarsk defenses. How many Americans do you suspect have landed?"

"Two—possibly three thousand, sir," answered the colonel—now General Fyodor Malik.

"Bozne moy!" My God! "You outnumber them two to one. Outflank them and attack immediately. Do you hear?"

The newly promoted general had to ask Litvinov to repeat the order; the line was fading by the second.

The demoted general was in shock, not knowing whether to feel relieved, insulted, or both. He knew he was afraid. Family connections had got him his command, but Uncle Vilna couldn't help him now. He was shaking. He could hear Litvinov's voice on the phone again through the frying sound of the static.

"All you have to . . . General," Litvinov advised his newly promoted colleague, Malik, "is . . . send a message to . . . ort Baikal. Give them the coordinates of the U.S. Airborne and they'll take care . . . Tell them . . . release the Aists."

Malik frowned, but then, aware of his previous commander watching him, smiled knowingly. "Of course. I will call them immediate—" The line went dead.

The demoted general's voice, now wavering between outrage and unmitigated fright, was tremulous and rising. "And how will you get any message to Port Baikal now?" he shouted. "No phone! What are the Aists? How can we—"

"By helicopter," Malik replied, unsure as to how he should address his former boss. "We'll send two helicopters with the message," he explained. "They'll be there in two and half hours—less with drop tanks and no troop load."

"And what will happen then?"

Malik wondered if the comrade was serious, but merely put his confusion down to his hyperanxiety.

"The Aists," Malik explained calmly. "You heard, Litvinov has released them. Once they've got the coordinates, they'll slaughter Freeman and his troops."

"How do you know it's Freeman?"

"Because," said Malik, the new authority growing on him by the second, sweeping over him now like the pleasure of a mounting orgasm as he carefully but quickly wrote out the coordinates and gave a copy each to both Hind D chopper pilots. "Of course it's Freeman. It's his style—to attack where you least expect it." Malik straightened up from the desk. "Freeman loves the underdog's position. Makes winning all the sweeter for him. But now he's made a bad mistake, Gen—uh, Colonel. But now he's finished."

Malik told the two helicopter pilots that en route over the 350 miles of taiga between Nizhneangarsk and Port Baikal they must remain on radio silence rather than risk detection by an American AWAC. Even if the American advanced warning aircraft were hundreds of miles off, their rotodome radar could nevertheless pick the helos up if they used their radio and, though it was unlikely, might be able to get an American fighter through the fog and the ring of Baikal's AA gun and missile defenses. "Meantime," Malik told the commanders of his two motorized rifle regiments, "we'll prepare a little surprise for Freeman here." With that, Malik strode to the map and drew in two arrows aimed at hitting Freeman's Airborne simultaneously on the American's western and eastern flanks. "Get every civilian in town that you can find. Issue them with greatcoats and take them to the front. Any resistance to your order and they'll be charged with *gulgiganstvo*." It meant "hooliganism" against the CIS—the Commonwealth of Independent States—and just as in the old Soviet Union, it would get you one-to-five in a "labor" battalion. Malik turned and looked past the man who had been his commander to the infantry major who would be in charge of calling out the civilians. Malik's tone was steely, brooking no objection. "Have them surrender to the Americans in twos and threes over the next hour."

The major was stunned.

"It will slow them down," Malik explained. "The Americans are soft about prisoners. Freeman will also be slowed down by the blizzard coming south. It will be here in a few hours. By then our Aists at Baikal'll do the rest."

Malik couldn't hide, nor did he wish to hide, the look of satisfaction on his face as he now saw the wisdom of Novosibirsk's long-standing insistence, based on the experience of the Nazis, that all military garrisons be manned as far as possible by troops from another oblast. A garrison made up in part of local conscripts or volunteers were naturally tied too closely to their fellows in the town, rather than to the iron fist of military necessity. It meant there would be no difficulty in having his troops round up the locals for the surrender.

As Freeman's troops continued to advance on Nizhneangarsk, fog was rolling over the frozen marshes, and the general ordered Dick Norton and his two aides in the Humvee to pray for good weather. "God damn it," opined Freeman, "the Almighty answered Georgie Patton's prayers at Bastogne—He can answer mine." Only Dick Norton knew he wasn't joking. But later, as the cold front kept moving south, a disgruntled captain, whose Humvee windscreen was being constantly splattered with lumps of snow kicked up by the treads of Freeman's Humvee, was heard to mutter that apparently this day Second Army was out of favor with the Almighty.

"By God," said Freeman as he, too, saw any hope of close air support disappearing, "we're being punished for White House stupidity! If I'd been allowed to pursue these sons of bitches when we had 'em on the run before that goddamn cease-fire, we'd—"

"General, sir!" FORs—forward observer reports—were flooding in on the Humvee's FLAP—flat panel lap display—to the effect that Nizhneangarsk was falling without a fight. And apparently Intelligence had screwed up; those surrendering weren't crack troops at all, but the infirm and inexperienced—old men and young boys. "Even women, General . . ."

"Maybe," proffered an incredulous Dick Norton, "your prayers *are* being answered, General. Their Motorized must be pulling back."

"Possibly," conceded Freeman. It was difficult in the now heavily falling snow to tell whether the general was grinning with the anticipation of easy victory or whether he was grimacing.

CHAPTER TWENTY-NINE

HUNDREDS OF MILES to the south, atop A-7, the barrel of Aussie Lewis's Heckler & Koch 11 A1 was steaming in the early morning fog. "Like a bloody Chinese laundry," he quipped as he reached forward, right thumb squeezing the barrel's plastic-coated handle, rotating it hard left, pushing it forward, then back and hard right, dumping it out on the snow, slipping in the spare, the gun back on full automatic in less than six seconds. "Too fucking slow!" he told himself, and he was right, but he'd taken a second to make sure the spare barrel wasn't plugged with snow. In minus fifty degrees, snow would turn to ice in the barrel, and bam! You'd blow your head off.

In a wide left-right sweep, the gun's backwash warming his face, Lewis dropped at least five, maybe six, of the Siberians, but they kept coming, and a few yards to his right David Brentwood was tossing his last frag grenade even as they heard the beautiful, bowel-turning roar of the Spectre reappearing, lighting the clouds in giant, swelling red sores. The fire-spitting dragon went into a tight anticlockwise corkscrew, forcing many of the would-be attackers back into the heavy timber, crackling now from the Vulcan's forty-millimeter and 105mm howitzer rounds as if on fire.

"You bloody beaut!" yelled Aussie Lewis in praise of the Spectre. "Jesus Christ, you Yanks can make machines," he told David. "I'll give you that."

"One o'clock, two of—" called David, but Aussie—or was it Choir Williams?—had already fired, downing two Siberians. The real trouble, however, was that in the moat of snow-filled craters that lay between the heavy timber and the rough hundred-yard-diameter circle of SAS/D men still holding out on A-7's summit, any fighting between the circle and the timber confused the Spectre's operators. The gunship's sensors couldn't distinguish between friend and foe, especially when both SAS/D men and the Siberians were wearing American uniforms. Already David Brentwood suspected that several SAS men had been killed in the initial well-intentioned enfilade from the Spectre, and radio contact with the gunship confirmed the confusion.

"We'll try to keep 'em bottled up in the trees," the gunship's pilot told Brentwood, his voice fighting to be heard in the cacophony of air and ground battle. "But you guys'll have to establish a chopper zone . . ."

"Roger!" responded David Brentwood, asking urgently, "ETA for the choppers? Repeat, ETA—"

"Fifteen minutes max," answered the Spectre, the pilot's voice quickly lost in the roar of the twin Vulcans tattooing the gray blur of timber below with what seemed solid tracer, more explosions and flares, the Chinese now attacking the Siberians, who in turn were attacking the ring of SAS/D men.

"Fubar!" shouted Aussie, clipping in another mag of 5.56mm, by which he meant he was in the middle of a fog in a fog of war, confusing even for the usually confused state of close-quarter battle; a situation, in short, that in the SAS/D lexicon was definitely, undeniably fubar—"fucked up beyond all recognition!" Chinese were fighting Siberians who were fighting Americans who were fighting everybody. "Where are those fucking choppers? I'm out of ammo!" yelled Aussie. David Brentwood tossed him a drum. It was the most anxious he'd ever seen the Australian, the man who was normally so cool, stressed now by the fear not so much of dying, but of dying at the hand of his own mates. "Jesus Christ, Choir!" yelled Aussie. "Stop! You mad fucking Welshman!" Choir Williams had stopped, though just in time, his 180- degree arc of fire kicking up snow just short of Lewis and David's position. Salvini, on the far right, saw another two SAS men badly hit and sent up yet another purple flare for the Medevac choppers to see—if they ever came.

"Where are the bastards?" Aussie began, but then ducked, his Kevlar helmet pushed hard into the snow, legs drawn up into the fetal position, his right arm pulling David Brentwood down by the collar as a heavy mortar round went off, shaking the earth, showering them with a black-white spew of snow and earth. "Our chopper pilots wankin' themselves off or something?" He saw a tongue of machine gun fire in the timber and answered with a long burst with the HK 11.

"Well, I'm not!" It was a man called Edison, nicknamed "Lightbulb," who'd dragged himself over to Aussie and

Brentwood's position, his left leg a mass of bloody pulp, but Edison not yet in shock. "Down to my last clip," he told Aussie. David tore the last one he had from his vest and picked out a body twenty feet in front of him, one of the Siberians he'd stopped, whom he might ransack for ammo and—

They heard the distinctive *wokka! wokka! wokka!* of the Chinook-47 Evac choppers, closing.

"Fucking cavalry's arrived," said Lewis, and gave a shape moving through the aspen stand fifty yards away a quick, deadly burst. Suddenly the sky was brighter than the sun, so intensely lit that for a moment all firing stopped, as the Spectre turned to oxblood-red, then black, the sound of it exploding creating a ringing in David's ears. And only now did they hear the sonic boom of the MiG fighter, a Fulcrum-29 that had downed the Spectre and was now screaming low overhead, banking in a tight turn away to the west. No one had predicted a lone MiG would dare Bingo fuel—an empty tank—at the farthest extent of his plane's operational radius and try to interdict the gunship.

But nothing was predictable. Certainly no one in the SAS/D company could have had any way of knowing that the MiG-29 was flown by Siberia's top ace, Sergei Marchenko, whose Fulcrum sported the YANKEE KILLER motif left forward of the left engine's box intake.

Within hours Novosibirsk was boasting about Marchenko's bravery, which was undeniable, but the propaganda broadcast failed to point out the element of sheer luck involved in hitting the gunship in the thick fog. In its spiraling turn, the gunship, its guns ablaze, had quite unexpectedly presented Marchenko with a target that a child couldn't have missed. Having made only one pass, he easily downed it with a two-hundred-pound Aphid air-to-air missile traveling at nine hundred feet a second, before pulling out all the stops to disappear westward into the safety net of Baikal's AA ring.

To all Siberia, Marchenko was a hero. But to the SAS/D men—several of them wounded and dying in their fighting retreat into the choppers, where ironically the downdraft from the Chinooks was so fierce that it knocked them off the rope ladders—Marchenko only added to the sense of bitterness they felt with their discovery that it hadn't been the Americans who'd started the war. To them Marchenko was no better than a vulture. He'd come in not on equal terms, but merely to turkey-shoot the lumbering AC-130, and then he'd "hopped it," as Choir Williams described it, to the safety west of Baikal, out of the American air striker reach.

To Commander Soong, now the victor of A-7, the MiG pilot was a comrade hero, having made it all the easier for him to conquer the summit and plant the red flag.

In the La Roche chain, Marchenko got more space than the president's victory over internal saboteurs and the arrest in Central Park of the man who the FBI said had engineered the massive computer debacle.

For Sergei Marchenko, his downing of the Spectre meant another U.S. plane for his ground crew to paint on the side of his Fulcrum, his daring kill on near-empty only adding to his reputation in the Siberian air force for having *devyat' zhizney*—"nine lives." Even those who disliked his haughty manner, which included most everybody at Irkutsk, had to concede his bravery in going it alone, his sheer talent and his media-star status after what the western press had thought was his destruction over Korea earlier in the war.

It not only added to his legend at home, but burned the ears of all those Allied pilots who'd come up against him. This was especially so for Frank Shirer, who, seeing a MiG crash, had claimed the Korean kill. Adding insult to injury, Shirer was given the information in the mess of the B-52 squadron at Nayoro, Japan. Here, so far from home, his sense of being a has-been—"from Porsche to bus driver," as he'd put it—was confirmed when he was told of Marchenko's resurrection at dinner, where all the B-52 crews also heard it. Frank thought of Lana telling him it didn't matter a fig about Marchenko, that what mattered to her was that he, Frank, was alive, that if La Roche ever conceded to a divorce, they could get married. But her hopes were no consolation to Shirer. There were just some things you couldn't explain to a woman. Shirer's gunner, a gregarious Murphy from Philadelphia, tried to make light of it, but as Shirer cut into his steak, he pressed so hard on the knife that the screech of the steel on china went through the mess hall like nails on a blackboard.

"Don't worry about it, skipper," said Murphy, who, as well as resident optimist, was the B-52's "designated hitter"—the tail gunner, though he had not yet seen an enemy plane and didn't plan on seeing one. "This Mar—whatever his name is."

"Marchenko."

"Yeah—Marchenko. He'll get his."

"How are those tail guns coming along?" asked Shirer, shifting away from talk of the Siberian ace. "Wandering a bit on the way over, weren't they?" He meant on the flyover from the States to Japan.

"Ah, they're okay. It was me wandering, skipper. Had some of that sushi last night. Don't think raw fish agrees with me. Had the runs all night."

"You should stock up on Pepto-Bismol," said Shirer. Murphy thought he was fooling, but he wasn't. "You might have a long flight if the weather clears up north."

Murphy patted his left vest pocket. "Got me a whole packet. Ah, know what the target is, skipper?"

"No." Shirer's tone sounded like he didn't care, either. "Only that it depends on clear skies, or enough to see where we're bombing."

"Could be important, right?"

"Oh, sure," said Shirer, feeling as bitter as the coffee. "It's always important."

"Yeah, right," said Murphy, confident he'd helped shake his skipper out of his depressed mood. Then quite suddenly Murphy turned pale.

"What's wrong, man? You got the runs?" the crew's navigator asked Murphy. "Look like you've seen a ghost."

"Sushi," said Murphy, pushing himself away quickly from the table, obviously in pain. "Goes through ya like crap through a goose."

CHAPTER THIRTY

"BIG DICK!" SAID Aussie Lewis, wearily unloading his pack. "That's what got us out."

"*And* the choppers," added David Brentwood wryly. The weapon Lewis was referring to was called the minigun by some of the SAS/D commandos who'd provided the withering cover fire as they'd loaded the litters of wounded aboard the helicopters. The minigun, one carried by each of the ten commandos, was a modernized mini-Gatling gun, a weapon with a phenomenal—"almost theoretically impossible," the experts had said—rate of fire of over nine hundred rounds a minute. The ten of them fired by the SAS/D commandos had thrown up a steel wall of over ten thousand rounds a minute, the circle of SAS/D men clearing the LZ for the two Chinooks that supplemented the commandos' fire with the front-mounted heavy machine guns. The extraordinarily rapid fire, due in part also to revolutionary C magazines feeding both the M-16 scope-mounted sniper rifles with 7.62mm bullets and the MPK5s with nine-millimeter Parabellum, enabled the SAS/D team to secure the snow moat between the timber and the landing zone long enough to get the wounded and dead aboard the Chinooks; the wall of depleted uranium bullets not only keeping down the heads of the Siberians, but the Chinese infantry coming up behind them.

The SAS/D team had lost seven men and four wounded,

and for that they now had the hard intelligence for Freeman that the Chinese had been conned by what had been a Siberian artillery barrage into firing on American positions all along the northeast China-Siberian border, breaking the cease-fire. But Lewis's prediction was borne out—it made no difference. The Siberian member of the U.N., representing the largest of the Commonwealth of Independent States, said the American allegations were "groundless" and "a pathetic attempt by the Washington warmongers to rationalize American aggression against the peace-loving peoples of Siberia and China."

On the flight back to Kalga Field, northeast of A-7 mountain, before changing planes for a fast jet to Rudnaya Pristan' on the Siberian coast, the Chinook pilots had a bad fright when fighters, in finger-four patrol formation, appeared on their FLIR—forward-looking infrared—screens, the pilots thinking that, like the downed Spectre, they were about to be attacked by more MiG-29s. But instead, the dots were American F-15 Eagles sent away down from Skovorodino to escort the choppers back. It was a tight-lipped bunch of SAS/D men who deplaned at Rudnaya Pristan'.

It was one thing to lose seven of your own in an attempt to rescue your own, but the sheer waste of the A-7 mission not only gave La Roche's tabloids more screaming headlines, but was a waste emphasized by the failure of the Chinese to break off hostilities.

"You'd think they'd call their lot back," commented Choir Williams as he watched a medic bandage up Lewis's left foot. It was only a flesh wound but had made a mess of the boot.

"Nah," said Lewis, looking at the medic who, Lewis saw, was carefully, obsessively, putting on a double pair of rubber gloves and rubber mask before he went anywhere near the blood. "Don't worry, sport. I don't have AIDS." The medic didn't answer, and Lewis turned his attention to Williams. "Ah, forget it, Choir. Beijing doesn't give a shit who started it. Not now. They see their chance to gobble up more rich border territory—their price for helping the Sibirs. Anyway, what you think those old farts in Beijing are gonna tell the masses, mate? 'Sorry, but we made a mistake and started a war. All our propaganda about Yankee aggression was a bunch of bullshit.' '' Lewis watched the medic open a brown bottle of iodine, its smell bringing back unpleasant childhood memories. "They'd lose face, wouldn't they?" said Lewis, his eyes fixed on the iodine. "And all their bloody perks as well." The medic tipped the amber bottle against a cotton wad and stroked the wound, the astringent odor of the antiseptic rising, seeming to fill the barracks.

"Sting a bit?" Choir asked, poker-faced.

"Nah."

"Oh well, then, boyo," said Choir, "you'll be fit for further service, then."

"I will," said Aussie, undaunted, and confident that the SAS/D team would now have a bit of well-deserved R&R. Aussie turned to Salvini and told him he'd now managed to find out the name of the "bird" with the "big nungas" he'd seen in Khabarovsk just before they'd been called for the A-7 mission. "Olga's her handle," he explained.

Salvini was cleansing his minigun and looking down each barrel as he did so. He winked across at Choir. "Olga? Sounds like a wrestler."

"Don't care, mate," said Lewis. "She can wrestle me. Smother me to death if she wants."

"Squeeze the life out of you, I should expect," said Choir.

Aussie held his hands out, bowl-like, in front of him. "I tell you they're this big, and I've got her address."

"Ah, wouldn't get all excited, Aussie, if I were you," chimed in Salvini. "Might be a while before you see Khabarovsk, let alone any poontang. Rumor is they're got something lined up for us."

Aussie Lewis's glance shot from Salvini to Choir and back again. Lewis could usually tell when they were kidding him, but Salvini looked totally disinterested—as if the rumor was already known by everyone except Lewis.

"Where?" challenged Aussie, suspicious.

"South," Choir said, nodding in the general direction of China.

Aussie shook his head and immediately relaxed. "Horse shit!"

"No—dinkum!" said Choir, using the Aussie's own expression for the absolute truth—the genuine article.

The medic taped the bandage and left. The truth was, he was overawed by the men of SAS/Delta. Aussie thanked him, glanced again at Salvini and tore off a piece of cleaning rag to wipe down one of the high capacity C mags. Salvini didn't have a trace of a smile. He looked bored.

"All right," said Aussie, standing up, wincing slightly, shifting his weight to his right foot, his grimace quickly replaced by a knowing smile. "You're tryin' to take the piss out of me, Salvini. Bet you're wrong. Two to one on." It was odds on—you'd have to bet two to win one. You could make money, but you had to be sure of your information. Salvini looked up, shifting the blame to Choir. "Should've known Aussie would bet on it—Australians'll bet against the friggin' sun coming up. Forty-eight hours without a bet sends Lewis into delirium tremens."

"Aha!" said Aussie triumphantly, seizing on Choir's hesitation. "What's the matter? The cat got your fucking tongue?"

"I've never heard you speak, boyo, without a swear word. You always have to swear?"

"Don't fart round, boyo. Put your money where your mouth is. Is there a mission or not? Pay up or shut up."

Salvini began "black taping" his Heckler & Koch's two-notch pistol grip, Aussie squatting down beside him, giving Salvini a friendly elbow nudge that almost toppled him.

"Five bucks, then," piped up Choir, his tone, however, hardly enthusiastic.

Aussie stood up, mock shock all over his face, looking around the barracks in wide-eyed surprise. "Five whole dollars! Jesus, Choir, don't go overboard. Salvini—how about you?"

"Five."

"What a pair of wankers," Aussie said disgustedly, shaking his head. "Hardly worth making book."

"Then don't," said Choir, which only confirmed Aussie's suspicion that they'd just made up a rumor.

"Oh I'll take it," said Aussie. "A mission south, is it?" He was reaching up for the small, blue, indelible pencil and paper he had tucked under his helmet's Medevac band.

"Within a week," said Salvini, upping his bet to add credence. "I'll bet ten bucks."

"A week? And a high roller! Okay—a week." Lewis licked the tip of the indelible pencil, leaving a purple stain on his tongue as he wrote down the two wagers. Next, he cast a glance about the barracks, the rest of the SAS/D team in various stages of undress and/or busy cleaning weapons. "Anyone else?"

David Brentwood declined, as did the rest of the troop.

"Okey-dokey," said Aussie, slipping the pencil back beneath the helmet band. "The Welsh Wart and the Brooklyn Dodger—five and ten. Done! Takin' candy from a baby."

"Better not be so cocksure," cautioned David Brentwood.

"Don't worry about my cock. I'll have fifteen bucks to blow, and she'll blow me!"

David Brentwood shook his head—the Australian was incorrigible.

"Listen, Davey boy," said Lewis. "If these blokes are right, I'll run starkers into Freeman's HQ!"

"Promise?" someone yelled laughingly.

"Absolutely!" said Lewis.

"You all heard that?" said David.

"Copied!" came back an SAS/D chorus.

The jocular mood died suddenly with the sight of the unit padre walking in with the dog tags of the dead.

CHAPTER THIRTY-ONE

"PELE . . . I AM the goddess of fire."

It was all Robert Brentwood in the bow of Echo One could think of when he saw the fiery, incandescent ball of light, for Pele—played by a Polynesian beauty—had risen from the fake but realistic-looking volcano during a Hawaiian show he'd once seen on Kauai, the waterfall in front of the mountain turning molten red like lava as the lights behind it changed from white to pulsating crimson. Pele's right hand flashed quickly into the darkness like a karate slice, and a ball of fire—perhaps it had been done by lasers— had shot with incredible speed across from the fake volcano to the rain forest like a bolt of lightning. But the red ball he saw now streaking through the darkness across the river two miles from the Nanking Bridge was no conjurer's trick. It was the tracer flash of a PLA eighty-two-millimeter 65RPG, a recoilless rifle round, in reality a short-range artillery shell tearing across the Yangtze darkness at five hundred miles per hour, striking Echo Two midships only seconds after her bow had hit a 'tween channel wire, the sudden increase in tension triggering the RPG. The outboard's fuel ignited, ammunition was exploding, the boat, its spine broken, in the air, afire and coming apart. Bodies and equipment spilled into the boiling brown water of the Yangtze illuminated by the fire, both sections of the boat still turning in air as if in slow motion, water pouring from one half in a gossamer spray. The acrid reek of burning rubber and cordite floated back to Echo One a hundred yards behind and to the left of what had been Echo Two's Zodiac.

In that split second of Echo Two being hit, Robert Brentwood had to make his decision: to go and try to save whoever, if any, of the SEALs had survived, or to head immediately left, closer inshore, to avoid the mid-channel trip wire. He told Rose in a harsh whisper, "Hard left!" instructing Dennison and Smythe to man the paddles. Almost immediately he felt the Zodiac picking up speed, water slopping over the gunwales as it moved beam-on to the current, heading at a sharp angle inshore.

Ten seconds later the cold darkness was lit up again as the Yangtze was swept by searchlights, their stalks reaching out like long, white fingers from the right bank, and from the city beyond came the distinctive wails of sirens. Robert Brentwood pulled hard on the front starboard paddle, all the time wishing to God he'd given the order to row to shore a second after the searchlights had appeared; the searchlights would have vindicated his order—his decision not to go looking for the men from Echo Two. Even though he knew he'd made the right decision—that the mission was the thing that counted, that every man knew that—his gut was still in a knot. Machine gun fire was now raking the river at the floating debris several hundred yards ahead of them.

"They're just guessing," whispered Dennison.

"Right," said Smythe, unconvinced. Rose kept paddling.

"Soon as we get ashore," instructed Brentwood, "we hide the boat—swim down to the bridge in two pairs. Dennison, you're with me. Smythe, you go with Rose. Rendezvous extraction point in two hours. Remember—no grace period. Chopper'll come in and out. No chance for a second run. Understand?" Rose, Smythe, and Dennison nodded, intent on putting on their Litton M983 B night vision diving goggles and closed circuit oxygen apparatus. In their quarter-inch-thick neoprene wet suits with the flexible breathing hose and small front oxygen tank attacked, the four looked more like jet pilots than divers as they deflated the Zodiac, making it, the outboard engine, and paddles easier to hide on the bank in the vegetation that spilled down from the rice field to the very edge of the river.

Cloud broke, revealing the moon, and for a moment or two the three-mile-wide Yangtze took on the sheen of molten quicksilver. As Robert Brentwood chalked his rubber shoes before slipping them into the long flippers, he was struck again by how cumbersome, even absurd, they looked. But he knew that once in the water—a small amount of which would almost immediately form a body-heated layer between his skin and the rubber suit—with the first breath in the rebreather suit and the first kick of the long fins, a metamorphosis would occur. Probably they would have to go deep—thirty to thirty-five feet—to avoid the kind of trip wire that Echo Two had triggered, but not below the safety limit of forty-five.

The searchlights were still sweeping the wide race of the river, beams splitting then reconvening like flocks of ghosts finding their way over the floating body parts that had been the men in Echo Two. Brentwood heard the distinctive, long rattling sound of a Chinese RPK machine gun on the more heavily defended right bank. But because of the RPK's limited nine hundred-meter range, its bullets didn't pose any problem for Echo One, the rounds plopping in the mustard-colored, spotlit water like tired hail around the flotsam of Echo Two—the boat's halves floating now like two dead manta rays, wings torn and shredded by the explosion.

The moonlight breaking through clouds revealed what looked like staggered platforms in the river, several hundred yards apart, of the kind Robert remembered kids in the States used in the summers to push out in the lakes and dive off. It told him how the river traffic they'd heard earlier was able to get past the trip wire or wires without incident, whereas Echo Two had been blown up. The ChiComs had anchored the floating platforms and mounted them with RPGs—not in a straight line across the river, but rather in staggered fashion, as one would place a series of overlapping gates at a sheepdog trial. You would have to know where they were, of course, in order to weave through

them; for the sampans, he guessed, it must be akin to a
motor vehicle driver in any other country having to negotiate
a series of overlapping staggered speed bumps, like those
the Communists had rigged up at Checkpoint Charlie in the
days before the Berlin Wall had come down and the United
Siberian Republic had arisen.

As clouds closed back over the moon like a cloven hoof,
not even the night vision goggles could pick out the
platforms, except for the one from which the RPG had just
been fired, a residual infrared blur from its heat still hugging
the platform. The brief glimpse of the platforms—he'd seen
at least six of them—told Brentwood he'd made the right
decision in bringing in his boat. He'd spotted at least one
pair of platforms, possibly two, between him and where
Echo Two up ahead had been hit.

He listened carefully for any increase in the putt-putting
sounds of the river, for any indication of a patrol boat
moving cautiously around the trip wires—but could hear
none. Perhaps one of the sampans' or barges' putt-putting
was in fact a patrol boat. He didn't feel lucky—not after
Echo Two being hit. The odds against a single round from
an RPG hitting it smack on like that weren't good, and if the
Chinese luck kept up like that, well . . .

"Sounds like the sampans are bunching up downriver,"
whispered Rose. "About the bridge."

"Yeah," added Dennison. "Maybe they've closed the
upriver channel on our side. Sounds as if they're working
the river traffic like a single-lane bridge—opening it for
down traffic for an hour, then to up traffic." Smythe agreed,
pointing out the ChiComs could watch one channel more
easily than two.

"Maybe," acknowledged Brentwood, simultaneously
smelling the polluted stench of the river and hearing the
heavy, somehow ominous-sounding heavy breathing of the
other men testing their COBRA circuits. The flexible air
bladders, designed not to give off any telltale bubbles of air,
rose and fell like an anesthetist's bag, responding to inhale

and exhale as dangerous carbon dioxide was absorbed by a soda-lime compartment and oxygen bled in from the small, eight-hour waist tank.

To Robert Brentwood the flexible breathing bags rising and falling imparted a tension that was unrelieved by a new development: smoke from a factory on the eastern bank wafting down over the river. Though cooling rapidly over the water, the smoke was joined by water particles to form a rolling mist which, because it was still relatively warm, interfered with the infrared goggles. But even if he could see whether there were any patrol boats, Brentwood knew he couldn't do much about it. Anyway, he told himself, it might simply be that the PLA had thought they'd already got all the saboteurs; probably content to pick up the bodies from Echo Two, or what was left of them. Maybe the ChiComs thought the Zodiac had been manned by Democracy Movement underground saboteurs and not U.S. SEALs. Yes, said Brentwood's alter ego, and what happens when they pick up the debris and discover they were Americans? That'll bring out more than a sampan or two.

But he knew he had to put such worries on hold and press on to the bridge. And the thought of the tens of thousands of Americans whom Echo One might save if the SEALs could sever the vital supply artery helped him quell his fears.

Easing himself quietly down the riverbank, from which the Zodiac was hidden beneath a camouflage throw wrap, Brentwood went over the equipment, giving most attention to the four "Javex" bottles, as the "upgunned" M2A3 conical-shaped charges were called. Twenty-four inches long by sixteen wide, the charges looked like four big magnums of champagne sawed off at the neck. If they could "earmuff" the charges on the south side of piers four and five, the four pairs of earmuff TNT charges having a 26,000-foot ROD—rate of detonation—pentolite detonating cord, the two simultaneous explosions should create shock waves to penetrate over four feet from either side of both piers into the solid concrete. Brentwood hoped that the ChiComs, always afraid of high-altitude bombing attempts despite their wall-to-wall AA SAM missiles about the bridge, would keep the bridge in darkness, observing their full blackout. But he thought it a vain hope. The PLA troops guarding the bridge mightn't be first-rate—most of those would already be at the front—but if he were the ChiCom commander in Nanking, after the destruction of Echo Two he would order the bridge lit up and have every available man on and around it looking for and shooting at anything that moved in the river.

Quickly having gone over their recognition codes, call signs, and hand "squeeze" underwater signals, the four SEALs entered the water, but not before Dennison suddenly realized and pointed out to Smythe, Rose, and Brentwood that the emergency code "Mars," chosen by the Bullfrog, was the same as the name of the Zodiac's outboard.

"Well, if we have to use it," whispered the more taciturn Rose, "our guys'll know we don't mean a frappin' outboard."

"Don't sweat it," Brentwood said. "We won't need it."

Submerged, Brentwood and Dennison as one pair, Rose and Smythe the other, were connected by a nylon feel line, Brentwood and Dennison heading for pier four, Rose and Smythe toward pier five barely a mile ahead.

The current was swift, and it seemed that in no time they were closing, only a quarter mile from the enormous black shape of the double-deck Nanking Bridge, hearing the rumble of the motor traffic on the bridge's top lane and the roar of three steam locomotives in tandem thundering across the lower. Brentwood could also hear the putt-putting of the sampans through the water, a sound that was progressively overwhelmed by a slower but heavier and more persistent beat, shot through with a sound of metal on metal and then a lazy *plump-plump-plump*.

Dennison tugged the feel line, but Brentwood already knew—he'd heard it all before aboard both the *Roosevelt* and the *Reagan*—the sound of depth charges rolling off a boat's stern. Brentwood estimated that he and the other three SEALs were now five hundred yards from the bridge. The *whump!* of the first explosion sent shock waves racing through the water at over three thousand feet per second, even the outer rings of the depth charges' detonations so gut-wrenching that Brentwood felt a wave of cold nausea, and he could only hope for the safety of Smythe and Rose.

CHAPTER THIRTY-TWO

FLYING SIDE BY side, the better to communicate while they observed radio silence, the two Siberian choppers, bulbous-eyed Hind A's, taking the coordinates of Freeman's position from General Malik in Nizhneangarsk south to Port Baikal and Irkutsk, beyond the blizzard, were halfway down the 390-mile lake. The overcast was still thick, metallic-looking and low, but visibility was at five kilometers when they spotted what looked like a SPETS chopper coming toward them. It appeared to be a Hind D but, given the near whiteout conditions, when depth perception suffered, it was possible that it could be a bogey, an American Sea Stallion—one of the enemy choppers that, coming in low over the frozen lake, were attempting to pick up remnants of the retreating and decimated American III Corps, whose tiny fleeing figures looked like white ants amid the black and burning detritus of their rout.

The Hind A pilot wasn't about to take any chances, and had his copilot use the flashlamp to signal his comrade in the other Hind A—a hundred meters on his right side, nearer the western shore of the lake and Port Baikal—that he was going to warn off the oncoming chopper, even if it was a SPETS. The pilot in the other Hind gave a thumbs-up acknowledgment of the message and put his Hind in a tight right bank toward Port Baikal. The remaining Hind headed straight for the oncoming bogey, now only two miles away, but still indistinct in the blur of snow, and began a hard left-right, right-left swaying motion, signaling the other chopper to land. The chopper kept coming, and so now, Malik's order in mind, the Hind's pilot hesitated no longer and began to "jiggle" and "jinx" in response to his weapons officer's commands coming up from the nose bubble below him. Switching on his "flowerpot" infrared suppressor, he fired two Aphid air-to-air missiles. The other chopper turned sharply, rose, then dropped like a brick, both missiles missing him, their white contrails now clearly visible to the fleeing Americans of III Corps beneath. But the chopper's evasive action was to no avail, its cockpit disintegrating, the attacker's undernose 12.7mm gun, slaved to the pilot's sighting system, already pouring a deadly fire into the bogey, bits of rear rotor flying off. Now the attackers could see it *was* a U.S. Marine Sea Stallion as it fell hard to the right, hitting the ice with a *whoomp*, sending spidery fissures racing along the ice, its main rotors striking the frozen lake, wheeling the chopper around in ever-increasing circles until the rotor blades snapped. Six-foot-long segments of rotor flew into a fleeing American sapper company like errant boomerangs, making a heavy "chunka-chunka" sound, beheading and disemboweling clumps of U.S. troops trying desperately to cross the lake, their blood and entrails smearing the ice.

CHAPTER THIRTY-THREE

ALEXSANDRA MALOF'S TONGUE was raw from licking the rough, wet stone wall of her jail cell. Chained to the wall, she had lost twenty pounds in ten days in the Harbin Number One Jail. On Ilya Latov's express orders, her jailers hadn't given her any food or water for the last three days. They were further instructed not to give her any until she told them who helped her in her escape from Baikal to Harbin and what information she'd given to the underground Chinese Democracy Movement which had aided her before she was captured.

Though she hadn't been fed, her licking the condensation off the cell's cold stone walls prevented her from becoming fatally dehydrated. But the stones were so rough, her tongue had become badly lacerated and swollen, and now her mouth was filled with the metallic taste of blood, her nostrils filled with the stench of her own waste emanating from the small wooden bucket by her side. But only once—during the moment of her arrest in the hutong—had she weakened, considered telling them anything. And even then she had been determined not to tell them about sending the message about the Nanking Bridge to Khabarovsk via Ling's underground cell.

She had been afraid her determination would weaken with her body, but her refusal to talk had become the one thing that had kept her going—the one thing to which she could tether her sanity. Even so, Alexsandra knew that all the will in the world to resist couldn't prevent her dying. Soon she must eat. But what? She had no strength left to try to catch the rats and roaches that scrabbled over her at night when she tried to sleep. And even if she could think of a way of killing them, the thought of eating them raw revolted her. She had managed to squash several of the cockroaches, but could not bring herself to devour them, the thought of their hard shell crackling beneath her teeth enough to make her almost vomit. Yet she knew she must eat if she was to survive.

One of the Chinese guards, whom she knew only as Wong, a middle-aged man—in his late forties, perhaps— took particular pleasure in her plight. In any other country Wong could have looked merely well-fed, but here in Harbin he looked positively rotund compared to the other guards. Wong smiled a lot at Alexsandra, and on the third day of her imprisonment—when he had come in to take out her toilet bucket—he had stood over her, holding a fresh stick of *youtiao*, the long sweet bread, undoing his fly with the other hand and pursing his lips, his gesture with the *youtiao* telling her what she had to do to get the bread. Contemptuous, she turned away from him. He laughed and left, making a snorting noise as he ate the bread, telling her that soon she would submit, that he had seen it all before. At the door he turned and declared that a prisoner would do anything for a scrap of bread, let alone sweet stick. It was a basic instinct. She refused to look at him, keeping her head facing the cell wall, but she'd been badly frightened, afraid he was right.

If he offered her the bread again tomorrow . . . She could feel her resolve slipping. Remembering the time she had spent in the hands of the Siberian secret police, and now this squalor and degradation, she began to cry. Half choking, she ordered herself to stop, knowing that her very tears were robbing her of vital moisture. She thought of the Russians starving, of her great-grandfather in Leningrad during the Great Patriotic War of 1941–45 and of how they had begun eating the wallpaper paste and . . .

Even with her fear of how she might be tempted to satisfy him, it still took all the courage she had left, but slowly she did it. Dragging the toilet bucket over, she removed the lid tentatively, the flies so insolent they didn't even bother to move. Steeling herself, remembering how her forebears had survived, she stared at the putrid stools—at the tiny imbedded scraps of undigested rice and chicken innards. Here and there a speck of corn. If her forebears had found the will to do it—to survive—she could. She would not give in.

One of the guards who'd heard Wong laughingly tell everyone in the station house that the white *jinu*—"whore"—in number 12 "is eating her own shit," had told his brother-in-law Chen, who'd laughed, too, and who was a blood member of the June Fourth Movement—Harbin's offshoot of the Democracy Movement. Chen knew it meant that Alexsandra Malof hadn't broken—hadn't told her captors about the bridge message. But all evening Chen was grumpy, shouting at his only child, calling him a "little emperor." "That's the trouble with the government's one-child policy," he told his wife. "It turns them into spoiled brats. When I was young . . ."

Later that evening, his wife mentioned that Wong had asked another guard and his wife and them over for dinner. Wong could afford it, she told Chen. "While everyone else is on war rations, Wong gets extra food from the prison." Her unspoken question was, Why can't you scrounge more food?

"*Wong ba*," muttered Chen disgustedly, his wife gaping. It meant "turtle"—the very worst kind of insult. She knew that night they would not be making love.

CHAPTER THIRTY-FOUR

PERSONALLY OVERSEEING THE first prisoners brought in, Freeman noticed that their greatcoats were surprisingly devoid of snow, which was coming down in tiny balls so hard that it bounced off the coats, collecting at the collar folds.

The moment he saw that the surrendering Siberians were wearing civilian clothing underneath, Freeman got on the Humvee's radio and ordered the entire Airborne to ignore prisoners giving themselves up unless they opened fire, in which case they were to be cut down. Apart from that, prisoners were to be simply disarmed and left to find their own way to the rear. "I'm not about to fall for that old ploy," he informed Norton, "letting columns of refugees cloy your advance."

General Malik's planned attacks against Freeman's flanks by his two motorized regiments were foiled by the U-shaped area of chopper-dropped mines, the two 155mm howitzers meanwhile laying deadly fire on Nizhneangarsk. The blizzard afforded more cover for Freeman's foot soldiers than for the squeaky Siberian T-80s whose laser range finders were cut by the blizzard, four of the tanks erupting in flame, hit by American LAW 80 rounds, and in one case engulfed by flame thrower. It didn't mean there wasn't hard fighting, Freeman's first battalion engaging a company of SPETS troops in the open area immediately northwest of the Nizhneangarsk tower, where the brine of the salt marshes had turned the edge of the lake a dirty cream color. Here combat was often hand-to-hand, and the two Lynx helicopters with eight ninety-five-pound Hellfire missiles apiece attacked, having dealt with another six of Malik's lead tanks. One of the Lynx helos that had helped lay the mines, so that the Siberians had only a quarter-mile-wide front on which to attack, was temporarily downed because of shrapnel from a prematurely detonated mine whose fragments were too big for the self-sealing fuel tank to handle. Nevertheless, the Lynx had taken down one of Malik's vital forward Hind D spotter helos just before the blizzard promised from the north hit full force.

But if there was a general collapse of morale among Nizhneangarsk's regular troops, there was no such weakening of the Siberian Sixth Guards Regiment aboard the enormous air-cushioned vehicles—Aists—whose huge propellers were speeding them north from Port Baikal under orders from Irkutsk HQ. Though Freeman had as yet no report of them, they were now only a half hour from his paratroopers.

The Siberian Sixth Guards, quite apart from being the best *shturmoviki*—"trouble shooting"—regiment unit in the Siberian army, had a special reason for wanting to close with Freeman. The Guards were veterans of the Sixty-fourth Siberian Division, which boasted among its battle honors the defeat of the Wehrmacht at Stalingrad, but who had been routed and humiliated by Freeman's Second Army before the cease-fire. Indeed, it was in part the devastation wrought upon the Sixty-fourth by Freeman's breakout at that time, following the destruction of Baikal's sub base, that had convinced Yesov to yield and to sue for a cease in hostilities.

It was only when Freeman's paratroopers had reached Nizhneangarsk, securing the rail line—the surprise and rapidity of the American paratroopers' attack having overwhelmed the garrison—that the first of several reports came in from one of the Lynxes that the Aists—at least eight, maybe more—had been sighted. The report said they were approximately fifteen miles south of Nizhneangarsk, which meant they'd be at the railhead in fifteen minutes—Freeman knowing his paratroopers didn't have anything like the huge, heavily-armed and armored Aists with which to resist.

Colonel Dick Norton felt his throat constrict. "What now, General?"

Standing on a slight rise, arms akimbo in his characteristic, defiant pose, snow peppering him as he overlooked the white on white that was the expanse of the lake stretching south from him, Freeman thought he could see the Aists' blobs. Or was it a mirage or some other trick of the whiteout? It couldn't be them, as it was still snowing too heavily, reducing his visibility to no more than a quarter mile or so. It struck him that he may have momentarily been a victim of what he called "Hegel sight"—the ever-present danger he constantly warned his troops about: that in times of excitement, particularly in moments of high stress, you often see what you expect to see, projecting your worst fears outward—in this case to the ice. To a small boy at night, for example, an old coat on a doorknob could easily become the feared intruder. It took training and a victory over fear to see what in fact was there. "Dick, I want those two howitzers up here right now, plus heavy mortars and sappers. Fast!"

As Dick Norton radioed back to the main force, now collecting about the railhead a quarter mile back, he knew they were in serious trouble. There was nothing, absolutely nothing, a couple of howitzers and heavy mortars could do to stop the giant 250-ton, 155-foot-long, fifty-five-foot-wide air-cushion assault Aist crafts. These amphibians, propelled forward by two push, two pull props and driven by two gas NK-12 MV turbine engines at over seventy-five miles per hour, could move about a hundred times faster on the mirror-smooth ice than could the two 155mm guns or their crews. And each of the ten 250-ton Aists, in addition to carrying 250 fully armed shock troops, boasted eight surface-to-air Grail missiles which could make very short work of the remaining choppers—and of anything else.

As if to support Dick Norton's pessimism, the snowfall eased and Freeman, through the ten-power binoculars, could see white blobs on white, the tiny, hard snow racing at him like huge tracer. Through the dancing screen of the snow particles, he could see what appeared to be clouds of steam—the "up-blow" of snow and moisture from the Aists' one-foot-high cushion of air, billowing out from beneath the bulbous rubber skirting on each of the huge craft.

Behind and all around him, Freeman could hear the sappers and mortar crews arriving, and behind them the clank of the two howitzers' anchor spades in the snow and ice.

Norton, too, could see the Aists—there were not eight, but ten—still out of the howitzers' effective range but steadily growing bigger, like blunt-nosed destroyers, their superstructure bulky and bullying in appearance. They were big targets, but Norton knew there was no way two howitzers could handle the Aists, with the Siberian crafts' maneuverability. Freeman announced that if he were the Siberian commander, he would deploy the 250 troops aboard each Aist into the taiga for a flank attack before using the PT-76 tanks, four aboard each Aist, and their five-mile-range Grail SN-5 missiles. The second thing he'd do, he said, would be to use the Aists, which could not traverse the timber taiga, for a swerving S frontal attack against the railhead. Norton's accurate estimate that such a maneuver would mean no less than two and a half thousand enemy shock troops coming at them was interrupted by someone shouting that the fleet of Aists—which Norton could now see clearly through his binoculars—were moving closer to the taiga. They were about a hundred yards apart and five miles away, to the right of the American position, and now turning to their left—to the Americans' right—the up-blow from the assembled Aists' skirts forming a huge flour-white cloud of snow. Norton could see their shock troops unloading, streaming out of the white cloud like small wooden sticks, disappearing into the snowy umbrel-laed taiga.

The Aists closest to the forest having spewed out their

human cargo, now moved off and were forming up in single file so as to deny Freeman any effective lateral fire. Their commander was obviously intent, as Freeman had predicted, on a frontal attack against the Americans, the second part of what was obviously going to be a scissor offensive. One blade would be made up of the shock troops from the Aists moving now through the timber, cutting in toward Freeman from his right flank and putting stiffener into Malik's two motorized regiments, which had been driven back into the forest from the railroad only a short time before. The other blade would be the Aist attack itself.

Freeman grabbed the field phone and relayed his instructions, his paratroopers taking up positions all along the rail line left and right of his Humvee, picking the spots where the rail lines, encrusted with ice, formed the rim of a slight rise in the ground, the rise having been man-made in order to lift this section of the Trans-Siberian above flood level. It created a natural firing mound behind which Freeman's sappers also set up their mortars, several of the crews already crouching over the dial sights, the two howitzer crews—pathetically, it seemed to Dick Norton, yet bravely—aligning the guns against the missile-armed Aists.

Freeman's two remaining Lynx choppers, one of them with the patched fuel tank, rose like huge dragonflies frightened by noise, their cargo nets of pressure mines slung pendulously beneath them as they headed to the right, west of Nizhneangarsk, to do what Freeman, still glued to his binoculars, called, "A little oat sowing." Still watching the Aists for the first wink of a missile, he shouted over the roar of the choppers to Dick Norton about the mines. "Mightn't help stop their infantry, Dick . . . but it sure as hell'll slow 'em up. Damned if I'd like to be feeling my way through the forest, fearing any moment I'd be wearing my balls for a necklace."

"Yes, sir," said Norton. "But the Aists—I know their missiles aren't any good over five miles, but what are you going to do when they—"

"Oh, you beautiful bastards!" yelled Freeman without taking his eyes from the binoculars. Norton took up his and, in the circle of eye-blinding white, saw the Aists—or rather one of them, obscuring any view of the others, which had apparently lined up behind the leader. It presented Freeman's artillerymen, for all the good the two 155mms could do, with the smallest possible cross-section of target, and only one target at that. It was a frontal attack, all right, just as Freeman had predicted. Hopefully, thought Norton, the hero of Pyongyang and Ratmanov had also figured out a defense!

"We've only got two friggin' guns," said one of the loaders, pulling on his helmet but careful not to strap it lest an explosion's concussion tear his head off. "Why the hell doesn't the old man open up, now we've got 'em in range? Might be lucky and pick off the lead one, anyway. Least do some friggin' damage."

"Don't ask me," commented the battery officer. "General told us not to fire until he gives us the green light."

After calling the Aists "beautiful bastards" for the second time, and several of his treetop spotters reporting there were twelve and not ten of them, Freeman gave the two-howitzer battery and the sappers the order to fire. Norton involuntarily jumped, startled by the feral roar and crash of mortar bombs and sapper charges. Freeman was pushing him down for safety behind the Humvee as the frigid air came alive with the singing of deadly ice particles whizzing overhead.

At first Norton thought the Aists' frontal attack had begun already, although he knew that the Grail missiles were still not in range. It was a minute later as he glanced back at the two 155mm howitzers, seeing their belching flame and hearing the clang of ejected casings, that he realized what was happening and why all the explosions seemed so close. It was because they *were* close. The two gun crews, like the sappers, were following Freeman's orders to the letter, ignoring the rapidly approaching Aists, now only seven miles off and closing fast. The mortar crews were firing their bombs in a 180-degree left-right "fan arc," its farthest point only a hundred yards or so in front of them, and *not* at the Aists, now less than six miles—four minutes—away from them, racing toward the Americans at seventy-plus miles per hour across the perfectly unobstructed ice. Instead of firing at the Aists, the Americans were firing *into* the three-foot ice several hundred yards out into the lake. For the howitzers it was point-blank range.

"Give the bastards a bit of their own medicine! Goddamn Mongols!" declared Freeman as ice chips smacked into his Humvee, the explosions from the heavy mortars and the sappers' C-4 HE packs acting like depth charges, chopping and smashing up what had been the mirrored surface of the lake. Within minutes it was a boiling jumble of mini icebergs, rolling over and over in the man-made turbulence, some of the bergs' jagged tops rising over five feet above the water.

Then Norton saw it in a flash: the Aists, with a draft of only one foot, might have difficulty negotiating above a bumpy terrain. As it turned out, there was no difficulty; there was only disaster, the Aists balking for a moment or two, clearly decelerating, their up-blow of snow increasing, then, ironically, rapidly decreasing as they hit full throttle, hoping to get enough air cushion to overrun the Americans. In Freeman's elegant phrase, the icebergs, sticking up like giant knives, "ripped the ass off" the Aists, causing a pileup the likes of which Norton had never seen. One Aist's Drum Tilt fire-control radar took off like a flying saucer. Another Aist's bow ramp imploded, pierced by the ice, the Aist rolling, its lift fans coming to pieces with the sound of some monstrous air conditioner suddenly filled with metal chips, particles of ice having passed through the protective mesh, buckling the fans' blades.

The Aist, still rolling, now capsized, the display of its enormous black bottom looking somehow obscene, covered as it was in a froth of chocolate-mousse-colored bubbles; one of the hovercraft's enormous push propellers, still functioning, having whipped up hydraulic fluid into a frenzied spill that soon all but obscured the rubber skirting.

"God damn it, Dick!" yelled Freeman, one hand putting his helmet back on after a concussion had blown it off, the other hand pulling out his Sig Sauer nine-millimeter. "Looks like Tacoma Demolition Derby out there! Goddamn Mongols!" He fired until his magazine was empty, oblivious of shots being fired his way, slapping in a new clip, firing again into the boiling sea of blood and ice and dying Siberians amidst which Norton again didn't feel it politic to point out that these weren't Mongols, but Siberians. He knew what the general meant. Freeman had told Washington he would avenge the slaughter of III Corps. But even so, Freeman had given strict orders that any Sibir who put up his hands—gave any sign of surrender—was to be treated accordingly, fished out, assisted as required, and put in line to be airlifted back to Khabarovsk.

CHAPTER THIRTY-FIVE

THE IMMEDIATE EFFECT of the Aist disaster meant that now Freeman's paras could give all their attention to preparing in-depth defenses of Nizhneangarsk. Freeman opted for a "broken diamond" of razor wire, two hundred yards a side, the pattern which had been used to telling effect against the Japanese in the jungles of New Guinea in '42 to '45. The fact that there was so much snow to help hide the spring-coiled razor wire as it was unraveled to form a diamond shape helped his plan. The left top run of wire went out for fifty yards or so beyond the end of the top right run, creating the impression to anyone approaching the railhead that the top of the diamond was open—that there was a gap blown open in the perimeter defense. Either that or they'd assume there'd been a break in the wire. But once through the break, they would in fact have entered a trap, wire on their left and right, coming to a closed V. Dug in behind the bottom of the wire V would be a corresponding V of American machine guns.

To keep the approaching Siberians unloaded earlier from the Aist occupied, Freeman sent patrols a mile east of Nizhneangarsk around the lake's edge so as to avoid the mines and to engage any Siberians who tried making their way out of the taiga to the less obstructed lake edge. In this way, the Siberian shock troops were being herded back into the forest and ultimately into the diamond of wire. In this, Freeman, as he'd anticipated, was aided by the slow going of the Siberian troops due to the mines that had been scattered by the Lynxes in the forest between Nizhnean-garsk and the Aist troop drop-off point.

Personally directing the layout of the razor wire at the railhead, Freeman was pleased to notice that while they had plenty of snow with which to hide the bottom V, the blizzard itself was letting up, which meant that he could soon expect air drops to resupply and thus consolidate his position. It meant he could also now order M-1 tanks westward on the Baikal-Amur-Magistral line to Nizhnean-garsk to meet any counterattack that might be contemplated by Litvinov's northern army around Yakutsk.

The long-range effect of Freeman's taking the railhead, quite apart from the fact that M-1 tanks were now rolling westward to Nizhneangarsk under heavy fighter protection, was that he had, as hoped, not only struck the Siberians a counterattack on their home ground, which would strike a blow at Siberian morale in general, but in doing so had created the massive diversion of vitally needed Siberian troops from the south around Baikal. This not only caused Yesov to lose the momentum of his eastward lunge, but simultaneously enabled what was left of III Corps to make the eastern side of the lake and to escape into the taiga and join the troops heading south. In all, Freeman having thrown Yesov off his stride had bought valuable time for Second Army to continue its buildup on the Chinese border.

Still, Freeman knew that a breakthrough of his in the south—any attempt to take the general offensive against the Chinese—would be impossible unless the Nanking Bridge was blown, cutting the logistical tail of the PLA, the vital line of supply for Cheng's northern Chinese armies.

As if to underscore the tentativeness of his Nizhneangarsk victory, there was a sudden swish of air, like that of an automobile passing another at high speed on a highway, and Freeman was yanked down into oil-stained snow by Dick Norton, both of them lifted bodily by the concussion of the hundred-millimeter shell hitting Freeman's Humvee twenty yards away. There was a soft *woof*, the Humvee—or rather, its buckled chassis—split and afire, the scarred snow around it a junkyard of Humvee parts, its burning engine spewing out a thick, churning column of soot-black smoke.

"What in hell—" began Freeman, but immediately hit the ground again, as did Norton and the others, a second round hitting the burning hulk with a loud *whang*, the chassis disintegrating, filling the air with shrapnel. For a moment Norton, deafened by the noise of the impact, couldn't hear what the general was saying. Freeman hauled himself out of the snow, dusted himself off and pulled out the Beretta from his belt band. "God damn it! That's the second time. No need for that!"

The general's outrage was directed at something none of the Americans had seen during the chaotic fighting amid the Aist pileup: some of the Siberians being hauled out of the frigid waters of Lake Baikal were still fighting.

The last three Aists had floundered, but seven of their twelve PT-76 up-gunned cannon amphibious tanks had been able to roll off the Aist before the latter had been taken out by the now point-blank howitzer fire. These seven tanks were now firing their hundred-millimeter cannon even as they swam with flotation boards out toward the American positions at ten kilometers an hour, navigating their way through, and largely protected from American fire by, the very icebergs that had incapacitated their mother ships.

Perhaps Norton was the only one who fully understood Freeman's outrage at the appearance of the amphibious PT-76s. They had been the nemesis of his armor earlier in the war. The "goddamned coffeepots," as he called them, had been used to killing effect in North Korea, the relatively light, amphibious PT-76s, at only fourteen tons, able to move with much more maneuverability in the flooded Korean paddies than could the heavy Abrams M-1s' sixty tons. But if the NKA had unleashed hundreds of them in the flooded rice paddies where they could move much more easily and could ford swollen streams with their flotation skirting, and the sixty-ton M-1s were often stuck and found it difficult if not impossible to negotiate on the flood plain, at least here at Nizhneangarsk the game was over for the PT-76s.

Or so it seemed.

For some inexplicable reason—perhaps because the driver of the PT-76 was concussed by the enfilade of 155mm and heavy mortar fire raining down about him, one PT-76 of the seven now approaching the Americans' position had its lights on, and in the snow made a wonderful target, attracting fire from every kind of weapon the Americans had. Its turret suddenly imploded and it was gone in a huge bubble, along with a cheer from several of the mortar crews. Only Freeman and the paratroop commander woke up to the ploy at once and had started to yell at the mortars and antitank LAW crews to spread their fire among the others, but a quick-thinking and brave Siberian commander had succeeded nevertheless. While every "Tom, Dick, and goddamn Harry," as Freeman later reported, "was throwing everything but his socks," including infrared homing rounds, at that PT-76 with its lights on, the remaining six amphibians had precious seconds to find "breaching" aprons of ice that allowed them to get a grip onto the mainland at the edge of the fan-shaped sea and to fire back. In those few seconds at least three got off a hundred-millimeter round each, one of these taking out one of Freeman's 155mm howitzer crews. There was another round, screaming overhead—so low that Freeman and Norton could feel its heat wash a split second before it hit one of the two Lynxes, which had come down to refill its "string bag" with antipersonnel mines. The explosion of the chopper was more a burst of black oil not yet alight, then a crimson flash followed by a deep, steady roar as the antipersonnel mines went off, filling the air with fragments that killed or wounded thirty-six of Freeman's paratroopers nearby.

The PT-76s paid dearly as the one-man portable one-shot LAW antitank weapons nearest them were brought to bear, the six-pound AT rounds sinking all but one of the remaining six amphibians. Some of the Siberians afire inside these tanks were trying desperately to get out, the sound of them beating against the inside of the cupolas whose seals had been warped under impact of the antitank rounds clearly audible to the LAW teams. Only one cupola managed to open, and a gunner, aflame, tried futilely to abandon the tank, falling forward as the tank went down, its gun coming up, striking him face-on and knocking him back into the water. The man was pushed toward the edge of the ice by a wave from the sinking tank, its gun, now at a crazy, sky-pointing angle, disappearing into an enormous bubbling, the tank's chopped-up flotation boards ripped, letting the tank slide backward into the oblivion of three thousand feet of water.

"I'll tell you, Dick," said Freeman. "I don't envy those poor bastards."

There was no reply. When Freeman turned about, Norton was out cold, his left hand lost from view in the blood gushing from his left eye.

"Medic!" yelled Freeman.

With the medic came more bad news. SATINT over China showed what the G-2 officer surmised had been a pinpoint burst of light situated about a mile upstream of the Nanking Bridge. Freeman said nothing, kneeling by

Norton, who had been with him since his days in Europe, since Ratmanov.

"Sir?" the intelligence officer pressed, unsure as to whether Freeman had heard him.

"I know!" Freeman growled up at him. "You're telling me the Country Market team's been discovered?"

"Well yes, sir, but we're not sure about both boats. We think this photo is definitely of one boat, but there's a chance the second is still operational."

"So, they're in trouble," said Freeman curtly. "Can't do anything about it from here. Right?"

"No, sir. But whether they blow it or not, there's the problem of getting them out. ChiComs are sure to be looking for them around the bridge."

"Well, we sure as hell can't leave them there."

"No, sir."

"They issued an emergency call?"

"Not yet, sir. Extraction's scheduled in ninety minutes."

"What do you suggest?"

A line of Siberians, dripping wet, some shivering so much from the cold that Freeman could actually hear their teeth chattering, was passing them under guard. One man saw him and saluted. Solemnly, the general rose and returned the salute, hearing the small arms fire in the background at the edge of the taiga a half mile to the east. Freeman knew he had a formidable problem either way. If the SEALs didn't blow the bridge, there'd be no hope of contesting the invasion by the northern ChiCom armies. If there were some SEALs still alive and they did blow the bridge, chances were their original drop-off point would no longer be usable, ChiComs now searching upstream from whence they'd come.

"Any suggestions?" Freeman repeated.

"Well, sir, Tom Pierce, the Pave Low commander on *Salt Lake City*, says that if his helos went in under the radar undetected, they can go in—and out—again. Problem is, there'll be absolutely no chance of even a touch-and-go extraction on the riverbank mud. Apart from possibly bogging down if that chopper landed, the ChiComs'd swarm all over 'em.''

"Is there any other way?" asked Freeman.

"Well, sir, Pierce says it's possible. SEALs carry an IFF—friend-or-foe identifier. Pierce thinks he could try a STABO link—if you approve."

Freeman raised his eyebrows, watching Norton coming to, the colonel having involuntarily soiled his pants in the shock of getting hit. The general nodded to his G-2 that they should move away, give the medic room.

"First problem those SEALs'll have," the general told the G-2, "is that damn bridge. Whether it goes or not, they'll know any attempted pickup'll have to be made soon as possible after. We'd have to have those helos from *Salt Lake City* in the air pretty damn fast. Have 'em almost to the China coast."

A Siberian officer, an American army blanket clutched around his shoulders, his face covered in oil, stumbled by, toward what he obviously thought was a vision or the grandest American invention since the Model T—the paratroopers' portable MUST, already inflated, taking in wounded, its sterile air filter unit humming a soft song in the din of battle.

"Well, you'd better get everything ready, son," Freeman told his G-2. "Use Black Hawks for that?" He meant one of the ubiquitous Utility-60 helos of Vietnam fame, the best for a STABO pickup.

"Pierce thinks the Pave can handle it, sir. He's all set to go."

"What's the SEALs' emergency call?"

"Mars."

"All right. Have those Paves airborne soon as you can."

"Yes, sir."

"And lieutenant . . ."

"General?"

"You tell those big, ugly Paves to add some firepower."

"Yes, sir."

Freeman's use of the phrase "big, ugly Paves" momentarily reminded him of the big, ugly, fat fellows—the B-52s he had ready at Nayoro should the weather ever clear over the Black Dragon River. With Americans and Chinese so close together in such foul weather, not even the B-52s' pinpoint bombing could avoid killing as many Americans as Chinese.

"Lieutenant . . ."

"Sir?"

"SEALs carry that STABO stuff?"

"No, sir, it's dropped."

"All right, you attend to that. I'll see if our navy boys on *Salt Lake City* can give us a few strikers offshore if we need them."

"I hope those SEALs blow that bridge, sir."

"They don't, son," Freeman called out, "you're gonna miss the World Series." He bent down again next to Norton, who was now sitting up, having his head bandaged. "And we, my friends," he told the medic and Norton, "will be up shit creek without a paddle."

"You think they'll—" began Norton, then stopped, feeling the bump of the bandage over his eye. He was having trouble seeing with his right, and it felt as if his head would fall off. He began again quietly. "You think Yakutsk will hit us from the north? I mean, the weather's still pretty bad for us having any hope of air cover. They might try it."

"They might," said Freeman. In the presence of wounded men, he always tried to sound confident, reassuring.

It was a commander's job. It was also a commander's job to look facts square in the face, and if he was the C in C of Yakutsk, and American cover was socked in, then he'd go for broke: release his armor and attack the railhead. Overwhelm it with armor. Still, Freeman didn't regret having brought his airborne to Nizhneangarsk, for it had achieved its aim of stalling Yesov's eastern advance and given him time to move his M-1s west to Nizhneangarsk. The next move was Yesov's—to stay put or . . .

"Maybe," said Norton, his voice dry, groggy from a shot of Demerol, "maybe they're already on the move."

CHAPTER THIRTY-SIX

LOOKING UP FROM thirty feet below the river's surface, Robert Brentwood could see a tan-colored sheen—moonlight on the water—which would make it easier for him and his co-diver, Dennison, and for the other Echo One pair: Smythe and young Rose. But Robert Brentwood also knew that it would be welcomed by the ChiComs, the better to see anything moving on the river. Already the Chinese were holding up traffic on the right-hand channel off the eastern bank, not allowing any vessel under the bridge. Brentwood estimated he and Dennison were now two hundred yards from the bridge. Smythe and Rose, though farther out in the river, were presumably about the same distance away from the piers. For a moment he toyed with the idea of using his penlight on the handheld GPS affixed to his weight belt to get their exact position, but decided that even at this depth it was too much of a risk with the ChiComs up and about. He and Dennison would have to reorientate themselves visually regarding pier four in a minute or so, the current moving them more swiftly now that the river was narrowing from three and a half to three miles wide as it approached the straightway leading into the big left-right hook of river that lay beyond the bridge.

Dennison's mask was misting up as he closed his eyes, fighting the temptation to scratch an indescribable itch that was moving malevolently up from his testicles to his backside, where the friction caused by the heavy flippers and explosive loads was exacting its toll. Or maybe it was something he was allergic to—something he ate on the *Salt*

Lake City before the mission. The carrier was a world away, and he yearned for the safety of it, even though he'd joined the SEALs precisely to get away from the bigness of the surface fleet, where you were lucky to get to know your own section, let alone anyone else in the five-thousand-man crew. Or rather any of the five thousand men and women aboard, now that Congress had empowered females, including those in the air arm, to be combat soldiers. He wouldn't mind one of *them* scratching the itch. It was crazy thinking about that at a time like this, but it drained off some of the tension. Still, unable to resist the itch now spreading up his loins like spiders, he was careful to use his right hand rather than the left. One hard jerk of the latter on the feel line would have signaled to Brentwood they were under attack. Yet despite Dennison's precautions, Brentwood felt the tension on the line increase, and swam closer in the pitch-blackness, only to be reassured by the okay squeeze signaled on his upper arm by Dennison. Brentwood signaled him in return that it was time to go up anyway—this being as good a moment as any in Brentwood's estimation to reorientate themselves.

When they saw it, silhouetted by moonlight, both men's pulses quickened. You could practice all you wanted in Pearl, stare for hours at a scale model with wall-sized SATINT blowups, planning just where and how you were going to place the charges, but the Nanking Bridge, standing proud over two hundred feet high and over four miles long, its two decks separated and held in position by enormous X-shaped trusses, was massively impressive.

Only a hundred yards from it now, Brentwood and Dennison could quite clearly hear the movement of traffic, the faint sing of tires and boom-boom sound of wheels crossing the join grates between each section of the eight spans supported between the nine piers. The lower—railway—deck was see-through for a second, bathed in moonlight that silhouetted the crisscross trusses beneath it. Then suddenly it was blacked out by a long goods train, its boxcars traveling right to left across the moon, heading northward, carrying much-needed supplies for Cheng's army. From the mission briefing, Brentwood knew they could expect another train within the next half hour.

Off to the right, from whence the train had come, he and Dennison could see bright dots of lights, searchlights, starting to probe from atop the ancient city's wall. The beams were still concentrating on sweeping the eastern half of the river downstream from where Echo Two had been hit. For this reason the searchlights didn't worry Brentwood now as much as earlier, and besides, the mist coming down from farther upstream, caused by the smoke from the factory, was spilling over both banks from flooded levees, helping to protect them. Brentwood was confident that unless they were actually caught, fully illuminated in the beam's circle—the latter a hundred feet or so across—there was a good possibility of avoiding detection. And even if you had your head out—provided you stayed absolutely still in the light and betrayed no motion—you would stand a fifty-fifty chance. In any case, much better to have the searchlights up on the wall, if you had to have them at all, rather than farther down on the bridge itself. Now that they were on the surface and could see no immediate danger, Brentwood tapped Dennison's shoulder and whispered, "When we get to the pier, we'll wait till another train starts across to place the charges."

"Copy," acknowledged Dennison, and, discarding the feel line, they disappeared once more beneath the muddy water, the current having moved them to within fifty yards of the pier, stratus cloud sailing across the moon, obscuring more of it by the second. It was now that Brentwood saw how the tragedy of Echo Two had unwittingly helped him and Dennison, for while the ChiComs had been concentrating on searching closer to the right bank, their searchlight beams faded in the mist over about a quarter mile on the three-mile-wide river, and so had given the remaining SEALs time to get nearer the bridge.

Brentwood's shoulders were already aching from the weight of his minigun and the heavy pack of his two

eighteen-pound, champagne-bottle-shaped charges, detonating cord, waterproof tape, grappling tackle, stable blasting cap, and timers. He knew that the big problem for the
two two-man teams now, providing Smythe and Rose
hadn't been picked up, was the question of the delay fuse
timer. With the Chinese already aroused, it couldn't be too
long, but time enough to permit them to make their
extraction point downstream. Brentwood decided that if he
and Dennison were lucky and managed to place the charges
as he'd planned, he'd be able to use a short-time ACAT—a
ten-minute acid ampule timer. He had to trust that Smythe
and Rose would do the same, "short fuse" being standard
procedure when any member of the mission had been
discovered and might jeopardize the remainder. He turned
his immediate attention to two things: first, where exactly
he would place the earmuffs on the pier, which was growing
by the second as he and Dennison neared it; and second,
how he would set the yellow-dyed and Play-Doh-like C-4
plastique between the flanges of two crisscross girders. The
C-4 explosive would have to be fairly high up in order to
literally cut through the girders with the heat generated by
the explosion rather than by the explosion itself.

Brentwood felt two sharp tugs—for danger—on his
weight belt, and immediately put his arms into a reverse
breaststroke position, his long flippers kicking hard against
the current to brake his forward motion, his backpack now
coming forward, thumping into his upper back

CHAPTER THIRTY-SEVEN

"WAKE UP, YOU Aussie bastard!" said Salvini. "You owe us money."

Aussie was already awake, but lying dead still from habit, as any SAS/D man did—not moving before you knew exactly what the situation was. "First, put your brain into gear," he could hear his instructor telling him. "*Before* you move."

"Aussie! C'mon, get up." Now he recognized Salvini's voice—knew where he was—safe in a warm kip at Rudnaya Pristan' after the abortive A-7 raid. His left foot was throbbing. "What's up, Sal? What money?" Outside it was still pitch-black.

"Yeah. Big-time spender," said Sal. "Let's go. Briefing in five minutes. We're outta here in twenty."

"A mission?" Aussie was sitting up on the edge of the palliasse, the SAS/D teams preferring the straw-filled hessian bag to regular Special Forces foam-rubber issue. Salvini, who had been on the eight-to-midnight watch, was handing him a steaming cup of coffee. "That SEAL outfit," said Salvini, "one Davey's brother's in . . ." He glanced about to see whether David Brentwood was nearby. "Well, SATINT shows at least one of the two Zodiacs bought it. We're on standby for assist. And you, sweetheart, owe me and Choir some bread!"

This jolted Aussie more than the coffee. "Hey, hey, fucking hold on there, Sal. Just hold on a mo. This just happened, right? Out of the fucking blue, right?"

"Yeah—so?"

"So this had nothing to do with any friggin' rumor. You and Williams here made up that bullshit!"

Choir was filling a C-mag for his squad automatic weapon. "That's right, boyo. We were just guessin'. Playing the odds. There's a war on, you know." He smiled across at Salvini, then down at Aussie. "Fact is, Mr. Lewis, sir, you owe us fifteen 'In God We Trust.' "

"All right, all right," said Lewis. "What a pair of bloody bushrangers."

"He means holdup men," Choir told Sal.

"I mean fucking con men," said Aussie good-naturedly. "All right, I'll pay you when we get back."

"I'd like mine now, please," said Choir, giving Salvini the nod.

"Oh, thank you, Choir," replied Aussie Lewis over his steaming coffee. "Thank you for your wonderful display of confidence in your mate. Think I'm gonna buy it 'fore I can square accounts, that it?"

"Had occurred to me, boyo."

"Jesus!" retorted Aussie, fixing Sal in his gaze. "Doesn't he take the fucking cake?"

"I'd like my ten, too," said Sal. "Now."

"Oh, I get it. It's fucking gang-up time on old Lewis, is it? All right, sticks and stones'll break my bones but names—I'm gonna report you fuckers to Davey."

"What for?" joshed Salvini, gathering his kit.

"For being assholes—detrimental to my morale." Suddenly Lewis remembered David Brentwood's brother. "Did his brother cop it?"

"Don't know," said Salvini. "Can't tell from the satellite pix."

"What's the problem? POE out?" He meant the point of extraction.

"Yeah. Freeman's HQ says the second team, if they're still alive, probably hid their kit a few miles upriver, and ChiComs've probably found it by now. So if there are any

SEALs left, they won't be able to use the Zodiac to get to the original POE.''

"How do we know they're still alive?" asked Lewis.

"We don't. But we will if the bridge goes," chipped in Choir. "Make one bloody great splash for a satellite picture, it will.''

"A satellite'll be overhead, then?" pressed Lewis.

"Don't know," said Choir. "We'd probably find out via Chinese underground radio, anyway. Same outfit in Harbin that put us in the know about the bridge.''

"Yeah," added Salvini. "They tell us the poor bitch who passed it on to us is now in a Harbin lockup.''

Choir made a face. "Chinese jail. Wouldn't change places with her, boyo.''

"Well, she's not goin' to be much friggin' good there," said Lewis. "She's not gonna see whether the bridge goes down or not from fuckin' Harbin.''

Sometimes Salvini got teed off with Aussie's insensitive streak. Still, it also was what made him a good man in a tight spot.

"No," agreed Salvini. "But Choir's right. We'll hear through the Harbin underground if anything happens in Nanking.''

"So what's the plan?" said Lewis, draining the coffee. He saw David Brentwood come in. "Sorry to hear about your brother, mate.''

David nodded. The fact was, he was trying to push any thought of Robert out of his mind by thinking only of the plan. That it was family made all the difference, but it couldn't make any difference. If you were going to let it get in the way of a good, clear, standby plan, you might as well withdraw. He motioned down at Aussie's bandaged foot, the iodine stain now a dark saffron on his left ankle and arch. "You up to it, Aussie?''

"Don't be bloody silly," answered the Australian. "Got to help a mate out, right?''

David Brentwood could feel his throat constricting with

emotion. The simplicity and spontaneity of the Australian's response to go so willingly into danger—though it was the same quality he himself had—momentarily threatened to overwhelm him. It was an unspoken pride they all shared, and he wondered whether anyone outside could ever fully understand. But perhaps they did. It had often struck David that there was many a civilian in the suburbs of America who, like the Chinese underground, carried on an everyday life with an unspoken commitment—to an aged parent, a handicapped child—with the same kind of devotion, and no one knew what it took. He thought of what his brother Ray had gone through after being so terribly burned aboard the USS *Blaine*; of his own wife, Georgina; and Robert's wife, Rosemary. And his sister Lana, still bound to La "Creep" Roche. They, too, had to cope with unspoken fears and the absence of loved ones.

"Standby plan is this," explained David quietly. "If we get a go from Freeman, we'll be flown—Mach-plus transport—to the carrier *Salt Lake City*. It's moving in as close as possible to the coast. Then we go into the area north of Nanking under the radar screen via a Pave—one of the two that took them in. But we don't go for the actual assist unless we get an emergency call sign. No call sign, we assume they're all dead."

"What is it?" asked Salvini.

"Mars."

"No," said Salvini. "What's the assist?"

"STABO."

Choir Williams shook his head at the acronyms the bureaucrats had thought up. STABO technically meant "stabilized tactical airborne body operation." And like most military acronyms, it made it all sound banal and straightforward, like taking the bus, the danger obfuscated by the bloodless officialese.

"Well hell," said Aussie, "we weren't planning anything for today, were we?" He looked around.

"I'd rather be playing football," said Choir wryly, adopting Aussie's tone, knowing that no matter what they said,

David Brentwood would feel badly about them all being involved in the mission, figuring that in a way they were doing it as a favor for him, inadvertently making him feel responsible.

"Football!" said Aussie, a mock sneer on his face. "D'you mean *real* football, Choir? Australian rules?"

"Australian rules?" echoed Choir, looking bemused at Salvini and David. "Now there's a contradiction in terms."

"Don't be so fucking rude!" said Aussie, picking up the mags for his 7.62mm mini and turning his attention to David Brentwood. "How many of us, Davey?"

"Four," answered David. "I'm going, but if any of you don't—" He stopped; the others were already picking up their gear.

"Maybe they won't need an assist," said Salvini.

"Right!" said Aussie.

"And pigs fly," replied David, looking straight at him. "Right?"

"You mean Welshmen?" said Aussie. "Oh yeah—they fly all the time."

"I hope we don't have to go in," said David. "I mean, I hope they get the bridge and—"

"They'll get it," said Salvini, though knowing he'd fail a polygraph test.

"One for the books, hey, Davey?" said Aussie.

"What's that?"

"Our mob—SAS/D—helping out the navy. Jesus, they'll never forgive us."

"Hadn't thought of it that way," said David, momentarily cheered by the Australian's light banter in the face of the odds.

"Well, you should have, mate. A Pave can accommodate us all, I take it?"

"No problem."

"Well, if it gets too heavy, we'll just throw Choir out."

"May I remind you, Mr. Brentwood, sir," said Choir, "that Sergeant Lewis here owes me and Salvini fifteen bucks. I authorize you to collect in my absence."

"Mercenary bastard!" riposted Aussie. "That all you think about? Dough? Filthy lucre?"

What Choir was thinking about was a filthy river, three miles wide, and trying to extract SEALs—if there were any survivors—by STABO.

The quartermaster caught up with them in the mess. He told them the STABO harnesses were ready. David Brentwood looked solemn. "Thanks."

They sat there waiting for the transport to the jet that would whisk them southeast to the carrier. His hands cupping a second mug of coffee, Aussie's head suddenly shot up like an eagle spotting unsuspecting prey. "Hey, you jokers," he said, looking at Salvini and Choir. "We're only on standby unless we get the SEALs emergency call. As of now I owe you sweet fuck-all."

"Technicality," charged Choir.

"Technicality my ass. Ha! And you thought you could pull one over—"

"Mr. Brentwood, sir?"

David Brentwood looked around. It was the quartermaster again. "Yes?"

"Sir, General Freeman's HQ says, 'Go.' Bridge down or not, he wants to have you guys in the area if they call."

"Hey," said Aussie, his eyes turned on the hapless quartermaster. "Shouldn't you be in fuckin' bed?"

CHAPTER THIRTY-EIGHT

THE SHEEN ABOVE Dennison and Robert Brentwood, now like a dull mirror on a darkened ceiling, wasn't moonlight, for in patches it was particularly intense. A minute later they realized that the blobs of concentrated light, not moving, were fixed floodlights on the bridge, and crisscrossing the dull, silvered roof of light that was the river-air interface were enormous black rectangular shapes—the shadows cast on the water by the gargantuan X-shaped truss girders.

They surfaced slowly, silently, in one of the shadows, and their worst fears were confirmed. Bridge floodlights, spaced a hundred yards apart, were switched on along the southern side of the bridge, and far over to their right, toward the eastern shore about two hundred yards from that side of the river's edge, was a long, black, snakelike object. As his eyes adjusted to the infrared lenses, Brentwood recognized it as a long line of river craft of all shapes and sizes, from small sampans and medium-sized junks to the big propane barge, all halted and forced to cast anchor a quarter mile upstream from the bridge.

And it was then that he saw the two men—Rose and Smythe—tied to the outer rail of the bridge, a hundred feet above the midway point on the span between piers four and five—like two black crosses, still clad in their rubber wet suits. Far below them, in the penumbra of the floodlights, the huge black shadows of the trusses shivered in eddies about the massive concrete piers, and now there was a lot more noise—shouted commands on the bridge, the distant rumble of another approaching train, only this time an empty one coming down from the north.

Brentwood knew it would be impossible to scale the pier and place the "earmuffs" as planned. But just as quickly, with the speed of a sub captain firing a snap torpedo shot, he knew what he must do, like seeing a fuzzy slide jump into focus.

There was barely time to convey the information to Dennison, including the GPS coordinates of the new rendezvous point he'd decided on. Even with the racket on the bridge added to by the rattle of the goods train, Brentwood was cognizant of just how far the human voice could carry over water, and quickly reverted to sign language during the lull that followed the train. It took him only a minute to explain it, but to Dennison, who expected a searchlight from the right bank to have him in its beam any second, it seemed much longer.

As Dennison checked his COBRA pack, he got a whiff of foul air blown down by the north wind from the flooded levees. Slipping beneath the dark water, the last thing he saw through his mask was the two blurred cruciform shapes of Rose and Smythe tied against the outer pedestrian railing of the seemingly endless black bridge. Going deep to forty feet, he took out the penlight and, pressing it hard against his watch, arched his body to prevent even such a dim light as this from being seen. It was 0133. He started the count, Brentwood having told him he must wait twenty minutes before he could go back up, and even then it would perhaps take another half hour before Brentwood was ready. But even now Dennison found his thumb impatiently slipping the safety off the Remington 7188 machine/shotgun, his left hand feeling the ventilated barrel shield beneath the waterproof plastic sheath that held the gun and its eight-shot 00 rounds. He was eager yet nervous, because along with the new rendezvous point, Brentwood had also told him that even with this quiet shotgun he didn't want any more fuss than was necessary—that he must be able to do it with two clicks—two shots.

CHAPTER THIRTY-NINE

NORTHEAST OF LAKE Baikal the five hundred Siberian tanks due to roll south from Yakutsk Oblast to engage Freeman before he could build enough armored strength to capitalize on his victory at Nizhneangarsk were held back for four hours at Udokan. Clear skies were reported in the sector above which American planes ruled supreme at the outermost limit of the Siberians' formidable AA network. But soon, invading the clear skies, there came threatening scuds of the storm line of cumulonimbus anvils which would soon swallow the clear sky and further engulf Nizhneangarsk to the south.

The storm, as in the case of those preceding it, was also coming down from the Arctic, blowing over the permafrost with a polar wind whose chill factor drove the thermometer in the Yakutsk Oblast to minus fifty-six degrees with the mercury still falling. It hadn't yet plunged to the minus eighties, but it was cold enough for exposed flesh to freeze in seconds, and metal was becoming brittle.

Still, the Siberian armored division from Yakutsk had pressed south under Yesov's orders. "You are fighting on home soil," the marshal exhorted his men, pointing out that the Americans might have made a name for themselves in Iraq at Mediny Ridge against the Soviet-built T-72s, but that was in another world—one of sand and baked earth—and the lessons of Mediny had been learned. Also, here the advantage would be with the Siberians, for whom winter was not so much something to resist but to act in concert with, to use, so much so that the Siberians' knowledge of snow fighting was said to be *Vsosano smolokom*—"bred in the bone."

When Dick Norton heard that the Siberian armor was on the move south from Udokan, he knew that Freeman, with nowhere to retreat even if that was his style, was now in a make-or-break situation, whether he liked it or not. And every other officer on Freeman's staff was as deeply worried as Norton, several unhesitatingly expressing their concern to Norton that this time "Fighting Freeman" might well have "bitten off more than he can chew." With several officers using the same cliché, Norton was concerned that the growing air of uncertainty among the senior commanders would spread by that rapid process of osmosis whereby fear is borne effortlessly like a virus from the officer corps to the grunt. He knew they wouldn't tell Freeman of their doubts—that was *his* job, and he was dismayed, for when the second storm struck, American planes would be yet again denied the opportunity to move effectively against the Siberian armor—this time consisting of main battle tanks moving south with formidable surface-to-air missile cover.

It wasn't as if Freeman was unconcerned with the weather. He had all but driven Major Harvey Simmet, the HQ met officer, to distraction by calling for hourly reports. But he seemed overconfident to Norton, as if he knew as much about the terrain as the Siberians who had lived there all their lives.

"What you have to understand, Dick," explained Freeman as he stood proudly watching his M1A1s heading north, "is their permafrost. In places it's over a thousand feet thick. Siberians worried for years about how to get their oil and natural gas up from beneath that goddamned concrete. Buckles everything you try to drill it with. Diamond bits wear out here faster than anywhere else in the world. Then this bright spark comes along from Novosibirsk and figures out you don't need miles and miles of piping underneath to tap the natural gas—or anything else, for that matter. Know what he does?"

Norton shook his head. It was time for what the general's headquarter staff called "Jeopardy." If you didn't know the answers, Freeman took you prisoner in a ten-minute rundown on little-known minutiae.

"Well, it was costing them a fortune in piping, Dick—not just for drilling stock, but for pipe to pump the natural gas through."

Dick Norton was finding it difficult to concentrate on what the general was saying, feeling too sleepy from the Demerol and too worried about the Siberian armor—already reported only sixty miles away. "Pipe?" he said, trying to sound interested, but imagining what would happen when the Siberians' T-72s with the laser sights and all the lessons of the tanks' shortcomings in the Iraqi War now known and overcome met up with the hastily assembled American defenses, only 227 American tanks having arrived on the BAM so far.

"Yes, pipe!" replied Freeman. "Don't you see, they didn't need it. Holes they drilled through the permafrost—vertical or horizontal—were natural aquifers. Natural pipes! Permafrost's so thick and hard, you don't need damn pipes. Use the permafrost."

So, thought Norton, good for Freeman, resident U.S. expert on permafrost, but had the general thought through his battle plan to engage the Siberians with their two-to-one advantage? Worse still, Freeman had ordered his tanks to proceed north from Nizhneangarsk line abreast. Any first lieutenant knew that a well-dug-in enemy tank or AT missile battery had a much better chance to pick off tanks if they were coming at you stretched left to right rather than in line of column. And so Norton used Freeman's homily about permafrost to alert the general, as unobtrusively as possible, to this potentially fatal tactical flaw.

Freeman, left hand on his hip, right clenched, thumb outstretched, was giving the hurry-up signal to an M-1 that had slewed off the Marsden matting that the resupply C-5s had dropped along with the howitzers also being taken north.

Freeman didn't acknowledge that he'd heard Norton. Hands back on his hips, his collar up, eyes squinting in the first snow of the new storm, the general shook his head— not in dismay at the coming battle, but with unbridled admiration for his men. Norton could see the general was in his "attack mode," as it was known among his officers. His holster's metal clip was undone so that it wouldn't freeze up and inhibit what he had, within earshot of a La Roche reporter, inadvisably called his "fast draw." The La Roche tabloids had picked it up and gone wild with a "Cowboy General" headline, asking in the lead, "Does He Care About His Men?"—a headline that Norton had taken care the general hadn't seen. Nevertheless, despite himself, Norton remained deeply troubled—not about whether Freeman cared about his troops, which was an insulting charge, but whether he had thought enough about the tactics of the coming battle of massed armor. Or was he simply flushed with the win at Nizhneangarsk? If the Nanking Bridge wasn't blown, everyone on his staff knew the victory at the BAM railhead would be a strategic nonentity, a mere side blow to Yesov's army rather than a knockout.

"You haven't been listening, Dick!"

"General . . . ?"

"Well, damn it, man, weren't you at the briefing last night? All commanders?"

"Un, no, General, I was checking the situation vis-à-vis the, uh, Nanking Bridge."

Freeman scowled. Whenever Norton had screwed up— which thank the Lord was rarely—he started this academic "vis-à-vis" bullshit, a leftover from his postgraduate days after West Point. "Vis-à-vis" really meant, "Give me time to think up a good answer." Probably sitting on the damn can during the briefing, his good eye soaking up the "interviews" in *Playboy* vis-à-vis some tart's tits, 'bout her posing nude just so she could afford the tuition at the Sorbonne.

"Colonel—goddamn it! Don't you slack off on me and go letting the logistical boys run line convoys through this stuff." He meant single file through the permafrost. "Permafrost is hard as concrete, like I said, but you run a line of vehicles over it and the tire friction and exhaust spittle'll melt the top couple of inches, and before you know it you'll be bogged down. Like running warm water over an ice tray. Won't melt the damn ice, but the top layer'll go to mush, slick on you—half black ice, half mush. Armored tracks'll be slewing and sliding like beginners' day at the rink. Sitting ducks for the Siberians.''

"Yes, sir." Maybe Freeman had been thinking permafrost tactics all along. Still, that didn't change the two-to-one advantage of the Siberians.

The general's expression had changed, his tone quiet now. "Ever tell you I met my wife at a skating rink?"

"No, General."

"In California. Can you imagine? Middle of summer, too. High summer. God, it was beautiful, Dick. Cool. She had this kind of green stuff . . ."

"Costume?" said Norton.

"All green," continued Freeman, "like the color of that water in Hawaii. Translucent, and every time she went into a spin it was—well, hell, I knew I'd marry her right there and then." He paused. " 'Course, never had much time to skate. I mean, go around with her, you know."

"Yes, General." In the howling of the approaching storm, Freeman stared up at the snow, then shifted his gaze toward the last of the tank support vehicles moving out. There were too few for the M1A1s, the tanks ideally needing a maintenance check every 120 miles. But "ideally" was always somewhere else. For every fifty of his 270-plus tanks, he knew he could expect twenty to twenty-five breakdowns. Most could be fixed in the field, but all would be time-consuming. The essence of being a good soldier and a good commander, as Freeman had lectured his officers so often, was to make the best of what you had. Seize the moment rather than wait for a logistics wish list. And Norton remembered, "Never let your own fears be known to the men."

"Dick?"

"Sir?"

"Get Harvey Simmet up here, will you?"

"Yes, sir."

Once again Norton, this time apologetically, called Harvey out of his warm cubbyhole of isobar charts, SAT pics, and other meteorological data, the printout piling up in a small hill by his printer. The hourly reports demanded by Freeman had now become half-hourly, and Dick Norton didn't take it as a good sign. In his experience, senior officers, including the best of them, often—albeit unwittingly—gave in to the temptation to switch their attention to factors they couldn't control whenever they had a deep-seated apprehension about their own strategies. It was a form of escape.

But if that's what "George C. Scott," as his troops called him, was hoping for, Norton saw that Simmet couldn't offer the general any encouragement by way of the weather. In fact it was getting worse, a sullen sky overcast enough to sock in any air cover for the outnumbered M1A1s. And Harvey Simmet said there'd be no letup in the Arctic storm for at least thirty-six hours, its epicenter not yet having passed through the Yakutsk region.

And if Freeman thought anything, including his prayers, would change the weather in the *next* half hour, Harvey Simmet knew the general was about to be bitterly disappointed. All the incoming data told the same bleak story, reaffirming his earlier forecasts. Even the Khabarovsk relay printouts showed that temperatures were likely to drop into the minus sixties and below—not unusual for Oymyakon, a town in the Yakutsk Oblast, officially recognized as the coldest town on earth, a town where minus *ninety* had been recorded.

Freeman took the message sanguinely, and as well as Norton knew the general, he didn't know whether this betokened superb acting, resignation, or resolve. The thought of Second Army suffering the same terrible fate that had overtaken III Corps, with over four thousand men slaughtered on the ice, was too much for Norton to contemplate. And what would be the reaction back home? The very thought of what the La Roche tabloids would do to Freeman, to him, to them all, likewise didn't bear thinking about. As Norton and his most senior officers saw it, this northern battle was quickly turning out to be Freeman's greatest risk so far, and except for the Second Army armored column now heading south from Skovorodino to the Siberian-Chinese border, awaiting the outcome of Operation Country Market, it constituted the spearhead of Freeman's entire army. In the end Norton knew it was a question of faith in the man—a calculated risk, based on past performance, that he had not gone definitely and finally bonkers like some evangelical who, though he was of the earth, was not in it, lost in a quiet reverie of past glory. One general, Norton remembered, had smilingly declined all help to cross the Rhine. "No bother, Sar'major," he'd said. "I shall walk across. I have been sent."

The circulation of La Roche's tabloids throughout the world was skyrocketing once again. The predicament of Freeman's Second Army, on a tightrope between defeat and victory, allowed La Roche's chain to make millions by describing the terrible arctic conditions under which Freeman's soldiers were about to fight the Siberian spearhead rumbling south of Yakutsk. If Freeman managed to pull it off—which quite frankly neither La Roche nor any of his tabloid editors believed he would—then the papers could ring their hosannas and they'd make millions on the victory. If he was defeated—the prevailing opinion of the editors— then it wouldn't be the Siberian winter that was so much to blame, but rather what their headlines would declare had been FREEMAN'S FOLLY! the leader paragraphs and descriptions of Second Army's incompetence already in the word processors of every La Roche paper. Either way La Roche couldn't lose.

The only impediment to his high, his only loss, was Lana Brentwood. From his Manhattan penthouse he looked out upon the dazzling city, much of which was owned by his Asian conglomerates, a fact unknown by the millions of

Americans over whose lives the conglomerates nevertheless had financial control.

Buoyed by the prospect of setting yet higher circulation records, La Roche took a snort of angel dust, felt the rush, and right then and there determined it was time he made another takeover bid—but he knew it mustn't look like that. He turned about and spread the two headlines—one for victory, one for defeat—that his New York editors had sent over by courier for his approval. Francine, shuffling over in her mink slippers and carrying two Bloody Marys, had never seen him so self-satisfied. "Whose side are you on?" she asked, glancing at the headline.

"My side," said Jay, picking up the courier envelope and smacking her on the butt. "Number one, baby—me." He took her Bloody Mary from her and put it on the polished burl coffee table.

"Not now," she said, half pleading, but trying not to look too annoyed. That only made him mad.

"Hey!" he said, and a moment later he was looking down at her, kneeling before him, the wispy negligee so transparent he could see it all. "You ever been to Alaska?"

"No," she said. "Why?"

"Because we're going there, that's why. Dutch Harbor."

"Sounds cold."

"It is—it's a berg."

"Then what's the big attraction?" asked Francine, swishing her auburn hair back.

"My wife."

"Oh—I don't wanna go."

"You'll do what you're told." She knew she had no choice. He'd bought her, and if she didn't like it, he told her she could always go back to working bar—for peanuts.

"When are we going?"

"Soon. La Roche Chemicals says thanks to the boys and *gals* at the front—all that shit. How's that grab you?"

She shrugged disinterestedly.

"Come on," he told her, brusquely pulling her face to his unbuttoned fly. "And for Chrissakes watch your teeth."

CHAPTER FORTY

ON A-7 IT was quite obvious to Colonel Soong, despite the American propaganda, what had taken place: the enemy SAS/D teams landing on the mountain were sent in with the Flying Dragon to rescue the American gunners, but instead, when they found they could not stop the Chinese attack, they did the next best thing to hide their aggression from the world by removing all the dog tags from the American dead, as he had found done on the American bodies. Ah, but they had not had time to remove the incriminating evidence of the shoulder patches, which he had sent back to Beijing and which were being exhibited to the world to show that America was guilty of aggression.

Of course, the Americans denied it and said that army patches could be bought by anyone from military surplus stores all over America and that they would be willing to let a neutral country verify this and examine whatever bodies were returned to them. And of course the running dog lackeys of America—such as Canada and England—on the Security Council supported the Americans' attempted cover-up by what Beijing rightly called "the outright American imperialist lie."

CHAPTER FORTY-ONE

WHILE ROBERT BRENTWOOD began his two-mile swim away from Dennison toward the far side of the river, Colonel Soong, more than a thousand miles to the north, was consolidating his capture of A-7 from what he still believed had been an American battery. He was determined that A-7, with its panoramic view of the Siberian-Chinese border, would never again be taken by the enemy. When the Siberians had effected their pincer movement against the Americans with their northern armored columns from Yakutsk, then Beijing would claim this territory around A-7 in the traditional buffer zone between China and Siberia as China's. They had captured it—it should now remain theirs, a price that Novosibirsk would surely cede to Beijing in payment for the assistance that had been rendered them by the peace-loving Chinese people against the American imperialists.

Soong had tank traps dug around the entire ten-mile base of A-7, and radiating out from these there were more traps and antitank ditches for another thousand meters.

The weather was bad generally but good for such work—little trouble from the odd U.S. Air Force fighter patrols that dared to risk empty tanks at the outer perimeter of their defense zone west of Khabarovsk. Besides, the hard manual labor warmed the soldiers, and as they carefully covered the traps with snow-laden vegetation, like soldiers anywhere they began to treat the traps as their own habitat. The snow atop them—even though no fires were permitted, so as to prevent infrared emission to any U.S. satellite overflights—acted much like an igloo. And so the deep tank traps became the best cover they could hope for, along with their Gore-Tex sleeping bags, the best the Chinese army had ever seen, purchased from the American firm of La Roche.

The irony of American sleeping bags making it possible for the PLA to better rest up and so kill Americans, if and when the counterattack came, gave Colonel Soong the first good laugh he'd had after his grueling, twenty-four-hour-a-day exertions—making sure all the antitank fortifications were up to standard.

Two miles south of A-7 Soong could hear a noise like that of insects climbing over a metal dish. It was the sound of the reinforcement Shenyang Brigade, deployed from Harbin and amply supplied with the shoulder-launched HN-5A surface-to-air missiles and Red Arrow tube-launched, optically tracked, wire-command infrared anti-tank missiles, these having a kill probability in excess of eighty-six percent.

Even if the weather broke and the Americans managed to launch refuel-in-air attacks to drop napalm—their most popular aerial weapon against high concentrations of ground troops—they would have to come down five hundred meters or so in order to have the free-tumbling petroleum gel pods hit the general target area. And Soong knew that one of the best-kept secrets of modern warfare—certainly one not known by the general public—was that any plane, no matter how fast, flying under a thousand meters into a phalanx of saturation, small-caliber, high-velocity AA fire, had no better than a fifty-fifty chance of survival. And Soong had such a phalanx of AA weapons, including the nine-and-a-half-ounce thirty-millimeter fired from the PLA's mobile, multiple-barreled, tripod-mounted turrets, one quad of ZSUs capable of throwing up a near impenetrable shield of over 35,000 rounds a minute. The ZSUs, ammunition for them purchased from La Roche, were so deadly that their fire was akin to ancient hunters letting clouds of mosquitoes and black flies swarm onto a galloping caribou until its mouth, ears, and anus were oozing with them and it finally fell from sheer exhaustion. Soong recalled how a U.S. observer who had seen the Chinese thirty-millimeter ZSUs in action earlier in the war in Korea had, in a mixed metaphor, described how the quads had ''nickeled and dimed the fighters to death.'' And only one or two bullets in a jet intake or in one of the black fly-by-wire boxes would be enough.

Soong started to relax. With the arrival of the Shenyang brigade, A-7 would be bristling with gun and SA missile quads for which the tank traps doubled as ideal cover, bamboo ladders at the ready should the PLA need to move out of them quickly in the event of a U.S. armor attack. For Soong, however, it seemed doubtful the Americans could muster the wherewithal to attack, given that their general, Freeman, was in for a surprise during the big tank fight looming in the Yakutsk Oblast, and given that the logistical pipeline pouring weapons and food over the Yangtze at Nanking north to the Shenyang army was still intact.

CHAPTER FORTY-TWO

THE TWENTY MINUTE count over, Dennison surfaced in the dark shadow of one of the trusses, his Remington machine/shotgun in his right hand, his left reaching forward to tear off the plastic protector cap. He found himself exactly where he wanted to be: no more than thirty yards from piers one and two. Flicking down the infrared overlay goggles, he could see Rose and Smythe still strapped to the railing above piers four and five, the white blur of their body heat eerily present as a ghostly outline around their wet suits, the radiant heat telling him they were still alive.

He lifted the Remington, its unfolded butt now pressing firmly but not too tightly in his shoulder. The gun's telescopic sight was filled with the huge white sun of the floodlight high above the concrete base of pier one. Deliberately shutting out the noise of the bridge so he could better concentrate, Dennison took a breath, exhaled slightly, stayed his breath, and squeezed the trigger. Not even he heard the click, but he felt the kick. There was no explosion, only the "whoosh" then tinkling sound of the floodlight's glass disintegrating, the light dying. Dennison gave a push with his right flipper, lifted the gun again, sighted pier two's light and fired, the noiseless Remington expelling nine .33 bullets from a single 00 buckshot casing, taking out the second light, leaving him six shots in the mag and seven lights to go.

Now there was a lot of screaming up on the bridge's top, four-lane motor vehicle deck; the first light's demise, Dennison thought, probably being attributed by the Chinese to a bulb going. But two lights in a row had no doubt spurred the bridge's guards into action. Yet they couldn't have heard any other sound than the splintering of glass. Dennison noted the distance to the next girder shadow cast by the trusses in front of lights three and four, and once there—only a matter of three minutes swimming—he surfaced and took them out within ten seconds.

Now the searchlights from the city side were probing frantically out through the mist, crisscrossing one another. But after a quarter mile the beams were eaten up by the mist, the light too diffused, producing phantom images of light on light, one of which caused the PLA gunners to blast away with RPGs and a barrage of small arms at two of their own trip-wire platforms, obviously mistaking the shapes for enemy boats from which the light-destroying shots must be coming. This allowed Dennison, who was on his fourth "Hail Mary, full of grace . . ." to get off, his next two shots taking out lights five and six, leaving him only two shots, with lights seven, eight, and nine to go. But as he took aim at the seventh, a wash wave, perhaps from a patrol boat mid-river, slopped over him, knocking him off aim at the precise moment he pulled the trigger. His last shot took seven out cleanly. This left him with an empty chamber with lights eight and nine still on, and the other seven out. Most of the southern side of the bridge was in utter darkness anyway, except for the pinpoints of flashlights frantically dashing back and forth like fireflies on the top deck.

By then Robert Brentwood had reached the logjam of black shapes—the riverine craft that had been held up before the bridge and which were now tethered to the right bank. Taking the load of the explosives off him by tethering one end of the explosive line to the keel guard of the propane barge, the other end to his weight belt, it was easy for him to do a chin-up on the stern rub. Water dripped from the 7.62mm minigun slung around his neck as he hauled himself over the stern and crouched on the mist-slippery deck, every muscle taut. He could hear two voices approaching the stern on the narrow walkway that ran alongside the flat-roofed bamboo wheelhouse. Quickly he slithered back over the stern, holding on to the prop guard as he submerged, his head about a foot or so underwater directly below the prop. The voices above him were muffled, but he could still hear them, and then another sound—a sprinkling above his head—then more of it, the two Chinese continuing to talk as they urinated off the stern. In a few moments they were gone and he was back up and over, drawing his K-bar knife from its ankle sheath. Through the slats of bamboo he could dimly see a small coal fire, like a ruby heart, in the darkness, a man squatting beside it, brewing tea. The other man was still walking forward, disappearing on the catwalk a couple of feet above the decking of the barge, between the two huge cigar-shaped tanks which Brentwood guessed were about thirty feet long and ten feet in diameter. He knew earmuff charges alone would have been enough to weaken a pier if he could have climbed up on the bridge to place them. The idea had been that shock waves from either side of the pier meeting then rebounding would have stretched the molecular structure of the concrete to its limit. But there wouldn't have been enough elasticity in the concrete to take the shock, resulting in a fracture. But with Echo Two gone, Rose and Smythe prisoners, surprise had been lost. He and Dennison wouldn't get onto the base of the concrete piers, let alone high enough above them to place the earmuffs. What he needed was to cut the trusses, as with an oxyacetylene torch—use the C-4 plastique as a primary charge to raise the propane to its flashpoint.

Making his way quietly forward by walking around the starboard stern walkway, Brentwood felt for the stern line, his knife cutting its hemp with surprising speed, as if it was string.

The man in the wheelhouse immediately felt the slight shift, the barge yawning slowly out from the bank, the man no doubt alert to every nuance in the barge's movement. As he turned about and stepped outside of the bamboo wheelhouse to investigate, Brentwood's left arm closed quickly, the man's hands instinctively coming up to pull Brentwood's arm from his neck, leaving his chest completely exposed, into which Brentwood drove the K-bar to its hilt and twisted sharply before he lowered the man to the deck. Quickly, almost slipping on the blood, he moved up toward the dark crevice between the propane tanks, and saw the other man coming back toward him. The man called out something.

"Chow mein?" said Brentwood. The man stopped, then turned, but Brentwood was already on him, the man's body hitting the slick decking hard. For a moment Brentwood feared he'd broken the man's neck, but he was only winded, gasping for air and dissuaded from yelling by Brentwood's blood-warmed knife against his throat. The man was rigid with fright. Brentwood lifted him up, turned him about swiftly, slamming him belly first against the side of the port tank, and within four seconds had a slip knot of primacord tying the man's wrists behind his back. Next, taking him by the collar, Brentwood steered him up toward the bow, the bowline—now extremely taut—cracking and creaking as the barge strained to be free. As he cut each strand, it protested with an anguished spitting and splitting. Then, just as quickly, the big barge was floating out into the channel, bow swinging out slowly, caught by the eddies at the periphery of the main channel's current. Someone in front of the barge shouted up from a small sampan, and the shouting became a tirade. Then other sampan skippers joined in, cursing the barge and its turtle owner as the barge's wash, if not its sheer bulk, threatened to swamp them.

Invisible in his black wet suit, Brentwood took the man into the bamboo deckhouse, lashed him to the tiller spar, then just as rapidly hauled up the bag of explosives from beneath the prop guard. He heard a voice yelling aft of the barge, and another. *"Huo!"* yelled Brentwood. Next to *pi-jiu!*—"beer!"—it was the most important phrase for any U.S. serviceman in prewar China. *"Huo!"* Brentwood yelled again. Fire!

There was pandemonium.

Suddenly the long traffic jam of riverine vessels came alive, the shouts of *"Huo!"* galvanizing every Chinese throughout the long string of backed-up craft. Frantically, vessels began casting off, terrified they might get caught in the fire, the sampans nearest the propane barge using their long stern oars, as well as the putt-putting motors that were coughing awake, trying to put as much distance between them and the barge as possible. But it was chaos as sampans collided with other sampans and junks, the air filled with accusation, counteraccusation, and ancestral insults both in Mandarin and Cantonese. The docile water was slapped with jettisoned tether lines under the orders of the PLA guards, themselves running about confused on the riverbank, screaming orders to the boat owners, many of whom instructed the guards to perform acts that were anatomically impossible.

The extent of the confusion was a bonus that Robert Brentwood hadn't counted on, but one he felt the SEALs were due for after the disastrously unlucky beginning of Operation Country Market.

Standing by the man at the wheel, gripping his arm in a half nelson, cutting him loose, Brentwood held him under the threat of the knife and directed him to start the barge's engine. The man nodded furiously with a string of imprecations which Brentwood took to be a plea for his life. Once the huge barge was under way, nosing out under its own power, the cursing from the motley flotilla trying to escape through the darkness rose to a frenzy as the sheer bulk of the barge overruled any questions as to who had right of way. To add a touch of authenticity to his shouts of *"Huo!"* Brentwood tore a rag strip off the hang curtain from the wheelhouse's sleeping compartment, stuffed it into a large Tsingtao beer bottle of cooking oil by the stove, lit it and tossed it astern. There was a small *whoof!* as it exploded, a flash of light, and a sampan afire. It was now definitely *huo*. What had merely been angry profanity rose with hysterical urgency all down the line, and in the added mayhem Brentwood indicated to the bargeman exactly where to steer. The man nodded again, talking quickly, not one word of which Brentwood understood, but the man's terrified tone revealed a universal language. It said, "You're in charge—whatever you say."

As the barge entered the channel proper, Brentwood heard a dull thud, then a slight vibration—a junk rammed amidships, followed by a string of obscenities in the dark night, made blacker by the moon now being totally socked in by cumulonimbus. The PLA on the bank were shooting in the air, not knowing exactly who was responsible for the sudden exodus in direct violation of their orders, but none of the shots was aimed at the sampans, junks, and especially not at the propane barge. One shot into either of the tanks and the ensuing blast, in its heat alone, would be the closest thing to an A-bomb going off that Nanking had seen in its thousands of years on the Yangtze. Brentwood tapped the 7.62mm minigun about his neck and gestured the man to move away from the wheel or he'd get it. After already losing the four men of Echo Two to the Chinese, and seeing Rose and Smythe tied up on the bridge, Brentwood was in no mood for half measures.

On the bridge itself, off to the left a quarter mile downstream, black squares, army trucks, were pulling up, blocking oncoming traffic from either side, searchlights mounted on their flatboards, the beams now beginning to sweep over the water, around the concrete piers and upon the dozens of boats farther aft heading toward the bridge or, more specifically, toward the two deep channels between piers four and six. Collisions continued on the way, but the putt-putting of the two-stroke motors kept up with what would have struck Brentwood as a comic insistence had it not been for the task and dangers that lay ahead of him. There was another bump, then another, more obscenities, but the barge moved inexorably toward the bridge, slowly at first, then like a monster possessed as it caught the full thrust of the current, smacking aside any craft that was so impudent as to get in its way.

Then everything changed.

Dennison, seeing the barge on its way, had dived and was already on his way downstream, jettisoning all equipment, save the Browning nine-millimeter automatic pistol and GPS with which he would rendezvous at the grid reference pickup point two miles downriver on the western bank, as agreed on by him and Brentwood. If Brentwood managed to carry it off, the GPS should bring him within a hundred feet of Dennison.

Dennison had been under way only two minutes, submerged and beneath the bridge, when he heard the muffled drone of a loudspeaker coming from the vehicular deck. Or perhaps it was from the lower railway deck, the noise being too indistinct to betray its exact point of origin.

On the barge, Robert Brentwood had no such difficulty in hearing the loudspeaker, the PLA interpreter shouting that the two prisoners tied to the rail would be beheaded in ten minutes unless all American commandos surrendered.

CHAPTER FORTY-THREE

"WHAT'S THE FORECAST, Harvey?"

Simmet, red-eyed from fatigue, which gave his face a peculiar, rodentlike stare, glared at Norton as if he was to blame. It was misdirected anger at the general, anger for asking what Harvey called "the fucking forecast for the fourth fucking time in the last fucking hour!"

Harvey Simmet snatched the latest computer printout from the isobar printer and took it through to Freeman.

"Storm's still heading south, General. Gusts to sixty kilometers per hour and rising. Visibility near zero."

"The temperature, Harv—the temperature?"

"Minus fifty, General, and falling."

"Thank you."

"Yes, General." As Simmet walked away, Freeman turned to Norton. "Dick, I think Harvey's a bit pissed off."

"Oh?" It was so painfully obvious to Norton that he didn't know whether the general was kidding him or not. Norton had no time to decide, for the next order Freeman gave him was a shock.

"Radio our tank commanders—burst code—to fire, then to fall back ten miles and go into defilade positions. When I go up there, I don't want to be able to see one turret. Tell them to camouflage the guns with snow netting if the snow lets up—which it doesn't look like it will."

"*Fall back*, General?"

"Something the matter with your hearing, Dick?"

"No, General, but you've never—"

"*Now*, Dick! Tell 'em to fall back!"

What in hell did Freeman think he was doing? Norton wondered as he took down the pad and pencil for the number-for-letter burst code. He knew it would be nearly impossible to hide every one of the 227 M-1s. If the Siberians' forward patrols were to spot even one or two hidden behind the snowbanks, experienced Siberian scouts would be sure to guess that there were many more around, and before the M-1s could move, hundreds of T-72s would be all over them.

For these troops, who had been brought up on the legend of Freeman as the swift attacker of Pyongyang and the unstoppable general who'd kept pressing home the offensive against Ratamanov Island—despite appalling losses—and won, the fallback order smacked of impending defeat. And wasn't it Freeman who had preached that "withdrawal is the first step to disaster"? The enemy, he had said, can smell it, and it "spreads like a great fart across the battlefield—gets 'em riled, eager for the kill."

Ten minutes later Freeman got the report from *his* forward patrols that the Siberian tanks had split up into echelons of five, eighty feet between them in line abreast, the classic attack formations that the Siberians had used earlier in the war, swarming through Fulda Gap. Freeman sent Dick Norton back to what he called Harvey Simmet's "cubbyhole" for the latest outside temperature as reported by the men who were now hurriedly retreating to defilade positions, behind either already existing snowdrifts or any fallen timber they might find close to hand. Some of the M-1 tank crews, with the rapid sarcasm troops the world over can call up for even the most popular leaders, were already calling Freeman "Dig-in Doug."

No one liked to be a sitting target.

Norton returned from the met room. "Sir, Major Simmet's indisposed."

"What?"

"He's on the can. Taken the met printout with him apparently."

"Well get him off the can, Dick. He's the best goddamned met officer we've got, and I want him to tell me the forecast.''

''Yes, sir.''

When Norton entered the ''latrine module,'' a series of prefabricated stalls, he could hear the wind and snow beating wildly against the aluminum exterior. When he saw Simmet's feet and told him the general wanted another forecast, Harvey jerked the chain so hard it came right off the S arm. ''Jesus, tell him it's fucking cold and going to get colder!'' bellowed Simmet.

''C'mon, Harv!'' It was the general. ''How cold's that?'' When Norton turned to face the general, Freeman winked at him, gesturing toward the cubicle wherein there was a furious unraveling of paper. ''You say something, Harv?''

Norton was starting to get worried. It wasn't uncommon for commanders to come a bit unglued, albeit temporarily, under extreme stress. Schwarzkopf could lose his temper— blow a gasket. At times Freeman dealt with the pressure by trying to be the Far East Jay Leno. But any hope of a joke with Simmet died as the outside door slammed. It was a messenger coming in from Signals. A forward American observation post was reporting that the spearhead echelons of the Siberian tank army were less than seven miles away from the dug-in M-1s.

Harvey Simmet, pulling his trousers up, was reading off the printout, ''Snow gusts increasing to one hundred kilometers—sixty miles per hour, General. Visibility zero.''

''Not zero visibility for infrared and laser sights, Harvey!'' Freeman commented.

''They've got infrared sights and laser, too, General.''

Freeman said nothing, but his frown told Harvey that Jay Leno was gone for the night. Coming out of the cubicle, Harvey looked apprehensively at Norton for reassurance that Freeman hadn't miscalculated. Norton couldn't give him any.

''Temperature?'' Freeman asked Simmet.

Simmet dropped the printout in a puddle of melted snow by the urinal as he was lifting his suspenders. He cussed.

"Minus fifty-five. Going to get worse," he warned, looking up at Norton.

"Norton," ordered Freeman, "signal all commanders to fall back another ten miles."

Norton didn't argue. He didn't know what to think. It made sense to withdraw, given the odds, but that wasn't the general's style. Was Freeman finally seeing the light, or had Jay Leno metamorphosized into "Duck-Away Doug"?

Watching the vertical and crisscross-trussed girders of the lower railway deck coming at him like huge X's in the darkness, truck-back floodlights above them on the vehicular deck, Robert Brentwood took off his Mae West vest, cut the Chinese bargeman free, pulled the cartridge on the Mae West, handed the inflated vest to the man, and gestured back over his shoulder to the river. The man was off the stern in three seconds. Brentwood heard the faint splash even amid the babble and excited yells on the Nanking Bridge and all around him in the jumbled bumping of sampans and junks, caught in the wash of the searchlights, scattered every which way, putting as much distance between them and the oncoming barge as possible.

Fifty yards from the channel, between piers four and five, he reached over to the rope trailing from the barge's capstan and jerked out the holding bolt, the resulting run of the anchor chain sounding like a dump truck upending a load of marbles. Now there was a splitting sound that grew rapidly: a volley of gunfire aimed at the bamboo housing but well aft of the propane tanks, in the PLA's desperate attempt to stop what they now realized was a boat with American commandos aboard.

The barge's bow struck the pier and shuddered, its stern swinging about, pivoting on the anchor chain, the stern bashing into the concrete midway under the bridge along the base of pier four. The barge was now completely covered by the rail decking above it, the small arms fire ceasing because of the danger of ricocheting off the crisscross trusses into the propane tanks. Brentwood had determined that to spend time trying to rescue either Rose or Smythe would be to jeopardize the whole mission, and against impulse had to weigh the lives of thousands of Americans that lay in the balance to the north should the Nanking Bridge not be blown. He pulled the ten-minute acid-ampule timer. But then, with heart-stopping suddenness, he realized that with the PLA's fear of firing down at him for fear of hitting the tanks, he had a sudden chance, albeit a short one, as he climbed off the barge onto the narrow maintenance ladder running from pier five's base to the rail decking and the vehicular deck above it. A roaring like another great river entering the Yangtze could be heard off to his right, the glaring headlight of a northbound goods train starting across the bridge. Halfway up the ladder, his left hand on a rung, he swung the mini machine hard right, firing from the hip, several of the long bursts crashing into the train's headlamp, denying the PLA any clear sight of him. Immediately above Rose he saw several PLA figures silhouetted against the rail. He fired another burst, and cut Rose loose as the PLA clambered over the rail, still too frightened to shoot but determined to exact a price.

"Go! Go!" It was Smythe yelling, tied high above pier four off to the left, cheering them on.

"C'mon!" hissed Brentwood, Rose following him down the ladder above the propane tank so quickly that, his muscles stiff from having been tied up, Rose almost fell, his left heel smashing into Brentwood's nose.

With only three minutes to go before the acid ampule would eat through the primacord, igniting the charges, Brentwood went back up the ladder another two rungs, putting himself above the level of the passing train, its hot slipstream buffeting him. He saw three black figures on the northern side ladder under the bridge and fired a long burst. Two men fell, their screams barely audible above the rush of the goods train, one body bouncing off a boxcar into the girders, the other falling into the river over a hundred feet below.

The moment they hit the barge deck, Brentwood handed

Rose his penlight. "Rendezvous point with Dennison—two miles down the river. If we get separated, head for the west shore. One flash—I'll respond with two, ten seconds apart. Got it?"

"Got it." Suddenly the train was gone, and in the half slice of a flashlight's beam on a girder Brentwood saw two more PLA figures fifty feet above him. He fired a burst, saw one slump, and holding the gun tightly to his chest, dove off, feeling the cold current moving him swiftly downriver, feet kicking as he submerged more powerfully than in the most rigorous training session. Immediately in the underwater blackness he made for his left, where the current would carry him to the west bank. For several seconds time raced as he tried to make as much distance between him and the barge as possible, waiting for the sound of the detonation. Then it seemed as if minutes had passed, that something had gone wrong, that the primacord had—

There was a tremendous flash of orange light, turning night into day, the barge going up in a feral roar, lifted ten feet out of the water, flames from it shooting hundreds of feet high, engulfing the two spans between piers four and six, the ball of fire a quarter mile across quickly narrowing about its central concentrated core beneath what seconds before had been cold steel but which was now plasticized. Brentwood could hear the steel groaning, starting to cave in, dropping then toppling like some enormous Play-Doh Lego set just behind him. In fact, swept down by the swiftly moving current, he was already a quarter mile from it. Still, the shock wave of the explosion hit him like a baseball bat in the small of the back, and a moment later his body was literally surfed toward the downstream shore by a series of five-to-eight-foot waves radiating from the explosion. He could see the river crimson behind him, its turbulent surface reflecting variegated colors, the blues and orange of the burning propane eating into the curling, thick black smoke that was tumbling over the water. Through it here and there he saw that not only the space between piers four and five, but that between five and six, had sagged, buckled, and come apart, pieces of them still falling into the river in a hissing stream; and he knew that Smythe was dead, vaporized in the fiercest fire he'd ever seen.

"Mars! Mars! Mars!" radioed Dennison, his message immediately picked up by the Pave Low as it banked hard south toward the GPS coordinates. The moment he finished the message and heard, "Fire delay flare," he pulled the flare from his pack, stuck it into the mud at a thirty-degree angle and pulled the cord. It hissed off, the delay seven seconds, its chute opening two hundred yards farther downriver, the flare beginning its flickering mauve burnoff, the delay a safety precaution to divert the PLA away from the actual rendezvous point, which, it was hoped, would give Brentwood time to rendezvous. In fact it was Rose he saw, Brentwood nowhere in sight.

"Set, Aussie?" David Brentwood yelled over the thunder of the rotors.
"Set!"
"Right. Sal, you and Choir—cover fire from the chopper."
"Right!"
The Pave Low's electronic wizardry didn't fail as its automatic fix took it down to a hundred, then a bare fifty feet above a marshy levee; for it to go lower and risk a wind shear in the unstable air currents from the fire would be to risk slamming down or getting bogged.
Within two seconds Aussie and David Brentwood were rappeling down two of the five dangerously swinging STABO lines. Dennison put himself in the spring harness at the end of one of the STABO lines and Rose did the same.
"That's it?" yelled Aussie. "Anybody else?"
"Yeah," called out Dennison, having no way of knowing he was talking to the brother of Robert Brentwood and making no effort to lower his voice under the roar of the Pave's blades. "The boss."
David Brentwood knew it was up to him. Now they saw

more searchlights frantically sweeping through the smoke
south of the burning midsection of the bridge. At least two
patrol boats could be heard. David couldn't risk it. This was
where the speed of a STABO extraction was worth every
penny of the taxpayer's money. "In harness, Aussie!" he
ordered.

"But—"

"In harness!" David shouted.

Aussie took a firm stand to snap on his harness and fell
down, his injured foot having given way.

"We can wait a—" began Dennison.

David shouted into his throat mike. "Let's go! C'mon,
Aussie!"

There was a delay of another ten seconds before Aussie
was in harness, but with that done the Pave climbed—as
slowly as possible, but in a steep, almost hovering angle.
The jerk would be abrupt when it came, and even as the
men braced for it, they knew the spring STABO links
wouldn't cushion them from possible injury if they didn't
do it right. Without an order, they stood close to one
another, linked arms, each man's fingers interlocked in
front of him as if in solemn prayer, and bowed their
heads—pulling firmly on one another's elbows, waiting to
be literally lifted off their feet once the slack on the STABO
lines had been taken up.

There was a grunting, slopping noise behind them.
Dennison felt something gripping his ankle, trying to pull
him back, and he kicked hard with the other foot and heard
a crunch of bone. Suddenly the STABO lines lurched
forward with a gut-wrenching sensation. The cold wind hit
them, and then they collectively felt the steady tug of the
five wires that, attached to the brace of harnesses being
hauled up, were making a singing noise in the wind as their
linked bodies swept forward into the void. There wasn't a
shot fired in their direction, or if so, they couldn't hear it,
the chaos on and about the bridge so panic-ridden and
smoke-filled that they were away and being pulled one by

one inside the Pave by Choir Williams and Salvini, most of whose effort was taken up hauling the last man in—who was not in harness, but hanging on to Dennison's legs like a very heavy rag doll.

Within five minutes, well below the radar screen, they were on their way back to *Salt Lake City*. No one spoke, everyone utterly exhausted save for the crew of the Pave, who now gave the craft full throttle, their side gunners still alert should they be unlucky enough to give off a radar echo or two. And it wasn't until they were low, north of the Yangtze's wide estuary, that anyone, least of all Dennison, realized Robert Brentwood was aboard but unable to declare himself, his jaw and nose broken by Dennison's vicious back kick. Thereafter, Dennison would be forever known as "Stomper Dennison."

"Temperature's minus sixty, General," reported a weary Harvey Simmet.

The change in Freeman was to be remembered by Norton and Simmet and indeed everyone in their HQ for a long time, and was to become part of the Freeman legend. "We've got the sons of bitches!" declared Freeman. "By God, Norton, full attack! Hit 'em!"

No one understood it for a minute or two, several of the officers in the buzzing HQ signals hut quite frankly thinking Freeman had flipped his lid. But later even Norton conceded that he should have known that Freeman's attention to detail, which bordered on the compulsive-obsessive, was about to deal a crushing defeat against the Siberian tanks.

"Well," pressed one bemused captain, "what's it all about?"

"The temperature, I guess," said Harvey Simmet.

"So what the hell is it?" asked the captain.

"Minus sixty," answered Simmet.

"No—Christ, I mean what's—what happens at minus sixty? The old man grows horns? Becomes invincible or what? What the shit's going on?"

"Captain!" In the babble of the communications hut the captain hadn't been aware that Freeman had overheard him. "Yes, sir. Sorry, General, I—"

"You get my goddamn Humvee around here. And fast. You're about to get an education, son!"

"Yes, General."

"You coming, Dick?" asked Freeman, looking remarkably reassured, confident now that his tank commanders would do the rest.

"Do I have any choice, General?"

"No. You coming along, Harvey?"

"I think I'll sit it out back here, General. It's gonna get a lot colder."

"Hotter, Harv. Hotter!"

As they took off in the Humvee, armored cars fore and aft, a TOW missile launcher atop the Humvee's cabin, Norton couldn't believe the intensity of the cold. With the heater's full blast there was only a four-inch-diameter half-moon clearing in the windscreen through which they could see—the rest a sheet of ice. Already he felt his toes were going into frostbite, though he knew as long as he could at least feel them there was no immediate danger of that.

"By God, Norton," said Freeman, "Harvey looks like hell. You watch him when we get back. Make sure he gets more sleep—valuable man, Harvey."

As Norton spoke beneath his balaclava, he swore his breath was turning to ice particles before his words were out.

It wasn't simply a victory for Freeman—it was the slaughter of the entire Siberian armored division, and within forty minutes Norton had seen why. The T-72s and the "little surprise" Colonel Soong had known about—over seventy T-80s with up-gunned 130mm cannon, also with laser sighting—were stilled, sitting ducks while the M1A1s broke cover, bursting forth like wild animals from snow-laden lairs, careening and wheeling and wheeling back again at over fifty miles an hour, and with unerring precision belched flame and shot, most of it APDS—armor-piercing discarding sabot—the projectiles hitting the Siberian tanks at over six thousand feet per second, often puncturing a hole only a few centimeters across. But through that hole came a molten jet of white-hot metal that, spraying inside the tank, created injuries and explosions unimaginable to any but the American gunners and tank crews who saw the T-80s and T-72s buck, snow flying off them like white flour, then engulfed in red, black-streaked flames. Many of the tanks, still a moment before, were suddenly jolted by the heat, moving—some forward, some backward—spewing sparks and lavalike flows as their ammunition stores exploded, the human and matériel detritus bubbling forth from the moving carcasses of what were once five hundred of the Siberians' crack main battle tanks. The reason: long ago, Americans whose names were not known, who had attended to the dull, analytical side of war and who were driven by the demons of perfection and Department of Defense specifications—specifications in this case insisted upon by none other than Freeman himself—had produced lubricants for the M1A1 that would not freeze. Or, more accurately, lubricants in which the waxes would not separate out and, like cholesterol in the blood, clog the vital hydraulic arteries of the world's best main battle tank. It was a tank that, thanks to American know-how, would keep running to temperatures below minus sixty degrees, at which point the Siberian tanks, good enough in themselves, simply shuddered and stopped, the petroleum waxes, because of more crudely refined oil, thick in their blood, with only the implosions of the American 120mm shells which killed them capable of heating them up enough to move.

Harvey Simmet forgave Freeman for disturbing his peace on the can, for when the temperature had fallen below fifty and showed no sign of easing up, Freeman knew all he'd had to do was wait. It was the kind of American can-do know-how that allowed Johnny Ferrago and the other "sandhogs" to dig the third tunnel under Manhattan.

CHAPTER FORTY-FOUR

WITH THE NANKING Bridge knocked out, the effect was not felt in the north for another three days, during which the southern arm of Freeman's Second Army readied themselves for counterattack in the vicinity of A-7. But if it took three days for Colonel Soong to see the stream of ammunition and food slow to a trickle, the effect of the Americans having taken out the vital crossing across the Yangtze was felt within hours in Harbin.

If the American commandos could strike that deep in China from their carriers in the East China Sea, then, Chen argued to his Harbin cell of the June Fourth Democracy Movement, it should not be too long before the Americans would drive south from the Siberian-Chinese border—so that now would be the opportune moment for the Harbin underground to strike. It would be a signal and example to all the underground movements in China to rise, for, as he pointed out, something the American commandos could not have known was the enormous symbolic power of the Nanking Bridge.

Quite apart from the vital strategic importance that the bridge had held for the Chinese Communists, its spans across the mighty Yangtze, joining north and south after the revolution, had been touted by the Communists as the joining of old enemies, of two Chinas, into one—a Communist China ever after. Now the link between the two Chinas, the northerners and the southerners, had been broken.

"What do you propose?" Chen's comrades asked him.

"The jail!" he said.

"To get the Siberian out?" asked another, not particularly enthusiastic about risking his neck for any long nose.

"To get our *friend* out," responded Chen.

"It will be dangerous."

"Living is dangerous, comrades. She is our friend." Chen said it to save face. Even so, he was lying. They were all lying. A long nose was a long nose, and in their view would not stand up to torture as well as Chinese. Friendship was not enough to move them. The truth, he knew, was that if the Public Security Bureau broke her—if she talked—the Harbin chapter of the Democratic Movement, and their own escape line through Manchuria should they need it, would be finished.

Chen gave them another reason that they should act. "We should begin to sabotage. Start the fire here, comrades—in *Harbin*! The Americans will now push south. Harbin is the first major city in their path of liberation."

"And what if the Americans don't attack?" asked a comrade. "If this Freeman doesn't come through?"

"He will," answered Chen. "The bridge is gone, and now we hear the Siberians have suffered a major defeat in the north around Baikal, which will leave the Americans free to turn all their forces south against our border and push the PLA back."

There was a show of hands. Chen won the vote.

His plan was simple. They would pretend drunkenness and call on Chen's brother-in-law Wong.

"Wong's a turtle!" said someone. Against this grievous insult, there was no defense from Chen. Wong was, indisputably a turtle. But he could help, Chen told them.

"How?"

"We will ask him to show us this crazy foreigner who eats her own shit."

CHAPTER FORTY-FIVE

IN HARBIN THEY would call it the night of the west wind. For the PLA guards on duty at Harbin Number One Jail, however, it would be the night of the hornets, for the Democracy Movement guerrillas swarmed all about them like a wild sea and seemed to be everywhere at once.

Within minutes of Wong having self-importantly opened the door to show off his power and to show his brother-in-law the foreign devil who ate her own excrement, the guerrillas were upon them in a kind of fearful ferocity, and the already grimy, yellow-bricked walls of the police station were streaked in blood.

Harbin was shaken to its core, and within an hour of the attack the PLA had rallied sufficiently to be scouring the streets in an outburst of officially sanctioned panic and revenge, the death knell of several guerrillas being the fact that to distinguish one another in the melee they had used cheaply dyed neck kerchiefs whose blue dye ran easily under the heat of their perspiration, so that even though they had taken the kerchiefs off, a stain mark was left on their necks. Less than half of the 150 arrested as Democracy Movement terrorists and "enemies of the people" actually belonged to the Democracy Movement, the others having been people, both men and women, unable or unwilling to account for their whereabouts to local granny committees or to the investigating police. Several were beheaded in public executions for no other reason than a cheaply dyed shirt left a blue stain on their skin.

Ling and his wife were immediately taken out and shot in

the tiny exercise yard, the bullets deliberately not aimed at their spinal cords, so as to have them bleed to death over a number of hours. Their small boy was sent the next day for adoption to Shanghai, but with it being known that he was the offspring of enemies of the state, no one would have him. He was then sent to the Fourteenth Reform School for thought correction.

But if Chen had predicted success in the raid on the jail, then his prediction that Freeman would immediately drive south couldn't have been more wrong. Freeman, his Second Army now casting all its attention southward, was on the verge of just such a massive counterattack on A-7 and beyond when Beijing, seeing the writing on the wall, sued for a cease-fire in the U.N. on the grounds that, as they told the people, "the enemy imperialist aggressors on A-7 have been repelled at the border and we are satisfied. The freedom-loving peoples of China are not warmongers, and now that a lesson has been taught to the aggressors, the Chinese people wish to normalize relations."

Without Chinese support on their eastern flank, and with the massive defeat of their armor out of Yakutsk, Novosibirsk quickly joined Communist China in asking for "peace talks." Washington readily agreed to a cease-fire at midnight.

In the southernmost part of the lake around Kultuk, General Minsky's troops, only hours before exultant over having helped rout the American III Corps, were defiant to the end. Their feeling of having been denied a victory because of Yesov's failure to hold in the north was further inflamed by the news of the severing of the Nanking Bridge. Minsky was hard put, and indeed did little, to discipline his troops.

After having looted the American dead, they were now withdrawing back through the taiga like a plague. A company of them occupying their southernmost flank position sought to vent their anger and frustrations on anything

and everything in their path. One such target was the small
house in the woods near Kultuk that Minsky had used as a
fire-control point. They burned it to the ground and then
moved to the next target, Major Truet's Charlie Company,
where Private Thomis was dug in with the others, waiting
for a helo evac that had been hampered by the midair
collision of two Black Hawk choppers, one of which would
have taken out Thomis, who now stood in the blood-soaked
ice of his foxhole.

Though injected with morphine for the pain, and fully
conscious, Thomis was unable to move his right leg because
of his self-inflicted wound, which the medic and Truet and
the others around him had quite reasonably believed had
come from an enemy bullet during the earlier Siberian helo
attack.

After the first attack wave of Minsky's company against
Charlie Company's foxholes and trenches near the tunnels,
the Siberians were beaten back. But Charlie Company was
left with no more than fifty-two men out of what had
originally been a hundred—several abdominal cases having
priority over Thomis and others in the pre-cease-fire evacuation now under way. Now it was Thomis's turn, but the
taiga a hundred yards in front began trembling, snow sliding
down the thickly laden branches from the reverberations of
the Siberians' machine guns. Amid all this, smoke flares
were being fired for cover by the Siberians even as evac
helos arrived in an effort to take out the last of Charlie
Company. Thomis had to help himself out of the foxhole,
Brooklyn and the man from Georgia both dead in foxholes
nearby, Thomis using his M-16 as a staff to haul himself out
with his left foot, but exhausted at the top, lying panting
like a whipped dog in the snow, trying to catch his breath
long enough to hobble his way to the nearest helo.

As the Siberian company broke cover under flare light
and closed for the kill, a section of eight or nine of them,
though white figures in the white smoke, nevertheless cast
long, dark shadows spearing toward the nearest loading
helo. Thomis knew that one good bullet in the right place

and the helo would be out of operation, and from the darkness beyond the flare light he opened up at twenty yards, downing two of the Siberians, the others diving for cover behind the wreckage of one of the earlier disabled choppers. There was a sharp crack by his ear, but Thomis had already tossed two grenades at the downed helo's carcass, the first going wide, blowing up snow and dirt, the second exploding in a purple crash by the helo whose wreckage suddenly spewed rivers of flame, two of the Siberians rising, afire. At fifteen yards Thomis couldn't have missed them if he'd tried, the other four or five Siberians heading back to the taiga.

"Jesus!" someone yelled at the helo now loading its litters with the last of the wounded. "Look at Thom!"

Thomis was glimpsed in the smoke for a second changing magazines. Having tried to hobble toward the chopper, he'd found he couldn't do it. The next moment he saw Emory, the black man moaning, his dark face shiny with blood draining down his left side. "Can you walk?" yelled Thomis, firing from the hip into a new rush of Siberians from the taiga trying to get close with their wildly spraying automatic Kalashnikovs. He heard the whack of several bullets hitting the chopper and was filled with panic that if the chopper bought it, he'd be left behind. "Get up, goddamn you!" he yelled at Emory. Emory was on his knees, blood still dripping from him, dazed, unsure of what was going on. "Go on, get up, goddamn it! Move your ass!" commanded Thomis.

The black man rose, and Thomis's right arm wrapped itself about his shoulder. Emory would be his transport. Using the butt of the M-16 as a walking stick, they limped toward the chopper, fell, got up again, and now the chopper was rising into swirling smoke, its litters full, arms and legs sticking out of it from every angle, it was so crammed with bodies. Several Siberians were charging through the smoke. Thomis fired again from the hip, saw one man literally thrown back, another go down face forward into the snow, the third literally shot to pieces by Thomis's last clip.

Suddenly another man appeared on Thomis's left, the smoke clearing because of the downdraft of the slowly rising chopper, the Siberian's Kalashnikov aiming up at the chopper when Thomis, with one hop, brought his M-16 around like a baseball bat, knocking the man off his feet and falling on his face, butt first. At this point the helo, dangerously overloaded, barely managed to make its turn away toward the lake, and the last thing Truet and the other evacuees on the chopper saw was Thomis yelling something up at them, fist raised defiantly.

The Siberians had had enough, and moved on to Irkutsk. All that later historians would note about the "small action" at a place called the Kultuk Tunnels was that Americans had come under "repeated Siberian attacks during a last-minute evacuation." Nothing was mentioned in the historical account—because no one knew—that Thomis had shot himself in the foot in the hopes of being one of the first "wounded" taken out, but had in fact been one of the last, along with Emory.

Major Truet had been told at West Point never to exaggerate a man's exploits when writing him up for a commendation, that battle-experienced officers could smell a "puff" job a mile away. And so he simply wrote what he saw as the truth: namely that Private First Class John D. Thomis of Charlie Company Second Battalion U.S. III Corps had, despite sustaining a leg wound from the enemy and being under repeated attacks by the enemy on C Company positions, not only held his ground, but in the best traditions of the service, had thrown himself into the breach, fighting off repeated attempts of the Siberians who were trying to destroy the helicopter evacuating his comrades. Private Thomis had kept firing until he ran out of ammunition, at which point he used his rifle itself as a weapon in close-quarter combat, securing precious seconds during which the helo, with his comrades aboard, could take off.

For his "valor at the Kultuk Tunnels," Private First

Class Thomis was awarded the Silver Star. Only Emory, his head swathed in bandages now, and some said still suffering from concussion, opined, "Shit—that son of a bitch couldn't walk to the chopper. That's why he was shootin' where he was, man. Otherwise he'd have been the first son of a bitch on the Huey."

"Bullshit!" they told Emory. Thomis had the 7.62mm slug that had penetrated his foot. It was Siberian, all right.

"Shit!" countered Emory. "There was enough bullets on the ground for you to start a collection. Son of a bitch couldn't walk, so he tried usin' me as his goddamned crutch. I got to be the nigger again, man!"

It made no difference—the La Roche tabloids were making Thomis a hero. The photograph on page one showed him in Alaska, Dutch Harbor—the first stop on his repatriation home—smiling broadly, his leg in an impressive cast, which seemed to reach out to you from the picture, and with an enormous cigar given him by a smiling Douglas Freeman, before Thomis had left Siberia. It was the only smile the general had given anyone that day.

Freeman was so angry, Norton thought he would self-destruct. There were only ten hours till the official cease-fire went into effect.

"By God, those bastards in Washington are doing it to me again! I swear to God, Norton, if you were getting laid and near climax, those sons of bitches would tell you to stop. My God, don't they understand?" His right fist slammed into the map of Manchuria, badly denting the area around Manzhouli and causing a red rain of ChiCom unit position pins to fall to the floor. "Those rice-sucking jokers in Beijing have no intention of withdrawing." Not caring that a group of reporters who had suddenly materialized like rabbits from the warren upon word of the cease-fire were entering the HQ hut, Freeman whipped off his reading glasses, jabbing them at the line that marked the Siberian-Chinese border. "Can't they read a goddamn map in Washington? These Chinks have no intention of relinquishing the territory they've taken from Second Army."

"Isn't it, uh, Siberian soil, General?" asked a correspondent from *The London Times*.

"No, by God. It's ours! We paid for it—at Skovorodino and Baikal. Or have you forgotten? *We*, the Americans, kept the Siberian-Chinese border intact. Why, hadn't been for us, there'd be no border. Chinese'd have moved in ages ago."

"But General," interrupted the *Paris Match* correspondent, "wasn't the A-7 incident started by the Siberians who were there? How do you make it out to be American?"

It was a trap, but Freeman saw it immediately, the reporter trying to get him to say it was Americans who had started the fighting, given that he said the area had been won and paid for by Americans.

"It's American because we lost good men on that damn mountain. Special Forces. That's why. Good men."

"Sir?" It was the stunning redhead from CBS. "General, does this mean you have no intention of ceding A-7 and the surrounding areas to the Chinese?"

"One more question," interjected Norton, quickly giving his warning glance to the general, giving Freeman a second or two to think about his career as well as the political implications of a no answer—which would in effect be going directly against the president.

"I," began Freeman, "am going to obey my orders, as General Schwarzkopf did."

Norton felt the tension draining out of him. It was a brilliant answer under pressure, at once making it clear that he would obey the president, yet it was politically obscure enough, Schwarzkopf having had to withhold his impulse to pursue the withdrawing Iraqi army because of the presidential order, and in so doing, allowing Saddam Insane to begin rebuilding his entire army both during and after the ceasefire. Which was precisely what Freeman was afraid the Chinese would do—rebuild the bridge and start shunting divisions, massing them all along the Manchurian-Siberian border from A-7 eastward.

What wasn't so brilliant of Freeman, what Norton hadn't

been able to run interference for, was when Freeman, going full bore, had used the word "Chinks" instead of "Chinese."

Jay La Roche loved it. On his private jet en route to Dutch Harbor to see Lana—who was "playing at nurse," as he derisively put it to Francine—he shook his head with undisguised glee at the headline his tabloids had seized:

CHINKS LIARS! CHARGES FREEMAN
CEASE-FIRE OFF TO ROCKY START

The fact that when the tabloids hit the streets in the U.S. there were still eight hours, till midnight precisely, until the cease-fire would actually begin and the special mandate of the Emergency Powers Act would be rescinded, was lost amid the outcry of every minority group in America. They charged that Freeman, protected by the Emergency Powers Act, had shown his true colors, indulging in racism and bigotry.

With the naiveté that often coinhabits genius, Freeman frequently underrated the wiliness of the press. He had no such prejudice against the Chinese and had meant no harm—said he meant no harm. He recanted, indeed he told the press how highly he respected the Chinese as a civilization. "A great people. By God, first ones to invent gunpowder!" Norton nearly had a stroke the moment Freeman said it, and had to corral the female correspondent from the *L.A. Times* who had heard the remark to tell her that if she used the "gunpowder" quote, she'd never again receive press accreditation anywhere in the Far East theater. "Will I need it again?" she challenged shrewdly.

"Well, miss," Norton had replied, completely unashamed of his outright act of censorship, "what do *you* think the Chinese will do during the cease-fire? Go home to Beijing?"

"Are you saying this is a Yugoslavian cease-fire?" she asked, smiling.

Norton gave a noncommital shrug. "Your phrase—not mine. Look at the map," he said casually. "What would you do if you were the Chi—"

"Norton!"

"General?"

"Pardon me for interrupting, miss, but you can hear this, too. We've reports coming in from Baikal that some Siberian fighter aircraft haven't got the message. About the cease-fire. There's been reports of strafing. I have to go and talk with this—this Chinese joker at A-7. Goddamn colonel. I won't go till they have a three-star commander there. The bastards!" He looked at the reporter. "And that's off-the-record."

"Which part, General? The strafing or the three-star bit?"

He forced a grin. "The three-star bit. Don't want people back home to think I'm . . . proud. What I *am* proud of is my boys."

A lie and a truth in one sentence, thought the correspondent. He *was* proud of his boys, but as vain as any Manchu that had sat on the Peacock Throne. "I'll just report that enemy elements are still—"

"*Elements*—hell! They're MiG-29s and they're shooting at my boys."

"Are the reports reliable, General?"

"Hell, yes. We've got SAT pics of them rising from forward fields around Irkutsk."

It was another half-truth, though the general didn't realize it. The Siberians *were* still fighting, but they weren't strafing. What they were doing was trying to shoot all the Marsden-matting forward air strips being laid down at a frantic rate by Seabees flown in, under Freeman's orders, from Khabarovsk. The general was doing a little last-minute reinforcing himself.

Indeed, while he was talking to the correspondent, in response to an AWAC report that four of Yesov's MiG-29 Fulcrums were flying in diamond formation over Baikal, a nine-plane mission of B-52s from Nayoro under his orders with midair-refueled F-16 Strikers were flying high, 35,000 feet above the AA missile envelope, toward Lake Baikal.

"Sleduyte menya." Follow me, intoned Sergei Marchenko in the usual calm, devil-may-care voice that had become as legendary as his Fulcrum's "Yankee Killer" motif. Suddenly caught in a series of buffeting air pockets, his left wing dipped, and just as quickly his *tetka*— "auntie," as he called his *rechevaya instruktsiya*, or voice guidance system—came on, telling him to correct the yaw.

"Yes, sweetheart," he responded, heard a bang, and felt his right wing going. He was in a spin. The sound and sight of black smudges against the blue told him that he'd been hit—orange speckles of American AA could be seen erupting from the blackish-green taiga that was spinning up at him at a frightening rate. In eight g's, the crushing pressure on his chest feeling like a locomotive rolling over on him, Marchenko involuntarily gasped for air, his wing man hearing him on the intercom. Disorientated in the spin, Marchenko punched the *krasnuyu knopku ChP*—red panic button—on his control column, but it couldn't stop the spin. He hit another series of air pockets, the spin momentarily decreasing.

Finally managing to reach down between his legs, he felt the rubber loop and pulled. He heard the bang of the eject rocket, felt the jerk, was thrown two hundred feet into the air, heard another bang—the small drogue chute out, slowing him. Then the main chute opened, the ejection seat dropping away from him, his chute a black mushroom in the late evening's cerulean-blue, the Americans not shooting at him as he floated down, swept westward in a fast airstream across Kultuk into the Siberian taiga.

In all, Marchenko had bailed out only three times, but his reputation for survival fed more stories, eagerly pumped up by the sleazier western tabloids, that it was six times. Novosibirsk encouraged the lie, for the defeated Siberians were badly in need of heroes. The fact that he had been

downed by AA gunfire became quickly changed to him
having been hit by some new kind of Stealth missile the
Americans were developing, or possibly by one of the new
Mach-3 needlepointed AA Starstreak missiles. Marchen-
ko's photo, the bruises to his face caused by the ejection
carefully masked by makeup, appeared on page one of
Novosibirsk's official *United Siberian* next to his old
MiG-29.

"What will you do now?" asked a reporter.

"Get another plane. Fight again!" Marchenko had answered. It was understood by the Novosibirsk reporters to
be a joking, quick-witted response. Quick-witted it might
have been, but it was no joke. Marchenko meant what he
said, fully expecting to be called on once again.

For Shirer, later that night, the sight of the long stick of
bombs falling away into the blue, and the trails of silent
orange explosions blossoming rapidly in the green-black
taiga, should have been more rewarding than it was. But
while gunner Murphy was chatting away excitedly on the
intercom about how there wouldn't be any "motherfucker
airfields" left for the "mothers to fly out of," so accurate
had been the nine-plane load of over 380,000 pounds of
five-hundred-pound contact bombs and cratering munitions,
Frank Shirer felt guilty that he couldn't join in Murphy's
excitement. No matter that in the closing hours the B-52s
had rendered the Siberians' three most important airstrips
beyond Irkutsk useless. For Shirer, the news of Marchenko's downing by an AA battery was a bitter disappointment,
for his determination to get back to flying—real flying—
had once again been thwarted.

CHAPTER FORTY-SIX

FROM HIS FORWARD HQ at Nizhneangarsk, Freeman insisted that before he would go to A-7, all prisoners must be exchanged. This list included the commando, Smythe, whom, or so it was claimed by the Democracy Movement, the PLA had cut down from the pier five railing as soon as they'd seen Robert Brentwood rescuing the other prisoner. All other prisoners would be exchanged, responded General Cheng on the phone, but not the man Smythe. "He is a spy." This told Freeman Smythe was alive and that the underground information was correct, that the PLA, fearing his rescue, had got him off the bridge only a moment or so before the explosion.

"I insist he be returned," said Freeman.

"This is not possible," retorted an implacable Cheng. "He is ill."

"Then we will release all Siberian prisoners but not PLA prisoners."

"As you wish," said Cheng.

"I told you, Norton," Freeman said after the phone hookup. "Those Communists bastards don't give a shit about their own people."

"Maybe so, General, but should we press the point? They won't kill Smythe, now that we've made a public issue of it. Besides, our contacts with the Chinese underground report that Beijing wants too much info from him to let him die. Reports are they'll feed him up first."

"A show trial?" Freeman proffered.

"Possibly. Smythe'll have to hold up a sign saying how it was us who began the war, I suppose."

"He won't," opined Freeman. "He's SAS/Delta."

"I hope he will. It'd be easier on him."

"I agree. Can you try to get a message to him via the Chinese underground to say whatever the hell they want him to say. Nobody outside China'll believe a public confession. You know that. Let him 'confess' and we'll get him out on a fifty-to-one trade." The general shook his head with the frustration he knew he'd have to live with. "God, Dick, I'd hoped to wrap things up tighter. Wanted to beat the bastards so bad they'd never—"

"If the underground movement rises up, General, maybe you can."

Freeman's head whipped around. "How do you mean?"

"General, Taiwan has the best air force and navy in Asia. They've never given up the mainland as their home. It's through their agents we have contact with the Manchurian underground. If people inside rise up like they did before the Beijing massacre, Taiwan could go in—if they thought there was enough internal support."

"How about external support?" probed Freeman, his blue eyes as intense as winter cold.

Norton gave one of his noncommittal shrugs, but Freeman knew that what it really meant was, I'm not going to say it.

Freeman was plainly excited. "Dick, who's their head honcho? Taiwan?"

"Political or military?"

"Don't fart around, Dick."

"Admiral Lin Kuang."

"We train him?"

Norton nodded. "Annapolis. Cum laude."

"Dick, I want you to invite Admiral Kuang to Tokyo HQ. Incognito. We'll 'do' lunch. Everything top of the line. American."

"Yes, General. You have anything in mind?"

"Yes. I want that man back. He's a brave man, Dick, and good. Brave men don't belong in Chinese jails."

"Yes, sir, but I mean the menu for Admiral Kuang."

"What—oh, yes. Well, let's see . . . soup for starters, clam chowder—Boston cream, not Manhattan. Main course—prime rib. *American* prime rib, Dick. Range fed. None of that damn chemical-feed crap."

"Yes, sir," said Norton, taking notes, the mention of "prime rib" making him hope he'd be at the table with Freeman and Kuang. He asked the general about dessert.

Freeman looked up into the cold blackness, and even though it looked like winter, he could smell, feel, that spring was stirring.

"What was that, Dick?"

"What kind of dessert will we offer?"

Freeman turned to him. "You haven't been listening to me, Colonel."

Norton looked at him, nonplussed. The general moved closer toward him, his face no more than six inches from Norton's. "China, Dick! That's the dessert. China!"

Norton felt himself taking a deep breath. The general, ice encrusting the stars on his helmet, looked southward across the vast taiga. "This is a wanker's—a Yugoslav—cease-fire, Dick. Those bastards in Beijing are pinning the logistical tail back on their dragon. Well, if it starts breathing fire again, I'm going to give it something to roar about. I'll chop the son of a bitch off at the neck! You still got that wolf dung in storage?"

Norton looked about nervously for any sign of reporters around the general's Quonset hut, its frozen arch dripping in the darkness as spring's thaw crept upon them. Norton saw a "covey," as the general called photojournalists, waiting for them by the headquarters. They would probably want some answers about Cheng's refusal to release Smythe and, now it was suspected, several MIAs—air crew lost along the Amur. Sometimes, as now, Norton was convinced that the photojournalists and others were less interested in a news story or a picture of Freeman next to his wall charts than they were in the headquarters coffee, said to be the best brewed in the entire Second Army. Proof of his theory came as they entered the HQ with the reporters, not a question being answered before everyone had their mug of steaming brew. Freeman was still agitated following his conversation with Cheng, and Norton knew he'd probably have to run interference for any of the dumber questions asked by any of the neophytes among the group.

Before the correspondents were upon them, Freeman instructed Norton to make sure they had lots of wolf dung ready in the event of a breakdown in the cease-fire.

"Yes, sir, I will."

"General?" asked the redheaded CBS beauty. "Have you any plans to run for public office?"

"Hell, no. I'm not that old." There was the usual smatter of polite laughter. "B'sides, my opinion of politicians—"

"Next question!" cut in Norton, pointing to ABC.

"General, it's rumored you sent a message to the president that this is a Yugoslav cease-fire."

"Yugoslavia no longer exists," said Freeman.

Very adroit, thought Norton.

"General?" It was a CBC woman with a French-Canadian accent. "Sir, is it true that a Siberian woman is to be granted the Medal of Freedom?"

"It is. That's no secret. Her name is Alexsandra Malof. She's done a magnificent job for us. Magnificent. She's in hospital in Khabarovsk at the moment, but we intend to recognize her—soon as she's well enough."

Norton thought it a nice point the general made—its international implications would rebound against Cheng. He'd have to be a lot more careful about how he looked after his prisoners, particularly American prisoners.

"What's wrong with her, General?" It was a stunning Estonian blond photojournalist who had already driven several junior aides gaga.

"Ms. Malof," replied Freeman, "is suffering from acute malnutrition, visual impairment, and severe gastric disorders due to her imprisonment by the Chinese Communists.''

Norton smiled approvingly. Cheng would now definitely be on the spot. No way would they kill Smythe. By the time they put him on the stand, he'd probably look overweight.

The press conference lasted another ten minutes, and then Freeman took time off for coffee, the young blonde from Estonia handing him a cup. "It is very nice of you, General, to agree to the film opportunity. You are a great hero in Tallin." She could see the general didn't understand. "Tallin is the capital of—"

"Yes, yes, I know that," said Freeman, scrambling quickly to recover good manners. "Yes, of course, I realize Tallin—"

Norton came to the rescue, which was just as well, for though he had omitted to inform the general, it was he who had okayed the Estonian request for a short picture opportunity with the general.

"Estonian press wanted to do a, uh, little profile on you, General. You know the kind of thing . . ."

No, Freeman did not know the kind of thing. Never had known the kind of thing the general public were interested in—pictures of where you ate, your favorite colors, your favorite food—damn wonder they didn't want to see you take a piss. But the blonde was smiling, and having taken off her parka, her figure poured into a white angora wool body suit momentarily caused a pause in all radio traffic in Freeman's tent.

"Very well," Freeman conceded. "Where do you want me to stand?"

"We were hoping, General, that we might get one or two pictures of your planning table—"

"Planning table?"

"Uh, I think the lady means where you figure out tactics and—"

"Yes, yes, I know," said Freeman, neither wanting to offend the blond goddess nor appear in any way inept. "Well, I do most of my planning here—at the large wall map, and in my room. Now if you like, we could have a picture here, but I'm afraid the background board will have to go past the censor before I can let you—''

"No, no," said the blonde sweetly. "Of course I understand, General. Nothing classified. Perhaps just a shot or two of your sleeping quarters. Would that be all right?''

"Yes, certainly. Right this way," said Freeman; another blonde, this one a photographer, bringing up the rear.

The communications duty officer walked over to Norton. "Think the old man can handle that?" he asked Norton, nudging him.

"Oh I think so, the general's—"

"Christ! You all right, Colonel?"

Suddenly Norton had remembered the press question weeks ago about the rumors of a possible OMON attack. He put down the coffee cup and ran quickly between the canyon of radio and communications equipment. He knocked on the general's door. There was no answer. He tried the handle. The door was locked.

"General?" he shouted.

Inside, Freeman turned when he heard the knock. So did the women. One reached behind her, and Freeman saw the glint of what looked like a long syringe. The other one was already coming for him. As she lunged, he swung out of the way, now the other woman coming for him.

Freeman didn't have time for the Sig Sauer nine-millimeter, barely making the Remington by his bed in time. He swung it in the general direction of the door and fired twice.

Outside, Norton heard the roar of the gun, a heavy thud, then another scrabbling noise. Freeman, his hair mussed, looked down at them. Nothing much was left of the photographer's midriff but the bone of her spinal column as she slithered in the bloody ooze that had been her stomach; the other blonde, the prettier of the two, literally spouting blood, dead the second after the darts from the Remington load had hit her, each dart wound now a tiny fountain of blood.

"General!"

Freeman, running his fingers through his hair, putting the shotgun on the bed, pointing it away from the door, stepped over the two bodies, told them outside he was all right, then opened the door.

For a moment no one spoke, several men quickly exiting to be sick outside.

"Jesus!" said the normally restrained Norton, not yet realizing that a splinter from the door had grazed his eye bandage and caused a trickle of blood down his temple. "What in hell happened?"

Freeman walked back to the bed and reloaded the Remington. He was whey-faced but steady as a rock as he looked back down on the two OMONS. "I guess it's what you call 'equal opportunity'!" he said wryly.

It was a remark, though said in the near heat of the moment, that all but ended his career. La Roche's tabloids went wild. FREEMAN JOKES ABOUT DEAD WOMEN.

"Christ—*women*?" Freeman raged. "Bitches were OMON-trained. They'd kill their mother and no qualms about it."

"I know," Norton counseled as understandingly as he could. "But I think for a while, General, you'd better let me handle all press releases. And I do mean *all*."

Back home every editorial writer was calling for Freeman to be disciplined.

It was a half hour before midnight when Jay La Roche's private jet approached Anchorage. La Roche, not caring that his lawyers and others were looking—indeed, hoping they were—told Francine to take her bra off, that he wanted "a bit of tit for good luck." This brought on gales of laughter from his hangers-on. Francine, trying to make the best of it, knowing she had little choice unless she wanted to end up getting another beating of the kind he'd handed out to his first wife, obliged.

*   *   *

Somewhat dreamy-eyed, but effusive nevertheless from what he called a "hand and nose job"—the nose referring to the snort of cocaine that now had him in its high—La Roche and his entourage were met at Anchorage airport by two well-dressed men who asked if they could speak to Mr. La Roche alone. He refused, saying grandly that anything they had to say to him they could say to his friends.

"Fine," said one of them, the other quickly slipping on the handcuffs while the first arrested Jason La Roche for treason, specifically for "knowingly trading with the enemy of the United States in a time of war."

There was near pandemonium as La Roche began screaming at the FBI men and telling his lawyers to pull their finger out and get "fucking moving."

"Why—Why—you haven't even read him his rights," one of the lawyers whined.

"And I don't have to," reported the FBI agent. "Emergency Powers Act. You're out of luck, mister."

By this time, the FBI having alerted Anchorage airport earlier, several security officers were quickly on hand to help them board Jay La Roche on the next Alaska Airlines flight from Anchorage to Seattle, where he would be arraigned before a grand jury.

In Brooklyn, police were called to a domestic dispute, a man suspected of beating his wife. The couple's two kids were being looked after by the neighbor who'd phoned. They got the woman out, but the man wouldn't budge, and his wife, a Mrs. Lenore Ferrago, said that something had snapped in her husband since the war.

"Is there a gun in the house?" the SWAT team captain asked.

"Yes. An old pistol." But she said she didn't think he'd use it.

When they went through the door, they saw him at the fridge, the door open, and told him to put his hands up and not to move. He banged the door shut, turned toward them and shoved his hand inside his jacket. They felled him with two shots. There was no gun on him.

"It's like he wanted to go," said one of the cops. "Why?"

The SWAT captain shrugged. "Who knows? War's over—you think everything's gonna quiet down, and then all of a sudden, boom!"

In a ceremony set for March 30, Alexsandra Malof was to be presented with the Medal of Freedom. General Douglas Freeman, not for the first time in his career, was "recalled to Washington for consultation." It was rumored that he would lose his command. Before he left Khabarovsk, he instructed Colonel Norton, on his behalf and in the interests of the long-standing friendship between the United States of American and her allies on Taiwan, to invite Admiral Kuang to have lunch with the general in Tokyo, where the general would break his journey en route to Washington.

While this meeting was taking place in Tokyo, in Khabarovsk a naked man with a small, red flag trailing from his rectum streaked through Freeman's HQ.

Ten minutes later it was rumored that Aussie Lewis was taking bets—two to one on—that despite his wired-up broken jaw, Robert Brentwood would be eating solid food within six weeks. The bet was taken by Choir Williams and Salvini, but there was a great argument over what exactly constituted "solid."

Later that afternoon, in Khabarovsk, along the bank of the Amur, two children watched a soldier who, without any formal introduction whatsoever, walked up to one of the members of the Polar Bear Club and said, "Olga?"

The big woman turned. "Da?"

"Name's Lewis. Aussie Lewis. Pleased to meet ya, Ol. You like green horses?"

ABOUT THE AUTHOR

Canadian Ian Slater, a veteran of Australian Naval Intelligence, has a Ph.D. in political science. He teaches at the University of British Columbia and is managing editor of *Pacific Affairs*. He has written several thrillers, most recently *WW III*, *WW III: Rage of Battle*, *WW III: World in Flames*, *WW III: Arctic Front* and *WW III: Asian Front*. He lives in Vancouver with his wife and two children.

Don't miss a single battle of WW III.

WW III
Off the east coast of Korea, Russian-made bombers prepare to attack. North Korea's invasion of South Korea sparks a chain reaction of local conflicts that leads to a worldwide war.

WW III: RAGE OF BATTLE
WW III continues. Japanese forces are poised to invade China, while the Atlantic Ocean has become a nuclear-submarine battleground. U.S. nuclear missiles are aimed toward Russia and no one is safe.

WW III: WORLD IN FLAMES
NATO armored divisions have broken out from near-certain defeat. The Russians are readying a submarine offensive against the American West Coast, and there is no way to know how it will end.

WW III: ARCTIC FRONT
World War III is over. Or is it? Moscow has surrendered, but Siberia defies the ceasefire and the battlefield shifts to this land that harbors the ultimate weapon.

WW III: WARSHOT
The war on the Siberian front intensifies. General Freeman orders the greatest "cavalry charge" in history, throwing every last American resource against the massed Chinese and Siberians.

WW III: ASIAN FRONT
American forces seek to maintain a cease-fire between China and the new republic of Sibir (Siberia). Then the truce collapses and the battle rages on.